THEY CALL ME BLUE

LOREN HUXLEY

TWISTED HEART PUBLICATIONS, LLC

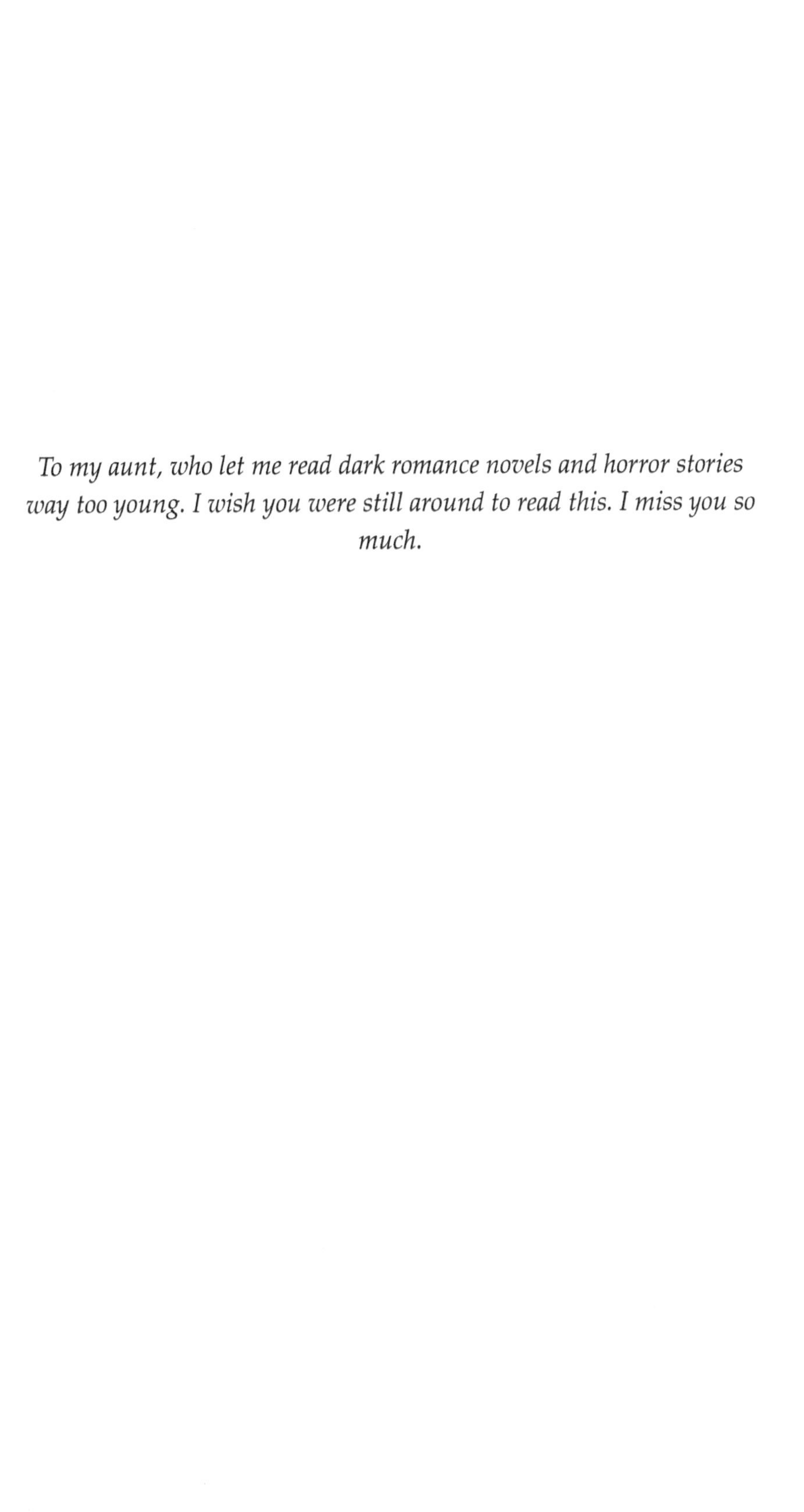

To my aunt, who let me read dark romance novels and horror stories way too young. I wish you were still around to read this. I miss you so much.

Author's Note

Content Warning

They Call Me Blue is a grimdark fantasy and horror novel. It includes dark romantic elements that may not be suitable for all audiences. For a complete list of content warnings, please visit the QR code below or go to Loren Huxley's website lorenhux ley.com

Unless specified, all of the triggers listed are explicit and graphic in nature. If any of these are unsettling for you, please do not continue. Self-care is best care. I tried to be as thorough as possible when creating this list, but if I've missed anything, please email me at contact@lorenhuxley.com

They Call Me Blue is the first book in a trilogy, and will end on a cliff. It includes a slow-burn m/f romance that will get spicier and deadlier as the series goes.

Introduction

"Wood nymphs lived on Rayna long before elves. When our people first arrived on the planet, their species welcomed us with open arms. We became their friends, their neighbors, and eventually their mates. From our couplings, the elgrew were born. At first, we thought they were carnivorous. By the time we realized they relied on consuming elves to survive, it was already too late."

—Isthan of the Drift, Historian of the Kantelli Tribe.

I. Arden

"All elgrew possess an intrinsic desire to consume elves. Born twisted and deformed, they steal our faces and wear our bones so they can look beautiful like us."

—Seris of Darkmarsh, Chieftain of the A'sow Tribe.

The stench of charred flesh and burning hair permeates my nostrils. Nose crinkling, I roll in my hammock, somewhere between dream and sleep as heat and smoke congest the air around me. Crust fuses my eyelids shut, slows my reflexes, when I hear a deep, bellowing scream and finally come to, snapping upright.

Dark gray smoke billows high into the rainforest's canopy, consuming orange leaves and knotted vines, blotting out the surrounding trees and sunlight. More than fifty feet below me, monsters throw torches onto the sprawling root system, shrieking a sharp battle cry that sends shivers down my spine— *elgrew*—not just one, but an entire hunting party.

From here, they almost look like us. Their lithe bodies are tall and gray, with sharp-angled faces and pointed eartips. But up close, their eyes glow violet and their teeth form sharp points. Silver threads hold their beautiful bodies together, forming a near-invisible patchwork of elven skin. Those threads shine in the heat of the fire, giving them away.

Heart pounding, I instinctively reach for the go-bag that dangles on the tree branch above me. Then, I wipe the crust from my eyes, tighten my leather breastwrap, and climb—not down toward the flames, which is exactly what the elgrew want, but up toward my baby sister, to the tippy top of the canopy where jumping from limb to limb and swinging from vine to vine gives us the best chance at escape.

The second I touch the tree, my slender blue fingers flatten, turning bulbous at the tips. The folds on my fingerpads—my lamellae—thicken and spread, becoming tacky the longer I flex and retract them. Keeping them flexed, I climb the tree like a lizard might, like the elgrew can't, my sights set on the little black hammock so far up, it looks more like a small animal than a refuge.

Get to Nirissa.

Keep her safe.

My goals are singularly focused. This isn't the first time the elgrew have found us, and I know what comes next.

The anguished screams of my tribe pierce the falling canopy, driving me to move faster, smarter. If the elgrew catch Nirissa, they'll eat her. If they catch me, they'll do much worse.

Long blue hair falls over my face, into my eyes and mouth. Spitting it out, I force my exhausted limbs higher, until the dark green sky bleeds through the dense leaves. The smoke turns my vision hazy and my breathing ragged. Coughing up lungfuls of the nasty stuff, I peer over my shoulders into foggy thickness. My parents' tree is somewhere over there, but I'm not dumb enough to think all four of us will make it out tonight. Out of six brothers, an aunt, and two uncles, we're all that's left.

I try not to think about that as I ascend.

By the time I reach Nirissa, she's already sitting upright, go-bag in one hand, a little doll made from twigs and leaves in the other. Her silver hair is tucked into a braid, and her pointed ears twitch as she peers around me, searching for Mom and Dad. I shake my head before she even asks.

"It's just me," I croak, voice hoarse from the wretched smoke and the tears brewing in my eyes. "We have to go, bug. Climb on my back."

She doesn't fight me. This is the third time in two years.

Wordlessly, Nirissa wraps her arms around my neck, and her twiggy doll digs into my skin. It's difficult to carry her. Even at sixteen, I'm barely taller than her, and my muscles strain under the weight. But I force myself to keep going.

A loud boom sounds to our left. A section of canopy disappears as the tree beside us snaps in half, tumbling to the forest floor. I gulp, knowing better than to look down, but am unable to resist. Elf blood stains the leafy ground silver. Lifeless, gray bodies sprawl out below me—our chieftain, our doctor, our . . . I bite the inside of my cheek to keep from crying out. Our mother.

"Don't look, bug. Promise you'll keep your eyes shut until I tell you."

My veins turn icy, terror freezing me in place as a male elgrew approaches the pile of dead bodies. His flesh isn't like the others. It's lumpy and purple, twisted and mangled and *deformed*. The man limps on a leg half as long as the other, slow in his approach, obviously in no hurry to reach his prey. Hung over his neck is a black apron covered in silver splatters and violet guts. Tied around his waist is a toolbelt of knives and bone saws.

They brought Butchers.

The elgrew withdraws a cleaver from his belt and bends over our mother.

My muscles tense. My breathing stops.

He swings the cleaver at my mother's arm, and an anguished scream rips through the blazing sky as her biceps severs clean in half.

She's still alive.

Sour bile bubbles up my throat, but I swallow it down and wipe my eyes. I can't save her. There are too many of them, I'm too noticeable, and with Nirissa on my back, it's too risky. My sister's warm tears spill onto my shoulder, and I can't tell if she's crying because she disobeyed me and saw what they're doing or because she doesn't want to lose everything again. I'm too scared to ask.

Steeling myself, I crawl up the tree until we reach the top, where a sea of orange leaves span for a hundred miles before reaching the *Korring-Marr*—a Great Tree as tall and as wide as a mountain, made from orange leaves with bark as dark as obsidian. The dawning sun turns the green sky patchy—dark in some places, light in others, ugly all the same.

Like with all elves, the Korring-Marr calls to me, though I can't explain why. It's a soundless music. A soothing lullaby. It's also the elgrews' stronghold.

Around the Great Tree's base is a sprawling metropolis made of beautiful stonework that's painted silver with our blood. The longer I stare at it, the harder it is to look anywhere else. Calm overtakes me as wind whips through the leaves and golden sap oozes down its trunk.

The need to touch it pulls at every fiber of my being.

"Arri?" Bug's voice snaps me out of the trance.

I shake my head to clear it, turning south instead.

We need to get out of here. We're running out of time. Soon, every escape route will be ablaze and I'll have no choice but to descend. Damn if I'll let that happen—not with Nirissa to protect.

I take a deep breath before jumping to the nearest tree, then the next one, and the next, extending my arms as far as I can so my lamellae catch and stick to the bark.

"Hey, she's up there!" one of the elgrew calls. "Blue's getting away."

The name sends a fresh wave of nausea curling in my gut. The elgrew don't give us names; they give us labels, and that's mine. The only blue elf in existence and one of the reasons the elgrew keep finding us. The scent of kerosene invades my nostrils, and the heat of the flames comes next, slithering up the tree until it hisses and pops and my feet are burning.

Crack!

Crunch!

Boom!

The five trees surrounding me collapse. I have nowhere to go. The jump is too far. The fires are too thick. I'll never make it.

Panic blooms in my chest as I scan the canopy for a better solution.

"Come down, Blue," another taunts, switching from their native tongue to Elvish, ensuring I can understand him. I understand him all too well. "We'll be sweet to you. You'll make a fine pet."

I swallow, my eyes latching onto a slimy, moss-riddled vine beside me. Giving it a tentative tug, I flex my fingers, spread my lamellae, and then curl it tightly in both fists.

It's not long enough, the nagging voice in my head whispers. *It's not strong enough. You'll die.*

"Arri?" Nirissa's voice trembles.

It has to be enough.

"Shhh. We're going to be alright. Hold on."

Emptying my mind, I pad backward on my feet, putting as much distance between the spine of the tree and the tip of the branch as I can. Two tree lengths, a one-hundred-foot drop, and a sea of fire are all that stand between us and freedom, and we're going to make it.

Better dead than eaten.

Better dead than a slave.

I take a running start, and then I leap.

Letters

Whoever finds the blue elf and brings her to me will be given wealth beyond their greatest imaginings. Whoever harms her or attempts to Claim her as their own will be met with a punishment worse than death.

May the rains bless you and the gods guide you on your hunt.

—AZERIN OF KARISS, THE GRAND OVERSEER.

II. Lyrick

"The purpose of elgrew venom is neither to incapacitate nor to kill, but to Claim. When we bite someone, our venom is injected beneath the skin, permanently linking them to us. To bite an elf is to Claim them as yours—forever."

—THE EMERGENCE OF SPECIES, ELGREW BIOLOGY, VOLUME ONE

T angy silver blood floods my mouth. The elf's rapid pulse throbs against my lips. I can smell her fear—sharp and poignant—as I pin the creature's arms above her head and run my tongue along the side of her gushing gray neck.

Fucking bliss.

My prey whimpers. Her feet kick weakly as I flatten her body beneath my own and claim what's rightfully mine. Sinking my teeth into her tender flesh, I rip out a hunk of purple meat and chew. The muscle is sweet in my mouth, stringy and metallic as I squish it between my teeth and roll it over my tongue, savoring the texture, the flavor, the way her bright silver eyes turn into saucers when I take it.

The creature won't last long. I'm not a patient man, and I don't enjoy playing with my prey once it's caught.

"Please don't do this," she begs.

The words jar me, and I stop my ministrations. This *thing* knows the elgrew tongue.

"You can speak," I hiss. "Whom do you belong to?"

She doesn't answer.

I pull away then and scan the elf's gray body for distinguishable marks. A *Hunter* can get into a lot of trouble for damaging an owner's prey without consent. Chances are if she can speak our language, she's been living in our cities as a pet.

Sure enough, two rows of serrated dots form a circle over her right thigh—unmistakable teeth marks.

Flexing my jaw, I bite back every instinct begging me to finish her off. Instead, I wave my hand in the air, gesturing to the rest of the hunting party. Five elgrew approach us, slowly padding through the leafy undergrowth, their palms outstretched so I don't mistake them as thieves. Hunters aren't obligated to share our catches. Whoever gets the first bite lays claim.

And I didn't get the first bite.

My stomach grumbles its frustration. I wipe her blood from the corner of my mouth and press my hand onto the creature's gaping neck wound, stemming the flow. "Someone, get me a needle, thread, and some ossi dust. I need to seal the wound before it bleeds out."

Already, silver blood soaks the purple leaves below us, pooling behind her head and neck. I never miss an arterial vein —much to my detriment now when her life is on the line.

The elf thrashes beneath me, landing a good kick to my shin. Groaning, I smack her hard across the cheek, and those stupid silver eyes flutter shut, her body going prone beneath mine.

"Fucking bitch. I'm trying to help you."

Leaves crunch to my left. My second-in-command squats

over the mossy, mucky ground, then passes me a black, cinched bag.

"A runaway?" Conrin asks.

I grunt. "Looks that way. Probably found refuge with the A'sow Tribe. I'm guessing the fires displaced her."

Black scorch marks stain the underside of her hands and feet. Deep, oozing blisters drain from the surface of her skin. Even with the damage, she smells divine.

My throat burns.

I'm so fucking hungry, it's a struggle not to bite off a finger or a toe—claim it as payment for returning her—but my father would never hear the end of it, and then I'd be forced to eat meat from the kitchens like the rest of his staff. Cooked elf doesn't taste as good, and the creatures bred for slaughter never fight back.

I uncinch the leather drawstring and withdraw a pinch of ossi dust—a black powder made from our bone marrow. As I spread it along the creature's arterial vein, the bleeding ebbs, thickening and coagulating until it's safe to thread the mutilated pieces of her neck back together. Cursing, I snatch the needle and thread from Conrin, shove it through thick layers of flesh, and get to work.

MY MOUTH IS STILL SALIVATING by the time I finish. Anyone else in the group wouldn't have been able to stop mid-feed, let alone stitch her back up, but that's why they appointed me as their leader. Even so, the urge to taste her is a constant, gnawing ache in the pit of my gut. The others wouldn't judge me if I changed my mind. They'd join in, and we'd cover it up. Out in the forest, anything could have happened to her. Disease. Famine. Prey to any number of beasts.

I shake the thought from my head. I'm better than that. My

uncle raised me to treat my prey with respect, and I've honored that, even when my people don't. What they'd want to do to her in exchange for their discretion wouldn't be worth it.

Double-checking the stitchwork, I load her unconscious body onto Conrin's verncat—a large, muscular beast almost as tall as I am, with saberteeth the length of my forearm and mottled orange fur that blends into the tall grasses. Sprawled out on the cat, the elf could almost be mistaken for one of us.

Like most Hunters, my friends and I have meticulously replaced our skin with theirs, converting our lumpy purple flesh into something smooth and gray, both for camouflage and vanity. Tiny silver threads connect the patchwork, while ossi dust fuses it to our musculature, giving us the ability to feel their flesh as if it were our own.

Besides the threads, our eyes and mouths are the only things that give us away—glowing violet irises where they should be silver and sharp, pointed teeth where they should be dull and flat. We'd rid ourselves of those, too, if we didn't need the eyes to hunt them or the teeth to pick their bones.

I twist my long silver hair into a bun as Conrin hops onto his verncat and tightens his arm around the elf. His hand roams a little too far south, and I click my tongue.

"She's not yours. No touching."

He glares at me but obeys.

His verncat purrs as I walk past them, running my fingers through its sleek fur. Its long tail brushes against my leather pants. "If you touch her and she tells," I warn, keeping my voice low so the others don't hear, "I won't protect you this time."

Conrin rakes his fingers through his hair. "Shit, Lye, I won't. Stop acting like my dad."

"Someone has to."

A tense silence settles between us; it always does anytime his father is involved. The man is worth less than dirt, having earned their family a life's worth of gambling debt that Conrin's still paying off.

I break the quiet, throwing my head back to release a sharp battle cry. Trees and grasses rustle behind me before Prowler's orange eyes emerge from a thicket of purple berries. My pet is shorter than the other verncats, but faster and with a wider body too. Jagged scars run along his back, cutting through the mottled fur.

The instant Prowler reaches me, I rub his chin in greeting. "Good boy. Did you have a successful hunt?"

Purring vibrations travel up my palm.

"Thought so. Your mood's much improved since this morning."

He nuzzles into my chest, and I nearly topple over. The damn beast has no idea just how large he actually is. Grinning, I scratch lower, until my fingers glide into something warm and wet. When I pull them away, silver blood glistens on my palm.

My stomach rumbles.

I glance between my friends, Prowler, and the orange grasses swaying in the humid breeze. I don't like sharing food, and unlike them, I haven't eaten in weeks. Salted meat rations sustain most Hunters, but I can't stand the stuff. I need my kills hot and alive and fighting.

"I promised Azerin I'd bring back oo'ren moss," I tell the others. They've already mounted their verncats and are on the mucky, uneven road that leads back to Kariss through the heart of the jungle. Audible groans escape their lips, and I screw my face into something apologetic.

"I'll be back soon. Give me until sundown."

I don't wait for an answer before gesturing at Prowler to follow me through the purple bushes to the orange grasslands behind them.

Brushing aside leafy plants, I gently but firmly pinch the tip of Prowler's ear, indicating he take me to the creature. The cat obeys, his muscular body slinking through the tall grasses, dragging his belly close to the ground. While Prowler sneaks, I straighten, feigning alertness like an elf about to be snatched. If I'm lucky, my prey will hear me walking then come to me for help.

The prickly grasses bend as I stomp on them. Mud squelches beneath my hunting boots.

Twitching my pointed ears, I inhale long and deep and scan the clearing for signs of *it*. Scents of ash and charred flesh linger here. On the other side of the field lies total devastation—downed trees and razed shrubs as far as I can see. The wildlife is either dead or gone. The sky around me is silent.

No chirping birds.

No buzzing insects.

This place is a graveyard.

My brows furrow as Prowler continues in that direction. No one survives something like this, yet his steps are sure as we approach the tree line.

"I know it hurts, Nirissa," comes a faraway voice, spoken in the Elvish tongue.

I can't see her, but saliva pools in the back of my mouth all the same. Not one elf, but two. Enough to sell one to the Butchers if they're big enough or to fill my growling stomach for the next week if they aren't.

I stalk toward my prey, ducking under a section of downed spine trees with thorns as large as my fingers.

Perfect.

There are no trees for them to climb up. No vines to swing from. If the elves want to run, it'll have to be on foot, and I'm exceptionally fast on my feet. Scratching Prowler's chin, I point toward the ground and snap, ordering him to stay put as I push aside the grasses and spot her.

Blue.

The elf every elgrew in Kariss is after. The elf my father,

Azerin, paid handsomely to track and import. My people hunted their kind to near extinction, and now my father is spearheading the campaign to bring them back.

Find her.

Breed her.

Make her a showpiece in his collection.

His instructions were very clear. No one eats the girl, but I lick my lips regardless. Everyone knows blue elves taste the sweetest.

A twig snaps underfoot as I move to get a better look at her. Cursing under my breath, I duck behind the fallen trees as she scans the forest and grasslands.

"Is everything alright?" another voice whispers. Her words are slurry, sleepy, and childlike.

"It's fine, bug. Just an animal."

My heart races. My limbs twitch with the need to give chase. Still, I wait several minutes before taking another peek.

Blue's skin is a lighter shade than I imagined, but her hair is as dark as azurite, and it glimmers in the midday sun. I'm too far away to see her eyes, but I know they'll match the hair, the nails, maybe even the blood that pours from her scraped arm.

Tiptoeing closer, I keep my mouth closed, my eyes lowered. Maybe she'll recognize me for what I am, or maybe, just maybe, she'll let me get close enough to take her down. I'm not like the other elgrew. I won't torture her, or breed her, or add her to the games. I'll make it quick and then I'll make it slow, savoring the taste of her long after her soul has left this world.

"We have to go," Blue says, turning to the smaller, grayer elf sitting beside her. "We need to find shelter."

Her voice quivers as I come into view.

That's right, little elf. Run from me. I'd love to give myself another workout.

"Stay back," she says.

I don't.

I reach behind my back, angling for the knife strapped to my belt.

"You're one of them, aren't you?"

Very clever.

My fingers tighten around the hilt. I lift my eyes and smile, flashing a mouthful of pointed teeth. I'm close enough now to see the deep gashes in her companion's thigh and the dark scorch marks on Blue's skin. The pair of them smell like smoke, tangy blood, and sweat. I can't stop salivating. When I speak, it's in Elvish, to ensure she'll understand.

"Would you like to run now, or are you content with lying there and taking it?"

Her blue irises home in on me, her chin rising ever so slightly.

Brave little elf.

Little *elf.*

I freeze in my tracks, giving her a double take. The creature is no older than my youngest brother, still a child in many regards. No breasts to speak of. No muscle mass or height. I've never paid much attention to what elves look like, but I know enough about them to know this one should be well over six feet tall if she's reached her *Age of Majority.*

She hasn't.

The gray creature beside her is considerably smaller. Even from this distance, I can tell it would only reach my thigh.

Most Hunters kill, capture, and maim their prey indiscriminately, but not me. I like my prey to fight back. I like to chase them until their lungs heave for breath and their eyes glaze over in that final glint of acceptance. What I don't like is chasing children. It's not sporting or fun. It's pathetic, cruel, and way too fucking easy. It also goes against everything that I believe in.

My lips purse as I near the creatures, considering my options.

The blue elf jumps in front of her companion as if to ward

me away, and I let loose a throaty chuckle. "You think you can protect her? A smart elf would run."

Unhooking my knife, I flash the weapon in front of her. The metal blade gleams in the sunlight, blindingly bright.

Blue stands up straighter, squaring her shoulders as I close the last few steps between us.

"I won't leave my sister," she says.

"So you'd rather die with her?"

The creature doesn't move even when I'm a hair's breadth away and the knife is at her throat. She narrows her gaze at me instead, in a way prey never has before, like she's imagining our situation in reverse—me at her mercy, her holding the blade.

My heart skips. My thoughts spiral as I envision the same.

What would it look like to hunt this creature when she's no longer slicked in blood or charred to a near crisp? Oh, she would fight back. Of that, I'm absolutely certain. As an adult in her prime, this elf would pose a very real threat, too.

The idea is more thrilling than it should be.

"Give me your palm," I growl, my eyes never leaving hers.

She clenches her jaw, and the tip of my blade digs in deeper until silvery-blue blood beads to the surface.

"I said give me your hand."

"Why?" she asks.

The blood seeps down her throat slowly.

So . . . fucking . . . slowly . . .

I swallow, and it's like swallowing tree bark.

Snapping forward, I grab Blue's wrist and yank, lurching her into my chest. She squirms against me as I bend, sinking my teeth into her little palm, injecting my venom deep beneath the skin, into muscle and vein. Warm blood gushes into my mouth as she yelps and twists, but I drop her long before the bloodlust kicks in.

Her hands will make beautiful gloves one day. But not today.

"That marks you as mine," I tell her, sheathing my blade. "If another Hunter finds you, tell him your master is Lyrick."

"No."

The hackles rise on the back of my neck, but I smile down at her. "Do you know what my people want to do to you, Blue? Are you old enough to have been told?"

She shivers and covers her nonexistent breasts.

"Good. Then you already know what will happen if you don't have a master when they come." I pat the top of her pretty head. "I have no interest in that. I want to eat you, and I want you strong enough and old enough to fight back."

Terror flits across her expression, and without thinking, I riffle through my leather breeches and withdraw the pouch of ossi dust, a needle, and thread. "For your sister."

I grab Blue's palm, slowly dragging my tongue along the dotted flesh. The pain in my stomach is almost unbearable. My jaw widens involuntarily, my teeth grazing over the sensitive skin one more time. I close my eyes, take a deep breath, and pull away. Dropping the tools inside her palm, I take one step back, then another.

It's time to go before I do something I'll regret.

"See you around, Blue." Spinning on my heels, I wave over my shoulder and disappear behind the foliage. Her angry voice cuts through it.

"My name isn't Blue!" she spits. "It's Arden."

Arden.

"I'll remember that when I'm tearing through your throat."

III. Arden

"Elgrew can sense their bite up to a mile away, making it nearly impossible for the Claimed to hide. It is for this reason most tribes refuse to grant the Claimed sanctuary, including ours."

—Tanlis of Brekken, Historian of the Lok'owe Tribe.

I stare at the bite mark long after Lyrick has left. It doesn't hurt, but it feels *wrong*—like a piece of him is trapped inside me. I want it gone. I *need* it gone. Every second that it remains makes me want to crawl out of my skin.

"He bit you," Nirissa says.

I force my gaze away and hide my bleeding palm behind my back. "It's nothing, bug. Let's get you patched up."

Lowering myself to the forest floor, I drop my go-bag and scoot closer to her, examining the wound that stupid cat left. Her pants are shredded, and silver blood oozes from the deep claw marks on her thigh. It isn't fatal—not unless infection sets in. Still, it'll be impossible to walk on.

One-handed, I fumble with the pouch Lyrick gave me, not

quite sure what to expect inside. Relief washes over me at the sight of black ossi dust—more than I've ever seen in my entire life. An amount no singular person could ever hope to use.

Why would he give me this?

Briefly, I scan the tree line where the Hunter disappeared, my brows furrowed in confusion. Mercy isn't a trait I'd expect from their kind. Then again, neither is restraint. Nirissa should be dead right now. *I* should be in the city, under the Grand Overseer's thumb. Instead, Lyrick has given us a chance to survive—to get stronger and fight him another day.

I won't squander it.

Pushing him from my mind, I dig through my go-bag in search of first-aid supplies. A pair of ivory shears and spooled gauze lie near the bottom, hidden beneath a thick hide blanket, jarred food rations, fire-starting equipment, and water skins. Unraveling the gauze, I cut a portion off and wrap it around my bleeding hand, tying the ends into a knot with the help of my teeth. Dry cotton clings to my tongue, but I ignore it, returning my attention to Nirissa.

Her pants are ruined. Still, snipping them feels wrong. Unlike elgrew, we don't have textile manufacturing. Everything of ours is made by hand, using plant fibers and animal skins. A new pair might take weeks to make, and in the meantime, she'll be exposed to the elements.

It physically pains me to cut along the hem, the *snip, snip, snip* loud in the otherwise abandoned forest. I slice to the very top of her thigh, then peel the fabric back, exposing Nirissa's ripped flesh to the humid air. Choking back a sob, she clamps her eyes tightly shut. Her body goes painfully still as I grab a pinchful of ossi dust and sprinkle it over the wound.

Like magic, the bleeding ebbs then stops. A thin layer of dark gray skin grows over the deep crevices, but it's too weak to support her weight, and it'll still need stitches if the muscle is to fully heal. Even then, she may never walk right again.

"This is going to hurt," I warn her. "But I need you to hold still. Can you do that for me?"

Sniffling, she nods, clutching her wooden doll to her chest. "I'm ready."

The needle and spool Lyrick gave me are finer than anything I'm used to. The silver thread is hard to see—almost invisible. After several tries, I force it through the eye of the needle and bend over my sister.

"I'll be fast," I say, and then I plunge the needle in, recalling old lessons the healers taught me. Sewing hide isn't much different from sewing elf skin, and I *am* fast—my fingers steady and sure as I join the wounds together. Snipping the thread, I scoot back to examine my handiwork.

Perfect.

"You did such a good job," I tell her. Nirissa doesn't cry, but I can tell she wants to, so I scoop her into my arms and soothe her the way our parents used to when she'd injure herself. "You were so brave today."

"I want Mom," she says.

"I know, bug."

Nirissa stares up at me with glassy, hope-filled eyes. "Maybe she'll be at camp."

I can't bring myself to lie to her, so I stroke her hair instead. In three days, we'll join the other survivors at our predesignated meeting spot. Until then, I'll let her pretend. It's the least I can do after everything she's been through.

Nirissa curls into my chest. She holds me until her limbs grow heavy and her eyelids fall shut. Once I'm certain she's asleep, I lay her against the tree stump and cover her in a hide blanket, then I contemplate my own injuries.

An eerie numbness spreads from Lyrick's bite mark up my fingertips and wrist. Indigo blood seeps through the gauze in the shape of a circle—thirty-eight dots that brand me as his.

I have to get rid of it.

Not only can he track me through the bite, but he can use it to track my friends too.

Wiggling my ears, I listen to the burned forest. Vibrations travel through my *sezin*—a small, crescent-shaped bone in the center of my ear canal—and the sounds around me amplify. The gentle breeze becomes a cyclone. Grassworms slither deep beneath my feet. From a mile north comes the faint, *thumping* pawsteps of what can only be verncats headed toward Kariss. No other animal or elgrew is within hearing range. *Thank Marr.*

Still, the tension in my shoulders doesn't ease. Predators or not, I'll need to act fast. The forest never stays safe for long.

I keep Nirissa in eyesight—close enough that I could protect her, or at least try, if the verncats change course. Then I begin gathering charred sticks, piling them into a small, makeshift campfire the way Dad taught me. The sun sinks lower and lower into the downed canopy, the sky shifting from chartreuse to emerald to a green so dark it could almost be black. By the time I'm finished, puffy gray clouds litter the sky, and the air turns humid with the promise of rain.

It'll start any minute now.

Squinting into the moonlight, I pull tinder from my go-bag— an edible yellow fungus in the shape of a fan—and set it onto my pile of scrap wood. A jar of flammable oils lies amongst my food rations. Holding my breath, I uncap it and douse the camp-fire, then I grab the pointiest stick I can find and drill it into another, rolling it back and forth in my palms until it sparks. I scoot the tinder closer, then fan that spark into a flame. The yellow fungus goes up in a plume of bitter smoke.

My eyes water.

My nose burns.

Sniffling, I wipe my face before scooting back to watch the orange flames hiss, and crackle, and lick across the wood. Thunder rumbles in the distance and lightning streaks across the skyline, igniting it in a flash of silver.

It's now or never.

I unwind the bandage that conceals my palm. The skin is raised and raw near each puncture, but there's still no pain—just that cold numbness spreading to my forearm, then my bicep. I clench and unclench my fist, hesitating, my courage wavering as raindrops patter onto nearby leaves.

"I'm not his," I whisper, my voice cracking.

I repeat the words until I believe them, and then I do what's necessary to make them true.

Closing my eyes, I thrust my palm into the raging fire and fight back a scream. Burning pain shoots up my palm, blistering hot, but I bite my tongue and force myself not to jerk away.

I refuse to be branded by one of those things.

Skin melts. Blood boils.

I count to ten, then to fifteen.

My body sways, and finally, I fall back, my head smacking into the dirt. Burned and bleeding—with no strength left to get back up—I lift my heavy palm into the sky and crack open my eyes. Scorched and blackened skin greets me, everything a mess of blood and ash. But there's no bite mark.

I grin—a big, toothy smile. Laughter bubbles up between my cracked and peeling lips as the icy rain starts to pour.

I'm not his and I never will be.

A RAINBOW SHINES OVERHEAD.

Silver fish dart from one side of the river to the other, disappearing into crystalline jade-green water. I hiss when my improvised spear strikes cobble—not the *roundtail* I'd intended—and drives all the other fishes away. That was the third miss since this morning.

The steady current carries my sharpened stick downstream, and I sink onto the muddy river bank—no more spears left.

Unrelenting sun plasters the clothes to my body, covering me in a layer of body odor and half-dried, sulfurous mud. A fingerless leather glove protects my charred hand, but it still burns. Even with ossi dust, the skin's regrowth is agonizingly slow.

Sun-blistered and tired, I groan, rolling onto my back beneath the shade of an orangeleaf tree. Within eyesight, Nirissa refills our water skins.

We're almost home.

"Got it!" she says, lifting the flasks triumphantly. Nirissa juggles them in her too-full hands, sharing the space with her twiggy doll. Limping, she climbs the bank to sit beside me.

"No fish?" she asks, the disappointment heavy in her voice.

"No fish."

Nirissa sets the flasks down but hugs her doll close. "Maybe I can help."

I wipe the sweat from my brow and shake my head. At Nirissa's insistence, I let her throw the first stick; it didn't even hit the bottom before floating off—not that I thought it would. At five years old, she can hardly be expected to do better.

I *was expected to do better. Mom and Dad didn't baby me.*

I push aside those jealous thoughts, burying them deep. It doesn't matter anymore. It's good that one of us knows how to survive.

"This is my job," I tell her, ruffling her short silver hair. "Why don't you look for fish eggs near the bank?"

"*Ewww.* I don't want fish eggs again." She scrunches her nose at me. "I saw *jurry* berries across the river. Why can't we eat those?"

"Because neither of us can swim. It gets deep in the middle."

At my sound logic, her protests fall silent. Still, my mouth salivates as I picture those dark berries squishing between my teeth. It would be so good to taste something that isn't fish eggs, or mushrooms, or jerky for a change. But even if we could swim, it wouldn't be safe. Elgrew trap those areas, knowing our food preferences as well as we do. At least with the river between us, we stand a chance at escape—albeit, a small one.

I swallow down the cravings as quickly as they emerge. Practical and alive beats foolish and dead any time. Pushing off the ground, I smooth out my clothing, loosening dried flakes of mud and moss. "Let's walk a little farther upstream. If the jurry bushes are fruiting, I bet the *bluewood* trees are too."

Nirissa's face brightens. "Bluewoods? Are we almost there?"

"We'll reach camp by nightfall."

She hops up and hugs my pant leg. The doll digs sharply into my thigh. "I bet Mom and Dad are worried about us."

My insides twist, but I say nothing, just hum in agreement. I've never been great at comforting people; surely Dad will know what to say to her when the time comes. He always does.

Snatching my go-bag from a low-hanging tree branch, I readjust it before lifting Nirissa into my arms, grunting at the heavy weight. Only a few more hours and my aching muscles can finally rest. A few more miles and I can close my eyes without fearing the elgrew will find us.

"Let's head out," I say, reaching for our flasks. I take a long swig of cool water, soothing the ache in my dry throat. Then, I get my bearings and head south.

This close to the river, I can't use my sezin—amplifying the current's sound would deafen me—so I'm forced to rely on my eyes instead. Tall grasses hide almost everything from view. Orangeleafs surround us, promising their protection in the canopy, but Nirissa is still too injured to climb on her own, and she isn't strong enough to hold onto my neck for more than a few minutes.

We're condemned to walking, and I've never felt so exposed.

My hairs stand on end as we weave through the undergrowth, twigs snapping and mud squelching underfoot. Between our body odor and lack of stealth, we're practically beacons to predators—not just elgrew, but black bears, wild cats, and snakes too.

Slowly, the grasses fade into thin bluewood trees as tall as the elgrews' tenement buildings. The noises of the forest vanish —insects, birds, skittering rodents all going silent. Each step sounds as loud as a thunderclap.

I keep scanning for threats, still too close to the river to use my sezin. Something *thumps* to my right and I swivel my head in that direction, only to find a large stone at the foot of a tree. My brows furrow in confusion.

"Why'd you stop?" Nirissa asks.

"Nothing." Goosebumps spread along my arms, but I force myself forward.

Another thump. Another stone falls to my right.

Wind howls through the trees, and I hug Nirissa tighter, quickening my pace. Behind us, leaves rustle. Heart pounding, I turn to investigate as something large leaps from up above—a dark shadow in my periphery.

My bloodcurdling shriek rips through the afternoon sky as it lands beside us and lunges.

IV. Arden

"When an elf dies, their spirit becomes one with the Korring-Marr, transcending time and space to integrate with our ancestors. It is the only time we know true peace."

–Selik of Cliffstone, High Priest of the A'sow Tribe.

"**A**sshole!" I smack my would-be-assailant square in the chest. It's like hitting a rock. "You scared the crap out of me."

Fenris—the chieftain's son and my "supposed" best friend—takes a step back, raising his hands in a show of peace. *There can be no peace between us. How dare he scare me like that?*

I shove him harder this time, and he snickers, barely budging from his spot on the ground. "I got you good, didn't I?"

Frowning up at him, I set Nirissa down and bare my teeth. Although we're both sixteen, Fenris reached his Age of Majority last year and is nearly twice my size, with the body of a fully grown elf. Dressed in hide armor, I've never felt so small in comparison. But small or not, I'm not about to let him push me around.

"I may not be able to out-fight you," I say, "but I can still poison you in your sleep."

He sticks his tongue out like we're twelve. Leaves are tangled in his long silver hair, only adding to that boyishness.

"She wouldn't really poison you," Nirissa says, raising her arms, silently commanding Fenris to pick her up. "Arri loves you too much."

My cheeks burn as hotly as my bandaged hand, and I bare my teeth at her too. *Just whose side is she on?*

Bending low, Fenris scoops my sister up and sets her on his shoulders. Nirissa winces when he readjusts her the wrong way, and the playful mood sours, a somberness filling the air as he examines her exposed thigh. "What happened, bug?"

She tells him about the verncat. I cut her off before she can mention Lyrick's name. "Nirissa didn't cry at all when I stitched her back up. The healers are going to be so proud when I tell them. Do you know if Morena made it?"

Fenris shakes his head. "I haven't been back to camp yet. I . . . I wanted to find you before the funeral." He lowers his voice to a whisper and leans in close. "I need to talk to you in private."

"Hey, keeping secrets isn't nice," Nirissa pouts.

"I'm sorry, bug," Fenris says. "It's just boring grown-up talk."

Unconvinced, she crosses her arms and glares at him.

"You must be hungry. I have some jurry berries that I'd love to share with you." Fenris points to the tree he jumped from. At the midpoint swings a black hammock—not at all concealed by the tree's thin black branches and even thinner blue leaves. The fact that I didn't notice it speaks volumes to my survival skills, and I know I'm never going to hear the end of it.

At the mention of jurry berries, Nirissa forgets what Fenris was talking about and demands he take her to them. I resist an eye roll as he obliges, swinging her onto his back and carrying her up the tree. Their voices echo as she chatters away about how I forced her to eat fish eggs and wouldn't let her bathe in elgrew-infested waters.

When Fenris climbs back down, he's got a leather sack hung over his shoulders. Nirissa remains in the hammock, shoving green berries into her mouth, their sticky yellow juice dribbling down her fingertips.

The perfect diversion.

Fenris swallows. "You should sit."

"What's in the bag?" It's huge and lumpy and, judging by the darkness in his cheeks, much heavier than my baby sister.

He doesn't answer right away and instead hefts the bag to the ground, letting it drop in front of me. Metal clangs inside it. "Please, Arden. Sit."

His serious tone prompts me to obey.

I lower myself to the muddy ground, short blue grasses crunching beneath me. Fenris does the same, letting that big bag obscure his face. A leather cord holds it together at the top. He takes a deep breath and unknots the laces, the edges unfurling into a large blanket. My heart sinks at the contents.

Biting the inside of my cheek, I reach for my dad's burnt journal. It crumbles beneath my fingertips, the scorched pages flaking off into the dirt. The rest of his stuff lies in a sprawling heap: a blackened telescope that doubles as a walking stick, the lenses warped from heat and cracked beyond repair, cogs and wheels attached to nothing, dried sealants and shriveled pastes stuck to their bronze containers. A life's worth of research and invention, gone.

"I salvaged what I could," Fenris says, his voice gravelly.

Wiping my eyes, I glance up from the pile. "Why do you have this?"

"I . . . I was assigned scouting duty outside your dad's hide-out. He saved my life."

Fenris reaches into his cuirass and withdraws a pair of goggles with green-colored lenses and a strap made from sinew

—an invention Mom and I created that hadn't been tested yet. He passes the goggles to me, and I run my fingers over the smooth glass, remembering the mornings I spent with her hand-carving them, coating the lenses in that slimy green goo before tempering them in tongs over the fire.

Those mornings are gone now.

She's gone now. And Dad . . .

"What happened to him?" I ask, already guessing the answer. There's only one reason Fenris would be carrying his belongings to me.

"I didn't see the elgrew until it was too late." He looks at the ground, his head hung low, his voice even lower. "When the fires started, your dad took his goggles off and gave them to me. He said I was faster anyway. That I'd have a better chance at escaping. I shouldn't have accepted them. . . I should have . . ."

"They worked?" I ask, my voice cracking.

"They worked."

Around us, dusk speckles the horizon in shades of orange and emerald green. As the sun sets, Fenris's pupils expand, consuming his gray irises, then his sclera until they're entirely black. *Darkeyes* like him and my dad are rare. At night, they have perfect vision, but they're also sensitive to light. A single fire can blind them for hours—or at least it could have before now.

I reach across the ruined objects and grab Fenris's hand, my vision watery. "It's okay," I tell him, swallowing hard. "Thank you for bringing his stuff back."

He pulls his hand away, still not meeting my gaze. His black eyes are dark-rimmed. "I'm sorry I couldn't bring *him* back."

For a moment, neither of us speaks. I turn the goggles in my hand—goggles I made for Dad, goggles that might have saved him if he hadn't been so selfless—and pass them back to Fenris, setting them in his lap. "You should keep them," I say. "He wanted you to have them. *I* want you to have them."

"Arden—"

"Go. I need to tell Nirissa before she finds out for herself." Blinking, I force myself to stand. I have to be strong for her; I'm all she has left.

Fenris doesn't move.

"Get out of here," I snap. "I'll meet you at the funeral."

Slowly, he rises then pulls me into a tight hug.

All the fight drains from my body. Burying my face into Fenris's stomach, I collapse against him, and for the first time in three days, I let myself cry.

GLOWFLIES BUZZ OVERHEAD, igniting the night sky in pulsing purple dots. Frogs croak in the distance and the air becomes heavy with the stench of algae, rain, and sulfurous muck.

Though we haven't reached the swamp yet, I can smell and hear it everywhere—which is more than can be said for Nirissa, who limps silently beside me. She hasn't spoken a word since I told her about Mom and Dad. She hasn't let me hold her either.

"Bug, your stitches are starting to tear. Please let me—"

She swats my hands aside like I'm an annoying insect, then hobbles past me, feet squishing through the decaying leaves. I follow closely behind, gently turning her by the shoulders when she starts going the wrong way. The solid ground becomes wetter, softer as we near our tribe's sacred burial grounds. Silver moonlight bathes our surroundings, peeking through the heavy rain clouds.

"You're wrong about Mom and Dad," Nirissa says finally. "They're going to be at camp, and you're going to look really dumb."

I wish that were true, but wishing won't bring them back. Still, I don't argue with her; I don't see the point when she'll see the truth soon enough.

Up ahead, spotters guard the edges of the Lycean Swamp, hiding in blue reeds that are twice as tall as I am, wielding long-bows crafted from spine trees. Thorns jut from every surface of their bows and the tips glint red with *varn*—a stinging poison. Masks conceal the spotters' faces. Dark leather armor conceals almost everything else.

As we approach, the spotters stiffen. They scan the moonlit forest behind us, then lower their bows once they realize who we are . . . Well, most of them do.

The spotter closest to us steps out of the plant cover and angles an arrow directly at my chest. Her fingers tighten around the grip of her bow, gray knuckles turning white. "Of course *she* made it," the woman hisses. "Of all the people who deserved to live—"

"Drop your weapon. Don't start that shit here." Another spotter steps from his post, walking toward her.

She glances over her shoulder, bowstring still drawn tight, voice cracking. "I don't know why you're defending her. It's her fault they're all dead."

I blink. "What are you talking about? The Hunters would have come with or without me."

The woman scoffs. "Is that what you think? Is that what they told you?" Lowering her bow, she withdraws a crinkled letter from her cuirass and stomps toward me, shoving it against my chest. "Hunters travel in groups of six, Arden. They don't bring armies unless they're hunting you. None of the other tribes have losses like ours do. None of them—"

"I said that's enough." The other spotter steps between us, and the letter goes floating into the mud. I bend to pick it up, my fingers curling over the ripped and tattered edges.

"Now isn't the time or the place," he reminds us. "This is sacred ground. It's disrespectful to our ancestors." The spotter guides me away from her, brushing aside an armful of blue reeds to reveal a hidden trail that leads deeper into the swamp. "You should go, Arden. The funeral is about to start."

I glance between him, the other spotters, and the letter in my hand. He's right. Now isn't the time. Nodding, I pull Nirissa through the prickly plants, and the opening closes behind us. Heated whispers come from the other side, but the words are inaudible.

Thumbing the letter, I guide us down the moonlit path, silver puddles rippling and splashing beneath our feet. I replay the woman's words, letting them sink in.

My fault.

"What did she mean?" Nirissa asks, as if reading my mind.

Curiosity eats at me, and I unfurl the letter, my throat tightening as I scan the contents. It's a conscription notice from the Grand Overseer, employing hundreds of elgrew for one purpose —hunting me—and offering great rewards to whoever succeeds in my capture. I knew he wanted me in the city, but this . . . This is something else.

I don't answer Nirissa. I can't bring myself to.

Would Mom and Dad be alive without me? Were they just collateral damage?

The heaviness in my chest makes it difficult to breathe. I shove the note into my back pocket as if hiding it can erase the words from my memory. It doesn't.

I'm still mulling them over—stewing in them—by the time we reach the end of the path. Reeds part to reveal a shallow expanse of murky water that stretches for miles. In the center, a thick and twisted tree root arcs into the air, as pale as the moonlight. A low hum escapes from it, revealing it for what it is—a piece of the Korring-Marr. Though our Great Tree is nowhere in sight, the roots have always run deep, as if trying to find us.

Gathered around the root are the last remaining members of our tribe. Standing atop it is High Priest Selik, dressed in his customary funeral robes made from thick animal fur. Bone necklaces, bracelets, belts, and earrings adorn the outfit, all taken from the high priests and priestesses who came before him. His gaze is downcast, focused on something in his fist that I can't quite see.

No one notices us at first—not even Fenris, who whispers something to the elf beside him. But then, Nirissa and I splash our way forward, toes squishing in the muck, warm water seeping into our breeches. Selik's gaze meets mine, gray eyes dark rimmed from crying. His lips press into a hard line, and as I get closer, I notice that thing in his hand is a carved wooden flower.

My heart cracks.

All married elves wear flowerpins in their hair, only removing them when their spouse dies.

Selik's eyes narrow into thin slits—an unspoken accusation. His fist tightens around the pin until silver blood drips onto the root below, rippling the stagnant water. The other elves follow his line of sight back to us, all holding similar objects—flowerpins, toy blocks, rattles. Nirissa and I are the only children present.

My fault.

I can see it in their eyes, in their tense postures, in their clenched teeth. How did I miss it before? How did I convince myself this is normal?

No one speaks to us as we take our places in front of Selik, the air so thick with tension it could be run through with a knife.

"Are they mad at us?" Nirissa whispers, loud enough I'm certain they can hear.

"No, bug, they're mad at me."

Selik shoves his fingers in his mouth and whistles three sharp blasts. Behind us, the blue reeds swish and part, and our spotters emerge near the water's edge. They don't come any closer, instead choosing to remain as silent observers with their weapons raised preemptively.

The elgrew won't hunt us here. The sawgrass is too sharp. The mud below our feet is too wet and too deep. Still, that doesn't make us safe. Instinct has every one of us scanning the surface of the water for rising bubbles or hissing pops, for the twenty-foot mudsnakes that accompany them.

My spine prickles when a section of sawgrass bends at an unnatural angle. Then, the breeze comes and the grass rights itself just as Selik clears his throat.

"We are gathered here to say goodbye to our loved ones," he says, voice wobbling. "When an elf loves something strongly enough, that love transcends death, taking root in the objects and people they've left behind. Because of this, it is our tradition to plant a seed alongside their most treasured possessions, so that from their death, something new may grow."

Sniffling, he wipes tears from his bloodshot eyes, then reaches for a leather pouch tied at his waist. Unfastening it, Selik flips the bag upside down and pours something into his hand, then leans forward and gives the pouch to Fenris—whose parents are just as absent as mine. Face stoic, my best friend repeats the gesture, then passes the bag to the elf beside him, and so on and so forth until it's in my hand.

I shake the bag until two fuzzy, arrow-shaped seeds fall into my injured palm. The elf beside me snatches it away, but I barely feel it. I'm too busy staring at the sawgrass seeds—at the glove concealing my burn marks—a surreal numbness overtaking me.

This can't be happening.

It can't be my fault.

Nirissa wraps her arms around my thighs and hugs me tightly. She might as well be hugging a statue. It's like I'm trapped outside of my body, seeing this moment through someone else's eyes. When Selik speaks again, my arms move mechanically, reaching for the leather duffle strapped to my shoulder, withdrawing the only thing left of our parents not burned in the fires—Nirissa's wooden doll.

"Until integration," Selik says. He kisses the flower pin with reverence, then places his seed atop it and lets it drop. The hairpin splashes as it hits the muddy water and sinks into the mud.

"Until integration," the crowd repeats.

They place their seeds into their objects and drop them in. I do the same, plunging both seeds into the doll's leafy chest. When it lands in the water, my hearing turns garbly, like there's wax trapped in my ears. Somewhere faraway, my sister's distorted voice begs me to pick the doll back up. Tells me that it's her toy. *Hers.*

I shush her. I stroke her hair. I do all the things I'm supposed to do because that's what Mom and Dad would have wanted.

The truth is, my baby sister was the only thing they loved. Every waking moment of my life, they spent training me for the day the elgrew Claimed me, teaching me their languages, their customs, anything that might help me stay alive in the capitol. Not Nirissa. Our parents played with her and built her toys. They sang her to sleep at night and poured their hearts and souls into making that wooden doll so she wouldn't be lonely in her hammock.

They loved her so much, but me . . . To them, I was always a lost cause, a child destined for capture.

The high priest chants something in an old language that I don't understand. We bow our heads, just as we've bowed them for the last dozen funerals, and the Korring-Marr's root starts to glow, bright and white and blinding. It pulses with the beat of my heart, thrumming with energy as dark and as ancient as the world itself.

In unison, we hum in tune with the Great Tree to a song that only exists in our bones and blood, that the elgrew will never hear. Then, the light fades and it's over—the rite complete.

Water splashes around us as the spotters join our gathering, their weapons still raised, their eyes still scanning the waters for danger. Fenris and Selik exchange places, the root wobbling as he jumps atop it. Fenris doesn't meet my gaze, though. His eyes sweep over everyone else.

"Tradition dictates that any survivors reconvene here three days following an elgrew attack." Fenris's throat bobs. Normally, his father would deliver this speech, and it seems unnecessarily cruel that they've asked it of him. "Anyone not present at roll call will be presumed dead. An election will be held tomorrow at sunrise to fill any existing vacancies."

Moments pass as he reaches into his pocket and withdraws a crumpled, ancient scroll. The silence of our people is punctuated by chirping insects and hooting birds as we stare at one another and count how many of us made it.

Twenty-seven.

Three days ago, there had been one hundred and twelve. Now, almost everyone I've ever known is gone. It doesn't feel real—not even when Nirissa reaches for my finger, curling her small fist around it like she used to do with Mom.

I wade closer to Fenris, wanting to offer him my comfort, my support, but he sidesteps me and climbs higher onto the root, the wood groaning beneath his oversized frame.

"Alysa of Darkmarsh," Fenris says. He reads off the scroll, a stick of charcoal between his fingertips.

"Present." The spotter behind me raises her hand.

It's the same one who confronted me earlier, or at least I think it is, judging by the way she carries herself. Alysa—the historian's daughter—has always been kind to me. She taught me how to sew, how to clean my blades. It's hard to picture that woman pointing an arrow at my chest. Then again, her daughter is missing too.

"Aman of Cliffstone," Fenris says.

Silence.

"Aris of Redden."

Silence.

Fenris scratches the names from his list, keeping his eyes on the parchment. "Arden of Ashwood."

"Present," I whisper. A few heads turn in my direction, scowling. I wipe my hands on the front of my leather breeches and keep my head low as roll call continues.

"Brenan of Razorwood. Caris of Smoke Valley. Clent of South Vale."

Silence. Silence. Silence.

So much silence.

Each name pounds against my chest like a war drum, made all the worse by the sound of Fenris's scribbling. Slowly, that numbness inside of me transforms into guilt. The letter burns white hot in my back pocket as Alysa's words repeat.

I don't hear the rest of the roll. It isn't until Fenris pockets the scroll and straightens that I realize it's over. Effortlessly, he hops from the top of the root, water spraying as he lands. "We'll discuss elections and relocation at sunrise. You're all dismissed."

An elf shoulder checks me as they leave. I don't see their face.

"Hey—"

Another elf does the same. And then Alysa steps in front of me and shoves me into the swamp. My butt sinks into muck. For a minute, no one says anything, no one *does* anything as algae and water scorch my nostrils, soaking into everything I own. Nirissa glances between Fenris and me, as if waiting for him to defend me, to help me.

He hesitates before offering his hand.

SLEEP DOESN'T COME EASY. Everything is strange out here. The trees are narrower. The canopy is sparse. Silver starlight gleams through diamond-shaped leaves that are too thin, too shiny, and too blue.

I'm so freaking sick of that color.

Somewhere above me, Nirissa snores loudly in her hammock, the cloth so dark it blends into the bark. I keep rolling in mine, knotted cords squeaking with each turn. The tossing has been endless. Whenever I close my eyes, I see Lyrick, the Butcher, Mom, that stupid letter. So, I stop closing them. Instead, I stare at the starlight, tracing an invisible line through the planets bright enough to see.

Corova—a red giant shrouded in swirling gray mist.

Sarinya—purple and small with a corona of darkness around it.

Precipi—this ugly green thing full of craters, surrounded by ring rocks and dust clouds.

From this distance, without my dad's telescope, they all look like white dots, but almost everyone knows how to find the Great Three. Sighing, I imagine there's an elf on one of them, looking at the same stars as me, fortunate enough to have never met an elgrew.

The elders say our people once colonized the universe—through what means, I have no idea. It's likely a fairy tale, but it's comforting nevertheless to imagine that not all of our people are living in this nightmare. Some of us must be happy . . . somewhere.

Twigs snap below me, and I bolt upright.

Peering over the edges of my hammock, I watch a shadowy figure climb the tree—not like an elgrew but like an elf, with their lamellae extended. Fenris's goggled face emerges from the darkness and relief washes over me. As he nears my hammock, he pulls the goggles down around his neck and crawls beside me, eyes as black as the night sky.

The cords groan as he settles in. The frame rocks in the humid breeze while I readjust my body to accommodate him.

For a moment, we exist in total silence, both of us sitting crisscross, close enough our knees touch. His body is so warm, I have to twist my hair into a bun to alleviate the heat, peeling sweat-soaked tendrils from my neck. I don't know what to say to him—or why he's here—but it's nice to not be so alone.

Fenris wipes the moisture from his brow and clears his throat. "I should have defended you back there. I'm sorry."

I bite my bottom lip. I didn't expect an apology—I'm not sure I deserve one. Reaching into my back pocket, I withdraw the worn letter and pass it to him, staring at my lap while he reads it over. "Do you think it's my fault?" I ask.

"I don't think you deserve the way they're treating you."

"That isn't an answer."

Fenris refolds the letter and returns it to me. Then, he takes my gloved hand in his, the way he has so many times before, through so many funerals, so many deaths. "My parents chose to take you in, knowing the risks," he says, staring at me with those depthless eyes. "They wanted you here."

"And you?"

"I always want you by my side." Fenris squeezes my hand and I wince. His brows draw together when he notices the twisty scars and blue scabs that climb up my fingertips. "What happened to your hand? Can I look?"

"The fires," I say. "It looks worse than it is."

Gently, he peels the glove back, exposing a wound I've spent the better part of three days ignoring. The skin is bright blue and swollen, so thin it could be pierced by grabbing bark the wrong way. The darkness is too thick for me to see the details properly, but not Fenris. His expanded pupils allow him to take everything in.

My best friend stiffens beside me. "How did you get this?"

More twigs snap.

I pull the glove down, cringing when the leather scrapes my scabs, and peer out into the moonlit forest. A team of masked spotters surround the bottom of the tree. "Elgrew sighting a mile north," one of them says. "The canopy is too thin to hide us here. We're taking shelter in the caves."

On reflex, I reach for my go-bag a branch up and flex my lamellae, but Fenris places his palm on my shoulder, stopping my ascent toward Nirissa.

"Arden—"

"What?" I snap. "We don't have time for this."

He recoils, the words dying on his tongue as he slips his hand away.

"What is it?" I try again, gentler this time, softer. "What's wrong?"

His mouth opens, but the spotter's voice cuts him off, making both of us jump. "Get your asses down here. *Now!*"

V. Arden

"In Rayna, there are two types of elves—those who live in the trees and those who dwell beneath the ground. Topside, elves prioritize family and peace. Underground, they form a militia capable of committing atrocities that rival those of the elgrew. Children are banned from their society, and the Claimed are used as bait to lure Hunters in. They are brutes and monsters. They are the Resistance."

—Esin of Ashwood, Chieftain of the Lo'kowe Tribe.

Shoulder Squish Cave is all but invisible—a solid wall of bedrock with an opening so narrow it can only be accessed by squeezing sideways through it, thus the name. Teal oo'ren moss glosses over the entrance, giving it this iridescent sheen that glitters in the moonlight. Carved into the moss, into the very rock itself, is a sigil—a vertical line with two dots on opposite sides of it.

Starra'lee. The underground elves.

Nirissa squeezes through the entrance first, then Fenris, then me. I suck in my nonexistent gut and feel the cool, slimy rocks press against me still. They scrape along my stomach, catching on my hide breastwrap half a second before the cave opens up. I nearly stumble inside.

It takes a moment to gather my bearings and adjust to the sudden brightness.

Knotted cords hang from the ceiling at varying lengths. Attached to the bottom of them are glass orbs filled with glowflies that crawl up the sides, blinking magenta light. In the forest, light is a luxury we can't afford; it'll lure elgrew in. Here, we're bathed in it. Pink flashes illuminate a damp, low-rising chamber. Water glistens off stalactites and stalagmites that try to join in the center, forming jagged columns that look like teeth.

The members of our tribe gather in small clusters, half-hidden by the cave's rock formations. They have to duck to get around, but not Nirissa and me. We're short and small enough that we can still fit almost anywhere. Swinging the go-bag from my shoulder, I point to an empty corner of the cave and urge Nirissa to settle in. She rubs her sleep-filled eyes and trudges there, curling up around a stalagmite. Fenris remains in place, his black eyes watery, his pupils slowly contracting back to normal.

"You alright?" I ask. "You could put on the goggles."

"I'll be fine." He wipes the moisture from his eyes and blinks a half dozen times, his vision likely reduced to shadows and light spots. "Go get settled. I'll join you in a few minutes."

I nod, then follow Nirissa's path. No one speaks to me as I pass by; they're too busy setting up camp, laying out blankets to sleep on, and rebandaging wounds. Whispers echo through the cave, but none of them are intelligible. In my periphery, Fenris bumbles not toward me, but toward High Priest Selik and a group of healers who unload their medical cache onto the floor.

Odd.

Fenris isn't injured—not that I'm aware of.

He leans in close to Selik and whispers something in his ear. The high priest stiffens.

Unease settles low in my belly, but it's probably nothing. Fenris is acting chief until morning elections, so it likely has something to do with security or resources. Still, I wish I could use my sezin to listen in. Amplifying this many voices would deafen me, though, just as easily as using it near the river or in the rain.

The healers join in on Fenris's conversation. They fumble with leather pouches on their belts, withdrawing clay, corked vials in every imaginable color—red with blue swirls, yellow with green stripes, pinks, and blues, and something coal black. They lay the medicines next to their surgical equipment, displaying them in neat rows.

"Whatcha doing?" Nirissa asks. I jump when I see her standing behind me.

"You should be in bed," I say, my cheeks flaming at getting caught.

"It's too cold. You have my blanket."

"Oh." I stare down at the go-bag I'm still holding. *Oops.* "Come on, let's get you to sleep."

Hand in hand, I walk her back to our spot. As she gets comfortable, I unfasten the buckles on my bag and fish out our only blanket. Then, I tuck her in. Nirissa sucks on her thumb and curls into the fetal position, her big eyes roaming the cave.

"I don't understand why we have to sleep in here," she says, slurring the words around her thumb. Drool dribbles out the side of her mouth. "It's so . . ."

Suffocating?

Crowded?

Bleak?

I feel the strangeness as much as she does. Elves belong in the forest, surrounded by fresh air and starlight—not in tight, enclosed spaces. "I know it's weird, bug, but it's just for tonight. Tomorrow, we'll find another orangeleaf forest to stay in."

"Will they still be mad at us?"

My gaze drifts back to Fenris, Selik, and the healers—all still chattering away. As the chieftain's son, Fenris has always been popular, but I've never felt left out until now. "Don't worry about that, bug. Everyone's a little sad because of the funeral, but they still love us. We're family."

I wish I felt as confident as I sound. Nirissa takes my word for truth, though, and rolls toward the wall, closing her eyes. It doesn't take long for the snores to start.

Lowering myself onto the floor beside her, I cringe at the cold dampness. Goosebumps prick my arms and I resist a shiver, rubbing my biceps to generate warmth.

"You look cold," Fenris says, appearing beside me. "Good thing I have this." Smirking, he holds two clay mugs of steaming liquid, the contents blood-red.

A quick glance around the cave shows others with drinks as well. Selik and the healers have begun to brew it in a large cauldron, heating it not with fires, but on wooden chips engraved with magical runes. Neither elves nor elgrew can cast magic, but the fae who came before us could, occasionally imbuing artifacts that we stumble across. The wooden chips glow bright-hot, activated with secret words only leadership knows.

I wonder if they shared that information with Fenris.

He offers one of the cups to me and the warmth provides instantaneous relief, the steam heating my cheeks and burning my fingertips in the best kind of way. I breathe in the sweet floral scent of scarlet tea and take a sip, groaning in pleasure. It's spiced with cinnamon and cloves and something I can't quite place. Something weird. Something bitter that makes me crinkle my nose.

"I hate caves," I tell him, drinking deeper, adapting to the flavor.

"Me too." Fenris takes a long swig then sits across from me. "It makes me nervous when I can't use my lamellae." He flexes his fingers, pressing them to the cave floor. They slide right off. Stone—especially wet stone—and fingerpads don't mix. We're defenseless in here if we're caught, unable to climb, unable to flee because there's only one exit.

The hairs rise on the back of my neck—a trapped panic threatening to consume me.

Fenris shakes me out of it. Literally. Brows furrowed, he grabs me by the shoulders and points to the entrance as someone new squeezes through it.

"Is that . . . ?" He trails off, his mouth hanging half open.

I don't recognize the woman, but she's dressed in fighting leathers and armed to the gills. A bandolier of knives hangs across her chest, and her face is covered in war paint—lips and eyes a dark black. Like Fenris, her pupils are fully dilated, and tears stream down her cheeks, streaking the kohl.

"Do you think she's in Starra'lee?" Fenris finally asks.

"She can't be."

As far as I know, no one in our tribe has ever seen the underground elves before. They're more myth than anything—monsters who hunt elgrew for sport, who move like ghosts in the night, unseen, unheard, deadly. Children are banned from their camps. The only way to join them is to be recruited personally.

Nausea turns my stomach, and suddenly I'm not thirsty anymore. I set the cup down with a click and slide it away from me.

Will Starra'lee punish us for using one of their sanctuaries? Will they kick us out?

This cave has always been empty in the past. Up until now, I assumed it had been abandoned.

The stranger closes her eyes and pinches the bridge of her nose. "This is a Starra'lee bunker," she growls. "Unless you plan on enlisting, get the fuck out—and take those damn lights with you!"

Everyone freezes, including me. Selik is the first to stand. He rises from his spot near the cauldron and approaches her open-palmed—not that she can see him. Her darkeyes are still closed, still watering.

"We need the space tonight," Selik says. "There's been an elgrew spotting nearby."

"And why is that my problem?" She glares at him—at all of us—a pale gray rim forming around her enlarged pupils. Tight braids cling to her scalp, and an orange-furred cloak peeks from the duffle strapped to her shoulder. "We agreed to stay out of each other's spaces. Or have you forgotten?"

"You're outnumbered," Selik says calmly. "We don't need your permission to stay."

Her teeth flash. They've been filed into points like an elgrew's. "Is that how it is?"

"That's how it is." Arms crossed, Selik stares her down in a way I never could.

And then she relents.

The woman rubs her face, smearing kohl, then stomps past Fenris and me—the stone shaking beneath her thick military boots. Sighing, she throws her go-bag to the floor and crouches low like a verncat ready to strike. Her angry gaze lands on me, and I jerk my head away, looking at anything else. I get the distinct feeling none of the other Starra'lee members are nearby; if they were, we'd be mudsnake food by now.

A sharp pain travels through my stomach. For half a second, my vision blurs and I moan, pressing my forehead against the cool cave wall. Then, it passes.

"Are you alright?" Fenris asks.

I've never enjoyed being vulnerable around him—around anyone really—so I deflect. "Did you notice that she's wearing shoes? Who does that?"

Fenris shrugs. "Starra'lee lives in underground caves. They can't use their lamellae, so it doesn't matter."

Good point.

"I don't know why anyone would choose to live like this." I gesture to the stuffy walls around us. Beads of sweat gather on my forehead, and I swipe them away, but not before they sting my eyes.

Has it gotten hotter in here?

"I don't think they have much choice," Fenris says. "My dad told me Starra'lee mostly recruits the Claimed. When an elgrew bites someone, they can't get rid of it. It's either kill or be killed."

"What did you say?" My head lolls, and the words come out all jumbled, like I've drunk too much ale. A sinking weight lands in the pit of my gut, my burned hand throbbing. Frantically, I yank the leather glove free, my whole body trembling.

I need to see that it's gone. I need to know Lyrick can't find me.

Through hazy vision, I stare at the twisty blue scars, the scabs, and the thirty-eight faint dots growing back—right where he left them. I shake my head. "No. That isn't possible."

"I'm sorry, Arden." Fenris grabs my cheeks between his palms, and my eyelids grow heavy. I blink once, twice, and then I close them fully, my muscles going lax. I'm vaguely aware of him laying me on the floor, covering me with something heavy and warm, whispering in my ear two words. "Forgive me."

And then I fall asleep.

Dozens of Hunters amass outside the Grand Overseer's estate, lined up against the silver, blood-soaked battlements surrounding the property. Their backs are to the wall, eyes faced forward toward me—toward the orangeleaf forest behind me where Conrin and the rest of my unit waits. Kerosene lampposts illuminate a long, winding road that leads from Kariss—our capital city—to the front gates here. Made of blue mosaic tiles, the road should gleam yellow in the lantern light, but there's so much dirt covering it, it's hard to see.

My father—the Grand Overseer, Azerin—exits the front gate, his polished shoes clicking down the pathway. As always, his outfit is pristine: a blue, tailed suit, freshly pressed and wrinkle-free, a ceremonial sword sheathed at his side, gilded and sapphire-jeweled, and a plain metallic-blue diadem. Purple-skinned Butchers guard him, flanking him on all sides, their bodies twisted and deformed, adorned in all black, with matching aprons around their necks.

Swinging my legs from Prowler, I approach the battlements, dragging my captive behind me. Ankles and wrists tied, there's nothing the elf can do to stop me, and she's smart enough not to try. Grass bends and twigs snap beneath her. Tears streak her face, but I was smart enough to gag her on the road, so I don't have to listen to the sniveling.

No one seems to notice us as I approach. Not my father. Not his guards. Not the Hunters lined against the wall. It's . . . unusual. The whole thing is unusual. I can't begin to fathom why they're here or what my father's plans for them are. With Azerin, sometimes it's better not knowing.

Facing away from me, he clasps his hands behind his back and paces down the line of elgrew. I stop dragging the elf and lean against a tree—not quite hiding, but not making my presence known either.

"You invaded the A'sow Tribe," my father says, the silver stitch-work in his gray skin glinting in the moonlight. His long gray hair is only a shade away from being black. "You displaced them and lost the survivors. Now we have no idea where my elf is."

Not yours. Mine.

The taste of Arden's blood lingers on my tongue. When I close my eyes, I feel like I can see her. Visions of murky water, of glowing tree roots, of things I've never laid eyes on before creep into my subconscious in a way that seems so real. It's unnerving. Bites don't connect us that way, and I can't help but wonder if I'm losing my sanity.

"It took years to find her," my father continues, his voice icy. "How difficult can it be to catch one small elf? I've given you endless resources and yet you've failed me. Again."

No one speaks nor tries to defend themselves. When my father makes up his mind about something, pleading and excuses only make the punishment worse. Unprompted, the Butchers guarding the Grand Overseer unsheathe their weapons with a loud shink.

"Someone must pay," Azerin continues. "I've discussed it with my council and we've come to an accord. Tenok of Kariss, Karesai of Hunters, come forward."

A man steps from the lineup — the current leader of our caste who organized the botched raid. Still clad in fighting leathers, still covered in ash and silver blood, he's nearly a head taller than my father. Against anyone else, the man might be intimidating, but Azerin earned his position through bones and gore and nearly two-hundred years of fighting.

My father stares up at him, and I'm thankful I can't see the vitriol in his gaze or hear the quiet words that must transpire between them.

Tenok goes pale.

The Butchers step in front of the Hunters, pressing their blades to their throats so they won't intervene. Calmly, my father withdraws a shimmering silver flask from his breast pocket and slowly unscrews the cap. The man flinches as Azerin douses him with the stuff, shaking it until every drop of liquid has been emptied. The sharp stench of kerosene is carried on the humid breeze.

Oh, fuck me.

The man could fight, but archers guard the battlements. Either they or my father would have him felled before he'd land a killing blow. And then Azerin would craft an even crueler punishment, perhaps with his unit, perhaps with his children. Tenok must know this because he barely flinches when the matchbox comes out.

A bright spark fills the darkness. Azerin tosses it toward him and takes a step back, the flames enveloping Tenok's body, the screams and smoke filling the night. I snap my gaze away at the stench of burning meat, trying to forget the last time I watched an elgrew punished this way. My uncle's face burns into my mind, and I feel his loss all over again, my fingers tightening into fists around the rope that holds my prisoner.

The screams seem to last forever.

I get this uneasy feeling in the pit of my gut, wondering what the punishment would be for catching and releasing Arden, for branding the creature as mine. For the thousandth time since last week, I wonder what in Demtin's name came over me—and yet she is mine, and I wouldn't have it any other way. The creature will be my greatest challenge, not my father's prize jewel.

Still, I'm not about to tell him that.

As the Hunters file out, the Grand Overseer pivots on his heels and strolls toward the forest, his face obscured in shadow. The Butchers don't follow, though their eyes linger on him—hands poised on weapons. "You brought a gift," Azerin says. My father's nose is every bit as good as a verncat's, but so is mine.

I clear my throat. "Found it after the raid. Lost and Found says she's Sorso's bitch. Figured it would be better if you gave it back, not me."

"You didn't participate in the raid." It isn't a question, but an observation.

"Tenok didn't invite me."

Azerin rounds a tree, his silhouette as silent as a shadow. "That's because he viewed you as a threat. You're competition for his leadership. Now that he's gone—"

"I don't want it," I say flatly. The Karesai of Hunters live notoriously short lives, either felled by Azerin's hand, disgruntled Hunters, or the elves they track. It's a thankless job full of busywork, often based in the capitol rather than the forest I've come to love.

"I didn't ask if you wanted it," Azerin says. "That would imply you have a choice. Now come inside so we can discuss your future."

I WAKE in a cool sweat to the rhythmic sound of scraping wood. I scan the dark room around me, searching for Azerin, ready to plead my case about how I can't become the next Karesai—and then I remember where I am, *who* I am. Chest heaving, I stare at the throbbing bite mark on my palm, spiders crawling down my spine.

I was in his head.

I *was* him.

There's not enough alcohol on Rayna to lessen my disgust.

Is that normal? Do all the Claimed see their masters' thoughts?

Resisting a shiver, I force myself to breathe normally, then remember what I overheard. The Hunter sees me too, and it's just as strange for him. This is something to keep secret, even from Fenris. If the others found out Lyrick could see into my head, that we're connected beyond the bite—

The others!

I bolt upright and scan the cave again, this time with a clear head.

The cavern is empty. No Fenris. No tribe. Even the lights are gone.

A lone figure whittles in the corner, a pile of wood shavings stacking up around her. She wears an orange-fur cloak—verncat fur, I realize, with the face and paws still attached. Saberteeth and fuzzy ears jut from the raised hood that conceals her face.

Wiping the crust from my eyes, I turn my attention away from her to the hide blanket where Nirissa should be, but isn't. "Where'd they go?" I ask, voice scratchy. "Where's my sister?"

The woman doesn't answer, but her knife pauses on the wooden figurine in her hand. Raising the blade, she points it toward the entrance, then returns to her whittling.

They left without me.

Jittery panic sends me scrambling for my things, stuffing everything into my go-bag. They couldn't have gotten far. I can still catch up.

Swinging the bag onto my shoulder, I take off into a sprint, squeezing past rocks and slime until I stumble into the muggy swamp. The bright daylight sears my vision, but I blink the sunspots away and squint into the reeds around me.

There aren't any footprints nearby, and the plants aren't bent. My tribe has been gone for a while.

A desperate scream climbs my throat, but I swallow it back down and count to ten. I need to stay calm and come up with a plan to find them.

Faint giggling comes from the blue reeds to my right. Relief floods my body and air fills my lungs for the first time in what feels like minutes. I brush aside the plants, sure there's been a misunderstanding, sure my tribe will be waiting for me close by.

I find Nirissa instead, sitting in the open water beside the Korring-Marr's root—wooden doll in hand. Its twiggy body drips muck into the water as she walks it across the rippling surface, playing with it, laughing and talking to herself as if she isn't in the center of snake-infested waters.

Heart pounding, I run to her—water splashing, feet squelching, the warm sun bearing down on my skin. She shouldn't be here alone. Fenris or the spotters should be with her.

Nirissa flashes me a toothy smile, completely oblivious to what she's done and where she is. "I found my dolly," Nirissa says, holding it up, victorious. "Can you believe it?"

Anger boils my blood. Soaking wet, I snatch her off the ground and hug her tightly to my chest, breathing her in. *She's fine. She's safe in my arms.*

"What were you thinking, Nirissa? You can't go out into the swamp alone. There are snakes here!" I squeeze her tighter, afraid if I let go, she'll disappear again. "You could have been hurt."

"But I found my doll," she says like that makes it ok.

I take a deep breath. Then another. Then I remind myself

she's too young to know any better. "Are you alright? Did you see where Fenris and the others went?"

"They were gone when I woke up."

I push aside the anxiety threatening to take hold. Drugging me had to be Selik's idea. He must have convinced Fenris and the others to leave us behind. If I can find them, I can explain what happened, and the elders might take us back. At the very least, they'd take Nirissa. After all, she isn't Marked like I am. She isn't blue.

"Let's get you cleaned up, and then we'll find them," I say, carrying her back to Shoulder Squish Cave. Begrudgingly, I set her on her feet and nudge her toward the narrow opening, not wanting to let her out of my sight even for a second but not having much choice.

We file in—Nirissa first.

As my eyes adjust to the darkness, a low, gravelly voice comes calling out. "You're back." The Starra'lee soldier lowers her hood, exposing her freckled, unpainted face. Thick silver hair brushes her shoulders, the braids gone from last night. Aside from her pointed teeth, she doesn't seem half as frightening. A poorly constructed wooden horse—or maybe it's a cat— sits in front of her, all lumpy and misshapen.

"You shouldn't have let them see your mark," she says. "That was incredibly stupid."

"Hey, bug, why don't you take off your wet clothes?" I suggest, not wanting to have this conversation with her around. "We'll hang them outside to dry."

She glances between the Starra'lee soldier and me but does as she's told. While Nirissa strips, I step deeper into the cave, the sound of her *splatting* clothes echoing. "We'll be gone by night-fall," I tell the woman, lowering my voice.

"Good. Starra'lee doesn't take children, and I'm not inter-ested in playing babysitter." She crosses her arms and leans against the cave wall, but her eyes are a sharp contrast to the aggressive posture—there's something soft in there. Or maybe that's pity. "Where will you go?"

"We'll find Fenris and the others. The Hunter who gave me *this*"—I flash her my swollen palm—"won't be a threat until I reach my Age of Majority. Once I explain that to my tribe—"

"You're delusional. Your friend drugged you last night," she says matter-of-factly. "After you fell asleep, he convinced everyone to leave you and your sister behind. Made a pretty compelling case for it too. I don't think they're interested in your explanations."

"He wouldn't do that to Nirissa."

He loves her.

He loves me.

The betrayal stings so sharply, I refuse to believe it. Fenris might've poisoned my drink, but he wouldn't have done so without Selik and the healers' encouragement. He might've suggested they leave me behind for everyone's safety, but not Nirissa; she got caught in the crossfire. The tribe's decision to abandon us was rash, caused by everyone's heightened emotions. Once they hear what happened, it'll be different.

I have to believe that. Anything less and we're as good as dead.

"My parents were inventors," I argue. "I know how to build things they can't. I'm the only one in our tribe who's fluent in the Elgrew tongue. I'm too useful to get rid of."

She scoffs. "Everyone's replaceable, *Blue.*" She says it like the slur it is, and the name hits like a physical blow. If that's the name she's calling me by, does that mean that's what she heard last night? Is that the way my people talk about me when I'm not around?

I feel queasy. The bitter taste of their tea lingers on my tongue.

"Tribes don't take the Claimed in. Full stop," the soldier adds. "It's too risky."

"Mine does." Our best forager, Trista, came to us Marked, and Fenris's dad took her in regardless. He protected her like he protected me.

But Fenris's dad is gone, whispers that little voice of doubt. *And Fenris left you to die.*

The soldier withdraws a dagger and begins picking her fingernails with it, clearly bored of this conversation. "And when they don't want you?"

"Then someone else will." I say it with conviction. And for my sister's sake, I hope it's true.

VI. Arden

"Two elves arrived at our camp today, carrying a blue-skinned child. I know little about them, except they possess forbidden knowledge from before the Great War. Their scientific research may finally give us the tools to protect ourselves against elgrew, but their child could doom us all. Only time will tell."

—Roskan of Blackwood, Chieftain of the A'sow Tribe

Personal Journal

"Leave. You're not welcome here." The elven spotter readjusts his dagger, but the blade quivers in his hand, giving away his lack of experience. It's hard to tell how old an elf is after they've reached their Age of Majority —we don't age past that—but if I had to guess, I'd assume this one isn't much older than me. His ears are pointier than most, the tips bound and stretched beyond their natural length. A common custom amongst the Lok'owe Tribe.

I hold Nirissa tighter and rest the bulk of her weight against my hip. My arms ache. My bare feet are covered in thorny cuts and weeping blisters. Eyelids drooping, I force myself to meet the spotter's gaze—not to stare at those hideously long ears his people consider beautiful.

"Please," I whisper. "We have nowhere else to go."

We've been to all the other tribes already—the Zel'nok, the Bra'ven, the Kantelli, and the Jakir. Like the Starra'lee soldier predicted, no one wants us.

A sympathetic look flashes across his features, but then it's snuffed out by the crunching of nearby leaves. We both whirl toward the sound, scanning a patch of orange razorbushes and violet canopy.

No one's there.

"I'm sorry, Blue," he says, sheathing his blade. It *shinks* as it hits the inside of a rusted scabbard. "I knew your parents. They were good fae."

"My name isn't Blue," I hiss, lowering my voice to keep from waking my sister. She snores against my chest, drool oozing through my leather breastwrap. "My name is Arden."

"Arden, then." He sweeps a silver, flyaway hair back into his bun. A sliver of black elgrew bone juts between the bridge of his nose. "I'm sorry, but you can't stay with us. Your skin draws elgrew like manure draws flies. We'd be found and burned in a week."

Every other camp has said the same thing since the last attack. Even with the bite mark covered, they believe we're harbingers of death. I haven't found our tribe yet, likely because they don't want to be found.

Tears blur my vision, but I blink them back and shove past him, toward the orange razorbushes where another spotter is likely seated. It's been weeks. Surely someone will show mercy on us and take us in. I can't do this on my own. I'm too young to have a child, let alone care for one; I barely know how to care for myself.

The spotter clambers behind me, rushing to catch up,

stomping over fallen leaves and tangled vines. Like me, his feet are bare.

"I know you're in there," I say, stooping in front of the bushes. Each leaf ends in a sharp, serrated point, thick enough to cut skin. A little boy pops out, barely older than my sister, his body covered in leather armor, his eyes hidden behind goggles with green-colored lenses—my father's goggles.

Fenris. I glance up into the canopy, but he's nowhere in sight.

It makes sense that my tribe would join up with a larger group, given their losses. There's safety in numbers. But if Fenris is here, why won't he show his face?

"How many times have I told you not to play around on the forest floor?" The spotter growls. Stepping between me and the razorbush, he yanks the child to his feet. "An elgrew could have found you!"

Nirissa stirs, rubbing the sleep from her matted eyelids. "Arri, where are we?"

I stroke her long silver hair and kiss her forehead. "Nowhere, bug. Go back to sleep."

The boy grumbles, wriggling out of the spotter's grasp. He stomps up to me and removes Dad's goggles, revealing one milky eye and one gray. His mutilated face is split down the middle. On the left side, he looks perfect, but on the right . . . I do my best not to stare at the lumpy mess of raised flesh.

"Your skin!" He beams up at me, but only half his mouth turns into a smile. "Did you know you're blue?"

The amazement in his eyes is unmistakable. So few elves are born anything other than dark gray, and the ones who are, are quickly snatched up by elgrew and either eaten, turned into jewelry, or bred. I'm probably the first elf he's ever seen that doesn't look uniform.

Before I can speak, Nirissa yawns. "Did you know your face is weird?"

"Bug, that's not very nice," I snap.

She only blinks at me. "But it *is* weird."

"I'm not weird. You're weird." The boy sticks his tongue out, and the spotter steps between us yet again.

"Excuse him. My son is…My son is not supposed to be here. Go back to camp with the others before an elgrew comes and snatches the rest of your face."

His body pales.

"Fine," he says, crossing his arms. "You're no fun anyway." The boy pivots and vanishes past the razorbushes. Grasses and leaves sway with his movements, and I track the steps, assessing the final moment he disappears. Bark crumbles and rains from a tree several yards away.

Got you.

I move to follow. If I can talk to Fenris or the tribal elders . . . If I can plead my case . . .

The spotter jumps in front of me and outstretches his arms. "No, Arden."

"But we'll die."

Phantom pains travel up the scars on my palm, reminding me my time is limited. I've been marked. *Claimed.*

"Please," I say again.

The canopy rustles overhead, so subtly an elgrew might mistake it for wind. At first, I had mistaken it too, only finding the spotter because I knew what subtleties to look for. Elven villages are safe—deadly even to the elgrew who hunt in small numbers. I need them to protect me.

No one can protect you, warns that gnawing voice in the back of my head. *Lyrick will come.*

"If we let you in," the spotter says, his gaze shifting to the glove covering my mark, "we'll all die. That bite will lead the Hunters straight to us. I won't trade my son's life for yours. Please don't ask me to."

"I'll cut my hand off," I blurt. What's a hand compared to

their protection? If I'm trapped out here alone, I'm dead anyway.

"That's not how bites work. The venom's in your system now. Hand or no hand, your master will be able to track you."

My nose crinkles at the vile word. "Then take Nirissa."

He shakes his head. "You share a bloodline. Her offspring could be blue, too, and then where would we be? I'm sorry, Arden. We can't."

The words are a punch to the gut. As they sink in, my knees buckle and I slide to the forest floor. Twigs dig into my worn, animal-skin pants. Dewy ground wets them. I fumble for words, but none come.

The spotter squats beside me and removes the blade from his belt. Reaching for my hand, he folds it over Lyrick's teeth marks. "Don't let yourself be taken. What happens in Kariss is worse than anything they might do to you out here."

"What are you saying?" I rasp.

His jaw hardens, and the softness in his eyes disappears. "I'm saying the blade will be a kindness to her and to you. When you die, your souls will be absorbed into the Korring-Marr. You'll be at peace."

Kill myself.

Kill my baby sister.

A small hand reaches for my cheek, wiping at tears I didn't realize I'd been crying. I can't bring myself to look at her, to admit I've failed, that my skin has condemned us both.

I blink past the burning in my eyes, holding onto Nirissa as tightly as I can as warm tears spill into her perfectly normal, perfectly silver hair. This is all my fault.

The sheath digs into my palm, and when I look back up, the spotter is gone. I know better than to think I'll find him or this tribe again. Still, I continue staring, waiting for my best and longest friend to show himself. Surely, *he* doesn't agree. Surely, *he* doesn't want to see us dead.

The silence is deafening.

"Arri?" Nirissa asks.

I take a hiccupping breath. Scooting Nirissa from my lap, I unsheathe the dagger. Rust falls from the pointed tip onto my wet clothes.

The spotter's right. This would be better for us.

My hands shake as I scoop her back up and lay her against my chest. I hold the dagger to her back, unable to speak past the swollen lump in my throat. It'll be over in seconds, and then we'll be with our parents again.

"Arri? Are you ok?" The blade wobbles as she wraps her tiny arms around my neck.

My stomach turns. Bile rises up my throat, but I swallow it back down.

"I love you, bug. You know that, right?" My cracked voice is barely audible over the wind that tangles in our hair.

"I love you too."

Sobbing into her, I angle the blade so it'll strike true. Then, I think of her lifeless eyes, her broken body on the forest floor. She'll never fall in love. She'll never reach her Age of Majority or undergo her Rite of Passage. Neither will I.

The blade drops.

It falls into my lap as I gasp for breath, the world so hot around me, I'm suffocating under the weight of my clothes.

I love my sister.

I don't want us to die. Not before we've had a chance to experience life.

"I'm going to protect you, bug," I tell her, brushing the hair from her eyes. "I'm going to keep us safe. I promise."

I glare up at the canopy and flip Fenris off.

MY GO-BAG THUMPS onto the cave floor. Green glass goes spilling out, clinking and rolling across the limestone. The Starra'lee soldier is here, lounging on a foldable cot. She peers at the entryway through half-lidded, disinterested eyes as Nirissa and I make ourselves at home.

"I told you, I'm not babysitting," she says.

"I don't need a babysitter. I need a place to sleep where the elgrew can't find us. The trees are too dangerous without spotters."

The soldier groans, rubbing her hand down her face. "Not happening. Find your own hideout."

"I can fix your eye problem," I say, dragging the bag to her, grunting with the effort it takes. I packed the duffle a little too full this morning, and my shoulder aches from carrying it. More glass lenses spill out, as do jars filled with viscous green fluid that only I know how to make. "My green glass dims the light without darkening everything else. I can make you goggles that'll save you in a raid. All I want is access to the cave."

She leans over and picks one of the lenses up, holding it to her eyes. "Starra'lee won't recruit you, you know? You'll have to hunt and forage for yourself."

"I know."

"It can't be official. If I say yes, this agreement remains between us."

I arch a brow. "Won't the others see me in here?"

She shakes her head. "No. I'm the only scout they send to this region. If that changes, you'll have to find somewhere else to sleep. It's the best I can offer." She holds out her hand and we shake on it. "My name is Giara, by the way."

"I'm Arden, but apparently everyone calls me Blue."

Five Years Later. . .

VII. Lyrick

"The first elgrew were of elf and wood nymph descent. The females of our species have always been infertile, whereas the males can only procreate by inseminating a female elf. Children born this way are always elgrew."

–Ancient Histories, The Emergence of Species: Volume 1.

A high-pitched shriek pierces the low chatter of the mess hall as the Butcher's cleaver severs 19764's arm from the wrist down. Silver blood sprays the glass divider between us. On the other side, the hunk of meat falls onto a blue ceramic plate next to the chopping platform. As the Butcher readies her elf for the next cut, her apprentice—a small female elgrew with bumpy purple skin—passes me the plate, sliding it through a thin gap beneath the divider.

"Thanks," I mumble.

"Always a pleasure to serve you, Lyrick."

She winks at me, and I grunt. I don't recognize her. Outside of mealtimes, I make a point of avoiding the Butchers and their ilk. It's fucking barbaric what they do to their prey, and I want no part of it.

The mess hall reeks of urine and sweat as row after row of elves line up for slaughter. It'd reek of shit, too, if the Butchers didn't have the foresight to starve them last night. Holding my breath, I poke the gray flesh with my carving knife, making a face as the blood coagulates. It's too bony. Too stiff. Eating it would be worse than starving.

My eyes snap to the creature standing across from me, and guilt twists my insides. Not only is this *thing* being tortured on my behalf, but I won't even have the decency to fucking eat it. We're still staring at one another when the Butcher pushes down on its shoulders, forcing it into a blue metallic chair made of *cold iron*, the one substance all fae are weak to save for us.

The elf's eyes roll to the back of its skull as the magical properties of the chair incapacitate it. Silver blood bubbles between its lips, its pleas morphing into nothing more than silent gurgles. By now, both its hands are missing—both ears too—and despite the drugs I'm certain they've plied it with, the suffering is evident on its blood and tear-stained face.

"Next!" the Butcher calls.

She fastens leather straps around the elf's arms, lashing them to the armrests. Then, she swings her cleaver again. No screams this time. The bicep lands with a *thump* and a *squish* as the next elgrew in line maneuvers around me and claims their prize, a serrated smile on display.

"Lyrick?" the apprentice asks.

I barely hear my name, my attention transfixed on the elf whose head lolls as it drifts in and out of consciousness. Butchers think the meat tastes better when cut from awake animals. It's only a matter of time before she withdraws her smelling salts, forcing it to endure—

"Is something wrong?" the apprentice asks. Her deformed

skin is covered in silver blood; her black apron sparkles with it. "Would you like a different piece?"

I shake my head emphatically. "No. No, I'm fine."

Blinking, I take one step back, then another, reminding myself where I am—how I'm expected to behave. It doesn't matter what I think about the Butchers or their methods. Speaking out would brand me a fanatic and get me killed. Besides, no one forced me to come here. My friends suggested it and my family expects it, but no one made me. There are more civilized eateries in the heart of the city, where they euthanize their food before they cook it, but no self-respecting Hunter would be caught there. Like the Butchers, we eat our kills fresh.

Except, these aren't my kills.

My stomach rumbles, the hunger, the aching emptiness almost unbearable as I make my way through the dining area, past rows of blue metallic tables and matching chairs. The bamboo floor groans beneath my military boots. Humid jungle air breezes through the wall-less space, the putrid odors dissipating the farther I get from the carving stations.

Everything around me is blue. Blue-painted ceilings. Blue placemats. Blue chalices filled with blue liquid. My father is obsessed with the color and has turned this entire city into a living reminder of the elf he hunts.

Too bad I'll eat her long before she's forced to see it.

I close my eyes, tugging on the mental connection between us, hoping to catch a glimpse of the forest through Arden's eyes. It remains as quiet and dark as ever. I have no control over what I see or when I see it, which is probably for the best. The bond between us shouldn't exist. It can only cause problems.

Pushing her from my mind, I scan the room for Eleesy, Conrin, and Sarvenna. They sit in the back, their uneaten plates in front of them, waiting for me to return. Like every Hunter here, the three of them are devastatingly beautiful—their bodies custom-made from their most memorable kills. It's a sharp contrast to the Butchers, who've maintained their twisted bones and malformed skin. But the Butchers don't need to be camouflaged like us; they need to be intimidating to the animals they keep.

No matter how often I see the Butchers, it's difficult to look at their hideous bodies without wondering what I might've looked like without the surgeries and body modifications. So, I don't look. I keep my gaze averted, ducking past their enclaves to reach my friends.

My plate hits the table a little too hard, silver blood oozing over the lip.

"Hands are the worst," Eleesy remarks, displaying the same cut as mine. "I swear to Demtin, if I get another hand this month, I'm going to jump across that damn divider and rip the elf's throat out myself."

I snort. Like the Butchers would ever let her get close enough to touch their property.

Nudging the hand on my plate, I stick my knife in and seesaw, almost retching when the blood slowly leaks out.

"Still struggling, I see." Across from me, Conrin happily cuts through his quarter thigh, having gotten the best cut the mess hall has to offer.

I lift a pinky finger to my mouth and bite down, the bone crunching between my teeth. Bile rises up my throat, but I force myself to swallow both it and the grotesquely lukewarm body part, shuddering when it slides into my empty stomach.

"I hate eating this shit," I say. "I need to be out there, hunting with the rest of you."

Where it's a fair fight.

"Then breed someone and get it over with," Sarvenna says, rolling her eyes. Her skin is mottled—dark gray, light gray, and cream forming a gorgeous patchwork across her face and neck. It ruins the camouflage, especially when her long silver hair is pulled into a pony, but fuck if it doesn't make her attractive too. Attractive enough, I can't keep my hands off her.

Our violet eyes meet, and I can tell she's thinking the same thing as I am. My bedroom won't be empty tonight.

"I have no interest in breeding animals," I tell them. "My cock is quite content as is."

Conrin groans. "Your father has some of the best pleasure slaves in the city. I don't see why you're making such a big fucking deal about this. Just give him a grandson already so you can hunt with us again."

He doesn't understand. None of them do. They eat meat just fine—cooked, salted, fresh, it doesn't matter. They fuck elves for pleasure as much as they fuck each other. But I'm better than that. I *want* to be better than that. I'm not about to fuck something that can't enjoy it. I won't torture animals by forcing them to carry my spawn or by coming in them when their eyes are half dead. It goes against everything my uncle taught me.

I'd rather be my father's prisoner indefinitely, which is all too easy to accomplish given his sentries block every exit.

"I shouldn't have returned from the last hunting trip," I snarl, dropping my knife and lifting the elf's hand to my teeth. The flesh gives way beneath me, and I do my best not to taste it as I rip and chew. "I hate living indoors and sitting in on the *Politic*. It's been five fucking years, and he won't take no for an answer. I wish my cock worked as well as their wombs."

I gesture to Eleesy and Sarvenna, who glare at me. If there's one thing elgrew women hate, it's being reminded of their infertility—that despite their physical prowess and cunning, they will always be inferior to elves in that one regard. I, for one, consider it a Marr-damn blessing. The last thing Sarvenna and I need is to bring a child into this world.

"Poor Lyrick," Eleesy says. "It must be awful having an endless supply of pleasure slaves to fill up."

"Truly torture," Sarvenna adds.

I hold my retorts. Admitting my disgust would raise eyebrows. It's a personal choice, not a political statement, but my father wouldn't see it that way. At best, he'd call me a traitor. At worst, he'd do to me what he does to the slaves—tie me naked to a bed and force me to fuck one. Living in Kariss means playing it smart, not making waves, not admitting the truth—that the mess halls, the pleasure houses, and the arena all make me want to puke.

I drop my mostly uneaten hand and reach for a clay pitcher at the center of the table. Sometimes *ya'esen* helps. Rather than pour the alcohol into my chalice, I chug directly from the source, face puckering with the bitter, burning taste. When it's a quarter empty, I pull away, gasping.

"You're in a mood today," Eleesy says.

I shoot her a vulgar gesture before taking another swig. Then, I fill my cup. Midnight-blue liquid—the same shade as Arden's skin—splashes against the ceramic, forming air bubbles in my drink. Clammy sweat beads my forehead as I imagine *my* elf strapped to the Butcher's chair, my father doing gods know what to her and forcing me to do the same.

I need to get out of here.

I need to be back in the forest, where everything makes sense. City life has made me soft. Five years ago, I wouldn't have cared about any of these creatures. Fuck, I would have sold them to the Butchers myself. But that was before I had to witness what was done to them day in and day out. It's easy to ignore what you can't see.

"He's always in a mood." Conrin snorts.

"Because he never eats anything," Sarvenna adds. "I can hear your stomach rumbling from over here."

I resist the urge to hug my traitorous belly and prove her right.

Outside, a series of rhythmic drum beats mark the start of

today's games. I practically jump from my chair, its metal legs scraping against the floor.

"Where the fuck are you going in such a hurry?" Conrin asks.

Bending over the table, I snatch my chalice from its placemat, then scoot my remaining food toward Sarvenna. "The games," I spit. "Azerin insisted I come. He thinks he can get me to take the victor as my *myrie*."

The mother of my child.

"Good luck with that," Conrin says.

Eleesy perks up, her eyes alight with something dark and playful. "Is he going to let you fight her? I've never fucked an elf outside of the pleasure houses, and the Trainers refuse to arm them, even when you ask nicely."

Groaning, Sarvenna rolls her eyes and takes a sip from her drink. "Don't be stupid, Leesy. Whoever wins is going to be the strongest elf in Rayna. Azerin isn't going to let Lyrick chase her just so fucking her will be more fun. Her womb's too expensive."

"As much as I enjoy this conversation," I say, squeezing the chalice so hard the stitchwork in my knuckles pulls, "I'm late."

Spinning on my heels, I polish off the rest of the ya'esen and leave. It's not enough to get me drunk, but it's a start.

VIII. Lyrick

"Elgrew are divided into five castes—Butchers, Bracers, Trainers, Hunters, and Stitchers. A single representative is selected from each to serve as Karesai on the Grand Overseer's council. This forms the Politic."

—Histories of Kariss, The Great Charter.

My father's newest *myrie* kneels on the stone floor, swollen-stomached and silent, with a golden collar around her neck. Her skin is so pale it looks white rather than gray, as does her long, flowing hair, braided down the center of her back. Like all *myrie,* she's dressed in clothes that showcase her pregnant form, indicating to the Hunters that she's to be handled with care on the off chance of an escape. A pair of dark blue harem pants hang low on her waist, but her chest is bare, accentuated by a net of golden chains and beadwork.

I avoid eye contact with her. It does no good to pity my father's pets, and if he mistakes my observation as interest, he'll insist I have her next, that we both breed her until she inevitably dies in childbirth, grows boring to us, or decides to take her own life . . . like the last three have.

Roaring crowds fill the octagonal stadium below us—Bracers, Trainers, Hunters, Stitchers, and Butchers all gathering to watch the show. Green reed papers wave in their raised fists, black ink scrawled on the fronts of them as they wager which fighter will emerge this year's champion. A young elgrew boy, some hundred feet below our private balcony, rushes up the stadium steps, collecting their papers in a wicker basket. My father will have placed his bets last night with the rest of the Politic, trading insider information with city officials, arranging the event so he doesn't lose.

Azerin never loses.

Turning sideways, I scoot between his myrie and the railing, making my way to the seat at his right. He doesn't look at me. I'm late.

Like me, my father's face is a near seamless patchwork of elf flesh, all uniformly the same shade of storm gray. Unlike me, his eyes have also been replaced—one of them, at least. The violet, silver combination has always been off-putting, even more so when he's angry with me and that silver eye swirls like it's made of mercury.

It's swirling now.

He clears his throat as I settle into my plush, blue-cushioned seat. "How nice of you to join us," Azerin says, grabbing the collar on his myrie. He tugs on the metal leash attached to it and rearranges her so that her face is in his lap. The chains jingle, but she doesn't make a sound, keeping her gaze down, her mouth closed.

I cringe knowing how much training—how many beatings—went into making her so compliant.

"I was with Conrin and Sarvenna," I say, leaning back on the cushion, pretending not to notice my father's myrie unbuttoning his silk trousers. "We were discussing—"

"Stop wasting time with them. You've already proven your-self a skilled Hunter. Now it's time to make a name for yourself here. I can't appoint you the next *Karesai* simply because you're my eldest. You have to earn it."

I don't want to earn it. I want to live in the rainforest where I can hunt and fuck and kill, free of this guilt. This shame.

Azerin's myrie opens her mouth and takes my father's purple cock between her lips, not pleasuring him but keeping her mouth full, her submission evident. He strokes her hair in affirmation, and sour saliva fills my mouth.

Fuck the cities.

Fuck him.

"Dad, this place . . . this life isn't for me."

He holds his hand up to silence me as another member of the Politic filters into our private balcony, his own myrie dragged by a chain and gagged with a glass ball to stifle her screams. I swallow when I see the bite mark on her neck that I inflicted all those years ago. The dotted scar glows amethyst in my presence, burning brighter and hotter the closer she gets.

My pit organs open of their own accord, expanding tiny pores near my tear ducts that change my vision. I can smell the heat of her. I can see it in the way the colors oversaturate her body and no one else's. I've never bitten an elf before and let it live; the result is almost euphoric.

Her master coughs, and I force my pit organs shut, severing the connection between us.

The elf glares at me with piercing silver eyes, but it's her master's stare that has me quickly losing interest. Sorso despises me. He's never forgiven me for tasting her, and I get the distinct feeling if I weren't the Grand Overseer's son, I'd be dead within the week.

Despite his obscene wealth, Sorso—the Karesai of Butchers—looks as hideous as the rest of his caste. He's kept his birth skin, leaving it purple and disfigured, with a twisted nose, a cleft lip, and a lumpy forehead that droops over his left eye. Dark purple lines have been scratched into his face and forearms. I imagine elsewhere, too, but if so, they're hidden by a loose tunic, a black butcher's apron, and matching trousers.

Sitting on my father's left, Sorso shoves down on his myrie's shoulders and forces her to the ground. Her knees crack against the pavement, and tears well behind her swollen dark-gray lids. He leans in close and whispers something in her ear, jagged teeth flashing.

All the fight drains away then. Shuddering, she wraps her arms protectively around her swollen stomach, then bows her head in submission.

I should have eaten her. It would have been better for both of us if I had.

"Lyrick, it's good to see you again," Sorso spits. Staring at me, his hand delves beneath the golden chains adorning his elf's chest, pinching her nipple in a demonstration of ownership. It's a struggle not to roll my eyes.

"Likewise, Sorso."

"Your father tells me you'll be picking a myrie this week."

I snort, but the sound gets lost amongst the roaring crowd. "Not likely."

Azerin's silver eye swirls. Unable to punish me without making a scene, he squeezes the roots of his myrie's hair, forcing her to swallow several more inches of him. She gags but doesn't struggle.

"We're considering Brawler," he says to Sorso. "Lyrick likes it when they fight."

I prefer it when they run.

Sorso's grip tightens on his myrie's shoulders—the topic of conversation reminding him yet again that I've fought his elf and won. My body has been between her legs, close enough to breed her if I'd chosen. And how can he be certain I didn't? It's not as if the other Hunters would rat me out.

Sensing his train of thought, I'm already expecting his reaction before it happens. Sharp fingernails pierce the elf's flesh until silver blood beads to the surface, seeping down her back. I lick my lips unintentionally, my stomach growling at the memory of tangy liquid and squishing flesh.

Azerin glares at me, and I work my jaw, fighting back the hunger. It's been too long since I last hunted.

"Excuse my son," Azerin says. "He's still adjusting to civilized society."

Sorso flashes those pointed teeth at me. "Tell me, Lyrick, why is it you've never taken a myrie of your own? Is there something wrong with you?"

I tense, but the words come out smooth as silk. "I don't find it very sporting to keep the elves collared and chained. I'd think you, of all people, would understand."

He arches a brow, and I indicate the scratch marks on his body.

A smart man wouldn't bait him, but if I'm to be forced into a leadership role, then these power moves are absolutely necessary, despite what my father might want.

"I'm guessing you let your myrie loose when you fuck her," I say, my lips curling into a smug smile. "It's probably how she escaped in the first place. Shame she was so easy to catch, though I don't think she fought me half as hard as she does you."

I let the implication hang in the air.

Sorso leaps from his seat, pulling her leash taut. "If I find out you touched her—"

"You'll what? Beg for advice?"

Sorso lunges, but my father shoves his slave to the ground and steps between us, a vein ticking in his forehead. "That's enough. Both of you." He opens his mouth to say something more, but before he can, feminine giggles sound from the entryway.

Turning, I watch the Karesai of Trainers and the Karesai of Bracers duck into the seating area, laughing arm and arm at some inside joke. Their patchwork gray skin is as mottled as Sarvenna's—their reputation just as brutal. One of the women dresses in a puffy, lacy gown, while the other wears purple fighting leathers, a pair of knives strapped to her thighs.

If either of them senses the tension between us, they don't say anything. Instead, they offer up customary hellos before selecting seats in the singular row behind ours. Usually, they bring pleasure slaves with them, but not today, likely because they're planning on purchasing a victor as well.

Straightening his apron, Sorso returns to his seat and readjusts his myrie between thick, lumpy legs. I've just made her life infinitely worse, and I can't help but feel terrible about it. Still, the need for self-preservation wins out.

It always does.

The Karesai of Stitchers is the last to arrive. He's dressed in a white surgeon's apron and matching silk trousers. His gray skin and eyes are so perfectly matched, he could be an elf were it not for the serrated teeth. Likely, he spent twice his weight in gold purchasing the elves who made him so attractive. The same could be said for me, Azerin, and half the upper class.

The Stitcher—the closest thing I have to an ally within the Politic—sits beside me and clasps me on the shoulder. "Are you still having trouble with your jaw?"

Instinctively, I rub at the square edges. Even with the ossi powder, Stitchers have limitations, and sometimes our bodies reject the transplant. It took six tries. *six elves*, before this operation finally took. "No, Yaklan. This is a perfect fit. Maybe a bit too angular, but Sarvenna isn't complaining."

Yaklan beams. "You know, she brought me an elf just this morning who has a beautiful nose... I think it would really match well with your face—"

"I like this one. My sense of smell is better with it than with any of the others I've tried."

He lowers his voice so the others can't hear. "Have you had a chance to test your new abdominals yet? I know the last pair . . ."

Wasted away because I haven't been eating enough.

"Don't worry, Yaklan. I'll let you know if I'm having trouble."

With a scalpel, the man is a fucking artist. He's hand-carved each of my muscles to perfection—not just for the aesthetic but for the hunt. And when the old muscles wasted away without warning, he didn't ask questions, just fixed me discreetly from the privacy of his estate, my father none the wiser. Yaklan has never asked why I only take transplants from wild-caught elves who haven't been tortured or imprisoned. Never pried into my ethical code of conduct.

Clearing my throat, I change topics. "Have you had any interesting surgeries this week?"

His entire demeanor changes, becoming livelier. In big hand gestures, he discusses his most recent transplant and the complications involved. I listen to him prattle on for far too long before the shrieking cry of a death whistle pierces the air, cutting off our conversation. In an instant, the stadium goes quiet. Thousands of elgrew turn toward the octagonal arena where a lone mound of dirt fills the center of an empty field. Bars of cold iron separate the lowest spectators from the fighting grounds, preventing the competitors from escaping or attacking someone in the crowd. Matching cold-iron bars hide this year's champions from view, storing them behind eight doors on eight sides of the arena.

A mottled gray elgrew approaches the dirt mound—one of the lead Bracers known for her grueling calisthenics and training regiments. A clay mask with a wicked grin hides her features from view, but the way the mouth is curved amplifies her voice, projecting it loud enough so that all of us can hear it.

"Purples." She nods to the lower class, all of whom sit at the upper levels of the arena, their mutilated violet skin marking them for what they are. "Grays." Her gaze drops a fraction of an inch to the middle and upper classes rich enough to afford skin transplants. "Members of the Politic." Her attention shifts lower, landing on our private balcony. "I welcome you all to the nine hundred and twenty-seventh annual games."

Cheers erupt. Hands wave high into the air, holding clay figures of this year's champions.

My stomach rumbles. My skin itches with the overwhelming need to be in that arena, fighting with them. Eight against one. All of them armed with knives and clubs. The fight would be more than fair, and I could finally fill this pit in my gut.

"Azerin says you never eat cooked meat," Yaklan whispers, pulling me back to our conversation.

"No," I admit. "The food in the mess hall is barely tolerable."

He purses his lips as the announcer clears her throat.

"For the next eight days, our best fighters in Kariss will face off against one another for a chance at being crowned victor on Ring Day. Eight finalists. Eight matches. One winner." The crowd goes wild, forcing her to pause. "As always, there is to be no killing. When a fighter is done, they're to raise their sash in the air."

Yeah, right.

Half the elves would sooner die than return to their Bracers —their coaches and masters—defeated.

"The betting is now closed for today," she shouts. "Let the fighting begin."

Thunderous applause rattles the stones beneath my feet as the Bracer rushes to take her spot in the stands, joining the other elgrew who've spent the past year—the past decade perhaps— teaching their slaves to fight. The Bracers all wear fighting leathers, the poorer ones concealing their purple and gray patch-work skin with longer sleeves than their wealthy counterparts. This event could change their lives, put them on a path toward the Politic if they trained the elf I'm meant to breed.

My fingers curl into fists. My father has told everyone I'll be choosing a myrie on Ring Day, which means I must choose.

I must.

I can't.

The iron gates lift. Eight well-fed and well-armored elves emerge from their cells with red sashes tied around their waists. There's only one female in today's group—Brawler—with a bald head and thick forearms that look strange against her other, more delicate features. Like all elves, she's pretty. If one can call chattel pretty. I can't imagine her doing anything for my cock, though.

I keep silent, watching her long legs carry her faster than all her male counterparts. As all eight of the elves run at each other toward the mound, she ducks and slides, kicking up a plume of dust. One minute, fists are flying, and the next, three of the eight elves are on the ground, silver blood spewing from the backs of their knees.

Brawler raises a small kitchen knife, kissing the blade as she faces the crowd. They chant her name, cheering her on, but my eyes are glued to the silver on her lips, pooling at her feet. *Did she . . . bite one of them?*

I can practically smell the tangy metal. My vision blurs, the hunger so great it's hard to breathe.

I grab the sides of my ringing head and close my eyes, imagining the forest surrounding me, jumping over vines and leaves, running, feeding, losing myself to the chase. For a moment, I see Arden's blue feet. I feel her pounding heartbeat as though it were my own.

"Lyrick, are you alright?" Yaklan's face is nearly pressed against mine, his soft gray eyes boring into my soul. "Lyrick?"

"I'm fine," I snap.

In the arena, all seven elves lie on the dusty ground, their sashes unknotted. Brawler beams up at the crowd, spinning in slow circles and flashing sharp, pointed teeth.

"When's the last time you had a proper meal?" Yaklan asks.

"I ate this morning."

He puts his hand over my chest and tsks. It's only then I realize how long I must've zoned out. Neither Azerin nor Sorso are watching the match. Instead, they're watching me.

Great. Now I've made a scene.

"Do you know what happens when an elgrew doesn't eat?" Yaklan asks.

"We go feral."

First, it's our bodies, then our brains. Instincts take over until we're no better than the verncats. If I don't breed someone, if I don't get out of here so I can hunt properly, there's a very real chance I may cease to exist. And no number of transplants will save me.

I cross my arms. "I'm fine. Really. It's just a headache."

But I think we all know that isn't true.

IX. Arden

"Spring, 986 A.T. Nine Hunters staged an attack on the Lo'kowe Tribe today. Upon interception, two of our operatives were captured, including Giara of Lycea and Parcy of the Drift. It is unknown how many of the Lo'kowe were taken."

—CHEEVY OF KARISS, STARRA'LEE DEMOLITIONS EXPERT.
BATTLE REPORT

I raise my bow, nudging aside thorny branches and bone-white leaves to scan the forest floor. White ivy blankets the landscape, consuming the other trees in a tangled mat. Blackbirds caw overhead as they trail a half-starved male elf through rising mist. He clutches his bare chest, silver blood oozing between his fingers through a rotting wound the size of my fist. The idiot probably thought cutting away his bite mark would free him from his master. It'll come back, though, once the skin heals . . . if he doesn't die of infection first.

The crunching of his feet is like thunder to my sensitive ears. To the silence of the forest. He stumbles over a vine, and I tense, loosing my arrow as a blur of colors stirs behind him.

My fletching whistles through the wind, sailing over the elf's head. Then, it thuds, hitting my mark. Behind him, a female elgrew drops to her knees, purple blood gurgling between her lips. Eyes wide, she wraps her hands around the arrow lodged inside her throat, realization taking hold just moments before those amethyst eyes glaze over.

Then, she collapses into the dirt.

Up until now, the Hunter had kept quiet, hidden in the brambles, tailing him so well I had trouble aiming. But those opportunistic bastards always fuck up one way or another.

The elf's gaze jerks upward. He inspects the tree line, and I duck behind my leaves. Hiding isn't necessary. He's a shit tracker, pointing his chin southeast of my location by several degrees. I could probably hold a jar of glowflies the size of a verncat and still be invisible to him.

Leaves rustle in the tree across from me, and I roll my eyes. It's just like Julian to reveal our location.

My friend and squad leader drops from the trees, landing on bare feet. He rocks back on his heels and examines the elf at the same time the elf examines him. They could be brothers—same towering height, same bulky muscles, silver hair cut short—but Julian has rounded and deformed ears where the elgrew lopped them off decades earlier.

Like all squad leaders, Julian is dressed in verncat hide, the orange fur making him stand out amongst the white leaves. He readjusts his armor as he steps past the elf toward the dead Hunter.

"Who…who are you?" the elf stutters, stumbling back.

"Starra'lee." Julian slows his steps and turns, outstretching empty palms in a show of peace.

I snort. As if there aren't several spotters pointing arrows at them.

"Starra'lee?" the elf repeats. His brows furrow like he doesn't understand the Elvish word. He probably doesn't. The elgrew never teach their pets anything but their native tongue, and even then, only the basics.

Sit.

Stand.

Spread your legs.

"The Resistance," Julian clarifies, switching languages.

The elf's jaw drops. He whispers a string of words—prayers of gratitude perhaps—as Julian sidesteps him to examine the elgrew's bloodstained body. I try not to feel offended that he checks to see if my arrow landed true before flipping her over.

As Julian fishes through the Hunter's pockets, he signals the rest of us down. I grit my teeth, knowing, *just knowing* he's going to give the new guy sanctuary. As if we need any more liabilities.

Strapping the bow to my back, I hop from the tree as effortlessly as Julian did, maybe more so given I'm half his weight and height. A pair of tight fishtail braids cling to my scalp, keeping the long hair from my face so it's easier to work. Unlike Julian, my leather breastwrap and matching breeches have been dyed to match the trees. White paint coats my body, too, leaving me nearly invisible on the forest floor.

I ignore the others who descend at the same time I do and march straight to Julian, who's kneeling in the ivy. He stares disapprovingly at my fingerless gloves—at the sawgrass reeds woven through them, so sharp they could skin a man. Before he can instruct it, I remove the gloves and pocket them, sighing heavily as I join him in the tangled mat.

Wouldn't want to wound the dead.

Chatter fills the air as the other members of our squad greet the new elf, exchanging pleasantries with him.

I close my eyes and count to ten.

"You were new too once," Julian says, lowering his voice. It's soft and placating the way a condescending parent's might be.

"Yes, but I had skills. *Several* skills," I add. "He had no fucking clue he was being followed. He didn't even know where to look when I shot my bow. You asked me to follow him, size him up, and give my recommendation. Why bother if you're going to ignore me?"

"Arden—"

"He has no foraging skills. No hunting skills. He can't suture a wound or prevent infection. The man can barely string together three words in our language. He would be a hindrance to the squad."

I can feel the leash on my temper slipping.

I hate it when Julian wastes my time. Five days of stalking and keeping quiet for nothing. I could have spent the week with Nirissa, doing something that actually mattered.

My squad leader tsks as we rummage through the elgrew's clothing. He detaches her emergency pack and peers inside. "Would you rather I turn him away like the other tribes did to you?"

"I . . . That's different. They weren't running military operations." The words sound as hollow as they feel.

Hypocrite.

Coward.

My conscience screams at me, blasting images of the spotter who'd rather instruct children to kill themselves than endanger his son. I *am* that spotter. But I don't have the luxury of guilt.

I spent years training myself. Fine-tuning my body into a weapon that can keep Nirissa safe. I *earned* my place here, and I'm not about to let some no-name, no skilled asshole fuck it up. If it were my life, it'd be different, but it's Nirissa's, too.

I'm about to say as much when Julian finds a black pouch—the same size and shape as the one hidden in my back pocket. He peers inside it, then frowns. Not ossi dust like he had hoped. It never is. As we continue searching, he schools his features to hide the disappointment. Flipping the body over, I slip a folded letter into her already-searched-tunic when Julian isn't looking.

"We'll train him, Arden," he promises. "I won't send him out until he's ready."

"He'll never be ready."

"That's for me to decide, not you."

The words are final. Resolute.

I spit at his feet, then slip my gloves back on, marching past the rest of my camouflaged squadmates. They clear a path for me, giving me a wide berth despite the fact that I'm the size of a child. Soft grasses bend beneath my feet. Ivy leaves blow over an air pocket, hidden well enough that an elgrew would have to know it's there to see it.

Dipping my fingers between the leaves, I find a crevice in the rock and dirt and pull. The trap door creaks as it swings open, revealing a dark tunnel path made from a centuries-old lava tube.

"Where do you think you're going?" Julian asks. "I haven't dismissed you."

I ignore him, flashing everyone a vulgar gesture before jumping into the black abyss.

***

"ARRI!" Nirissa throws her arms around me and squeezes. She's only a head shorter than I am now—too big for me to lift like I used to—so I tousle her hair instead.

"It's good to see you, bug."

The tightness in my chest loosens as I scan her over. No new cuts. No bruises. She still has all her teeth, thank Marr. Our mother's doll hangs from a belt on her waist, and she's dressed in snug clothing that shows she's well cared for and fed—the best-kept kid in Starra'lee.

The only *kid kept in Starra'lee.*

My presence here has always been contingent on my sister's safety. If the Resistance wants me, they have to take us both. It's why we have a private bedroom while the others share a communal barracks; no one wants a ten-year-old sleeping in their living spaces.

"Have you been minding your tutors?" I ask, peering around the room to make sure everything's intact. Sure enough, the bunks are made, the clothes in our closet have been folded, and there's a neat stack of papers on the stone-carved desk.

"Yes, Arri," Nirissa says. She tucks a strand of short silver hair behind her ear and sheepishly glances at her bare feet.

I stare at that short hair, remembering the last time I left her alone. When she snuck into the armory and spilled resin all over her braids, the tunnels, our weapons. The healers had to practically shave her head to get it all out, and I spent several weeks on cleaning duty.

She's had remarkably good behavior since then. Some might say suspiciously so.

I eye the room again, certain I've missed something. It's pristine.

"Did you do anything fun?" I ask.

"No." Nirissa makes a pouty face and huffs. "They never let me go aboveground when you aren't here. It's boring."

"Better safe and bored than outside and eaten."

She narrows her eyes. "You go outside all the time, and you've never been eaten."

I smile. If only she knew how close I'd come. "When you're older, you can go outside all you want. How about that?"

"When I'm older, I'm going to be a fighter just like you."

I blink away the burning in my eyes. "You don't want that. It's scary out there, and Julian only lets us eat gross food. You remember those dried vegetable packs?"

"The ones that taste like mud?"

I nod. "I had to eat three of those today."

"Ewwwww!" She makes a face, her nose scrunching in disgust, and I can't help but laugh.

"Told you, you wouldn't like it." I toss my arm around her shoulders. "Come on, bug, let's go find something good to eat."

"You're covered in paint," she says, staring at my clothes.

"So?" I arch a brow.

"I wish *I* were covered in paint." She sighs wistfully but lets me lead her out of our bedroom.

A thick canvas curtain conceals the small space. Pushing it aside, we step into the lava tube, the sides of our arms brushing against sleek walls as we walk. Even single file, the tunnel here is so narrow, Nirissa and I are the only elves small enough to fit. Raindrops patter overhead. Jars of glowflies hang from the ceiling, casting our surroundings in dim pink light.

"Julian wants me to run patrols next week," I tell Nirissa, my voice echoing off the blackened stone. "Will you be okay on your own?"

"If I say no, can I come with you?"

I glare at the glowfly lights, wishing I could glare at her. "No. And don't try to follow me like you did last time. I almost shot you."

The pattering rainfall fades into nothing. Our footsteps grow louder as we round the corner and descend a path of winding, uneven steps into the musty belly of Rayna. Nirissa doesn't speak. More importantly, she doesn't promise that she'll stay put.

"I mean it, bug."

She grumbles then mutters something that sounds a lot like, "You're not my mom."

It hits like a physical blow.

It doesn't matter. Mom or not, I'm all she has, and she *will* listen to me.

The stairway opens into a network of wider, taller tunnels meant for the other soldiers. Armed men and women ignore us as we pass, chatting amongst each other, glamorizing their most recent kills. The dewy admiration in Nirissa's eyes has me balling my hands into fists. If I could take her from this place, I would. But we have nowhere else to go. As skilled as I am, I can't be everywhere at once, protecting her while I hunt, hiding her while I scout; it's too much for any one person.

I miss Giara.

True to her word, she never babied me, but she did watch Nirissa when I hunted. We'd still be in that cave, living a quiet, solitary life, if she hadn't gone and gotten herself captured. Now, I'm stuck inside this shithole.

It takes us minutes to reach the dining hall, and I instantly regret it. A mess of crude language and familiar grunts comes from the other side of the curtained doorway.

"For the last time, Cheevy, no one wants to hear about your dick." Julian's voice cuts through the thick canvas.

"All I'm saying is that the hole's wide enough—"

Julian cuts him off. "Get your hands out of my fucking med-pack."

Cringing, I peek back at Nirissa, wishing I could cover her ears. Of course, she's absolutely enthralled. Practically glowing with excitement.

"Five minutes," I tell her. "In. Out. We're not stopping to talk with them."

She frowns. "You never let me do anything fun."

Shoving past me, Nirissa sweeps the canvas aside and marches straight into the dining hall like she owns the place. It's physically impossible not to roll my eyes.

The room dwarfs us. It's the second largest space in the underground, formed from an empty magma reservoir. The ceiling and walls extend hundreds of feet into the air, encircling us in jagged black and purple and red rocks. Stone tables and chairs fill the space—firepits too—which form plumes of thick gray smoke. A series of hidden air ducts and vents carry the smoke to the surface, but not fast enough to stop the room from hazing.

Through the fog, I spot my squad right away, having already ransacked the pantries and salted meat reserves. I sniff the air on impulse. Not salted meat. Fresh. Someone hunted and brought their kill to share.

My stomach gurgles at the thought of having fresh meat for once. It's not worth the cost of speaking to them—not when Nirissa is so young and impressionable. Still, my mouth salivates.

"To the pantries, and then we go," I remind her.

Quickening my pace, I step in front of Nirissa, guiding her away from the others, toward food storage at the other side of the hall. As we pass, I make a concerted effort to ignore whatever my squadmates are laughing or fighting about. I've nearly cleared them entirely when someone whistles at me, the sharp noise bouncing off the cavernous walls.

"Arden, come here."

I stiffen at Julian's command. The words *fuck you* form on my lips, but I hold them back, plastering on the biggest, fakest smile I can muster. Gesturing toward the pantries—deep recesses hidden in the rocks—I urge Nirissa forward. "Go. I'll catch back up."

She glances between my squad and me, huffs, then storms off. Her attempt at dramaticism is underwhelming; her bare feet hardly make a sound.

"Couldn't this wait?" I hiss, my smile dropping as I approach the fire. The warmth of the flames sends involuntary shudders up my spine, my frigid toes curling in relief. I refuse to settle into it. To get comfortable with them. "If this is about earlier—"

Julian jerks his head, gesturing to the others.

Our squad forms a circle around the new recruit, all four of them examining his infected chest wound like they're playing a game of *Find It*. Med-pack open, our field healer, Sora, grabs a magnifying glass, hovering it over the pus-filled, bloody mess.

"I'm no expert, but shouldn't you be doing this in the med hall?" I ask.

"Can't." Sora's fingers palpate the wound's edges. Sweat glistens off her bald head, collecting on a cloth circlet. "They're overflowing right now. Mission went topside in South Ridge."

Something shimmering and blue ekes past a lump of the elf's pale tissue. My brows furrow as Cheevy—our demolition expert *of all fae*—grabs a pair of tweezers and starts digging for it.

Metal? Rock? I can't tell.

To Chest Wound's credit, he doesn't scream when the tweezers split apart flesh. Aside from his ragged breaths, the elf is a perfect statue. Pupils dilated. Cock hard and pitching a tent beneath his trousers. If I had to guess, Sora drugged him with lavender oil—makes it easier to touch someone in pain. Makes it easier to pleasure them, too, according to my squadmates. Lavender oil is strictly forbidden. No one wants a soldier high as fuck responsible for staving off an elgrew attack, but the healers keep a secret supply.

The blue shard slips free of Chest Wound's skin. It tings on the stone floor as Cheevy drops it from his tweezers. Tears leak past his and Sora's eyes, but they don't stop working. Cheevy, digging. Sora, palpating. Another shard rises to the surface.

"What is that?" I ask.

No one answers.

I take a step closer, narrowing my gaze. Upon further inspection, dozens of tiny cuts cover Chest Wound's body, leaking silver onto the floor. Stitches close the worst of them, but most are narrower than papercuts. Sweat drenches his unusually pale skin. His lips and fingers twitch despite the oil.

This man is dying.

I'm not a medic any more than Julian or Cheevy are. I'm trained for the basic stuff—everyone in Starra'lee is—but none of us can do better than Sora. If the man looks like this . . . if she's resorted to lavender oil already and Julian hasn't reprimanded her for it . . . if we're doing Marr-damn medical extractions in the dining hall, I don't see how the fuck I can be of any use to them.

"What am I doing here, Julian?" I ask.

"There's been extensive damage," he says. "Torvin worked as a foreman in the cold-iron mine. His master embedded the metal into his skin to make it harder to run. Sora and the others are pulling it out, but the metal slows healing. The infection—"

"No." I practically spit the word.

"Arden—"

"No!"

I jam my hand into my back pocket, fingers coiling protectively around the pouch of ossi dust I keep there. Dust Lyrick gave to me. Dust only Julian knows about. It's rare—difficult to find because the elgrew hoard it in their cities and impossible to make because no one knows what it's made from. Tribes have fought wars over it; my own chieftain nearly died once protecting his stash.

"Absolutely not." I glance at the others and take a step away from the flames, the warmth. My heart splinters at the expectant look on their faces and the guilt in Julian's eyes.

"You told them?" My voice warbles but doesn't crack.

"We've never had inside knowledge of the mines before," Julian says. The words are velvety soft, like he isn't a lying, two-faced, trust-breaking snake. "Arden, we need him."

If I could claw his face off, I would. "I kept it for Nirissa," I say. "Not for your stupid missions."

Tears of anger threaten to leak free. *I won't cry in front of them. I—*

Cheevy rises from the floor. Unkempt hair falls over his freckled face and half-missing nose. Slowly, he approaches me, hands outstretched like I'm a feral animal, not his squadmate. I take another step back, only to hit Julian's hard, unmoving body.

"I'm sorry, Arden." He grips me by the wrists, wrenching my arms behind my back. "I wasn't asking."

I struggle against him, but I'm half his size. Moving him would be like moving a mountain.

Cheevy closes the gap between us, reaches into my back pocket, and snatches up the one thing that could save my sister if something went wrong. The pouch is almost flat now—a lifetime supply for most tribes whittled to nothing. Back when I was scavenging the marshes for scraps, still learning how to fight, it had been a literal lifesaver for bug and me. If they use it now, there won't be anything left.

"Don't do this," I hiss, my eyes burning with righteous indignation.

Julian doesn't let up.

Cheevy kneels over Chest Wound, offering the bag to Sora. "Is all the cold iron out?"

"I think so." She stops palpating then snatches the bag, frowning when she realizes just how close it is to empty. Sora doesn't waste time measuring or scooping. Instead, she turns the pouch inside out and lets the plume of dust settle over the new recruit's chest.

The whole time, I struggle, kicking and wriggling as my failsafe vanishes from sight, magically fusing Chest Wound's skin back together. When it's done, Julian releases me.

I say nothing. Words wouldn't change anything; they certainly wouldn't bring the dust back.

"Arden, it had to be done," Julian says.

"Of course it did." I laugh a bitter laugh. "The squad comes first, right?"

We stare at one another for a long time. There isn't a trace of remorse in his expression. Spinning on my heels, I try to compose myself as best I can before finding my sister.

"I just hope it was worth it."

X. Arden

"The Lycean Swamp is considered one of the least hospitable habitats on Rayna. Bordered by sawgrass reeds, it's nearly impossible to access without self-injury. Ancient beasts lurk within the waters, and snakes as large as verncats slither in the muck. If an elf chooses to seek refuge within it, elgrew should not pursue; they are dead already."

—The Stolen Journal of Jakil Orn, Hunter.

Status: Deceased.

Nirissa snores peacefully in the bunk above mine. Wood creaking, I climb the ladder that links our beds together and lean over her still form. Above us, a glowfly jar hangs from the ceiling, bathing the room in dim pink light.

"I'll be back by morning," I promise, my voice barely a whisper. Gently, I tuck a strand of hair behind Nirissa's pointed eartip, then kiss her forehead. She doesn't stir, but that's okay. The words are more for me than for her—a reminder that I owe it to her to return alive and well and in one piece.

It's bad enough that I'm leaving at all. Still, I can't force myself to stay.

Restlessness stirs my bones. Simmering anger threatens to boil over if I don't do something. Julian's betrayal happened hours ago, but with my sister around, I had to swallow those emotions for as long as I could. Now, the monster rages.

When I get like this, there's only one cure. Hunting. Dangerous as it is—reckless and stupid now, without the ossi dust—it's the only way I know to vent steam. I do everything for Nirissa. I do *this* for myself.

Hopping from the ladder, I check the tightness of my braids then dress, covering my leather breastwrap with a long-sleeved linen tunic and exchanging a pair of shorts for breathable black trousers. By elvish tradition, we're supposed to wear hide, but the elgrews' soft fabrics are more flexible, easier to dry. Besides, what's the point of killing those assholes if we can't steal from them?

The echoing sound of water rushing over stones comes from the hallway—rainfall draining through the air ducts. A lot of it. My skin prickles with anticipation, imagining the challenge of a low-visibility hunt.

Grinning, I crawl beneath my bed and retrieve the leather go-bag I keep tucked against the wall. A series of buckles and knots secure the contents and a large strap allows me to hook it over my shoulder. I unfasten the central flap and withdraw the rest of my nonregulation outfit—an oversized, long-sleeved shirt woven from blue sawgrass reeds, a pair of matching oversized trousers, and fingerless gloves. When I stroke down the outfit, the stems are as smooth as glowfly silk. Stroking up, they're sharper than razor wire with a penchant for embedding needle-like splinters beneath the skin.

When I first arrived at Starra'lee, Julian banned the makeshift armor. He said if healers couldn't touch me, they couldn't help. And if I couldn't touch others, I couldn't be an effective member of their team. Begrudgingly, I agreed. But I still keep the pieces for solitary missions, and Julian hasn't been stupid enough to confiscate them.

Carefully, I tug them on, adding linen liners to my gloves to prevent the reeds from slicing through skin. Once I'm fully dressed, I pluck my go-bag from the floor and double-check its contents.

Med-pack, check.

Emergency rations, check.

Fire starters, check.

Twine, check.

An extra set of clothing, check.

I buckle everything back up and swing it 'round my shoulders. Then, I walk to my weapons cache in the closet and retrieve my knife. Not my bow. Not my machetes. But that tiny, rusted thing the spotter gave me all those years ago. Jagged and chipped, the blade gleams in the glowfly light. It's pitiful, but I like the challenge.

The canvas ripples as I swat it open, sparing Nirissa a final glance before exiting into the hallway. She's still soundly asleep and blissfully unaware of the things I do at night. Sometimes, I wonder what would happen to her if I died on one of these excursions. Would Julian take care of her? Would he force her to fight?

My back pocket has never felt so empty.

Don't go, my conscience pleads. *Take care of her like you promised.*

But the walls are so tight around me, I can hardly breathe. I'm suffocating down here, drowning under the weight of my obligations. I may not belong to the elgrew, but I'm far from free.

"I'm sorry," I whisper.

And then I climb.

MUCK SQUISHES BETWEEN MY TOES, red blood and water mixing in a shallow pool beneath my feet. Kneeling in the underbrush, I sweep aside soaked leaves to reveal a hidden flap made from twigs and knotted twine. On the other side of the flap comes the pleating cries of a *korkuran* bird—a flightless, little creature that ventures out at night to hunt the grubs and earthworms. When it rains, the damn things are everywhere. The flooding drives the worms topside so they can breathe, and the worms draw the korkuran.

Starra'lee keeps dozens of these traps; I just take advantage of them. It's not suspicious if one or two turn up empty when the spotters go to check on them in the mornings.

A transparent thread of glowfly silk connects the trap's flap to a weighted mechanism held up by sticks. Pressing down on the flap makes the weight lift, and the trap door opens, inundating me with the bird's frantic cries. The leak-tight clay hole is full of water. Rain continues to pound overhead, plastering the wet clothing to my body, creating dozens of tiny ripples in the water below.

The blue korkuran thrashes its neck, hopping on webbed feet to hold its head above the surface. Wingless, its movements are ineffective.

With a *shink*, I unsheathe my blade. Then, I wrap my hand around the bird so it doesn't have to struggle anymore. The korkuran doesn't fight me—it thinks I'm its savior, and in a way, I am. The death I'm giving it is far more merciful than what the trap would bring.

I slash its throat. The movement is so fast the bird can't register it, and the cut is deep enough it won't have time to feel pain. Blood turns the water red. Once the bird is limp in my hands, I grab its taloned feet, then knot them to my belt using a ball of twine. Three other korkurans from three other traps hang by its side—the same slash across their throats.

Four is enough.

Julian will likely realize I screwed over the traps, but fuck him.

Blood drains down my legs, staining my clothing faster than the rain can wash it away. Wiping the wetness from my face, I squint into the darkness. Up ahead, a solid wall of sawgrass reeds denotes the start of the marshes. It'll rip the birds apart if I'm not careful.

Thunder booms overhead. White lightning streaks across the sky, illuminating the dark world in flashes. Still, I can't see. The rain blurs everything, turning the dirt into a slushy mess beneath my feet. I trudge through it all the same—feet schlooping, sticking, squelching in the muck. It's ankle-deep in some places and knee-deep in others. I have to practically crawl to pull myself free.

When I reach the reeds, I toss my go-bag onto a tree branch overhead. Shoving a hand into my soaked pockets, I retrieve a dozen small stones that I collected at the start of the hunt—skipping stones. Smooth and flat and black as my surroundings.

Hands outstretched, I wade into the marshes, sticking to the border where the water barely reaches my ankles.

Goosebumps prickle my skin, the warmth of the marsh at total odds with the chilly rain. Shivering, I keep my hands in front of me, using the backs of my gloves to brush aside the blue reeds—the same shade as my skin. My movements are slow. Deliberate. One wrong step and I'm done for. Cut by the grasses. Eaten by the beasts that lurk within them.

All around me, water ripples. Phytoplankton create bioluminescence under the constant onslaught of rain—tiny blue lights twinkling in an otherwise black expanse.

The grass bends up ahead. I let out a little prayer to the Korring-Marr that it's just the wind as I wade deeper into the marsh. The water reaches my knees, and my heart thumps against my ribcage.

Another boom.

The thunder shakes the mushy ground beneath me and I throw my first stone, skipping it across the twinkling lights. The water glows turquoise with every hit. Red eyeshine reflects despite the thick curtain of rain. *Swamp dogs.* Dozens of them. But I only need one.

I throw another stone in a different direction. Eight pairs of angry red eyes blink into and out of existence. I toss again and again until I find the social outcast—usually the biggest, most cantankerous of the group, who doesn't play well with others. In the darkness, in the rain, it's impossible to guess its size.

Retreating into the sawgrass, I move parallel to the swamp dog. Then, I draw my knife and slice the first korkuran loose, catching it before it hits the water. The plume of feathers is smooth beneath my fingertips. Sleek and thick. I pluck some free for Nirissa, pocketing them before I run my gloves over the freshly exposed skin.

Tiny rivulets of blood ooze to the surface; most of it has drained by now, but there's still enough for my purposes.

Reeling back my arm, I hurl the bird as far as I can toward the swamp dog. The rain slows it. But it hits close enough. Drawn by the smell of blood, the swamp dog swims to the bird and thrashes out of the water. Turquoise illuminates the spot, outlining a massive, scaled beast taller than Julian.

I swallow, palms sweating, chest aching. Adrenaline pours into my body, my muscles screaming in anticipation.

I can do this.

On instinct, I grab the next bird and the next, repeating until I've lured the swamp dog so close to me, I can see it despite the rain, despite the dark. Quietly, slowly, I backstep to the outermost edges of the marsh until the water has receded to the bottom of my calves. Out there, swamp dogs have the advantage. But on land, they're clumsier. Slower. They make mistakes.

I grab my last bird and cut it deeply with my knife until the slimy insides fall out. Then, I run.

Korkuran in hand, I make it out of the water just in time to see the swamp dog's shimmering blue-and-black scales. It lunges, paws thumping in the slippery muck. Dropping the bird, I dodge, squeezing the rusted blade in my right palm. The sawgrass can't help me win this fight. The swamp dog's back is thicker than armor. If I want to kill it, only two options exist—the underbelly or the eye.

Every time it lunges, it exhausts itself. The birds were a lure as much as a distraction.

Keep it busy.

Wear it down.

Trap it once it's too tired to fight back.

Julian wonders how I kill my prey. The answer is simple—I outsmart it.

Its massive jaws open wide, revealing pointy teeth the size of my fingers. Thrashing its body, it seizes what remains of the bird carcass and consumes it in a single gulp. Blood seeps between its crooked smile. Those glowing red eyes settle on me.

I circle it, and it lets out a low hiss.

Body squirming, it rakes its claws through mud in an attempt to keep me in its line of sight. It's fast, but I'm faster.

Lightning cracks, illuminating the marsh in brilliant white, showing me where to strike. I take the opening and dive onto the creature's back. It bucks against me. My fingers slip on wet scales, and my knife goes flying.

Shit.

Fuck.

Panic seizes my core. No weapons. All I have is a spool of twine on my belt. Above us, the rain pounds so hard, I can't see a damn thing. But I'm trained for this—I trained *myself* for this.

Emptying my mind, I clench my thighs around the creature's massive frame and grope blindly for a fingerhold. Soft, vulnerable skin grazes my fingertips—its neck.

As the swamp dog squirms and thrashes, I grab a fistful of skin with one hand, then reach for my twine with the other, my thighs and forearms burning with effort to hold on.

It roars, its whole body rumbling with the sound.

Twine in hand, I reach for the swamp dog's head, pushing down on its massive snout. Too late, it realizes what I've done. The creature tries to retreat into the water, but its movements are clumsy—slowed by exhaustion. I wrap the twine around its upper and lower jaw, forcing its mouth shut. Then, I ride its back until the thrashing stops and it's safe to retrieve my knife.

Smiling, I stare down at the massive, worn-out thing, my whole body tingling with exhilaration.

I did it. I won.

This is what freedom feels like—the ability to fight monsters and win. One day, I'll rid myself of the elgrew too. Not just for my sake, but for Nirissa's. I stare at my fingerless glove, Lyrick's bite mark throbbing beneath it. It's been months since I felt our connection, but I feel it now, like someone squeezing my heart.

I don't know if he can see me, nor do I care. I whisper the words regardless. "Letting me go will be your biggest mistake."

Gripping onto the swamp dog's tail, I drag it through the forest and return home.

XI. Arden

Long black claws rake across the bottom of the lava tube, scratching frantically. The swamp dog's desperate struggles have the opposite of their intended effect. Unconscious or dead, the beast would've proven too heavy for me to lift, forcing me to abandon it in the marshes. While fighting though . . . its kicking legs and twisting body propels it wherever I want. Still, my biceps scream with the effort of dragging this living creature, my grip so tight on its armored tail that my palms are numb.

Skittering paws and hissing snorts echo down the cavernous hallway as I drag the swamp dog toward the dining hall, my stomach growling. Water drips from my braided hair, pooling on the stone beneath my feet. It plasters the clothing to my body —tight enough that the sawgrass pricks through my linen underlayers, turning everything itchy.

Behind us, a trail of mucky water leads back to the trap doors—to the terrified spotters who had to let us in. I wonder if Julian will have the balls to tell me I'm responsible for cleanup.

"It's past curfew," spits an unfamiliar voice.

To my right, a bedraggled woman appears in the hallway, shoving past the canvas door that leads to one of several barracks. She's dressed in nothing but a leather breastwrap and panties, her arms folded across her chest. "Go to bed or I'll report you to—"

One look at me and the words lodge inside her throat. I'm not sure if it's the blood-soaked skin the dirt caked on my body or the giant beast that has her frozen in her tracks.

"Arden, I-I didn't realize it was you." She takes a cautious step back, her eyes darting between my prey and me. "I'll get out of your way."

Backpedaling into the barracks, she disappears behind the safety of her flimsy door. No doubt they'll gossip about this tomorrow once the other units are sure I'm not around. It always gets back to me, though.

The girl is a fucking animal.

I don't know why Julian recruited her.

She gives me the creeps.

I repeat the insults in my head, reminding myself for the hundredth time, these fae aren't my friends. Outside of Julian and Giara, the elves in Starra'lee don't know the first thing about who I am. They see a little girl half their size capable of downing a bear, a swamp dog, or a team of elgrew by herself and get spooked by it. To them, I'm as much a monster as the elgrew are. Which is fine by me.

Grunting, I pull the swamp dog down several flights of stairs, then push aside the canvas flap that leads to the dining hall. The scents of lye and musk greet me. Unlike earlier, the smoke is gone, the place abandoned—*almost*. Despite the fact that it's well past curfew and only active spotters or squad leaders are allowed to roam freely, the entirety of my unit sleeps around their makeshift surgery, wrapped in sleeping bags and blankets.

I roll my eyes.

Muttering curses at Julian, I drag my breakfast toward an unlit firepit. Suspended chains and metal hooks dangle from a makeshift platform beside it—high enough to hang and drain my meat. Buckets, cooking utensils, and plates lay atop an adjacent table, freshly washed from whatever sap got stuck with cleaning duty.

Dropping the swamp dog's tail, I sigh. Then, I crack each knuckle and brace myself for the arduous task that is killing, draining, skinning, and cooking an eight-hundred-pound monstrosity.

It hisses mockingly.

Ignoring it, I sling the go-bag from my shoulders, then carefully remove my scratchy layers of sawgrass reeds, dropping them into a puddle at my feet. Peeling the shirt from my body, I toss it too, the fabric *splatting* as it hits the floor.

"Shit, Arden, that looks terrible."

My head wheels at the sound of Julian's voice. He's leaning against the table, a ratty blanket curled around his shoulders.

"Fuck off," I spit.

Still, my eyes follow his as he assesses me. Raised, dark-blue rashes cover every inch of my exposed skin. It'll burn like a bitch when it's time to clean up. I cringe, imagining what the rashes will feel like once I'm fighting in unyielding leather armor.

"Told you not to use the reeds," Julian says, pushing the bangs from his forehead. "If you were going to disobey a direct order, you should've at least worn something thicker underneath."

Without a word, I step around him and withdraw my rusted knife, irritated that this asshole thinks we're still friends. Maybe others find his banter charming—maybe I did too, once—but it's not enough to make me forget I hate his fucking guts.

At least now, I have an outlet to channel that rage.

The swamp dog slithers across the cold, damp floor. My feet stomp behind it. Arms outstretched, I approach it from the side where its blind spot is, then lunge. Claws slash out. I dodge, burying my knife with a single thrust to its eye. A quick, painless death.

Julian would be so lucky.

Seesawing the knife, I rip it free of flesh and bone, then wipe the blood on my pants.

"Marr-damn, Arden. Remind me not to piss you off." Julian winks at me, and I grind my molars together so hard my gums ache.

"Don't tempt me," I growl, slamming the knife in its sheath. "If you're here to talk, it's not happening."

Julian arches an eyebrow.

"Either help me drain it or fuck off." Jumping, I stretch for the dangling metal chains and groan when I'm still too short to reach them. Shrugging off the blanket, Julian grabs one for me— not even needing to stand on tiptoes. *Asshole.*

"I've got it, Arden." He breezes past me and wraps the chain around the swamp dog's back legs, forming a makeshift harness. Then, he tosses the other end around the platform and raises the beast until it's hanging upside down. Julian is one of the only elves strong enough to do so. *Berserker*—that's what the elgrew call them—elves with supernatural strength and stamina, bred to make their games more entertaining. Though he doesn't look a day over twenty, he fought for decades in the elgrews' fighting pits before Starra'lee saved him.

He still doesn't talk about it.

"Go clean up. I'll cook," Julian offers.

I narrow my eyes at him.

"You're soaked and injured." Unsheathing the knife from his belt, he flashes me a crooked smile. "Consider it a peace offering."

"Not a fucking chance." Still, I grab my go-bag, my movements sluggish, my muscles gelatin as the adrenaline finally wears off. "This isn't me forgiving you."

"I wouldn't dream of it."

ROARING LAUGHTER BOUNCES off the cavernous walls. Savory smoke clogs the air—white and thick plumes separating me from my squad mates.

Of course, Julian invited them.

Their laughter dies the second I approach, padding barefoot toward the crackling fire. Julian forwent my original plan to carve the beast into smaller, more manageable chunks. Instead, he hoisted the whole damn thing onto a spit, combining several firepits into one massive inferno. It blazes heat, sending goosebumps up my arms and legs.

For the first time in months, my silvery blue hair is free of its braids. I'm dressed in a sleeveless elgrew top and shorts that barely reach my ass. It's the most vulnerable I've ever been around them, and it has me hugging my middle as I settle onto an empty, upside-down crate. A half-dozen other crates fill the space; I stare at them rather than at their traitorous occupants.

"Saved the skin for you," Julian says. "In case you wanted to make armor out of it." He indicates a bucket filled with unwashed gore. The gesture is not as half as kind as it would be if he'd done something—*anything*—to clean it.

I grunt, forcing my rashy arms to my sides, wishing I'd chosen to chafe in sawgrass rather than expose my flesh to them. I'd be totally fucked if I had to fight right now—all I have is the rusted knife strapped to my thigh—but it's too late to do anything about that.

"Food's almost done," Julian adds, speaking in Elgrew this time—no doubt to include Chest Wound in conversation. He passes me a smooth wooden plate and a pair of eating utensils, which I pointedly set on the floor. A jug of fermented grain— *glorified pisswater*—rests by my feet.

"I didn't mean to interrupt your fun," I say, the Elgrew words feeling strange on my tongue. Wood creaks beneath me as I lean back in my seat. "Carry on."

No one speaks.

It's so quiet, I can hear the meat cooking.

Typical. The fastest way to kill a party is to have me join in.

Julian clears his throat, ready to smooth things over as always. "I was telling the new guy about that time Cheevy asked me to pee on him to treat a yalka sting. Fucking moron."

"How was I supposed to know it'd make the infection worse?" Eyes narrowed, Cheevy wipes the snot from his half-missing nose. "Besides, Sora let me."

Sora chuckles. "Because I didn't think Julian would actually do it."

Rotating the spit, our squad leader smirks. "I think we all learned some valuable lessons that day."

They laugh, and my presence is all but forgotten.

One by one, my squadmates settle into casual conversation,

sharing stories of how they came to be in Starra'lee. Like me, their physical prowess, cleverness, or hunting skills earned them recruitment offers. Unlike Chest Wound, they *deserved* to be here.

I tune them out, having heard the watered-down tales a dozen times before. Focusing on the cooking meat, I let the cadence of their voices lull me into something almost soothing. The high of the hunt is gone now, and the worst of my anger is gone with it, replaced with an exhaustion that makes my bones feel like lead.

"What's *her* story?" Chest Wound asks, snapping me out of my haze.

No one answers—not right away. Eventually, Julian fills the awkward silence. "Two years ago, I found Arden half feral in the Lycean Marshes, fighting off a twenty-foot mudsnake with her bare hands."

"I was hunting it," I correct, "and I had a knife." I pat the blade the spotter gave me, and Julian chuckles like I said something funny.

"I'd never seen a child fight like that. I knew then, I had to have her in my unit."

Child.

I bristle at the insult.

"I wasn't a child then, and I'm not one now," I hiss, sitting up straight. Unfastening my blade, I stab it into the swamp dog's hind leg. Cartilage pops as I twist it free at the joint, the calluses on my hands thick enough I barely feel the searing heat.

"My mind is twenty-one," I explain to the new guy. "It's my body that hasn't caught up yet."

I bite into tender muscle, and grease dribbles down my chin. Seeing the look of absolute disgust on Chest Wound's face, I flash him an open-mouthed smile—teeth still full of meat.

"*You're* twenty-one?" he asks.

"Last time I checked." Swallowing, I wipe my mouth with the back of my hand then swipe the jug of pisswater from the floor, belching loudly.

I relish the way his nose crinkles in response. Being repulsive —feared—is far better than the alternative. I've spent years building my reputation across the squads, ensuring no elf will think of me as anything less than monstrous. As for the childlike features that haven't vanished? Well, that's an added bonus.

No one can breed me if I'm not fertile.

"I thought all elves reached their Age of Majority by eighteen," Chest Wound says, scanning me like I'm some kind of mutant.

"Most do," Julian interjects. "Some never reach it at all. What happened to Arden is rare, but her size allows our squad to do things others can't."

I tip the jug back. The soury bitterness makes me want to cough, but I chug my way through it.

"Can she . . . ?" The recruit has the decency not to complete his sentence.

"Can I what?" I ask. Slamming the drink down, I take another bite of meat, chewing open-mouthed and loudly— smacking my lips together as I do so. "Can I fuck? I don't have the sexual organs that would make it pleasurable, so why the fuck would I?"

His cheeks turn dark gray. "I wasn't . . . I didn't . . ."

"Can I become a citizen? Can I lead a unit?" A piece of bone snaps beneath my teeth, but I continue chewing. "Apparently, it takes a properly working cock or pussy to wield a blade correctly. News to me."

I stab the swamp dog for emphasis, and the new recruit stares at his feet.

I've made him uncomfortable.

Good.

Julian frowns at me then works to pacify the situation. "The Starra'lee charter says only adults who've completed their Rite of Passage are eligible to vote, marry, and, *yes,* lead their own units. We've been debating Arden's situation for a while now. If it were up to me, she'd have full citizenship, but the others aren't convinced."

"Because she's a fucking lunatic." The words are out of Cheevy's mouth before he has time to think them through. Everyone cringes, sucking in a collective, audible breath as they wait for my reaction.

I snort. "Better a lunatic than missing half my nose."

A grin spreads across Cheevy's face, and just like that, the tension breaks.

Slicing off a hindquarter, I eat directly from my knife. "It doesn't matter anyway. I'm fine being second-class if it means the elgrew have no use for me."

Chest Wound's eyes widen in realization. "You're the elf Azerin is hunting?"

"I'm the elf his son owns." The angry scar glares at me as I stare at the inside of my greasy palm. Thirty-eight midnight-blue bumps mark me as Lyrick's—to eat and breed as he pleases. But I've seen enough through our bond to know he doesn't hunt children. And he can't impregnate someone without a womb. So long as I remain this way, I'm safe.

"I'm too tired to get into it right now," I say, waving away whatever questions Chest Wound might have. "Maybe later."

"Maybe tomorrow?" Julian suggests. "He needs someone to show him around."

"No."

"Arden." Julian's voice is a low growl.

"I'm busy with Nirissa."

"I'll take you off scouting duty next week."

I know what this is—some desperate ploy to make our unit

function. To make us *friends*. But I also know that a few hours touring the underground, teaching a new recruit the ins and outs of Starra'lee is far preferable to the weeks I'd spend away from Nirissa. In the end, it's not a hard choice to make.

"Fine. But you're cleaning *that* for me." I point toward the bucket of gore. Then, I carve my next slice of meat.

Letters

Grand Overseer,

We tracked the escaped slave to the Ivory Forest, where our hunting party was then separated and attacked. Our unit leader, Farra of Rothstone, did not survive the ambush, and her killers remain at large. We intend to regroup in the grasslands to assess our options.

To note—your blue elf was spotted amongst the insurgents. Blue has left us three more letters, all clustered in this region. It is our belief it has taken refuge with the militia. If we find it, we find them. As we continue our search for the missing slave, Crawler, we implore you to send more Hunters to seek Blue as well. Anything short of an army could prove fatal to whoever stumbles upon your elf.

For honor and duty,
Hunter Esten of Kariss

XII. Lyrick

"All debts accrued in the gambling dens must be paid. Failure to do so will result in asset forfeiture, including all rights to any myrie or pets. If the borrower has no assets, restitution must be made in payments of the flesh."

—AZERIN OF KARISS, GRAND OVERSEER
ROYAL PROCLAMATION

The Gambling Block reeks of smoke, and booze, and body odor. It's a mystery to me why anyone would willingly travel here. An air of desperation clings to the patrons—mostly lower caste purples with no chances of moving up in life—all too stupid to realize the house never loses. *My father never loses.*

Dice tables fill the cramped walkways and city streets, their seats overflowing with elgrew. Even on slow days, this place is unnavigable by carriages or palanquins. In the heart of the city, purples might be tempted to clear a path for someone like me, but grays aren't welcome here even though we own it.

I'm all too aware of how my presence will be received, so I

pull my hood up and hide my face in shadow, like I do every time my father sends me on this particular errand.

Gods, I fucking hate being his go-between. Still, it's better than thinking about the arena.

My boots scrape across the cobbled walkways where kerosene lampposts illuminate multistory, multiblock buildings made from reflective black bricks. Tinted windows hide the patrons inside, and pleasure slaves decorate the front steps— male and female elves dressed in tasteless scraps of black fabric, so sheer it hides nothing. Their owners call out prices to every elgrew who walks past. Nightly rates. Hourly.

The sooner I find him, the sooner I can leave.

Turning the corner, I enter a street where green betting slips hang from crisscrossing clotheslines. I'm tall enough that I have to duck beneath them as I walk. Wriggling through the crowds, I make a concerted effort not to touch anything. Not the betting slips. Not the pleasure slaves. And certainly not the unwashed masses.

I hold my breath for as long as possible, but the stench of stale perfume and sex is unavoidable.

Eventually, the congestion levels out and the mossy-blue sky gives way to a green so dark, it could be black. By the time I reach the gambling den that Conrin's father frequents, any trace of daylight has vanished. Silver moonlight bathes the towering building to my right—*The Bronze Isle.* It's identical to the others, save for the gleaming bronze gate in front of it, barring entrance to anyone without an invitation or key. Two deformed Butchers guard the gate, one of them holding a list of approved patrons.

This is going to be messy.

I crack my knuckles then my neck, sighing as I approach the most exclusive gambling den in Kariss.

"Name," the Butcher on the left demands.

I pull on my cowl just enough to expose my silver hair, my

perfectly sculpted gray skin. "Lyrick. I'm here on the Grand Overseer's behalf."

Reaching into my silk cloak, I withdraw a scroll from a hidden internal pocket and pass it to them. My father's wax seal —a blue sun with an x through it—remains intact. Inside is a detailed ledger of outstanding gambling debts. "I'm here for Morcai," I add.

They glare at me, but I'm used to it. When Sorso despises someone, so do all his lackeys. Fortunately, they fear my father more than they wish me dead.

Without a word, the Butchers return the scroll to me and unlock the gate. Its hinges squeak as I step through it—sealed ledger in hand—and climb the half-dozen steps that lead to the front entrance. The black marble door is already open. Golden lamplight spills from it onto an overcrowded porch. Here, the clientele is dressed in expensive suits and puffy dresses, their skin a blotchy combination of purple and gray.

Drums pound from inside the building, shaking the stones beneath my feet. Shrill laughter joins it.

Jaw clenched, I thumb my father's wax seal and mentally brace myself for what's about to happen. If I'm lucky, Morcai will have the money and Conrin won't hear about this. If I'm not . . .

Maybe he'll forgive me.

I slip past the outdoor seating area, into the foyer of an unfurnished room. Black marble walls and a black marble floor greet me, reflecting the faces of the hundred richest merchants and inventors in Kariss—all of which are packed so tightly, it's impossible to wedge myself between them. Glittering blue powder covers their cheeks. Their lips are smudged with dark paint, which flash serrated teeth when they smile.

Unlike the other gambling dens, there are no tables in The Bronze Isle. No dice games. No cards. Here, the betting is much more sinister. Everyone circles around a bright red spinning wheel where an elven boy has been tied naked to it, its arms and legs outstretched like a starfish.

Three elgrew form a single file line in front of the creature.

"Place your bets, everyone!" shouts a Bracer. Clad in black leather, she paces the room, holding a bamboo wicker basket. The crowd parts for her as she passes, tossing green betting slips into a nearly overflowing pile.

A dozen conversations echo off the walls.

"I think Oris will kill it," whispers the woman in front of me.

Someone else snorts. "Selia's brother is a Hunter. She has better aim."

I scan the room for Morcai and clench my fists once I realize he's the third competitor. It's a desperate ploy to recoup the money he owes Azerin—one that costs a fortune in and of itself. Contestants don't just pay the betting fee. They pay for the elf. They pay the betters if they lose. And they pay the house fifteen percent of their earnings.

It's fucking psychotic that he's up there, owing what he already does. Conrin's bailed him out enough times already. If he goes through with this, neither of them will ever be out of debt.

For the first time in my life, I *want* to make a scene. Someone has to teach this man a lesson before he ruins my best friend's life. If I have to be that person, so be it. I'm glad Conrin isn't here to stop me—to *pay* me—he's already paid enough. And this stupid piece of shit deserves everything that's coming to him.

My hand reflexively goes to my bone knife—the one my uncle gave me when I was seven, first learning how to kill. The smooth hilt curves into my palm. A perfect fit. Slowly, I unsheathe it and lower my hood, intent on stopping this before it's too late.

"The betting is now closed," the Bracer announces, cupping her hands around her mouth to be heard above the chatter. "Oris, you may spin the wheel."

The room falls silent.

Kerosene sconces dim.

At the spinning wheel, the elven boy snaps its eyes shut, tears and snot leaking down its freckled face. The creature's bottom lip wobbles as Oris approaches it, his expensive boots clicking on the polished floor, his silk cloak swishing behind him. He ruffles the elf's hair playfully, like this is all a game. Of course, to him, it is. I'm the only one who seems to realize how fucking disgusting this is.

I take a step forward, nudging the woman in front of me as Oris places his hands on the wheel and heaves, putting his whole body into the spin.

The boy screams. The sound changes pitch, wavering as its head swings toward the ceiling then back down again. At least with me here, it won't have to suffer long. I'm nothing if not precise.

"Move," I hiss.

The woman turns to glare at me. "If you wanted a better spot, you should have gotten here sooner."

Her jaw drops when she sees my face. The Grand Overseer's enforcer—not *just* his son, but the person he sends to demand restitution.

"Lyrick . . ." She takes a step back, bumping into the elgrew closest to her.

The boy continues screaming and a knife *thunks* against wood.

"Move." I'm louder now.

More patrons turn toward me, then shuffle out of the way, clearing a direct path to the spinning wheel, Morcai, and the panicked boy. Not seeing me, Oris flicks his blade. The metal tip gleams as it shoots through the air and lodges into the boy's arm. Another knife goes flying in a blur of motion. And then it's buried into the elf's emaciated gut.

Silver blood oozes onto the marble floor, glittering like mercury. My stomach turns even as it rumbles.

He shouldn't be here.

This is wrong.

Anger simmers in my veins. Maybe I can't stop the torture that happens in this place, but I *can* offer mercy. I clench my jaw and throw before the other two competitors get a chance.

The boy's cries suddenly go silent—everything does save for the *swish, swish, swish* of the wheel and the clomping of my military boots. I don't look at the pathetic creature as I step past the frozen crowd, up to the macabre display. No—my eyes are on Morcai as I wiggle my blade free of its gushing throat.

A clean kill.

As painless as it gets for someone like him.

"Morcai, you owe the house a debt," I say, keeping my voice level, my face blank. Calmly, I wipe the blade on my thigh, spreading silver onto my black hunting leathers. The tangy metallic stench threatens to cloud my thoughts, but I force myself to blot it out.

I will not lose control here.

I sheathe the blade and proffer my father's scroll. "For you."

The retired Hunter narrows his violet eyes. Like Sarvenna, his skin is a mottled patchwork of gray. Too poor to maintain it, purple scars sprout from the flesh where he's been cut or scraped. A narrow line down his left eye. Another through his lip. He dresses in expensive suits that I know he can't afford, wasting his son's money and abusing his charity.

Gods, I fucking hate him.

The man makes no effort to retrieve the missive, so I close the gap between us. "The Grand Overseer requires payment," I say, shoving the scroll against his chest. "Now."

Baring his teeth, Morcai thumbs the wax seal open, breaking it. His cheeks darken with anger upon reading the contents. "That's twice as much as I owe."

"That's interest," I say. "Do you have the money or not? If not, I have permission to extract payment in other ways." Peeling back my cloak, I flash my blade. It wouldn't be the first time I've flayed someone here. Elf skin is worth a fortune, even as used as his.

He puffs out his chest. "You think you can best me?"

"I do." It's not confidence or arrogance. It's a fact. The old man is out of practice, and while I haven't been permitted to hunt, I've never stopped training.

"Get the money from Conrin," he says, shooing me away like he used to when I was a child. "We both know he's good for it."

My fist shoots out, connecting with Morcai's gut. The man grunts and doubles over, his chest heaving as he catches his breath. Gods, this asshole is pathetic—not just that, but weak too. It's hard to believe I ever admired him. Flexing my fingers, I walk a circle around the used-up has-been, my footsteps heavy and loud in the silence of the room.

No one interferes. They never do.

I punch him again—*one, two*—hard and in the side. Morcai stumbles forward.

At the edges of the crowd, several armed Butchers appear, ready to intercede if I need them. Ready to hold him down if it comes to that. But I don't need help. Fighting, skinning, putting Hunters in their place, that's what I'm good at.

"Your son's name isn't on the ledger," I say. "*Yours* is. It's time you took responsibility for your actions." I shove Morcai to the floor then join him, climbing over his body.

Morcai lashes out, grappling for me. Fingernails claw at my leather armor to no avail.

I pin his body beneath my own and rest my forearm against his throat, pressing down, cutting off his air supply. Choked off sputters escape the elgrew's mouth. His gray face turns dark, nearly black as he slaps and kicks at me with muscles that have long since atrophied.

A knock to my gut.

A kick to my calves.

He grabs a fistful of my long hair and yanks, lurching my head back so I look at the ceiling. Searing pain lances my scalp, but I don't budge. I've been waiting for this moment a long fucking time, and a little bit of pain isn't about to stop me.

I stare at our reflection in the dark marble, savoring the view as his eyes close and his limbs stop flopping around.

Still, no one moves. No one speaks.

They watch me in complete stillness as I flip Morcai's unconscious body over and reach for my blade. Expensive fabric rips as I trail the knife down his spine, peeling back layers of a three-piece suit, exposing a canvas of fattened muscle and scarred elf flesh.

Straddling him, I grip Morcai's nape and shove his face to the floor, holding it there while I angle the knife between muscle and skin. It severs so easily. So quickly. I'm loosely aware of how he moans beneath me. How he twitches and begs for mercy. But I'm more focused on keeping the cut clean, tracing a stable line through a river of oozing amethyst blood.

My hands are steady—as sure as Yaklan's—as I remove what Morcai owes my father, sweat beading against my brow. I blink past the burning in my eyes and throw the flesh to the floor with a resounding *smack*. "Pick it up," I order the Butchers. "Have someone deliver it to Azerin."

Purple blood sticks to every part of me. I have no desire to clean it off as I sweep the hair from my eyes and stand. I want them to see. *My father* wants them to see. No one fucks with us and gets away with it.

My legs wobble from how long I've been in the same position, but Conrin's father has gone eerily still. If not for his white breath fogging the onyx tiles, I'd assume him dead.

"My guess is that at least one of you has ossi dust," I call, speaking to anyone—everyone—in the crowd, stretching as I do so. I don't wait for a response. "If you feel so inclined, you may heal him. Fuck if I care."

And then I walk out—not bothering to see what becomes of the useless heap.

XIII. Conrin

"Butchers are responsible for maintaining order in the city. They are our first line of defense against invasion, rebellion, and civil war. Most purples cannot afford surgery—this is not the case with Butchers. They are purple by choice, to better represent the people they protect. Their loyalties lie first and foremost with the lower castes."

—CREATION OF THE CASTE SYSTEM, CHAPTER 3

"**D**ad?" My voice cracks when I see him all broken and bloody on the gambling hall floor. No one moves to touch him, to *help* him. He has no friends left.

"Dad." I fall to the marble tile, in a puddle of his sticky blood. More blood oozes from him, seeping from the exposed muscle at his back. "Who did this to you? Why?"

He doesn't answer. He doesn't move.

Is he . . . No. He can't be.

My hands shake as I reach for the pouch of ossi dust knotted to my belt. It's so much blood. *Too much.* And no one's fucking helping.

I fumble with pouch strings, cursing at my clumsy fingers as I pour the dust over my father's exposed back. The bleeding ebbs, then it stops. A thin layer of purple skin—so transparent it might as well be glass—stretches and expands over the open wound. Dad's eyes snap open, bloodshot and wet like he's been crying. Fuck. *Fuck.*

I've never seen him cry before. He's always been the stoic one.

"You're okay," I whisper. It's more to reassure me than him. "You're okay. I've got you."

Gingerly, I loop my hands around his armpits and lift—wincing when he moans in pain. This mountain of a man is too heavy to move. Too fragile. I don't know what I'm supposed to do with him, how I'm supposed to safely touch him. And everyone keeps fucking staring.

Useless sacks of shit—all of them.

The Butcher who summoned me here steps up to the circle. I don't recognize her, but that doesn't mean much. Hunters and Butchers rarely share the same social groups.

"We have a room upstairs," she says, smoothing down her black apron and matching trousers. Her purple face is a mess of twisted lumps and throbbing veins that I can't stop staring at. "We can summon a Stitcher if you'd like. It may take a while for them to get here though, given where we are."

I know there's an angle; Butchers don't work for free. Still, what choice do I have?

I nod, and the woman whistles, loud and sharp. A team of Butchers cut through the crowd—their black aprons appearing from nowhere, shoving past lacy dresses and pleated suits. Surrounding us, they grab my dad by his ankles and wrists, then hoist him into the air. His head falls limply back, eyes closed and unmoving.

At the woman's instructions, the guests clear a path to a

servants' staircase at the back of the room. Hushed whispers echo across the marble walls, but none of those assholes dare look at me as we exit the gambling hall.

The walk takes minutes, but it feels like hours.

The Bronze Isle is known for its luxury, but the upstairs is austere and plain. Bamboo floors and bamboo walls. Kerosene lanterns that swing overhead. The woman leads us down a hallway with three doors and opens the very last one, ushering us into a sparsely furnished, dimly lit bedroom. With a sweep of the hand, she commands her lackeys to set Dad down, rolling him onto his stomach on a mattress barely large enough to accommodate him.

The sheets, the air, it all smells like mothballs here, like no one's visited in a long time. It's windowless and quiet and sets my teeth on edge.

"Wait here," the woman says. She walks to a dusty wooden desk—the only furniture besides the bed—and pulls out a rickety wooden stool tucked inside it. Sliding the stool to me, she pats the surface and orders me to sit. "He'll be alright," she says. "I've seen worse."

Squeezing my shoulder, she offers me a reassuring smile that doesn't reach her eyes. Then, she and the other Butchers file out of the room, the door clicking shut behind them.

I collapse onto the wooden stool and grab my dad's limp hand. Pressing it to my forehead, I sit and wait. The silence stretches, but he doesn't wake.

As the hours pass, I feel myself drifting, my head lolling against the mattress. I dream of Dad taking me to the forest for the first time, hunting with him and his lover, Korun. I remember the moist grass beneath my feet, the cold rain on my face, the three of us laughing—always laughing.

Then, the memories turn sour.

Korun dies, and Dad refuses to hunt again. Then comes the

gambling, the poverty, the growling stomach I could never fill. I don't realize I'm crying—that I'm awake again—until someone pats me on the back. Wiping my eyes, I look up, expecting a Stitcher. I find Sorso instead.

"The Stitcher will be here soon," he says by way of explanation. It's the first time the Karesai of Butchers has ever spoken to me directly. His voice is deeper than I thought it would be, and his breath reeks of soury metal and rancid meat. Like the rest of his caste, Sorso dresses in an unassuming black apron and matching slacks. "She's in the washroom right now preparing some elves for transplant."

"I can't afford a transplant," I say.

"It's taken care of." Sorso waves me off dismissively. The floor creaks as he walks to the bed and leans over my dad, examining his shiny skin and fatty muscle. "Did my purples tell you who did this?"

I shake my head.

"Morcai owed Azerin a substantial amount of money."

It takes a moment for the implication to hit—Azerin only sends one person to collect.

"He wouldn't." But my voice comes out hoarse, unsure. The two of them have always hated one another.

"He *would*." Sorso sits on the edge of the mattress, nearly crushing my father in the process. Dad doesn't notice. He doesn't even flinch. Face-to-face, the Karesai of Butchers stares into my eyes as if to show me there's no deception hiding there. "Lyrick is a monster just like the Hunter who trained him. I could tell you things about him . . . things the Grand Overseer has worked hard to bury."

I turn away from him. I don't want to hear this, nor do I want to believe that my best friend—the boy who fed me when I was dying on the streets—would do this to my father. "Why are you here, Sorso? Surely, it's not out of the kindness of your heart."

He chuckles. "Of course not. I don't believe in charity." Sorso smiles at me in a way that makes the hairs rise on the back of my neck. "Your father has been looking for a way to legally kill Lyrick for years, and I'm going to provide one. The question is, are you going to help me, or are you going to stand in my way?"

XIV. Lyrick

"Korun of Olsenna was our shortest-lived Karesai. A paragon of justice, he was the only elgrew brave enough to punish those closest to the Grand Overseer. Perhaps in this case, bravery is synonymous with stupidity."

—On Elgrew Politics, Newspaper Entry
Author Unknown

25 YEARS EARLIER...

"What do we do with the boy?" Morcai asks, pacing the tent. He acts like I'm not here, gagged and bleeding, my head woozy from how hard he hit it with the back of his machete. My surroundings blur, blinking into and out of focus as Korun—the Karesai of Hunters—approaches me, crouching to inspect my injuries. His hand is cool on my forehead. Almost gentle.

"Do you have any evidence that he knew what Talin was doing?"

Morcai shakes his head. "But the man trained him. Gods

know what ideas he filled the boy's head with. It's too dangerous to keep him alive."

I shout behind my gag. I don't understand what's happening—why they took me from my uncle in the middle of the night or stashed me here. We've done nothing wrong. We hunt alone. We follow the rules.

"He's the Grand Overseer's son," Korun says. "We can't kill him on a hunch. There must be proof."

"If we can't kill him, then we'll make him watch. Let him see what happens to traitors, then he won't be so quick to follow in his uncle's footsteps."

Korun scratches his chin, considering. Then, he grabs me by the armpits and hefts me over his shoulder, carrying me like I weigh nothing. Like I *am* nothing.

"I want to see my uncle," I hiss. The words get lost in the dirty rag that tastes of mildew and wet grass. "Let me go."

Twisting and writhing, I struggle to break free, but Korun holds me in a vice. Pushing aside the canvas flaps, he carries me into a flowery field where a crowd of Hunters gather. In the center towers a large wooden pole surrounded by dry hay that reeks of kerosene. I squirm harder when someone drags my uncle toward it, past the quiet onlookers.

Purple and yellow bruising covers Talin's body. He's been stripped to his underclothes, which are dirty and covered in purple stains. Blood seeps from his missing fingernails, down a split, swollen lip, over his pit organs, and from bones bent at unnatural angles. The woman who drags him, ties him to the post, tightening the ropes until he screams.

The teeth are missing from his mouth.

I squirm harder. "Let him go!"

Korun passes me to Morcai, who shoves me to the dirt, forcing me into a kneeling position. His fingers dig bruises into my shoulder. As my uncle's light purple eyes find mine, he mouths something like, "Don't watch."

But Morcai doesn't give me a choice. He fists my hair and keeps my gaze level. "Turn away and I'll make sure you look just like him."

Body shaking in terror, in anger, I stare at Korun, who marches to the wooden stake, a matchbox in hand. Tears well behind my eyelids, but I blink them away.

"Talin of Kariss, you've been found guilty of treason. May the rains bless you and the gods forgive you. Demtin knows I won't."

He throws the match onto the hay, and my uncle goes up in a plume of smoke and screams.

XV. Lyrick

"A good teammate trusts their friends, a good leader trusts
their instincts, and a good Karesai trusts nothing."

—Talin of Kariss, Lead Hunter of the Nines
Status: Deceased

I crack my knuckles, then my neck before taking off into a
sprint. My bloody shirt lies discarded on the running track
—not a soul in sight. I leap over it, sweat drenching my
body, wetting the dried blood that still clings to my skin. When I
wipe my forehead, my palm comes back purple.

Another lap. A fourth, then fifth.

My lungs heave for breath, but I keep going. There's a knot
in my chest that I can't quite loosen, and it's not caused by guilt
or remorse for Conrin's shitty father, but by *her*. Stars shine
above me, but when I stare at them, I don't see anything but the
cold inside of a familiar yet foreign cave.

I'm in Arden's thoughts again, and I can't shake out of them.
I'm not sure I want to.

The hazy face of a male elf blinks into and out of focus. A

brother? A lover? She'd be old enough by now. I crack my knuckles again and run faster. The elf wraps his arm around her in an awkward half-hug that she doesn't pull away from. It makes me grind my teeth, but I'm not sure why. Fuck if I care what the creature does. She should have her fun before I escape my father's sentries and eat her.

So should I.

I reach for the connection between us and mentally tug, trying to sever it for the dozenth time in the past hour. This time, the images go black. Sighing in relief, I lurch to a stop, snatch my crusty shirt off the ground, and use it to wipe the hot sweat from my face. My sore muscles ache in all the best ways. I've spent hours on the workout field—lifting weights, flinging knives at straw targets, taking out my pent-up irritation with Azerin on everything in sight.

The only thing that hasn't been exercised and satiated is my cock—which Sarvenna will be more than happy to take care of.

Whistling, I make my way back to our shared accommodations. The workout field lies in the center of *Hunter's Square*—a large compound reserved for active hunting squads, with tenement bedrooms that can house teams of six. Technically, I'm not eligible to sleep here anymore, but Sarvenna and the rest of the squad makes room for me.

Long, external staircases lead up the sides of the building onto separate landings for each residency. I climb the stairs to mine, the shoddy metal groaning and shaking with each step. Seven flights later, I reach my apartment. Outside the door is a government-mandated posting of who dwells within.

Sarvenna of Kariss.

Eleesy of Olsenna.

Pel of Nordi.

Conrin of Kariss—Acting Squad Leader.

Beside their names are tally marks, tracking each capture and kill. None of them have less than fifty, but all have less than I do, were I on the list. It's two names shy of a full hunting party. We lost our combat medic last year, and they never replaced me on the team—still waiting for the day Azerin releases me from my obligations.

I sift through the key ring attached to my belt loop and let myself in, mentally bracing for whatever drama Conrin's about to start.

If the Gambling Block is chaos, Hunter's Square is order. No drinking. No smoking. And noise ordinances are in effect from sundown to sunup. The laughter I hear inside jolts me back, bright lantern light pouring from the living room onto the landing.

"Shut the door, Lye," Eleesy whines. "You're going to get us caught."

I oblige her.

Stepping past the threshold, I roll my eyes when I see the barrel of ya'esen in the center of our living room. Conrin is gone. Everyone else sits on threadbare couches around stacked wooden crates that serve as drink tables. Discarded weapons and armor clutter the bamboo floor, turning the terrain into a hazardous obstacle course.

It's always messy like this. Besides me, no one stays here long enough to warrant turning this house into a home.

Angling for my bedroom, I maneuver around a leather cuirass, my wadded, bloody shirt in hand. Now that the adrenaline's worn off, the last thing I want to do is party with them. *Shower. Fuck. Sleep.* In that order. Like a good girl, Sarvenna's already rising from her seat, close on my heels.

"Shit, Lyrick, what happened to you?" Pel asks from the couch. He's the youngest on the team and loyal to Conrin, who recruited him. With close-cropped hair and uniformly gray skin, the two are almost identical.

I grunt a response. I'm not interested in discussing this with the squad or listening to them bitch about how shitty of a friend

I am. I'm the only one with the balls to do what needs to be done, which is why they appointed me leader in the first place.

"It's not my blood," I offer when Sarvenna starts inspecting me for injuries. "Azerin had me on collections."

In my periphery, Eleesy perks up. Her lilac eyes glimmer with excitement. "What'd you take? Eyes? Ears?"

"Neither. Skinned his back."

And then I'm gone.

Refusing to elaborate, I shove into my bedroom, discarding knives and other weaponry onto the floor, metal *clanging* as they hit. I peel stiff leather breeches down my hips, wincing when Morcai's dried blood pulls on my stitchwork. Sarvenna leans against the doorpost, arms crossed, enjoying the show. "Rough night?" she asks.

"An annoying one." Images of that male elf hugging Arden blink into existence. He's familiar somehow, but I can't place it. "I'm not in the mood to talk."

"Who said anything about talking?"

She sashays up to me and curls her fingers in my blood-soaked, sweat-soaked hair, pressing her warm body flush against mine. Now that we're alone, I notice what Sarvenna's wearing, or rather what she *isn't*. Dark nipples tent her thin white undershirt. Matching panties made of sheer lace show off every inch of her smooth, mottled-gray skin.

She grinds against me like a verncat in heat, but for once my cock refuses to cooperate.

"I need a shower," I say, brushing her off. "Go have fun with the others. I'll find you after."

Sarvenna pouts—an annoyingly desperate expression that doesn't suit her at all. "We're playing *Secret Box*," she says. "You should join us when you're finished. Winner gets to pick tomorrow's training exercises."

I give a noncommittal answer and step into the adjoining shower room, shooing her away.

Thank gods she doesn't follow.

Of all the things I enjoy about being a Hunter, our bathing options aren't one of them. Most grays live in luxury, but we're efficient. The shower is small—barely large enough to accommodate me, let alone *two* elgrew—and boxed in by a metal cage. A lever with neither hot nor cold settings turns the spout on, which sprays a single stream of low-pressure water onto a grated floor.

Closing my eyes, I step into what should be room-temperature water. I feel delicious warmth instead. Steam thickens the air, loosening the tension in my muscles, and I groan in agonized relief. When I open my eyes again, the bathing chamber is foggy, roomy, and made of stone.

I half expect my body to be blue as I glance down, but it's still me. Sort of. My palm flashes gray, then blue, then gray again—the skin throbbing where I bit her.

"Who is he?" I ask. I don't expect an answer. We can't communicate like that, and even if we could, doing so would be idiotic. Besides simple commands, elgrew are forbidden from speaking to our pets and food.

"Lyrick?" Arden's voice sounds as confused as I feel.

But I'm still thinking about his damned face. Still lost in trying to figure out who the man was that I can't bring myself to think about the repercussions of what I'm doing. "Who were you speaking with earlier?"

"That's none of your business," she snaps at me.

"Everything you do is my business. I own you."

The rage that fills her is visceral. She grits her teeth—*we* grit our teeth—and the connection goes black again, my washing room reverting to its normal, claustrophobic size. Sighing, I rinse the rest of the blood clean and towel off.

It isn't until I'm dressed that I realize something even more troubling than my ability to speak to her. We weren't talking in Elvish, but in Elgrew.

A BLINDFOLD OBSCURES MY SURROUNDINGS. Feminine voices snicker as I sit up straight, taking in the faint floral scent of whatever lies in front of me. Pel is passed out somewhere on one of the couches—an early loser in this bullshit game.

"Shush." I hold my hand up to silence Eleesy and Sarvenna, then whiff again, deeper this time. Slower. Floral *and* bitter with a faintly sour back kick. A grin spreads across my face. *Too easy.* "It's acathia flowers. Just the roots."

The box in front of me snaps shut, the lid clicking tightly into place.

"Damn, he's good," Eleesy says. "Are you sure he isn't cheating?"

Bamboo floorboards creak as Sarvenna crosses the living room and checks the tightness of my blindfold for the seventh time tonight, ensuring no light peeks through. Her cool fingers send goosebumps down my arms and back.

Great, now my cock decides to work.

"Maybe the fabric is more transparent than it looks," Sarvenna suggests.

"I'm happy to trade places with you," I tell her. "Or I can give you a demonstration in my bedroom. Whichever you prefer."

I can practically feel her rolling her eyes at me.

Another box creaks open. The resulting smell is so potent and familiar that I call it out on instinct. "Korkuran feathers from the Lycean Marsh."

"How the fuck could you possibly know that?" Eleesy sighs in frustration and slams the lid shut. "Did you go through my stuff?"

No, I watched Arden hunt there earlier this week.

I snort. "Don't be jealous, Leesy. Not everyone can be as talented as I am."

Blindly, I reach for the low-lying drink table—an upturned milk crate—in front of me, my fingers coiling around a goblet of ya'esen. Drinking with them feels more tolerable now that the other options are stewing over Arden or waiting for Conrin to return. I should have taken sex when it was on the table.

I drink until the edges of my brain feel fuzzy. Another box creaks open and another scent replaces the last one.

"If this doesn't get him, nothing will," Eleesy says.

Sighing, I set the empty goblet down and scent the air around me. Admittedly, this game is only a challenge while drunk, and even then I can run circles around my friends. The constant starvation heightens my senses and makes me a better Hunter, but they don't know that. Nor do they know that when they win, it's because I let them.

At first, I don't smell anything. It must be old—either that or the sample is too small.

Leaning closer, I waft the air toward me.

Big mistake.

Venom floods my mouth, sending my salivary glands into overdrive. I swallow again and again and again, fighting the hunger in my stomach as I glare at Elessy and Sarvenna through the dark blindfold. "Elf's blood," I bite out. "Hardly a challenge."

"*Whose* blood?" Eleesy prods. "Can you tell?"

I risk another breath, shallower this time, and feel my thoughts slipping, the predator in me begging to be released. The creature's blood is sweet and metallic. Tangy and rich too, like a dessert wine. But underneath all that is a familiar buzzing in my ears that marks it as *mine.*

I rip the blindfold off and blink away the blurry brightness of the room. Eleesy and Sarvenna hover over me—Eleesy dressed in an outfit that matches Sarvenna's, exposing everything. I barely notice her. Instead, my eyes home in on the trinket-sized silver box in her hand.

My heart thuds against my ribcage.

Inside the velvet-lined box is a folded letter dotted with blue blood.

"Told you he couldn't get it," Eleesy says, beaming down at me.

I can barely hear her over the blood rushing to my skull, barely see her through my rapidly tunneling vision. Darkness edges in until all there is is me and that damned letter. I reach for the bond between Arden and me, needing to see her, to know she isn't hurt or captured or both, but it remains frustratingly dark.

Rationally, I know Eleesy couldn't have taken her in the span of a shower. But logic doesn't matter right now because I know what happens to her if she's brought here. My claim might not be enough to stop Azerin from breeding her or turning her into another myrie. *I might not be enough.*

Before Eleesy can close the box, I dart forward and snatch the letter from inside. Unfurling it, I smooth the crinkled edges over my thigh and stare at the contents, my brows furrowing in confusion. It's a number.

"She marks her kills like we do," Eleesy says. "And she's edging in on my record."

That small girl I spared in the forest has taken down sixty-three elgrew? Shit.

Hunting and killing her will be more challenging than I thought. My mouth waters at the prospect, even as another truth hits home. Owners are legally responsible for the elves we Claim. Her kills are *my* kills, and the families can demand restitution.

I'm fucked when they bring her in. *If* they bring her in.

I swallow. "How'd you get this?"

"My cousin Bolzeik was hunting one of your dad's escaped slaves," Eleesy says. "Apparently, the blue elf's taken a liking to it and they're traveling together. She killed one of the Hunters in Bolzeik's unit and left that note behind."

That's the elf I saw earlier. It must have been.

I turn the paper in my hand, resisting the urge to sniff it—*her* —a second time.

The front door swings open, and Conrin stomps in covered in what I can only assume to be his father's blood. I don't ask who told him; I made a big enough scene at the gambling hall it could have been anyone. Hair ratty, eyes dark-rimmed, he crosses the threshold and heads straight for me. Before I can stand, he grabs me by my loose-fitting shirt and yanks me to my feet.

The letter falls to the floor between us.

"What the fuck is wrong with you?" Conrin growls. I punch him in the side until he releases me, and he doubles over, coughing. "You're a fucking psychopath."

Eleesy and Sarvenna glance between us. Sarvenna speaks first, her voice quiet. "Lyrick, what did you do?"

I don't have time to answer.

Conrin lunges, headbutting me straight in the gut, knocking me back into the couch. The air goes whooshing from my lungs as he climbs on top of me, pinning me into the squishy cushions. In a blur of motion, his fists connect with my cheek—again and again and again. My jaw cracks. My left eye swells shut, half the world going dark. I squirm beneath him, fighting for a good angle to throw Conrin off, but I don't get the chance.

Eleesy and Sarvenna grab him by the shoulders and peel him from me, body thrashing, teeth bared. In the corner of the room, Pel rouses from sleep, groggily rubbing at his crusty eyes. It'll be a harder fight once he realizes what's happened and joins in.

"Do you have anything to say for yourself?" Conrin asks. His jerky movements calm the longer they hold him.

Cracking my jaw back into place, I offer a slurry answer. "Your dad's an asshole and I don't regret it."

He spits at me, the glob landing on my cheek. I swipe it away, ignoring the looks of betrayal that flash in Eleesy's and Sarvenna's eyes as they piece together what I've done. "I want you out of my apartment," Conrin says.

"That makes two of us." I straighten my clothes and snap at Sarvenna, pointing to the door. "Are you coming or not?"

Letting go of Conrin's arm, she glances between him, Eleesy, and me. Quietly, she gathers up her things and follows me outside. "You shouldn't have done it," she whispers, hugging her scantily clad body as the cool wind rushes us. "He's not an enemy either of us want to have."

"He'll get over it," I say. With my swollen tongue, the words don't come out convincingly. The taste of over-ripened fruit coats my mouth and when I spit, purple blood sprays the sidewalk. "If he doesn't, I'll deal with it. I'm not scared of Conrin."

"Maybe you should be."

XVI. Arden

"Metallic blue in appearance, cold iron is the single most crippling substance to elves. Looking at it can scramble the mind, leading to headaches, blurred vision, and slurred speech. Upon contact, even the lowest quantities are known to cause tinnitus, muscle weakness, and bleeding of the eyes, ears, and nose. It is to be avoided at all costs."

—General Ismas of Ashwood, Starra'lee Personal Correspondence.

"This is where our unit sleeps." Pushing aside the canvas curtain, I lead Chest Wound—*Torvin*— into one of several barracks. Twenty bunk beds hug the walls, creating a narrow hallway between them. "We share this space with five other squads. Leaders sleep across the hall, but entrance is prohibited."

Struggling not to slip on the smooth stone, I pad across the floor, wearing the soft, knitted socks I stole off an elgrew corpse. New guy had the common sense not to comment on my wardrobe. Then again, he's cold too, shivering as he hugs his bare chest.

I flash him a sympathetic smile. "They tell me it gets unbearably hot at night once everyone's loaded up. Our soldiers screw like korkuran too. So, if you're ever cold, just find a bed to share."

He peers around the room, glancing at go-bags that hang from every headboard. All the beds are made—covered by a thin sheet of white glowfly silk and topped with a downy pillow. It doesn't look like much. The mattresses aren't nearly as comfortable as hammocks, and the blankets aren't nearly thick enough. But it's safe, which is more than can be said for the forest.

I point to the occupied spaces. "It's technically first come, first serve, but if you take either of these, Sora and Cheevy will have your head."

"Where do you sleep?" he asks.

"Not in here."

"Because of your . . ." He gestures to my body. "I imagine it'd be uncomfortable for you to watch others . . . *share a bed.*"

I narrow my eyes. "I've watched them fuck plenty of times, Chest Wound. My physique has nothing to do with it." Gesturing to the door, I push aside the canvas curtain and lead him farther down the hallway, not bothering to check that he's followed.

The sound of ungraceful, thumping footsteps is confirmation enough.

In truth, touring with Chest Wound hasn't been as terrible as I thought it would be; the elf speaks almost fluent Elgrew, and he isn't half as dumb without the cold iron rotting his brain. But I'm not ready to make peace yet. Blaming him for the loss of my ossi dust is irrational—I know that—yet every time I look at him, I'm reminded of the emptiness in my pocket.

"I have a little sister," I say eventually. "It wouldn't be proper for her to stay in the same rooms as them, and I prefer looking after her when I'm home. We sleep down that tunnel up ahead." Stopping, I point to the narrow entryway that leads to our quarters.

Chest Wound shudders. "You can fit through that?"

"It's a little snug, but we manage."

His face is ashy pale. "We had tunnels like that in the mines. The elgrew used them to vent air so we wouldn't die as fast inhaling cold-iron dust. Before I reached my Age of Majority, they'd force me to clean them out. Even then, small as I was, I used to think I'd get stuck down there and die. You couldn't pay me enough to live somewhere like that."

"I used to be afraid of it," I admit. "Back when I first joined Starra'lee, I thought I might reach my Age of Majority while I was asleep and get trapped. But then I aged out of the transformation window." Shrugging, I continue down a set of stairs. "Now, it's not so bad. If the elgrew found the place, they couldn't reach us there."

Another canvas curtain separates us from the armory. I shove it open, holding the flap for him as he ducks inside. Chest Wound's eyes widen as he takes in the massive space—smaller than the dining hall but larger than three barracks combined. On one wall, go-bags hang floor-to-ceiling from metal hooks. On another, stone shelves contain folded sets of clothing, armor, and grooming supplies. Then, there's the weapons themselves. A cache of machetes, bows, arrows, quivers, and knives fill racks upon racks of storage. Several dozen feet above us, a hand-sized stream of sunlight creeps in, illuminating the dark rock walls.

I march to the clothing first, giving Chest Wound a long once over to assess his size. His cheeks flush silver—the gaunt hollows already filling out now that the cold iron's gone. Despite my nickname for him, the elf's wound is barely a scar. Courtesy of my ossi dust, a circle of thirty-eight dark gray pinpricks is the only evidence of last night. And I can't help but feel bitter about it.

"Everyone gets issued one outfit," I say, tossing him a hide shirt, then a leather vest to go on top of it. Surprisingly, the recruit catches. "If you don't like the armor that's assigned to you, you can make your own or steal it from others. Sawgrass is prohibited. I think Julian will have a conniption if another member of his unit breaks that rule."

Resisting the urge to scratch my rashy arms, I find pants that will fit him, then turn around so he can change. It's Julian's fault the itchiness is so bad this time. When I lived in the marshes, I'd built up callouses to protect against the friction. Here, I wear the sawgrass too infrequently and my skin's gotten soft.

While Chest Wound changes, I grab a go-bag and fill it with grooming supplies, a machete, a utility knife, and the other pieces of his armor—vambraces, bracers, greaves, and tassets. The bag is stuffed so full that the buckles barely latch by the time I'm finished. Holding my palm to my face, I peek between my fingers to check that he's done dressing, then I pass him the bag.

Chest Wound sinks under the weight of it, grunting as he hooks it over his shoulder.

"I'll let Julian know I didn't issue you a bow or arrows," I say. "Until you're topside, there's no point. It's too hard to practice down here."

"You said we can steal armor?" he asks, adjusting his leather vest. "You mean from the elgrew?"

I shrug. "From the elgrew. From each other. If you're dumb enough to leave it out, you're dumb enough to lose it. I wouldn't fuck with the squad leaders, though. They'll stick you with shit missions from now until the end of time."

I made that mistake once; it's how Julian and I became friends.

"Cheevy is our demolitions expert," I say. "He coats his body in flame-resistant oil and sews flammable patches into his cloth-ing. Don't steal from him unless you're prepared to be slow-cooked. Sora is fair game if you don't mind pissing off the elf who's responsible for patching you back up. Tari—you haven't met her yet. She's on scouting duty—got switched to our unit after stabbing the guy who took her chest piece. Generally, if you're going to steal, steal from someone else's team and don't get caught."

We return to the hallway, where I guide him down another set of steps, then another. In the center of a small, unpopulated chamber is a hole that leads into the deepest, darkest depths of Starra'lee. "Be careful on the ladder," I say. "It gets slippery near the end."

Expertly, I lower myself into the hole, my hands and feet automatically finding the metal guard rails and thick rungs. The walls are tight around me, and the vertical tunnel is so long and so dark, it's impossible to see where the next step starts. But I've taken this path hundreds of times, and climbing it is as familiar as breathing air.

One rung. Two. A half dozen.

The new recruit still hasn't followed.

"What's the hold up, Chest Wound?" I shout up to him. My voice bounces and vibrates off the stones.

"Do I have to go?" he asks, bending over the hole. His pale face blots out what little remains of the light. "If it's all the same to you, I'd rather not."

"It's the last stop," I tell him. "Trust me. You won't want to miss it."

"I can't, Arden. *Please.*" His voice trembles. His breaths grow rapid like he's on the verge of hysteria.

The mines, I realize.

Being here in these tight, dark spaces must be so much harder for him than it ever was for me. A shred of empathy sparks to life. I try to shove it back down, knowing he won't make it here if he can't climb a simple ladder, but fuck, I was new too once and I wish I'd had someone—*anyone*—willing to help me survive. "Get your ass on this fucking ladder, Torvin. My baby sister climbs this twice a day. If a ten-year-old can do it, so can you."

The ladder groans as Chest Wound lowers himself onto it and begins the descent.

We climb in silence, the only sound that of our thudding footfalls and joined breaths. He stops after a handful of minutes —at the halfway mark—and when I glance back up, I catch him staring at the abysmally small hole we left behind. Legs shaking, palms sore, I lean back on the railing and call out to him, aiming for a distraction. "Tell me about yourself. Julian says you were a *Watcher* in Azerin's mine. That's why you're so good at speaking in the Elgrew tongue."

"Yeah," he says, sniffling. "*Watchers* translate for the foremen so we get a bigger vocabulary than most—not that we can use it. If we're caught teaching it to the other slaves, it's considered treason. No trial, just execution." He takes another step, then another, and we resume our climb—distraction complete.

"It's not like anyone would talk to us anyway," Chest Wound adds. "When slaves fall behind, it's our job to punish them. Doesn't make for many friends."

I can relate to that. People have never rushed to be my friend either.

As we near the end of the ladder, my sezin crackles from the change in pressure. I imagine his do too. Grunting, I work my jaw until my clogged ears pop, and then I clear my throat. "How did you escape?" I finally ask.

There's a long pause. "It's not very exciting."

"Tell me anyway."

Still in the tunnel, my feet connect with solid stone. I lower myself onto all fours—onto a ground that's slippery and damp —and wait for Chest Wound to catch up. Herbal smoke and humid steam trickle in through a child-sized hole in front of me. Peering into it, I see pale flecks of green light blink on the other side.

"A few days ago, one of the mining tunnels collapsed and I was on the wrong side of it," Chest Wound says. Metal groans. His feet thud to the ground beside me. "I'd been close enough to the surface that I managed to dig myself out. When I realized the collapse was outside of Azerin's compound, I took my chance and bolted." Palms outstretched, Chest Wound feels around for me. "Arden? Where'd you go?"

"On the ground." I tug on his shirt and he follows me down.

"Where are we going?"

Some things are better seen, not heard.

Wordlessly, I crawl through the hole into the heart of our world. As we cross the threshold, a familiar humming sound fills my ears. The *Korring Marr*—not the one in the elgrew capital, but a secret seed grown down below.

XVII. Arden

"Elves exist on many planets, and on each one is a Korring-Marr. Most Great Trees are normal in color and match the world around them. Those like ours give birth to gods. One day, the Korring-Marr will gift us a champion, and they will free us from the elgrew."

—ELDER RISHA OF THE DRIFT, HIGH PRIESTESS SUPREME.

The Korring-Marr here looks nothing like the Korring-Marr topside. It's gnarly and thick with twisting vines that resemble veins. Nine trunks rise from nine pools of steaming, murky green water, braiding together into this massive thing. But it's not the shape of the Tree or even its leafless branches that make it so strange. It's the color. The Korring-Marr's bark is opalescent—as clear as glass near the edges and roots, with a prismatic rainbow in the center. Even in the near-total darkness, the Tree gleams brighter than anything I've ever seen.

Geodesic spheres that are twice as tall as I am dangle from the Korring-Marr's jagged branches on thick metal ropes, their glass panes dyed rainbow to match the bark. At night, our high priests and priestesses sleep inside them. Supposedly, it's a great honor, but it seems even more uncomfortable and impractical than the bunks.

"This place is incredible," Chest Wound breathes, taking in our most prized, most hidden possession. A gentle, soothing buzz emanates from the Tree, draining all the tension from my body and filling me with a familiar weightlessness that only comes from being down here. I know without asking that Chest Wound feels it too.

When I glance back at him, his gray eyes are glassy with tears; most are the first time they see the Great Tree. The elgrew think our Korring-Marr is just a plant, but it's so much more than that. It's the physical manifestation of our all-knowing, all-seeing god through which all other gods—all other life—is made. Though I've seen it a hundred times before, like Chest Wound, I still struggle to turn away.

In a daze, the recruit shuffles closer to our Tree, passing by at least a dozen hot springs and twice as many holy leaders, dressed in hooded black robes.

The Deep is massive. The floor is a solid sheet of glassy obsidian and volcanic pools that stretch as far as the eye can see. Up above us, glowfly orbs hang from the ceiling, casting flecks of pale green light over everything, reflecting it off the black floor. Still, I have to squint to see.

Grabbing Chest Wound's shoulder, I guide him away from one of the springs before he can stumble in. He doesn't notice. His gaze is singularly focused.

The closer we get to the Korring-Marr, the more crowded it is. Nearly a hundred holy leaders and their apprentices gather in circles around the pools, some meditating in prayer, others collecting water samples into glass vials. I catch a few dumping cartons of white powder around the Korring-Marr's roots, where it forms a chunky paste near the water's surface.

Chest Wound forces his way through a group of priestesses, and I groan in frustration.

"Sorry about that. He's new."

"Arri?" Nirissa pulls her hood down. "What are you doing here?"

Stepping away from the others, she wraps her arms around me and squeezes tight.

I can't stop the smile from tugging at my lips. Bug has been tutoring under Elder Risha, High Priestess Supreme, for the last two years, and while it's not exactly a surprise to see her here, I wasn't expecting it either. Risha keeps my sister busy with her studies and rarely lets her do fieldwork with the other apprentices. Most days, she's cooped up in private chambers that I'm not allowed to visit.

I return the hug and ruffle her hair. "I'm giving the new guy a tour today. Pretty sure I mentioned that this morning."

"I forgot." Nirissa bites her bottom lip and fidgets with the ends of her long sleeves. Tucked beneath her robe is the twiggy doll Mom and Dad gave her. "Can I come along?" she asks. "I promise I'll be good."

"I don't think Elder Risha would like that."

"Nonsense." Striding toward us, the High Priestess Supreme lowers her hood. Risha looks no older than any other adult, but her voice has this ancient, scratchy quality to it. Curly silver hair frames a face that's too thin. Too austere. Her cheekbones and nose are so sharp, they could probably cut a man. "Perhaps Nirissa could lead the tour to show us what she's learned?"

"Really?" Bug squeals, her body practically vibrating with excitement.

Elder Risha quirks a brow at me, and I relent.

"Go for it. I could use the break."

Clasping her hands together, the High Priestess Supreme smiles in approval. On the surface, her expression seems genuine—friendly even. But the two of us have never gotten along. When I first arrived at Starra'lee, she ignored me, telling Julian, and I quote, "I have no use for her. You can do with her as you please."

For whatever reason, though, all the things Risha found lacking in me, she found present in my baby sister—just like our parents. Even here, they all prefer Nirissa.

The thought rankles me, but I push it to the back of my mind, locking it up tight. It doesn't matter. I don't need Risha's approval. I don't need anyone.

The bite mark on my hand begins to throb, and I clench my fist tight.

Not now.

Not here, dammit.

I can't allow Lyrick to see the Tree, nor hear our militia's most tightly kept secrets. I need to get the fuck out of here before I ruin everything. But what can I tell them? It's not as if I can admit to the bond—they'd kill me for keeping it a secret for so long.

"Arden, are you coming?" Elder Risha's voice cuts through my thoughts. When I look up, she, Nirissa, and Chest Wound are nearly to the Korring-Marr.

Unease churns my stomach. Guilt weighs me down. I shouldn't follow them—it'll put everything at risk—but then again, I shouldn't do a lot of things.

Self-preservation wins out.

Shoving my hand into my pocket, I scramble to catch back up, my socked feet slippery on the glossy stone. *Please go away. Please, please, please, go away.*

I practically shout the words in my head, praying to the Korring Marr, to any god who might be listening, to sever our connection. Laughter reverberates in my ears—this velvety dark sound that slithers through me turning my veins to ice. But I force myself to keep walking, to not draw attention to myself.

"I found one of your letters," Lyrick whispers. *"You've made quite a mess for me."*

"Good," I hiss the word down our mental bond, not sure how this works, if he'll even be able to hear me. *"Then you know what'll happen when I find you."*

The cocky bastard snorts. *"We'll see about that. By the way, my number is two hundred and eleven."*

The connection goes blessedly dark. Starra'lee's secrets remain safe . . . for now.

I should feel relief, but instead there's this aching hollowness in his absence. As if he took a piece of me with him. *What the fuck is wrong with me?*

I shake the feeling off in time to see Chest Wound place his palm atop the Great Tree. His face ripples and a look of absolute serenity washes over him. Eyes closed, tears stream down his cheeks and he mouths something I can't hear. For a long moment, Nirissa, Elder Risha, and I watch him in silence, giving him the privacy he so desperately needs.

My fingers itch with the desire to touch the Korring-Marr too, but I refrain, afraid that doing so might somehow summon Lyrick once more.

After a long while, Chest Wound opens his eyes and dabs the moisture from them. But he doesn't remove his hand. "How is this possible?" he asks, staring at the dimly lit space, the lack of sunlight and soil.

Nirissa answers before I can. "See that powder over there?" She points to the apprentices and their cartons. "Our scientists use it to grow plants in the dark. And the green glowflies"—she gestures to the ceiling—"those help, too."

"And what about the glass vials?" Elder Risha prods, directing Nirissa toward the robed figures who are taking water samples. Once the vials are full, they place them onto wooden racks, labeling them in a language I can't read—the same one

Selik spoke all those years ago. "What are those things used for?"

Afraid to disappoint her mentor, Nirissa nervously twirls her hair. Her words come out more as a question than a definitive statement. "The priests and priestesses are testing for salt, acidity, calcium, nitrogen—the stuff plants need to grow that they usually get from the soil."

As she speaks, one of the figures swings a go-bag from their shoulder and lowers themselves to the ground. Unhooking buckles and dumping out external pockets, they withdraw dozens of glass dropper bottles and distribute them to the rest of the group. Notebooks in hand, each robed figure begins dripping the solutions into their water samples and furiously jotting down the results. Some vials change colors—yellow, pink, red. Others remain the same.

"They test the water at night to see what stuff needs to be added," Nirissa explains. "In the morning, they go topside to remove it from the soil with the army."

"How long has this been here?" Chest Wound asks.

"Almost a thousand years," Elder Risha says. "Though the Korring-Marr hasn't always been this large. It's grown rapidly in the last decade or so."

A crease line forms between Chest Wound's brows. "And you've kept it secret all this time? How? Why?"

"The Korring-Marr doesn't want anyone to know about this place. You'll find yourself physically unable to speak of it when you leave here. Elves may lack magic, but our Great Tree doesn't. You'll see soon enough." Elder Risha redirects her attention to my sister. "Nirissa, what else can you tell the recruit about the Deep?"

"Hmm . . ." She bounces from foot to foot. "Some people like to bathe in the hot springs. That's ok as long as you stay out of the ones with the roots. Around the edges of the cavern are study and prayer rooms. Those are off-limits. You can't take weapons around the Tree. Obviously."

Like I'd ever go anywhere unarmed.

Five daggers are in plain sight—two sheathed at my hip, another two at my thighs, a fifth strapped to my bicep. They're lucky I didn't bring the bandolier this time. Still, Elder Risha narrows her gaze at me in distaste. Fuck if I care. She doesn't have the power to disarm me. No one does—not even Lyrick with his two hundred and eleven kills.

"What makes the Korring-Marr look like that?" Chest Wound asks, thumbing the gemstone-like bark. "Is it something you add to the soil?"

Elder Risha smiles. "No. It's nothing we do. Legends say there's a Korring-Marr on every planet. Most of them look like the ones in Kariss, but the colorful ones like ours indicate the birth of a new god. We believe that god will one day free us from the elgrew."

I snort.

"Do you have something to say, Arden?" Elder Risha asks.

"Waiting for a savior is a bullshit excuse for the priests and priestesses to sit around and do nothing. It's no better than the elves topside who hide behind their trees while we do all the actual fighting."

"You think our work is cowardly?" Elder Risha challenges. Her voice is cool and calm. "It's the high priests and priestesses who keep our Great Tree alive, and it's the Great Tree that allows us to strategize our largest battles. You're no better than us, just because you're good at stabbing things. Nirissa, would you like to show your sister what we've been working on this week?"

My sister beams up at her. "For real?"

"For real."

Jumping up and down, she swings the robe from her shoulders and it goes floating to the floor, blending seamlessly into the obsidian slab. Nirissa sets her twiggy doll on top of it and approaches the Korring-Marr's trunk, or rather the pool surrounding it. An herbal, decaying stench rises from the steaming green water. Clear glass-like roots jut from the surface, covered in lumpy paste.

My sister tiptoes into the pool, lowering herself chest deep into the putrid water. She ducks beneath the roots and latches on, hugging them the way she does her twiggy doll.

"Some people are born with the ability to communicate with the Korring-Marr," Elder Risha says. "Your sister has a far greater, far rarer gift. She's a conduit. Not only can Nirissa speak to the Great Tree, but she can share its thoughts with others. Go on. Show them."

Bug whispers something in that strange language, and the roots around her start to glow—a soundless harmony that radiates up the braided bark. Her eyes roll to the back of her skull and she dunks her head beneath the water's surface, vanishing into murky green.

Air bubbles rise and pop. A minute passes. Two.

Each moment she doesn't surface is agonizing.

I charge after her, but Risha blocks my path, shoving her arm into my chest. "Nirissa knows what she's doing. Look."

The hot spring ripples and hazy images flare to life, swirling across the pool in a blur of colors. Silver ramparts. Narrow tunnels coated in shimmering blue dust. A diadem made from elf bones and a blue palm scarred by thirty-eight tooth marks. The images flicker faster—*too* fast for my brain to track. A pair of eyes blink open, revealing irises as opalescent as the Tree.

Shredding the images, my sister emerges from the water, choking and gasping for air.

I rush to her then, and the High Priestess Supreme doesn't stop me—no, her gaze has this faraway, distracted look to it. Water splashes. Wet warmth seeps into my hide pants as I pull Nirissa away from the roots and into my arms, asking her if she's alright, patting her back to get the water out. My sister clings to me, her whole body shaking like a leaf as she buries her face into my chest.

"I've never been down that long before," she whispers. "I'm so tired, Arri."

Her eyes close and her body goes limp.

Carrying Nirissa from the pool, I stomp toward Elder Risha. "What the fuck was that?"

"The Korring-Marr doesn't speak in words," she says. "It shows us things, and it's our job to decipher the meanings. I—"

"That's not what I'm talking about. Why is my baby sister risking her life for this shit? She's supposed to be studying books, not . . . *this*." I gesture to the pool. "I don't care how gifted she is. She's a child, Risha."

Blood pounds in my ears, muffling her response. But I'm not interested in her excuses. Snatching up Nirissa's cloak and twiggy doll, I storm off toward the exit. Clumsy footfalls follow close behind—*Chest Wound*. He scrambles to keep up, but Elder Risha yanks him back, her fist curling around his vest.

"Let her go. We need to talk."

XVIII. Arden

Brush in hand, I untangle the knots in bug's wet hair, working through each snarl with intentional slowness. Being soft has never come easy to me, but I force my twitching muscles into submission, forgoing efficiency for comfort. Eyes closed, Nirissa leans her back against my chest, the bedroom silent save for the *swish-swoosh* of the defeathered, korkuran-bristle hairbrush as it glides through her hair. The straw mattress crinkles beneath us each time we move.

Freshly washed, we both smell a little too floral for my taste. Like kissy lips or jurry berries. Like elves who want to get eaten. But I'm on leave now, so there's no reason to bathe with unscented lye or coarse salts. No one's going to hunt us down here.

"Hey, bug." I choose my words slowly, carefully. "I think you should take a break from studying with Elder Risha. I don't like that she has you risking your life."

"You get to risk *your* life." Nirissa opens her eyes to glare at me. "It's boring down here. What else am I supposed to do while you're gone?"

"Maybe you could stick to books."

"Books are stupid. I want to help. I want to go topside like you."

Stubborn kid. She doesn't get it. She'll *never* get it. Nirissa was too young to remember when Mom and Dad died. The fires. The elgrew. The Butchers and their cleavers. To her, all this is some sort of abstract danger. Maybe I've sheltered her too long, kept her *too* safe. Maybe it's time she saw with her own eyes what life is like up there.

The top bunk groans as I readjust, setting the brush on a blanket made from thick animal furs. Even here, Nirissa lives in luxury compared to the other recruits. Her bed is filled with soft blankets and thick pillows made from the animals I've hunted—not the standard issue, flimsy stuff the others have. Her clothes are luxurious too—taken from the elgrew I've killed and resized to fit her. She gets to bathe in expensive oils from the plants I harvest and read books in her spare time, when most of Starra'lee is illiterate. It's a cushy life. As cushy as it gets for people like us, but so long as she's cooped up down here, she'll never appreciate any of it. Worse, she'll resent me for it.

"I'm on leave this week," I tell her. "I think we should go topside."

Every instinct tells me that's a bad idea, but I know the safest routes. Unlike five years ago, I'm experienced enough and strong enough to keep her safe . . . at least for a few days.

"You mean it?" Nirissa's face brightens. She pivots on the mattress so we're face-to-face. "You want to take me with you?"

Want isn't exactly the word I'd use. "Just for the week. We'll harvest some jurry berries together, and I'll teach you how to hunt."

She throws her arms around my neck, clinging to me like a primate. "Thank you, thank you, thank you! This is going to be so much fun!"

"This isn't a vacation, Nirissa," I snap. "You're going to have to do what I tell you. You understand that, right?"

Scooting out of my arms, she rolls her eyes at me before climbing from the bed. "Of course, Arri."

My sister walks to the closet and begins gathering clothing, tossing it into the center of our bedroom floor. I arch a brow at her.

"What are you doing?" I ask.

"Packing."

Sighing, I join her on the floor. *I guess we're really doing this.*

"Okay, but first, let's make a list."

SEVERAL HOURS later and we're almost ready to go. A short trip to the mess hall to gather food rations. A chat with Sora to refill my diminished emergency med-pack. And then, of course, Julian's office—not to ask permission, but because someone should know what we're doing in case we don't come back.

Go-bag in hand, Nirissa and I exit our bedroom door, pushing past the canvas curtain. At the end of the dark, narrow tunnels is a silhouette sitting on the floor, blotting out the glowfly lanterns in the main chamber. Brows furrowed, I step in front of Nirissa, squinting to get a better look at them.

No one ever visits us. I'm not exactly a gracious host.

"Chest Wound?" I ask, blinking twice when his face comes into view. "What the fuck are you doing here?"

"I've been thinking," he says, rubbing his chin.

"That's dangerous territory."

Ignoring my barb, he stands up and ducks into the narrow passageway, coming as close to us as his gargantuan size will allow. "You said Cheevy is a demolitions expert?" he asks. "Meaning he knows how to make explosions and stuff?"

"That would be the definition." Hands on my hips, I force myself not to roll my eyes at him or shake him by the shoulders when he doesn't immediately get to the point of this little drop by. "Do you have something you want to blow up?"

"The cold-iron mine."

My veins turn icy. A lead ball drops into my stomach. "That's not possible. It's surrounded by Butchers and protected by hundred-foot walls. The Grand Overseer lives there, for fuck's sake. I know you want revenge, but—"

"I can show you how."

The confidence in his voice is enough to give me pause.

Even if he has no idea what he's talking about, I'd be stupid not to hear him out. Cutting off the elgrew's supply of cold iron would finally give the elves in the forest a fighting chance. It could save countless lives.

Turning to Nirissa, I ruffle through my pants pockets and withdraw the list of equipment we still need. "Why don't you finish gathering this stuff without me, and we'll meet back here when you're finished? I bet Sora would love to see you."

"Okay! Promise you won't leave without me."

"I promise."

Nirissa snatches the list from me, then the go-bag, sagging and grunting under the weight of a not-so-insubstantial cache of weapons. As she walks away, half-dragging, half-hefting the bag, I sit on the floor and pat the space beside me, gesturing to Chest Wound. "I'm listening. Now tell me your plan."

CHEST WOUND, Cheevy, and I sit at the war table in Julian's office, leaning over two makeshift maps—one of the cold-iron mines, the other of the Grand Overseer's estate. Julian paces the room, his lips pursed in thought. Tousled hair falls over his eyes as he returns to his seat and traces along the map's escape tunnels and airways.

"And you're sure this will work?" Julian asks, peering up at Cheevy.

Our demolitions expert nods. "If the air vents are where Chest Wound—Torvin—says they are and if Arden can fit through them like he says she can, it'll work."

"That's a lot of ifs." Julian sighs, scratching his head the way he always does when he gets nervous. "Leadership will never agree to it. Arden's size makes her too valuable to risk."

"It's my size that will let us do this," I snap. Then, I peer behind me to ensure my voice didn't lure any unwanted visitors. Feet pass beneath the canvas flap but don't linger. Still, I lower my voice. "If the plan has any chance of working, we need to ride out tonight. Otherwise, we miss the opportunity until next year, and by then, it'll be even riskier because the information will be out of date."

Chest Wound and I discussed this at length. Ring Day is the only time the mine shuts down, and it's the only day Azerin's property isn't flooded with guards.

Groaning, Julian rubs his hand over his face. "Are you so eager to die, Arden? Or maybe you're looking forward to a reunion with your master?"

I shrink back at the words, digging fingernails into my scarred palm. For once, the bond is quiet.

"What if Lyrick is at the estate?" Julian asks. "It's not so deep underground that he won't sense your presence. If he tracks you —if he takes you when you're anywhere near that city—there isn't an army in Rayna that could break you out of that fortress."

"Shit, I forgot about him," Cheevy says. "Arden, I don't know . . ."

But I *do* know. Lyrick doesn't live at Azerin's estate; he lives in Hunter's Square with his asshole friends. He doesn't like the games, nor the festivities that follow. For all "my master's" faults, for all his cruelty, Ring Day and the celebrations associated with it aren't one of them. Worrying about his presence there isn't necessary.

The chair squeals as I rise from it. "I can do this," I spit. "I know I can. I'm faster than anyone else in our unit. I'll climb through the air vents and place the explosives before anyone even realizes where I am."

"Have you ever been around that much cold iron?" Julian asks, his words sharp as steel. "You won't be able to tell your ups from your downs, let alone have the motor skills necessary to climb through a ventilation shaft. The answer is no."

Rage boils in my chest. My pulse pounds in my throat. Gripping the edges of the table, I fight to keep from breaking something . . . *everything*. "If I were anyone else, you'd let me risk it."

"You aren't anyone else, Arden. You're my best fighter and this is a suicide mission."

I flip the table, sending the maps scattering. It isn't fair. Julian's protectiveness over me will get everyone killed. "You saved Chest Wound because he had access to the mines. And now that you have that information, you're going to do fuck all with it? Because of what?" Angry tears blur my vision. "I'm not a child, Julian. Don't treat me like one."

He narrows his eyes. "The answer is no. You have a sister to protect."

"I *am* protecting her!" I groan in frustration.

But Julian isn't listening. He never listens to me. I'm not a soldier; I'm the little girl he pulled out of the marshes two years ago. It doesn't matter how many swamp dogs I kill or elgrew I shoot, he will always see me as less than.

Chest Wound crawls onto the floor and collects his papers. Neither he nor Cheevy rush to defend me, though.

Fuck them.

Flipping everyone off, I storm from the room, making a beeline to my quarters.

I don't need their help, and I don't need his permission. I can do this on my own, just like everything else.

The crowded hallway clears for me, the other soldiers smushing themselves against the walls to stay out of my way. Footsteps thud from behind, but I ignore them, pressing deeper into the underground, wiping hot tears from my cheeks.

I shouldn't have to prove myself to Julian. I'm the best Marr-damn soldier in the fucking army.

I make it to my room and push aside the canvas curtain. Rushing to my desk, I find a fresh sheet of paper and scribble out a hasty goodbye to Nirissa, hoping she'll forgive me, that one day she'll understand. Then, I scan the room for my go-bag and curse. Bug has it. She has nearly everything I need to survive a mission like this. I'm totally fucked. There's not a chance on Rayna that Julian will allow me to collect new materials from the armory right now. He's probably warned the others that I'll try.

Screw it. This shithole isn't the only place I've stored a weapons cache. It's just the most convenient. With no supplies and no armor, I return the way I came. Two soldiers guard the exit, their hands tightly gripping the hilts of their glittering bronze sabers.

"You're fucking kidding me," I scoff at them—neither of whom I recognize. "Get out of my way or I'll—"

I'll what? I don't have my weapons. I don't have my sawgrass. I'm entirely useless right now and they know it. Throwing my hands in the air, I curse them, their mothers, and every other person in this Marr-damn army before returning to my chambers.

It's a minor setback. I'll figure out another way. I'll—

Two thuds sound from the hallway. Metal clangs and reverberates as it hits the stony floor.

"Bug?" I call out to her, but it's a male voice that answers.

"Arden?" Cheevy asks. "You in there?"

What? A crease line forms between my brows. I pad through the tunnels where the guards lay unconscious at the exit—hands tied behind their backs, weapons nowhere in sight. Cheevy and Chest Wound bend over them, knotting their ankles together, pockets stuffed with maps and paperwork that had once been on Julian's desk.

"You're still going, right?" Cheevy asks. Hands on his knees, breathing heavy, he grins up at me. "We figured you might need a little help."

Emotion clogs my throat. No one ever helps me—not unless they think they can get something in return. Swallowing past a hard lump, I tiptoe over the bodies and join my squadmates; they're also empty-handed. "No weapons?" I ask.

"Julian posted guards outside the barracks and the armory. We couldn't go back for them," Cheevy says. "Don't suppose you have any hidden in your bedroom?"

"Not the kind I need. But I know where I can get some."

"*I?*" Cheevy quirks a brow. "We're coming with you, Arden."

That pesky lump gets bigger, making my throat all achy and sentimental. "What about Julian?" I ask. "You'll both be reprimanded."

"Fuck him," Chest Wound says.

"Yeah, fuck him."

Letters

Bug,

You won't see me for a couple of days. I'm on a super-secret mission right now that nobody knows about. If Julian comes looking for me, please tell him I've been eaten by a verncat. Or maybe say I'm stuck in slowsand. Whatever you tell him, make it sound cool! I'm sorry I didn't have time to take you topside this week. I promise we'll go first thing when I get back.

P.S. Please stay out of trouble. And no more lessons with Elder Risha.

P. P. S. Do you remember those feather necklaces we used to make? I gathered some korkuran quills on a hunt yesterday and thought maybe we could make jewelry out of them when I get back. Or maybe you can make some for me while I'm gone? Mom used to say they'd bring good luck, and I need all the good luck I can get.

Love you to the Korring-Marr and back,
Arden.

XIX. Lyrick

**"No elgrew shall bite or kiss another elgrew; this is our most
sacred law. We are born into freedom and shall die in it. A
mark of ownership is punishable by death."**

—CITY OF KARISS, THE GREAT CHARTER.

Sarvenna rolls off the bed, disentangling her legs from
mine. Breaths heavy, cheeks flushed, she steps into a
puddle of tight leather pants and shimmies them up her
thighs. Lazy afternoon sunlight streams through the bamboo
shutters, lighting the bruises on her patchwork skin—the bruises
on mine. Twisting her hair into a bun, she looks herself over in
the vanity before tugging on a long-sleeved linen shirt.

"You were too rough this time," she says, inspecting the
purple bruises on her collarbone. "People will talk."

"You weren't exactly gentle, Sarvenna." Blue bamboo sheets
slide down my legs, the bed creaking as I join her by the mirror.
My fingers ghost over a patch of superficial bite marks and she
shutters, goosebumps pebbling her skin.

"Lyrick," she moans, her nipples pricking through the flimsy shirt.

My exhausted cock twitches, not quite ready for round three but more than open to the suggestion . . . *if only we had time.* Cupping between Sarvenna's legs, I back her into my erection so she can feel just how much I crave her. My head dips, teeth grazing over a pale yellow splotch near her shoulder.

She spins on me faster than I can blink, her violet eyes blazing. "I mean it. Keep your mouth to yourself." Sarvenna pushes on my chest and the world flips. The mattress bounces as I fall backward onto it.

"If you want someone to mark, take a myrie," she spits. "I can't risk you breaking skin. It's *illegal.* If they found out I let you kiss me—"

"No one's going to find out." Groaning, I prop myself up on my elbows. She's so fucking serious all the time; it's exhausting. "If it makes you feel better, I'll let you kiss me too. You can even bite me if you want."

Sarvenna glares. "Can't you just . . . ?"

"Just what?" I ask, snatching my clothing off the floorboards.

"*Behave.* Eat like the rest of us. Take a myrie. Stop kissing elgrew. It's not normal, Lyrick."

I cringe at the disgust in Sarvenna's voice, my cock flaccid by the end of her little speech. I'm not normal—*I fucking know that* —but why should I have to lower myself to their standards?

Jaw clenched, I yank on black silk trousers and a matching tunic, shrugging Sarvenna off when she tries to cup my shoulder. I don't need her to placate me. I don't need her to fill my bed either. Dozens of other elgrew would be more than willing to accommodate my strangeness if only to jump the social hierarchy themselves.

"Lyrick, I'm only looking out for you," Sarvenna says. "The Politic will search you for weaknesses. They can't find one."

They already did.

The words are on the tip of my tongue, but I hold them back. I still haven't told Sarvenna about the scene I made at the arena earlier this week. She has no idea the depths of my depravity, my hunger, and I have no plans to enlighten her.

Leaning against the wall, I watch her don leather armor. First, a brigandine, then pauldrons and bracers, followed by a pair of thick military boots with grooves at the bottom for hiking. She'll be gone by the end of today. Who knows for how long. Her last hunting trip took her away from the city for well over a month.

Sighing, she leans against the wall opposite of me and glances at the door. "I wish you could come with us. Pel and Eleesy are much more tolerable when you're around."

"It's for the best," I say, forcing a smile. Even if Azerin would permit it—which he never would—our team still needs time to depressurize after the incident with Morcai and the gambling hall. "I think Conrin would burst a blood vessel if I showed up."

She scrunches her brows together in confusion. "Conrin isn't coming. No one's heard from him in days."

Strange. It's not like him to blow them off.

"I'm surprised you're leaving without him," I say. "Who's stepping in as team leader?"

"No one. We're joining up with Eleesy's cousin, Bolzeik, and the rest of his hunting party. They're getting close to finding Blue, and we want in on the reward money. It's going to be so gratifying to catch the bitch after all this time."

My spine stiffens at the word, though it has no reason to. Bond or not, Arden *is* an animal—a bitch meant to be bred, killed, or eaten—and nothing more. It's not an insult; it's a fact. Still, I work my jaw, this unidentifiable rage coiling inside me, turning my veins to molten fire.

"I'm sorry I'll miss it," I say, painting on a mask of indifference. "Maybe next time. Azerin can't keep me here forever."

The floorboards squeak as she crosses the room, boots thumping with each footfall. Sarvenna extends her hand, and I accept, squeezing her fingers in mine. It's the closest thing to hugging most female elgrew get. On good days, I can hold her in my arms and she'll pretend to be okay with it. But today clearly isn't a good day.

Still, Sarvenna squeezes back. "I'll miss you," she says.

I believe her. She cares for me more than anyone else.

"Same." My throat swells with emotion. Coughing, I pull my hand away, raking fingers through my hair. "You should go. My father will be here this afternoon to plan the Ring Day celebration. It would be better if he didn't see you."

Of all my friends, Azerin loathes Sarvenna the most. Every interaction they have is tense. I think because he assumes my disinterest in taking a myrie stems from her warming my bed. Most days, they avoid each other, which has been increasingly difficult now that I've been living at the estate. Perhaps it would be better to mend relations with Conrin sooner, if only so I can move back into the apartment.

Sarvenna grimaces. "If you manage to get away from him, we'll be hunting near the Lycean Marshes this time. Eleesy says Blue's been spotted in the area."

Arden. I feel this intense urge to correct her but hold my tongue.

Nobody can know that I've marked the creature—not even Sarvenna. If my father doesn't kill me for Claiming what's his, others might for my negligence. Sixty-four elgrew are dead because I released her, a fact that weighs heavily on my conscience, even as my heart burgeons with pride. Hunting her, killing her before anyone finds out will be all the more gratifying knowing she's as powerful a fighter as the members of my team.

"If Azerin allows me to leave the city, I'll be sure to find you," I promise. "Good luck on the hunt."

"Thanks." Snatching her duffle from the entryway, she swings it 'round her shoulder before exiting my bedroom. Like always, Sarvenna doesn't look back. She doesn't linger. The hunt is infinitely more exciting to her than my company ever could be.

The resulting silence is unbearable.

I shoot a warning to Arden down our bond, telling her about the search party so no one catches her before I can, but there's no answer. Just the stillness of my empty bedroom that reeks of sweat and sex.

Beyond the shutters, damp rainforest and dusty mining land extend for miles—the Grand Overseer's estate sits on Rayna's largest supply of cold iron. Compared to the city, it's quiet here. Occasionally, the faint clanking of chisels against stone or the garbled commands of the Butchers to their slaves will come through, but the thick limestone walls keep almost everything out.

Combing fingers through my hair, I tie it back, then finish dressing. No boots for me. Nothing nearly so practical. I slip into a pair of silk sandals with ornate patterns sewn into the straps. Pretentious. Impractical. My father will almost certainly approve.

My stomach growls as I exit my palatial childhood bedroom. It never stops growling. Were it not for muscle transplants and herbal supplements, I'd be entirely useless. Feral. Even now, the grip on my sanity feels featherlight.

In the hallway, blue bamboo floors and blue mosaic walls greet me. Butchers guard the stairwells and exit points, keeping tabs on the slaves' comings and goings as well as mine. Ignoring them, I descend a winding servants' staircase that leads into the drawing room, where my father waits on a plush, blue cushioned couch, his feet propped onto a shiny blue table made from a celestite geode. At his side, his myrie kneels on the floor.

Thud. Thunk.

Thud. Thunk.

Thud.

The sound of a hammer striking wood fills the foyer. Craning my neck, I see a Butcher nailing something to the wall. A shadow box of some kind. My stomach knots. Through the glare of its glassy, freshly polished frame is a sheet of mounted gray skin with purple scars running through it. *Morcai's payment.*

Azerin waves me over, gesturing to the matching blue couch across from him. "Do you like my new trophy? I was quite impressed with your decision to obey me. It seems your loyalties finally lie with whom they've always belonged."

"Take it down," I hiss. If Conrin sees that, it'll squash any chance at reconciliation.

"No. I like the way it looks, and so will our guests at the Ring Day celebration. They should know how you earned your place at my side."

"What are you talking about?"

High heels click across the waxed bamboo floorboards. Feminine humming follows. A moment later, Colette—the Karesai of Trainers—appears near the entryway carrying rolls of folded silks. Her ribbony yellow dress is a stark contrast to the rest of the room. It's a wonder she can breathe in it. A tight corset binds her breasts and stomach while a hoop skirt makes the bottom billow out like it's stuffed with hot air.

Trainers never dress for practicality. They dress for sensuality. Dramatics.

Violet powder dusts her gray, patchwork cheeks. Matching lipstick pulls tight as she spreads her mouth into a feline smile and drops the armful of silks. "Lyrick, it's so good to see you."

"You as well." Years of mandatory etiquette training snap into place, and I bow at the waist. "Are you here to help my father prepare the estate for our Ring Day celebration?"

"I'm here for you, dear," Colette answers. "You and I will be in the city today, getting ready for your inauguration."

I blink.

Brows furrowed, I glance between her and my father, my attention settling on Azerin. "You're appointing me the next Karesai of Hunters? I thought the council's vote needed to be unanimous for that."

"It does." My father frowns, stroking his myrie's pale hair. "Given your . . . *performance* at the arena, Sorso was not an easy man to convince. It cost me dearly."

Azerin's gaze lingers on his pet, and spiders crawl down my spine at the implication.

"Sorso doesn't seem the type to share," I say.

My father sighs, tracing idle circles on the elf's shoulders. "He isn't. His youngest daughter is a Trainer, though, and she's quite enamored with Chalk's hair."

At the sound of her name, the elf's head rises. Likely, it's one of the only words she knows—aside from the sexual ones needed to perform her duties. My insides curdle. This elf has done everything right. She's never fought, never screamed, never cried. Despite her near-perfect temperament, my father is still going to kill and scalp her. For Sorso.

For me.

"Did he make any other demands?" I hiss.

How much did you pay to force me into this role?

"I believe the words you're looking for are 'Thank you, Father.' And 'I'm sorry you've had to clean up my messes again.'" Azerin rises from the couch, tugging on his myrie's leash. Her swollen stomach brushes against the table as she fumbles to find footing. When she steadies herself against my father's pant leg, her innocent, wide eyes latch onto mine. She's so fucking oblivious—holding onto her captor when she should be fighting him with everything she's got.

I rip my gaze away.

It's worse than the mess hall. At least those creatures saw the blade coming.

"Will you be visiting the city with us?" I ask.

In my periphery, Azerin lifts the elf by her armpits and sets her gently on her feet. "I will, but Chalk and I must stop by Yaklan's surgery first. The babe is far enough along. It can be extracted now."

"I take it she won't be returning?" I ask.

Run.

Bite him.

Do something!

A thousand orders die on my tongue.

"He'll euthanize her at the office." Sighing, my father rubs the elf's belly then tuts. "I'd hoped to breed her multiple times. She's so much easier than the last one."

Colette smiles, brushing down her skirts as she tiptoes over the bundled silks. "I'm certain we can find you another myrie today. My girls have trained some very docile, very beautiful ones."

Stepping toward my father, she examines Chalk in a slow circle.

With a wave of the hand, Azerin cuts her off. "No need. My Hunters spotted Blue last week. She'll be a more than adequate replacement."

I smile to myself, knowing he'll never touch her. He'll never breed her, or eat her, or sell her body in parts to a man like Sorso. As long as that bite mark is on Arden's palm, she's mine. And I intend to finish what I started.

I just have to escape first.

Colette, Azerin, and I exit the house, Chalk stumbling behind us on the jingling metal chain that connects her to my father. Lush grass and blue wildflowers surround the sprawling estate. Insects buzz around us, flying in lazy circles as they collect pollen. It's almost peaceful were it not for the muffled but rhythmic hitting of chisels against stone.

Up close, my father's home is a paradise. Warm sunlight

bounces off a wraparound porch made of sapphires. Waterfowl nest on a turquoise lake that's so clear, I can see each individual stone at the bottom. But far enough away, the nightmare looms. Blue-leaved trees blot out the mining shafts where Butchers and slaves extract our cold iron. Silver buildings gleam with blood, not paint. It's a dark contrast no one seems to notice but me.

Two palanquins—portable rooms with bisecting poles through the frames—wait for us at the front entrance. One is a large bamboo box with a curtained window on the front door. The other is made of glass and gold and glitters brightly in the sunlight. A menagerie of elvish slaves stand at attention, ready to lift and carry the palanquins on our cue.

With a click of the tongue and a tug on her leash, my father orders Chalk into the glass one. He opens the door for her, then maneuvers her onto the blue cushions inside, waving us goodbye as he joins her in the seat. His arms wrap protectively around her swollen stomach, and she leans into the touch—all stupid and defenseless and cooperative.

Colette trained her well.

A sharp whistle pierces the air, and my father's slaves move into position. Three on each corner raise the bisecting poles, lifting it onto their shoulders. Doe-eyed, Chalk presses her hands to the glass as they march down the estate toward the hundred-foot limestone walls that separate us from the jungle. It's not the first time she's seen the property like this, but her eyes light up like glowflies every time. It's clear to anyone she's happy here. Content with the scraps she's been given.

Fucking idiot. If I could shake her, I would.

"Should we eat along the way?" Colette asks, her voice sweet like honey.

I arch a brow. "What?"

"The way you're staring at her, dear. You look hungry. I'm not a fan of the mess halls, but for you . . ."

"I'm fine."

"If it's her you want, I'm sure your father wouldn't mind sharing. Once the babe has been extracted—"

"I said I'm fine," I growl.

Fuck, I may never eat again.

My stomach roils at the very visceral image of Chalk splayed out for me, her belly open and bleeding, too weak to fight back. My father would let it happen, too; that's the worst part. He'd rather me give in to my most primitive instincts than embarrass him at the games again.

Forcing a smile to my face, I climb into Colette's bamboo box, the floorboards groaning as I settle into soft blankets and colorful cushions. She joins me soon after, forcing the hoop skirt through, shoving it up against the cramped wooden walls. Her lacy yellow dress spills onto my lap as she leans out the window and whispers orders to a slave.

Then, we're up.

We sit crisscross in silence, staring at the estate as it passes by. Blue-black leaves flutter. Orange fur darts between the tall grasses—Prowler, out for a hunt. My verncat is equally unsuited to city life and more bored than I am. But at least he's permitted to leave.

"What are you thinking about?" Colette asks.

Snapping every guard's neck and joining up with Sarvenna.

I turn my gaze away from the window, forcing myself to play my father's shitty political games. "Nothing," I say. "I'm just wondering what my preparations will entail."

Colette scoots infinitesimally closer, her expression that of a viper's. Patting me on the knee, she grins in that saccharine, unsettling way of hers. "You'll see."

XX. Lyrick

"Trainers are the backbone of elgrew society. As the name implies, they are responsible for training all breedable pets within the city, ensuring they're well-versed in obedience and bedplay. Elves who undergo training are reportedly happier than their counterparts who don't. They are also far less likely to pose a danger to themselves and to others. It is for this reason, training is mandatory before any pleasure slave or myrie can be sold or bought."

—City of Kariss, The Great Charter

The training houses are located at the center of the metropolis, shaded by the Korring-Marr's fiery orange leaves. Centuries ago, these buildings could be found all throughout Kariss—or so my father says—but that made it easier for the elves to escape. Here, they're far enough away from the city walls that any attempt would be futile.

Still, the elves try.

Colette's training houses are some of the most lavish build-ings in the city—glossy, black marble structures with long staircases and pillars so high they touch the lower branches of the Korring-Marr. Most of them have purple roofs; those are for the lower caste. Some have silver. But our palanquin stops in front of a blue marble building with golden veins running through it —the only one of its kind, reserved solely for members of the Politic, which apparently now includes me.

"What are we doing here?" I ask. My legs ache from sitting crisscross in the box for so long. From my father's estate, the training houses are nearly half a day's journey. Already, dusk approaches, scattering pink sunlight across the skyline. "I thought we'd be writing speeches or contacting event planners."

Colette snorts. "We have people who take care of that, Lyrick. There are many, many perks that come with being a Karesai."

Carefully, her slaves lower the box. Colette swings the door open, sighing as she stretches. Her yellow dress is wrinkled from travel. Her updo droops free of its golden pins. "Your father has asked me to prepare you for the celebration that comes after you're inducted. He thought you'd throw a tantrum if he suggested it in person."

"Prepare me how?" I step outside the box, cracking my back as I twist from side to side. The relief is instantaneous.

"Sorso won't agree to the appointment unless you take a myrie. He doesn't like the way you look at his. After the inaugu-ration, there will be a public breeding ceremony at your father's estate."

I clench my teeth. "How public?"

All breeding ceremonies require a minimum of five witnesses—one from each of the five castes—or else the joining is illegitimate as well as any children birthed as a result. Much to my chagrin, it was never going to be a private affair, but I'll be damned if it's a spectacle.

"All his guests will be in attendance."

All ten thousand of them? Fuck that.

"You can tell my father to take his appointment and shove it up—"

She holds up her hand. "I know. You're not interested in breeding a myrie *or* becoming a Karesai. You're a Hunter, and like all Hunters, you despise domesticity. But the thing is, you don't have a choice. Once the Grand Overseer makes an appointment, it's already done. Yes, Sorso, Yaklan, Ryla, or I could technically vote against him, but he would make our lives very unpleasant, like he's making yours right now." Colette cups my shoulders, her eyes full of the one emotion I didn't think a Trainer could possess—sympathy. "In two days' time, you will be a Karesai, like it or not, and you'll be forced to mate. I can train you for the role, as I trained your predecessor, but only if you cooperate."

My skin itches. I'm as trapped here as the slaves. Forced to rule over a society I despise. Forced to break the morals Talin so thoroughly engrained into me.

"I tried to run away," I admit. "But the guards know my face."

"The last Karesai of Hunters ran too," she says. Colette offers me her arm, and I accept, letting her guide me up the marble steps. "Now he's dead. When it comes to defying Azerin, I wouldn't recommend it."

Crisp air billows my clothes. Leaves as large as my face fall from the Korring-Marr, tangling in our hair before they sweep down the steps. The elves claim they can feel divinity when they touch their sacred tree, but if their god exists, it abandoned them a long time ago.

The front door yawns before us, a solid sheet of gold with a knocker shaped like a verncat head. Colette picks it up and slams it down. Once. Twice. The doors swoosh open in a flurry of motion, three slaves on either side holding it as we walk past.

Kerosene chandeliers hang from the ceiling, casting dim yellow light across the polished marble. A grand staircase leads to the second-floor overlook, where a gilded railing frames the rectangular space. To my surprise, there aren't any pleasure slaves milling about. There are no screams of pain or moans of pleasure. It's . . . quiet.

"We can speak freely here, Lyrick," Colette says, her voice echoing off the stonework. "The slaves don't understand enough Elgrew to spread rumors, and the other members of the Politic never appear unannounced. I can help you best if you speak candidly and honestly."

"What do you want to know?" I ask.

"Have you ever lain with an elf before?"

I peer over my shoulders, staring at the six elves who let us in. They're dressed in plain white gowns, not the netted breastplates or low-rise harem pants that would mark them as pleasure slaves. "I . . ."

She steps in front of me, blocking my line of sight until we're the only two people in the room. "Candidly and honestly, Lyrick. Help me help you."

Swallowing, I debate the intelligence of sharing such personal information with a political rival. It's nothing she couldn't guess. Still, I choose my words wisely. "I'm not attracted to them," I admit. "They don't *do* anything for me."

"You can't get hard," she clarifies. There's no judgment in her voice. It's a matter-of-fact statement.

I feel judged regardless.

Tugging on my shirt collar, I envision the floor swallowing me whole.

"No need to be embarrassed," she says. "I suspected as much based on what your father has told me. I have potions that will help with that."

Rifling through her pockets, she retrieves a glass vial that contains viscous orange liquid. Uncorking it, she offers the vial to me. "Reaction times and side effects vary from elgrew to elgrew. It's best to take it in an isolated setting the first time."

I sniff the potion. My nose scrunches at how sickly sweet it is —like fermented fruit.

"It's not poison, Lyrick. I'm not stupid enough to harm the Grand Overseer's son. Take it or don't. It doesn't matter to me, but if you refuse your father will hear of it."

"He expects me to drink it."

She nods. "He expects your full cooperation."

Of course he does.

Glowering at her, I tip back the liquid and shudder as it slides down my throat. Warmth settles into my stomach like a slimy lead ball, and my mouth puckers in revulsion. She hums her approval then collects the empty vial and recorks it, slipping it back into her puffy dress.

"Normally, elves are trained for months before they become a myrie. Your father has demanded we expedite that process." Colette whistles, and another plainly dressed elf appears, sprinting as she descends the marble staircase. Her footsteps are lighter than a fallen feather. In her hands is a measuring tape and a notepad.

"Brawler will not be like my other pets," Colette warns. "She speaks too much Elgrew, and she's trained to fight back. It will be dangerous to keep her."

"So, it's been decided then?" I hiss. "I no longer have a choice in who I breed."

"Apparently not."

The slave kneels at my feet, loose silver hair falling over her face as she takes my measurements for gods knows what. First, she takes my inseam, then my hip, moving up along my body with slow precision. My disgust at her touch is unmaskable, and Colette takes note of it.

"I promised Azerin you won't embarrass him at the ceremony. Trust me and everything will be alright. If you need something stronger, that can be arranged."

The elf finishes and darts away as quickly as she appeared,

saying nothing.

"I tried to dissuade your father from Brawler," Colette continues, "but he likes the statement it makes, and he likes the idea of a powerful heir. It's been a long while since a Bracer was born into your bloodline."

Colette offers up her arm again then leads me to the second story. At least twelve golden doors fill the space. She opens one of them and steps inside.

I expect a bedroom but find an apothecary instead. Shelves upon shelves of potions and ingredients line the walls. A large island in the center contains a mortar and pestle—crushed purple powder sticking to the inside of the bowl. Floral scents invade my nostrils, so pungent I cough, shielding my nose with my shirt.

I'm not used to strong odors, even pleasant ones. On the hunt, elgrew try to smell as neutral as possible to keep our locations secret—both to the elves we hunt and the predators who hunt us. Even in the city, we only frequent inoffensive places. The ones that won't assault our nostrils or weaken our sense of smell.

Colette crosses the room, high heels clicking across stone. A cabinet creaks as she peeks into it, withdrawing a clear glass jar filled with dehydrated silver berries. Hundreds of them.

"Do you know what these are?" Colette asks.

"Rowan berries." A single one costs the lower caste five years' wages. Harvested from the Korring-Marr once a century, they're the single most limited and valuable resource in Kariss. "Elves need them to ovulate."

Nodding, she taps her nails along the jar, clinking the glass. "One or two will make an elf fertile. But any amount can make them more … *accommodating* to your advances."

She passes me the jar, and I turn it over in my hands. While elves can live for millennia, it's more than most elgrew could use in a lifetime—although my father might come close. He's replaced his body parts enough times to avoid the decay that comes with old age, artificially extending his life for centuries.

"When my pets leave their training houses," Colette says, "they don't need the berries to behave, but with Brawler . . . it might be best to keep her under sedation so long as she's in your house. A pinch of powder added to her drinks every few hours will ensure she doesn't injure herself or others."

Sweat pools beneath my armpits, plastering the shirt to my skin. I feel sick, listening to her talk about drugging someone so casually.

"If you need more berries, come to me. The Politic has unrestricted access to our reserves." In demonstration, Colette withdraws another identical jar and sets it on the counter. "I have cold-iron shackles as well. They're messy, but they should keep her in her place. Still, I'd advise against using them in public. As the Karesai of Hunters, you must be seen as strong enough to manage without."

The room closes in around me, stealing the air from my lungs.

I need to sit down.

I need to run.

How the fuck am I supposed to get through the Ring Day celebration? My inauguration? Does Azerin honestly expect me to rape and keep one of those things?

"Lyrick?" Colette asks.

I sink to the floor, my pulse in my stomach, my mouth so dry it could be a desert. "I can't do this," I admit.

She presses the back of her hand against my forehead. Her skin is cool against my flesh. Shoving her hands into her pockets, she withdraws another orange vial, uncorks it, and forces it down my throat.

It burns this time.

As the seconds pass, the heat in my stomach radiates to my

limbs and arms, and the sickness settles, turning into something else. Raw, aching, need.

"That's better," Colette says. Her pointed teeth glint in the lamplight, and that saccharine smile twists into something sinister. Her breasts spill from her corset as she bends over and rubs my rapidly hardening cock. "Mmmm, you're so much bigger than I expected."

I groan at the sensation, my eyes rolling to the back of my skull. My thoughts are fuzzy, my brain scrambled. The room blurs as she tugs me to my feet.

I blink, and then I'm lying belly up in a bed, staring at a blue marble ceiling. Giggles fill the room. The bed creaks and dips as a naked elf climbs on top of it, her silver hair brushing her delicate shoulders. Red lips part as her tongue darts out to lick them.

My insides squirm in realization. This *animal* is trying to mount me.

No.

NO!

I jerk, but nothing happens.

Another elf joins us, breasts smooshing against my chest as she reaches for my elastic waistband. To my abject horror, my cock stays hard.

I clench my hands into tight fists. It's the only movement I can manage. My body is too heavy and my muscles are too achy for anything else. Closing my eyes, I disappear into the woods, vanishing into a hunt that isn't real. My hunger blots out the sensation of being touched. Stripped. Somewhere, I register a growl. A scream. The snapping of bones against my palm.

Then, nothing.

XXI. Lyrick

"Male elgrew are solely responsible for child rearing. Females have neither the temperament nor disposition for such a task; their talents lie elsewhere. Allowing an elgrew child to interact with their elvish incubator is strictly prohibited. If the myrie remains a household pet, they must be separated and supervised at all times. Failure to do so will result in the seizure of the child and the pet."

—CITY OF KARISS, THE GREAT CHARTER

"**W**hat the fuck did you do to him?" Azerin's voice flits across my consciousness, though my eyes are too heavy to open them. Groggy and disoriented, I try to sit up, but my muscles scream in protest.

"What you asked," Colette spits. "He had enough *rukin* in him to sedate a verncat. I thought you said he was eating."

"He *is* eating," my father insists.

"Try telling that to the two pets he killed. I know what I saw, Azerin. He was *feral*."

"I'll take care of it."

Colette huffs and the door slams shut.

Rough hands peel back my eyelids. Tears blur my vision, the brightness blinding. When I blink, a pair of silver-violet eyes come into focus, but it isn't anger I see reflected there. It's . . . relief. Azerin sucks in a breath, his arms wrapping around my shoulders as he crushes me to his chest.

Is my father . . . hugging me?

"I thought I lost you," Azerin says, smoothing back my hair. He cups my cheeks in his palms, his gaze more intense than I've ever seen it. "I *did* lose you. But the spirits gave you back."

He hugs me again, and I swallow, my throat burning and voice scratchy. "Dad, I didn't mean to kill those girls . . ."

I barely remember doing it. The memories are there but scrambled, like I was possessed. *Feral.*

"I know." He lets go of me, and I fall back onto the bed, too sore to hold myself upright—from malnutrition or Colette's potion, I don't know.

My vision blackens at the edges. My stomach rumbles so loudly there's no doubt he heard it. Azerin pivots toward a golden door to my right, and I reach for him, my heavy arm falling limply on the mattress.

"Where are you going?" I rasp.

He doesn't answer, but he gives me this resigned, exasperated look.

"I'll take care of it."

The door clicks shut, and unconsciousness pulls me back under.

I WAKE TO MUFFLED SOBS.

Head throbbing, I peel my eyes open and come face-to-face with a female elf lying in bed beside me. Cold-iron chains wrap around her ankles and wrists, pinning her arms behind her back. A thick ball gag made of glass pries her painted, violet lips apart. Hair in her face, tears in her eyes, she squirms against the bindings and, ultimately, gets nowhere.

The pit in my stomach begs for relief. The stench of her fear is a symphony on my tongue.

It takes a moment to remember where I am. And then the revulsion kicks in.

Bolting upright, I yank the golden silk sheets from my body and climb out of bed, my pulse racing. *Where are my clothes?*

Scanning the floor turns up nothing. I'm naked and hard in Colette's training house. My ridged purple cock is so fucking stiff, it could tear through glass. *Damn potion. Fucking bitch.* Cock bobbing, I race to the golden door on the other side of the bedroom and yank the handle.

Locked.

Golden sunlight streams through open shutters, bathing the room in warm light. The elf continues crying and my heart races, veins pumping with adrenaline, instincts kicking in despite my moral code. There are no clothes on her body. Nothing to get in the way of my teeth.

An arterial vein pulses at the surface of her throat, begging me to rip it out. It would be so fucking easy—and that's the Marr-damn problem. She doesn't deserve this; it isn't a fair fight. I stare at my trembling hands and will them to be still, begging the pain in my stomach to ebb long enough for me to think.

It doesn't.

The scent of moss and dirt floods my nostrils, my sentience slipping. It's only a matter of time before my instincts give in, even if *I* don't. Swallowing back saliva, I pound on the gilded door confining me.

I have to escape. I can't be in here with her.

My knuckles crack against the metal panels. Purple blood seeps between the stitchwork in my skin. "Let me out! You can't keep me here."

The door creaks open mid-pound, Azerin's face behind it.

My fist falls. I dive toward the opening, but Azerin blocks my path with his arm to prevent an escape.

"Eat, Lyrick."

Jaw clenching, I glare at him. "Let me leave the city and I will. I'll join up with the other Hunters."

"You'll go feral long before you reach the forest." He spins me around and forces me to stare at the creature. Silver blood streams from her eardrums, down her neck. Bile rises to my throat even as my stomach clenches. "How many elves do you think you'll kill once you can't even remember your own name?"

"Please." My voice cracks. "Don't make me do this."

"You're hungry, and she's food," Azerin says. "Hot. Fresh. You can even kill her yourself."

My pit organs open on reflex, taking in her heat, homing in on how fucking warm that arterial vein is. Twisting, I try to shove Azerin away, but his grip tightens.

"I will not lose you again, nor will I have rumors circulating about you in the Politic. You are my son, and you *will* eat. Only one of you comes out of this room alive. Is that understood?"

I twist harder.

In a blur of motion, something sharp nicks my throat. My father's blade gleams in the sunlight. "'Yes, Father.' Say it."

I swallow—the sharpness digs in, slicing deeper. "Yes, Father."

"Good. Now get on with it." Withdrawing the knife, he pushes me toward the bed. The door closes, but when I peer behind me, he's still there, leaning against the blue marble wall. Arms crossed, Azerin stares at me expectantly. Waiting.

There's to be no privacy. No choice.

Fighting back against everything that I am, I approach the creature. She squirms harder, the springs in the bed creaking, the chains on her wrists jingling hard enough to echo in the room.

Whimpering moans crawl past the ball gag as I climb onto the bed and lean over her body. Tears prick my eyes, knowing just how fucked this is, but the gnawing hunger doesn't care and neither does Azerin.

Glancing behind me, I see the steel in his gaze.

"I'm sorry," I whisper.

My teeth drip venom onto the elf's skin. I'm not strong enough to stop myself from lowering my head. Or strong enough to keep from sinking my teeth into her supple flesh. Unlike the elves in the forest, she doesn't scream or fight back; her tremors are strong enough to shake me.

Defenseless.

Caged.

I eat anyway.

Hot blood gushes from her neck in a steady stream, staining the sheets, my soul. Tendon and muscle glide over my tongue. I rip through it like it's made of paper, destroying years of self-restraint just as easily.

Then, the frenzy hits.

Ripping up fistfuls of flesh, I scarf her down—unable to stop, unable to slow. The hunger in my stomach ebbs, each bite bringing relief and a fresh pain all its own.

I am weak.

I'm no better than the rest of my species.

The metallic sweetness is bliss on my tongue. Euphoric agony. Only a pile of entrails and bones are left by the time I can pull myself away. My stomach convulses, the meat festering inside me as I look at what I've done. My eyes burn at the sight of her. Broken. Those chains still on her bones.

Chunks rise up my throat, my chest heaving over the carcass.

"Do not vomit," Azerin says, "or I will make you eat that as well."

I force myself to swallow, sobs racking my body.

I'm a fucking monster. Talin would be ashamed.

Azerin pulls me from the bed and holds my face to his chest, shushing me like I'm a godsdamned infant. And I let him. As the tears settle, he drags me through a blue door—not into a hallway, but into a bathroom.

Hot steam fills the chamber, and blood percolates from my body onto the gilded floor. I'm fucking covered in it. My hands shake as I grip onto the edges of a marble sink, staring at my silver-stained face in the mirror. Like something from a nightmare.

I'm faintly aware of levers and knobs being turned in a claw tub. Of Azerin dragging me away from the mirror and helping me into the water. The liquid shimmers silver as I step into it. There's not enough water or soap in the world to wash away what I've done.

"Do you know why I chose you as Karesai?" he asks, retrieving a bar of soap from the cabinets.

"Nepotism," I sniffle, wiping the snot from my nose.

Azerin shakes his head. His hand dips below the water, grabbing up my arm, washing me like he used to when I was a toddler. "I chose you for the same reasons I chose Yaklan." His words are surprisingly gentle. "You both show restraint and empathy where others do not, and while I may not agree with your approach or your beliefs, it does good to have those voices of dissent on my council. You are the most skilled tracker in Kariss. Your people respect you. As their Karesai, you will be able to influence their opinions, as well as policy."

He finishes washing me, dunking my head below the surface long enough to rinse the blood and tissue away. Then he guides me out of the tub, gore still dripping off my body. I stare at my reflection in the polished stone, wishing I could break it. The Hunters wouldn't respect me if they could see me now, being bathed by my father while crying over an elf. I'm a fucking disgrace to my species.

Bending, Azerin passes me a plush golden towel. He maneuvers his head until I'm staring at his face instead of mine. "This isn't a punishment, Lyrick. But I see now you may not be up to the job. If this is something you truly can't handle, then I will let you leave, but I think you would make an excellent Karesai."

"There's something wrong with me," I croak.

"There's nothing wrong with you." Azerin tucks the towel around my body. "I want you to stay in the city and rule by my side. But to do that, you must put aside your fanaticism and adapt to our way of life. Can you do that, Lyrick?"

I don't know.

I don't want *to know.*

I want to return to the forest where everything was easy. Yet, I can't bring myself to say that either. Part of me yearns to be the son Azerin wants me to be. The other part is fucking terrified at the prospect.

If I stay, what do I become?

XXII. Arden

"Starra'lee isn't a charity. If they offer you a spot within their ranks, it's not because they care about you. It's because they want something only you can provide. Don't become complacent. They aren't your friends, and they will betray you."

—Giara of Rothstone, Starra'lee Lead Scout
Personal Correspondence

TWO YEARS AGO . . .

Hot sun bakes a thick layer of sulfurous mud to my skin. Naked, half-submerged in the murky green swamp, I resist the urge to scratch it off and soothe the ever-growing itch in my nose. My sights are singularly focused on the air bubbles rising to the water's surface not three feet from me. It's almost time.

The silt shifts beneath my belly and my muscles tense. No weapons. No armor. A stupid dare Giara posed last night when we were both more than a little drunk. She wouldn't blame me if I backed out, but I'm not a quitter.

Shoving my hands through the squelching dirt, I knead the ground as if I'm walking, squishing the mud between my fingers. The bubbles move closer, pop-popping, and the ground dips another half inch, my sunburned shoulders slipping into the cool water.

Marr-damn, that feels good.

But there's no time to enjoy it. Right on schedule, something slimy and hard brushes up against my fingertips—the mudsnake I've been tracking all morning. With fingernails sharpened into points, I dig them into the creature's flesh, spearing it blindly, praying I've nicked something vital. It squirms and thrashes and thrusts up from the dirt, breaking through the air. I go flying back, the world a blur of colors as it knocks me hard on my ass.

Nose burning, I inhale lungfuls of water, decaying algae, and gods know what else. Through blurry vision, I spot the scaley, mucousy body of the mudsnake as it slithers through the water. It's my size. A baby.

Fuck. Where'd it go?

By the time I've wiped the water from my eyes, the mudsnake is nowhere in sight, but its red blood stains the swamp, ballooning outward like some sort of macabre dye. A string of curses falls from my lips as I roll back onto my stomach and crawl ever closer to the red patch. Almost there.

Behind me, the dirt shifts.

Oh shit.

Oh shit, oh shit, oh shit!

An enormous mudsnake bursts from the ground, coiling tight around my legs. Grainy red eyes. Vertical pupils. A triangle shaped head that glistens with water droplets. With a hiss, the mudsnake opens its impossibly wide jaw, baring long, red-tinged fangs that mark it as female—the baby's mother.

It compresses tighter, slithers higher. My face slips beneath the surface of the water and I choke on it. Panic coils in my chest, but I've trained for this. Stop. Assess. Move.

Forcing my body to go limp, I let the snake inch up my stomach, then squeeze my organs and bones so tight I hear a snap at my ribs, feel the sharp pain threaten to consume me. The tip of its nose roots around my sides and chest—not biting, not wasting its precious venom because I'm not a big enough threat. Eyes closed, I wait until it's at my neck, its thick muscles so strong, I couldn't free myself even if I wanted to.

Slowly, I move my arms toward the creature. It was too stupid to pin them to my body. Too confident that it could best me.

When it opens its mouth and its long slithering tongue licks along the side of my cheek, preparing to swallow me whole, I strike. Using my nails as claws, I spear all ten fingers into its eyes, scooping out the jelly faster than it can react. The mudsnake's muscles uncoil, just enough for me to crawl free. And crawl I do.

Sliding through the dirt, I scramble to the surface and gulp in stagnant, swampy air. It's the best thing I've ever smelled.

The mudsnake blindly lunges for me and its fangs sink into my thigh.

I grab its head, dig my fingers into its slimy scales, and claw at it. The asshole doesn't let go, even as its coppery blood pours into the water. Vision blurry, I wrap my legs around the beast's body, wrestling it, kicking and hitting, and . . . sliding. I can't get a good hold on it. It's too slick and gooey.

Heat pours into my leg where its fang—the length of my forearm—remains half sticking from my thigh. "Fucking let go already," I growl. Then I take a note from Giara's playbook and bite the snake where its heart is, sinking my teeth in as hard and as deep as I can. It's not easy. The skin is tough and thick, and unlike Giara, I don't have artificial fangs. But I'm determined.

Mucous seeps into my throat. The taste of metal floods my

mouth. I fling my head from side to side, spitting the skin out and biting again. And again. The heart bursts beneath my tongue, spraying hot blood into my face—fuck, into everything.

Finally, the mudsnake goes limp.

Sighing, I peel its fang from my leg, wincing when it comes free and my own blue blood gushes into the swamp. Fucking stupid Marr-damn dare. Never again.

A slow clap echoes just past a wall of blue sawgrass reeds that sway in the distance. And I see red. "Giara, you fucking bitch. Did you really just stand there and watch as it—wait, you're not Giara."

The reeds part and this elvish man steps through, weighted down by so much leather armor, I'm not sure how he can walk so stealthily, but he does. Despite the mud, the man moves without making a sound. Tousled hair falls over his conventionally attractive face, and suddenly I'm all too aware that I'm naked, covered in mud and blood and snake guts. And I couldn't care less.

Fuck this guy. He would have let me die before intervening.

Grunting, I shove my hand into the dead mudsnake's mouth and begin tugging its carcass through the swamp, toward Shoulder Squish Cave. When the man follows, I pause long enough to flip him off with both hands, the snake head thumping and splashing to the ground. "Fuck off. As you can see, I'm a bit busy."

Each time I put pressure on my bleeding leg is agony, but I'm not about to let this asshole know that. Even if I am on the verge of bleeding out. My ossi dust is just a few minutes and a couple hundred feet away. If I'm lucky, it'll neutralize the venom too.

"My name is Julian," he says.

"Good for you." I reach the near-hidden entryway—trophy in tow. "This is a Starra'lee bunker," I warn. "They don't allow guests."

"Well then, it's a good thing I'm not a guest. I command this posting."

———

I'M NOT LUCKY.

The venom has me in and out of consciousness, sweat dripping down my slippery, hot, still-naked skin. Pouch in hand, I lean against the cave wall and sprinkle a second dose of black ossi dust onto my finger. Then, I shove said finger through the hole in my bleeding, gaping thigh. The blood flow ebbs, skin and muscle weaving back together, though the fever remains.

Somewhere deep within the cave, Julian and Giara whisper-argue—though I can't see them and I struggle to hear the words. Bug kneels beside me and presses a cool, damp rag to my forehead, but when she tries to speak, I put a finger to my lips and shake my head.

Three years ago, I couldn't use my sezin in the cave. I wasn't disciplined enough to filter out the echoes without going deaf. But I'm better now. Stronger.

Wiggling my ears causes my sezin to vibrate to life and words as loud as a thunderclap threaten to overwhelm me. But I focus on the *drip-plink, drip-plink* of water on stalagmites instead, distracting myself so that what I hear of their conversation comes out at half volume.

"You were supposed to report back two days ago," Julian hisses.

"I was busy."

"Playing house with Blue." His words are as venomous, as volatile as the mudsnake. "Why didn't you tell me about her?"

"Because I knew what you'd say." Giara's voice wobbles with emotion. "But Julian, she's a skilled fighter. She's smart and quick on her feet. Arden deserves to be in a combat unit."

"You're on a first-name basis with her? How long has she been here?"

Drip-plink. Drip-plink. Drip.

Her response is muffled, and I strain to hear it over the condensation. "Three years—but listen, she's too old to transform. It doesn't make any sense to bring her to Starra'lee."

"That's not your call to make. Elder Risha will want to see her."

Hurt and betrayal spear through me as realization strikes. All this time, Giara kept me a secret from the militia. They had no idea I was here, fending for myself in the fucking wilderness. Without asking anyone, she unilaterally decided that my small stature made me worthless to the team.

And all this time, I thought we were friends.

I relax my ears, not willing, not needing to hear anything more. It's one thing to be too chicken shit to help a friend out. It's another thing to lie about it. How many times did I ask her if Starra'lee had changed their mind about letting me join? How many times did she offer me fake condolences?

Too. Fucking. Many.

Long tendrils of hair cling to my sweat-soaked forehead. Sweeping them aside, I peer toward the entryway in time to see a man stumble through, then two, then three. All of them wear a hodgepodge of coarse fabrics and hide armor, their hair shorn, their bodies covered in battle scars. One with a missing nose locks gazes with me before turning his sights deeper. Chest heaving, he calls out into the darkness, "Julian! We have a problem."

The Starra'lee commander groans. "When do we not?"

He and Giara emerge from one of the cave's many internal chambers, both of them grasping the hilts of twin daggers sheathed at their hips—battle ready at a moment's notice. Meanwhile, my broken ribs scream when I so much as lean forward.

"Well, spit it out," Julian says.

The other soldiers are staring at me—gaping, really—their jaws slack as they take in my blue skin. Apparently, no one taught them any fucking manners. But whatever spell I hold over them is broken when the winded one speaks again, wiping sweat from his flushed, deformed face. "Fires to the west. A lot of them. I think it's the Lo'kowe Tribe."

My heart squeezes, though it has no reason to. Fenris abandoned me. He convinced the others to do the same. I owe him nothing, and yet the thought of the elgrew raiding his home and taking him is too much to stomach. Eyes pleading, I meet Giara's hardened gaze.

Her jaw clenches, and she nods once. "Is there time to reach them?"

The messenger glances at his two friends—the other members of Julian's squad. They must've traveled here with him, searching for Giara when she didn't return to her posting quickly enough. I blame it on the alcohol.

"If we hurry, we might be able to intercept them before they make it to Kariss," the messenger says. "But we won't reach the settlement in time. Best we can hope for is to free the slaves they've captured."

"It's a suicide mission," one of the other soldiers says. His face is covered in so much war paint that it's unidentifiable. Black circles around his eyes. Dark lips. Lines across both cheeks. "I say we leave it lie. Those topside assholes would never risk their lives for one of us."

"He's got a point," Julian says, shrugging.

Grasping my stomach, I try to hold my ribs together as I rise from my spot on the floor, wincing at the pain of it. Warm venom travels up my thigh to my hips, inching ever closer to my fluttering heart. It won't kill me, but it will knock me the fuck out. The more I move, the more the blood circulates and the faster it spreads. But I don't have a choice. If these dickwads won't help them, I will. Because I'm better than Fenris.

Because, besides Nirissa, he's still the closest thing I have to family.

I brace myself against the cave wall, panting. Sweat rolls down my dirty, bloody body. "I have to save him—"

My knees buckle. Giara rushes to me and catches me before I crumple. "You're not saving anyone. Not looking like that." Carefully, she lowers me to the cold stone floor then turns to Julian. "Permission to intercept?"

"I'll go with her," says the messenger.

"Me too." The other soldier—the one who hasn't spoken yet —raises his hand. "I never miss an opportunity to kill some elgrew."

Face Paint stays painfully silent, his mouth set in a hard line.

Sighing, Julian nods at Giara. "Permission granted. But don't be a hero. The mission is to take out as many elgrew as you can without getting caught. If you can save some of the Lo'kowe, great, but your safety is priority. Get in. Get out. Stick to the shadows."

"And what will you be doing while we're out risking our lives?" Face Paint asks. Arms at his sides, he grips his hands into tight fists. "Sounds like you were excluding yourself from those orders."

"That's easy," Julian says. "I'll be making sure Blue doesn't get herself killed."

XXIII. Arden

"Killing is supposed to be hard, but I consider it one of the most freeing experiences in the world. I like watching the life leave their eyes, knowing that their bastard children might starve without them, that their friends and family will suffer as I have. Maybe that makes me a dick, but it also makes me a damn good soldier."

— ARDEN OF ASHWOOD
PERSONAL JOURNAL

"**S**tep where I step," I whisper, ignoring the blur of color that darts between the sawgrass reeds. "There are traps everywhere. Don't wander off."

Behind me, Cheevy and Chest Wound glance over their shoulders, their muscles already tensed to flee or fight. And to think, they haven't even spotted the elgrew yet.

Mouth shut, I keep my sights on the path ahead, my bare feet shlooping and splashing through the warm water and slick mud. The Lycean Swamp looks exactly as it did when I last came here three months ago. Like Giara, I'm the only scout Starra'lee sends this far, mostly because I'm the only one willing to brave the swamp dogs and mudsnakes alone.

My path is as familiar to me as the back of my hand. It's with ease that I zigzag through the sunlit reeds and blueleaf trees, angling ever closer to my cave and to the stockpile of equipment and weapons I've collected over the years.

Gnats and mosquitos swarm us. My tagalongs swat them aside, flapping their hands in the humid air, smacking at their slick, sweaty skin. I don't give myself the same distraction. As the buzzing insects bite my flesh, I watch in my periphery a wall of blue reeds to the east.

More colors dart in and out of focus. Orange verncat fur. Dark leathers. Gray skin.

I could warn Chest Wound and Cheevy that Hunters are following us—that they've been following us all afternoon—but then they might do something stupid, like tip the elgrew off by fleeing deeper into the wilderness. Their jittery nerves are just as likely to get them eaten by Hunters as they are to get them maimed by my own traps. No, it's infinitely safer to keep my squadmates oblivious. Besides, Chest Wound and I are the perfect bait. If we play our cards right, Starra'lee can slaughter more elgrew today than we have in months.

As we near Shoulder Squish Cave, I take a detour west, where the trees disappear and the sawgrass reeds fade into short blue sedges and irises paler than moonlight. At the surface, it looks like an exposed field that extends forever, but I know something my companions don't. It's not a field. Not a swamp. It's a floating bog—the sedges and flowers and mud are suspended at the water's surface, creating the illusion of stability.

Goosebumps prick my neck, this tight panic constricting my chest—in all these years, I still haven't learned how to swim. There's no place for it in the underground, and only a fool would put themselves in such a vulnerable position topside.

Giara taught me to map this place, to look for soft spots, but it's all too easy to fuck up and fall in. Still, it's the best option—the *only* option—we have to dispense of the elgrew chasing us.

Heart racing, I push onward, taking the first step onto unsteady ground. It holds firm just like I knew it would, just like Giara taught me. To Chest Wound and Cheevy, they probably won't notice the difference. I didn't either the first time I came here. "The cave's up ahead," I lie. "Cross the field and it's on the other side."

"Wouldn't it be safer to go the long way around? It's too exposed without the reeds and trees. If there are any elgrew nearby, we'll be sitting korkuran."

Gods, they're so fucking oblivious.

A quick glance over my shoulder shows the elgrew haven't caught up yet. Thankfully, my traps have slowed them down, made them take their time to not get scooped up in nets or snared by foot traps. We have plenty of time to position ourselves for their inevitable ambush.

"No," I tell Cheevy. "The direct route is faster. We need to get to Kariss as soon as possible."

My palm prickles in a way it hasn't for days, but I ignore it, the ground squishing and sagging beneath my feet. Chest Wound and Cheevy exchange looks, scanning the tree line for predators they're too fucking stupid to find, before following slowly behind me, their footfalls clumsy and loud and all over the fucking place.

"I told you to step where I step," I hiss, gritting my teeth. "No wandering."

It's like babysitting Nirissa.

"Someone's cranky today," Cheevy jokes.

I flip him off. "If you want to die, by all means, do whatever you want."

He narrows his eyes at me, his deformed, half-missing nostrils flaring, but does as he's told, taking more careful, measured steps. The ground wiggles beneath my feet, a bit like gelatin, but I press on, stepping only where the irises have been planted, where I know the "ground" is most stable. Once we're halfway through the bog, I wipe the sweat from my forehead and lower myself to the grass.

"We'll rest here," I say.

"In the open?" Cheevy asks.

"In the open." I unhook an animal skin flask from my belt and bring it to my salty lips. Cool, fresh water soothes my aching throat and I hiss in relief. Only then do I let my gaze drop to the thirty-eight pin pricks on my hand. *"Thank you for warning me,"* I tell Lyrick. *"You've made it so much easier to eliminate them."*

He doesn't answer. I haven't heard from him in more than a day, and the connection doesn't seem to go both ways, where I can summon him at will. If it does, I haven't learned how to utilize it yet.

Patting the ground beside me, I gesture at Cheevy and Chest Wound to join me. They stare at me like I've grown three heads.

"I don't think—" Chest Wound starts.

"I didn't bring you to think. Just trust me." I pat the ground again.

The two of them fixate on the tree and reed line, scanning the shaded blue spots for any hints of danger. When they find none, they kneel amongst the flowers and sedges. The plants are softer here, the sweet floral smell masking the sulfurous one from the water below. Songbirds chirp somewhere in the distance, and the sun warms the top of my head. In another situation, it would almost be peaceful.

I take another gulp of water and stretch my aching muscles, spreading my arms and legs as I stare at the clear green sky. No clouds. No storms. It's a beautiful day to murder someone—or in my case, many someones.

Setting the flask aside, I reach for my favorite rusty dagger strapped to my thigh and unsheathe it. When the others aren't looking, I slice a line through my palm, ignoring the biting pain as my blue blood beads to the surface. Fingernails extended, I claw through grass and muck, then shove my bleeding hand into the frigid water below. A moment later, something slimy and hard brushes against my wound and a grin spreads across my cheeks.

Slowly, I stroke the mudsnake I nearly killed all those years ago—not a baby anymore but as large and as formidable as its mother who nearly ended me. Healing it, feeding it, and training it is arguably one of the smartest things I've ever done. I wish I could say I did it because I felt pity for the poor thing, but the truth is, I always knew it would pay off.

Near the edges of the swamp, a mass of orange fur emerges —several verncats breaking through the blueleaf trees, their long, slinking bodies padding onto the unstable ground. More than a dozen Hunters follow, armed and armored, their skin a patchwork of our stolen gray flesh. Across the distance, I stare into two sets of familiar purple eyes—*Lyrick's friends.*

Sarvenna is just as hideous as when I've seen her through Lyrick's eyes. Her skin is a mishmash of various elf corpses that makes her look every bit the monster she truly is. Eleesy's hair has been cut short and spikes into the air. Teeth bared, she grins at me and points to her chest, then to mine.

I resist a shudder.

"Arden—" Chest Wound's voice trembles.

Finally, they've seen them. It took long enough.

"Stay where you are," I tell him. "Trust me. If you move, you're dead."

The Hunters charge forward, wielding daggers and swords made of glistening blue metal—*cold iron.* My head pounds. My vision blurs. Eyes weeping, I force myself not to look at it, not to run away. The chilly water cramps my aching fingers as I stroke along the mudsnake's mucousy body, waiting.

And then a verncat steps in the wrong spot.

Water splashes. A tangled mat of plants and mud gives way as the verncat slips beneath the bog and thrashes at the surface. My fingers fall away from the mudsnake and I snap. *Dinnertime.*

It slithers away from me at breakneck speed, and then the verncat slips under. It doesn't resurface.

Another splash. Clumps of mud and dirty water spray the air as one of the Hunters falls through, then a second, then a third. Their screams of surprise rend the air. They grasp and claw at the ground, trying to pull themselves back up, failing as my snake slithers beneath the bog and knocks them back in. Arms flailing, feet kicking, they each disappear beneath bubbling brown liquid that's more sludge than water. A few Hunters flee toward the tree line, but they don't know where to step and they sink too, unable to return to safety.

Eleesy flashes her teeth at me, growling when she sees the trap I've laid. Outmatched, she charges forward anyway, her cold-iron dagger glinting in the sunlight. But Sarvenna hangs back—glancing between her friend and the tree line—before retreating with the others, avoiding all the places they've sunk, her verncat's paws smashing into the ground as it takes the lead. The songbirds stop chirping. Hunters bark confused orders between one another.

"Kill the snake."

"Capture the elves."

"Don't let anything happen to Blue!"

Another plot of land gives way beneath the lead Hunter—a male elgrew clad in sleek red leathers stands out amongst the crowd. He sinks through and wails, his black blood pooling in the light blue grasses. The tip of a sharpened bone stake pokes through the shrubbery—one of Giara's old spike traps dug into the shallows, where the water isn't deep enough to be fatal on its own. The elgrew pulls himself onto the grasses, blood gushing from his ruined foot and shredded calf. A fatal injury without immediate treatment.

Grunting, he crawls forward on hands and knees and attempts to retreat. Then sinks into another crevice. I'm too far away to see the air bubbles—if there are any—but he's dead regardless.

"What the fuck, Arden?" Cheevy spits. For being an idiot, the man is smart enough to stay put. He's practically trembling in his seat, staring at the massacre slack-jawed like Chest Wound. I rise and pat the dirt from my pants. Dagger in hand, I wait for the bog traps and mudsnakes to do their job—bored at how fucking easy it is. Honestly, I expected better.

I hope it won't be so anticlimactic when Lyrick and I—

Cheevy grabs my leg and yanks, sweeping me to the ground as a blur of metallic blue swipes the air above me. The plants sag beneath my weight and cold water soaks into my civilian clothes —a simple pair of hide breeches and a thin elgrew top made from soft bamboo.

"Are you insane?" I hiss. "You'll risk the structural integrity—"

"*Move!*" Lyrick's voice bursts through my skull, and for a moment, my body isn't my own. My muscles move of their own accord—no, of *his* accord—and I roll left, dodging Eleesy's dagger as she swipes at me again, trying to pin me on the ground.

Fuck, fuck, fuck.

Woozy, I try to get my bearings, but there's no need. Like a puppet on a string, Lyrick takes command of my body and I jump to my feet, head rushing Eleesy's chest. She stumbles back and swipes again, but Lyrick knows her technique. He's sparred with her hundreds of times, maybe thousands. Duck, punch, kick, punch, kick again. She falls to the mud like she has in so many of our—*his*—practice sessions.

And then we're towering over her, prying the dagger from her closed fist, uncurling each bony finger one digit at a time. Her violet eyes widen and for half a second, I wonder if she realizes what's happening. But then the smooth hilt is in my palm, and my eyes roll to the back of my skull at the contact. The Marr-damn cold iron sears every part of me, vibrating my bones. Lyrick growls, and we fling the dagger as far away as possible.

The mud and sedges jiggle beneath us as Lyrick and I straddle her. Our thumbs wrap around her neck and her body tenses, kicking and slapping, then jerking and twitching. Eyes cloudy, she finally goes slack. There's this twinge of remorse. Of deep sorrow. Of horror at what we've done—what *he's* done to one of his best friends.

"I'm sorry," I whisper. And I know I shouldn't be, but I am. Something warm and wet runs down my cheek and I realize I'm crying, his emotions a physical thing inside me. I'm quick to swipe them away, my body suddenly my own again. For a breathless, exhausted moment, Lyrick says nothing. Then his words are a low timbre in my ears.

"Not sorry enough, but you will be."

The tingling in my palm fades to nothing, the connection going dark.

As I glance around me, I see the consequences of my actions. No more verncats. No more elgrew. Only the guilt of what I've done and Lyrick's promise of retribution.

XXIV. Arden

"In Starra'lee, the command hierarchy might seem straightforward: squadmate, squad leader, region commander, and general. Little do our soldiers know that their orders come from the High Priestess Supreme. Perhaps if they did, they would know to fear her more than anyone else."

—Clara of Ashwood, Former Starra'lee Priestess

Lost journal entry

"You have to talk to me at some point," I say, brushing aside the sawgrass reeds blocking Shoulder Squish Cave. My two squadmates remain silent behind me. Dejected. Bitter that I didn't warn them of my plan.

Fucking babies.

"You would have screwed it up if you'd known." I mutter the words before I can think them through. Cheevy storms in front of me, blocking my path to the cave. His fingers curl into fists.

"You know what your problem is, Arden?" he spits. "You don't know how to work as a team. You go off and do your own shit without thinking about how it'll affect the rest of us. You're welcome, by the way."

"For . . . ?"

He grinds his teeth together. "For saving your Marr-damn life. Or have you forgotten that Hunter would have stabbed you in the chest if I hadn't pulled you down?"

I did forget. With Lyrick puppeteering me, the whole fight is a bit of a blur, but it's not as if I can tell Cheevy that. This soft, squishy feeling wraps around my chest at the realization that not one, but two people saved me today without having any reason to—with having every reason not to. When I swallow, it's like swallowing tree bark. "You're right. Thank you."

He huffs in response and wriggles through the cave entrance, sucking in his gut to do so. I follow closely behind, as does Chest Wound. Inside, everything is impossibly dark. *Too dark* for an elf without darkeyes, which only Chest Wound possesses. On muscle memory, I tiptoe across moist, jagged rocks, avoiding the stalagmites and stalactites to reach the far side of the chamber. I fumble for a swinging chain I hung from the ceiling years ago, then for the glass and metal lantern fixed to it. A matchbox sticks to the bottom, attached by pine glue.

A bright spark of orange. An acrid, smoky odor as I remove a match and ignite it, lighting up a kerosene lantern—an elgrew lantern—normally banned from Starra'lee bunkers. Unlike the others, though, I don't care where my stuff comes from. I care about efficiency.

Pale light exposes an entire depot's worth of weapons, armor, food, and inventions that Mom and Dad taught me to make when I was young. Green-glass goggles. Cuirasses, gloves, and vambraces woven from sawgrass reeds. Daggers and swords. Pointed bows carved from spine trees, and red, poison-tipped arrows crafted from the teeth I pried off elgrew corpses. But even more important than all that are the explosives I smuggled out of Starra'lee. The key to completing our plan.

"Holy shit." Cheevy whistles low, taking everything in.

I feel this strange urge to defend myself. Back stiffening, I cross my arms and narrow my gaze at him. "The last time I trusted someone, I ended up getting poisoned and left behind. This was insurance in case it happened again."

"Gods, you're such a fucking psychopath," he says. "And I love you for that."

I roll my eyes at him. "Grab what you need and let's go. We've lost enough time already."

Grinning, he steps up to my arsenal and begins touching everything, trailing his fingers across row after row of equipment sprawled along the floor. "You've been holding out on us," he says, unscrewing a bronze jar filled with yellow paste—a topical analgesic meant to remove the sting from burns. "I didn't know Clara taught you how to make this. We've been going without for years."

Clara. My mom.

He sniffs the waxy mixture, unaware of what he's said. The hairs rise on the back of my neck as I try—and fail—to think of a reason he would know her name, would know she was an inventor, would have used a paste she invented. Not once have I ever spoken that word aloud—not even to Giara. "You knew my mom?" I ask, eyebrow raised.

Cheevy doesn't glance up from his sifting, but he does pause, his fingers hovering over a jar of fruit preserves. "Barely," he says. "She left Starra'lee around the time I joined. Took all her notes with her. Really pissed Elder Risha off."

"And none of you told me?" I don't try to hide the accusation in my tone. Across the cave, Chest Wound bites his fingernails to the quick, as if he's also been let in on this little secret. "Did Giara know?"

Cheevy shrugs. "I couldn't say. Giara wasn't exactly chatty with the rest of us." Snatching a bag off the floor, he shoves the yellow paste and jarred fruit inside. Then he moves on to weapons, as if putting this conversation past him, but I'm not about to let it go.

"What about Julian?"

"This isn't some grand conspiracy, Arden." Cheevy sighs—loudly. "A lot of us knew them—or knew about them—but we shun traitors who go topside. You know that. Speaking about them is forbidden."

His movements are more forceful as he grabs a bandolier and straps it across his chest, sheathing daggers through the leather loops. Maybe he's right. Maybe I'm being paranoid. As a rule, we don't mention the elves who go topside and decide it's more important to start a family than to fight. But this nagging voice in the back of my head can't help but feel . . . hurt? Betrayed? Lied to?

I shake the feelings aside—*for now*. Once our mission is finished and I'm back at Starra'lee headquarters, I'll confront Julian about it, but until then . . . I snatch an empty go-bag off the floor and follow in Cheevy's footsteps, grabbing equipment and tossing it inside. Then, I motion for Chest Wound to do the same.

"What's this?" Two rows from me, he plucks a fuzzy, rolled up blanket from the floor. Glass clinks inside it, and a wave of panicked nausea washes over me.

"Don't touch that!" I rush to Chest Wound, jumping over a pile of armor. Sweat dampens my palms. My heart roars so loudly, I can't hear anything over it. Snatching the blanket from him, I hug it tightly to my chest and breathe, slowly, deeply, inhaling the musky, loamy scent that marks us as safe. No sharp chemical odors. No dribbling liquid.

Marr-damn, that could have been awful.

My arms and legs tremble and my fingers lock protectively over the explosives cache. It takes a moment to stabilize my breathing, and by the time I do, my squadmates are staring at me like I've grown a third arm.

"Firecaps," I whisper in way of explanation, lowering myself to the hard stone. The projectiles clink together—albeit less dramatically—as I unfurl their protective cover and smooth it over the damp limestone. Dozens of round glass disks glimmer in the lantern light—the right halves filled with pink liquid, the left with something that resembles piss. A thin divider with a glass pull tab keeps the two sides separated.

Chest Wound leans over me, staring in fascination at the little disks. "What do they do?"

"Go boom," I say, imitating the sound. "Pull the tab and throw. When the liquids mix, you have about ten seconds before shit gets bad. It's not a big explosion"—*unless you have a bag full of them*—"but it'll light them up."

"We try not to use them in the field," Cheevy adds. "The noise lures in more elgrew than the firecaps kill. But if you're already in an unwinnable situation, it's nice to take some of those assholes out with you."

Before I can stop him, Chest Wound snatches up a firecap and holds it to the swinging lantern, examining it with one eye open. "That's so fucking cool."

"Thanks." Cheevy grins. "It's one of my better inventions."

Jumping to my feet, I pluck the glass disk from Chest Wound's fingers and pocket it. Then, I roll the blanket back up and tuck it deep within my bag, where the new guy can't access it without explicit permission. Last thing we need is some untrained, clumsy asshole fucking everything up. "Enough chatting. Grab what you need and let's go. We've got a lot of ground to cover before sunset."

I take my own advice and finish loading up, ignoring the "you're no fun" looks the guys keep giving me. I don't need to be fun; I need to be pragmatic.

And if we don't hurry, this whole plan falls apart.

Tightening the straps on my shoulder, I wedge my fat, over-stuffed go-bag between the rocks and exit the cave, listening with my sezin for any unusual sounds. Itchy vibrations travel through my inner ears, the noises of the forest amplifying. No thudding footsteps or purring cats. For the first time in hours—maybe days—we're free of the elgrew chasing us.

So why can't I shake the feeling of us being watched?

XXV. Lyrick

"In addition to delivering our young, Stitchers are responsible for all skin, organ, and bone transplants. A skilled Stitcher can begin the grafting process at birth; however, it is not without risk. To minimize complications, all transplanted parts should be from a healthy, whole, and infection-free individual."

—ADVANCED MEDICAL GUIDELINES, VOLUME 4.

My newborn sister is already gray. Her lumpy purple skin lies in a bucket next to the surgery table, amethyst blood dripping off it. Dressed in his white Stitcher's uniform, Yaklan gently raises her club hand and assesses the silver stitchwork. Smiling to himself, he moves on to examine her lumpy shoulder, then her malformed nose.

The more advanced surgeries will have to wait until she's old enough to crawl. Even then, finding an elf child of similar size with compatible genetics will be a challenge. I was seven before my body looked right, and I was lucky. Azerin had the money to pay for upgrades as I grew and underwent puberty.

Most can only afford the surgeries once, and they wait until adulthood.

"How is she?" I ask, leaning against the wall. It's only him and me in the surgery center—well past visiting hours—but my father insisted I retrieve her tonight before the Ring Day celebration.

It's a welcome distraction all the same. If I'm kept busy, I don't have to think about Eleesy or the training house—sacrificing my best friend to save a godsdamned elf, murdering an innocent to fill my aching belly. So much blood is on my hands. It makes my stomach turn.

"Your sister is fine," Yaklan says, shaking me from my tormented thoughts. "I placed her under anesthesia a few hours ago. It should wear off soon." He leaves Tyla on the surgery table and walks across the room, loafers clicking on the white marble floor. Metal tables and sinks line the back wall. Surgical implements, gauze, and disinfectant litter the countertops—all bloodstained from the operation.

Yaklan plugs one of the sinks with a metal stopper. "Your inauguration is tomorrow. How do you feel?"

"How am I supposed to feel?"

With his back to me, he reaches for a large glass bottle filled with clear liquid and wiggles the stopper until it pops free. The sour stench of vinegar follows, glugging and splashing when he pours it into the sink. "Your father sent you to me, so if I had to guess, you're having second thoughts. He mentioned we might need to speak."

More political maneuverings. Why am I not surprised?

"There's nothing to talk about. I don't want to be a Karesai," I admit. "Azerin's given me permission to deny the appointment and return to the forest."

He hums thoughtfully. "That must be very tempting for you."

You have no idea.

My palm tingles, right where I bit Arden. I flex my fingers, trying to ignore the aching possessiveness that flares to life inside my chest. It's only gotten worse these last few days. I need to return to the forest—to consume her and sever this twisted bond between us once and for all, before it gets anyone else killed.

Thank the gods Sarvenna escaped.

Metal scratches against metal as Yaklan scoots his bloody scalpels into the sink. Slowly and meticulously, he scrubs each one with a sponge, then soaks his hands in the vinegar mixture before drying them on his pristine white apron.

He returns to the surgery table and raises my sister, cradling her to his chest.

"Walk with me," Yaklan says. "I have some patients I need to look over before I leave for the day."

I obey.

My boots squeak as I follow him out the door.

Kerosene lamps flood the white hallways in golden light. Large bay windows reveal a small, moonlit courtyard where cobble paths weave through wildflowers and orangewood trees. Yaklan opens a closet near the courtyard doors, revealing an assortment of colorful baby blankets.

"Pick one," he says.

I select an indigo quilt with golden stitchwork, knowing that's the color my father will prefer. Together, we wrap my sister, *Tyla,* in it, and then he passes her to me. She's deadweight in my arms—a hideous little thing, but my heart melts all the same. As my father's eldest, I've held and cared for many of his babes, picking them up from surgeries, feeding them at night. It was one of the few tolerable things about returning from my hunting trips.

Resting her head against my chest, I marvel at how fast the stitchwork has healed. Ossi dust is a miracle. Our bodies— monstrous as they are—are miracles. Resistant to infection. Fast healing. Capable of regenerating skin and bone when cut. The elves never stood a chance.

Arden won't stand a chance either when I finally reach her.

Yaklan opens the courtyard doors and ushers me outside.

Humid wind whips at our clothing. Cupping Tyla's head, I shield her from the worst of it. Single file, we wind through a bumpy cobble path toward the recovery center on the other side of the facility. The twin buildings tower at the city's edge—its walls so close I can smell the musty rainforest.

Home.

"Do you know what the surgeries were like before I took over?" Yaklan asks, forcing me back to the present. We pass under a marble bench where luminescent white moths fly. They're everywhere—covering the seat, the manicured orange grasses, and the yellowberry bushes that shine in the silvery light.

I don't answer his question. Yaklan is over two hundred years old—he became a Karesai long before I was born.

"They didn't use anesthetic on the elves," he says. "If they needed a cesarean, they cut the babes out with no effort to preserve the mothers."

I swallow at his choice of words. No one calls them that here —it's forbidden. It's grounds for execution.

Yaklan continues as though he didn't say something fanatical. "Back then, disease and infection ran rampant in these halls. Elves were kept alive until all their parts were either used or rotted." He shudders. "It was a nightmare. When I took over as a Karesai, I ended the worst of it. Elves that are used for parts—*any parts*—are now euthanized on the same day. They don't have to experience their bodies disappearing little by little over months or years. We use anesthetic during surgery. Mothers can go on to have more children . . . if it's their master's intent."

That word again. Mothers. Not incubators. Not myrie.

We reach the recovery center, and he opens the door for Tyla and me.

Pushing fingers through his hair, Yaklan straightens and forces a fake, political smile to his face—the same one Colette and my father wear. It's not directed at me, but rather at the patients who face us. Transparent glass walls line each side of the hallway, looking in on the rooms of dozens of elgrew and elves. The former have curtains to draw if they so choose. The latter would never be granted that degree of privacy.

Most of the recovering elves lie in plain white beds, their stomachs wrapped in bloody gauze from having cesarean births —few myrie can deliver the natural way. Their pelvises aren't shaped to accommodate us, and trying to force it poses undo risk. A handful of elves tout injuries from working in the mines —either missing fingers or crushed arms.

"In the beginning, there was pushback to my changes," Yaklan says, peering into each of the windows. "The cost of surgery has more than quadrupled in the last hundred years, but as a Karesai, I've had the ability to ensure my policies remain intact. If you don't like the way things are, Lyrick, it's possible to improve them. You'll never stop the Butchers from butchering or the Hunters from hunting, but you can make incremental changes for the better."

Once he's finished examining the elves, he moves on to the elgrew, occasionally stepping into their rooms to check their vitals. I wait outside each time, not wanting to see the transplants when they fail.

Drooping body parts. Sloughing skin. The thought alone makes me gag.

We pause in front of Chalk's room—not Chalk, I realize a second later—but Sorso's daughter. She's taken more than the elf's scalp. Most of her skin is that same shade of pale, almost white. But her teeth are still razor sharp, and her eyes still glow amethyst. She sits in a wooden chair beside her bed, flipping through a voluminous black tome titled *Obedience Training: When Beating Doesn't Work.*

My mouth curls in revulsion.

Yaklan forces me away, placing a steady hand on my back. He maneuvers me to the end of the hallway—my baby sister snoring the entire time. Unaware of what befell the creature who birthed her.

"Chalk didn't suffer," Yaklan says. "I was quick."

My throat bobs. I can't bring myself to meet his gaze. "It's not my business."

"No, but it's alright to care. It's better if you do. Having compassion will make you a good leader."

"I can't live in this city, Yaklan. It's . . ."

Repulsive.

Rotten.

Sighing, he brushes the hair from his face. "Azerin has given you a gift, Lyrick. As a Karesai, you can affect real change. Your caste is rife with cruelty, but you can reduce it just as I have with mine. We can't save the world or stop what's in our nature, but we can be more *ethical* about it. I get the strong impression that's something you want."

I think of the mess halls and the arenas. Of the training houses and the Hunters like Conrin, who can't keep their fucking hands to themselves. Yaklan's surgery is perhaps one of the only places elves aren't tortured or abused. But it's far from kind.

Still, I see my father's logic in sending me here. He's offered me a chance to mold society into my image . . . on one condition. I behave the way he desires. I breed the elves, I eat in the mess halls, and I pretend that living here doesn't make me feel like spiders are crawling on my skin.

Fuck if it isn't tempting—not for me, but for them.

"Hunters are hard to control," I say eventually, thinking of Sorso and how easy it would have been for anyone to fuck and eat his myrie. If I hadn't been there, Conrin most certainly would have. "No one follows the rules that are in place now."

"You have to change their minds before you can change their actions. It's slow but worthwhile." Yaklan's politician face drops, and he lowers his voice. "Colette and Azerin told me what happened at the training house with her pets. That must have been . . . traumatic."

I swallow, swatting the memories of my assault aside before they have time to consume me. The last thing I need is to lose control of my emotions in front of Yaklan, too.

"I was the same way about touching them," he says. "But you don't have to drug the elves like Colette or force them like Sorso. There is a third path."

We stop in front of a large room, shielded by a spotted pink and yellow curtain. Golden lamplight streams through a gap in the fabric. Yaklan withdraws a chain from around his neck with a small key attached. He shoves the key in the lock, his fingers hovering on the crystal doorknob. "I expect your discretion, Lyrick."

I arch a brow.

Turning the handle, he ushers me inside then closes the door.

My jaw drops at what I see.

Sitting crisscross on the floor is a smiling female elf, surrounded by plush blankets and toy blocks. A small elgrew boy sits in her lap, gumming wooden cubes as she strokes his hair. His gray skin is the same shade as hers, but lumpy and uneven. A pair of golden pins hold a cloth diaper to his waist.

Their heads jerk toward us as Yaklan locks the door. At the sight of me, the elf's broad smile vanishes and her arms wrap protectively around the elgrew boy's stomach—her son's stomach, I realize.

"Yaklan, what is this?" My gaze flickers between them.

He merely crosses the room and sinks onto the floor, kneeling beside the creature. Yaklan cups her face in his palms and kisses her forehead. "It's alright," he says. "Lyrick is a friend."

They exchange words that I don't understand. Not Elvish, but something older, something *illegal*—the language before Rayna's takeover. Her eyes dart to me, then to the boy, then back again. But Yaklan strokes her hair, his voice placatingly soft. "Relax. Sit. You are safe."

In that ancient language, he says more until her shoulders finally slump. Once she's calm, Yaklan turns to me and pats the floor beside him in invitation. I shake my head. This is wrong. The elves are animals and incubators. Not parents. Not . . . whatever the fuck this is.

I feel sick.

I turn the handle. It rattles, but it doesn't budge.

"This is Vera," Yaklan says. "She's been my myrie since before I became a Karesai. I've never taken any others." He picks up the squirming boy and holds him in his arms. "This is our son, Luvin. He'll be two next week."

"Does my father know about this?" I hiss.

"Azerin knows everything that happens in this city. We have an understanding." Setting the boy down, he strokes the creature's head, and she closes her eyes, purring like a verncat. "I keep Vera confined to my domains. She isn't allowed alone in public spaces, and she knows no more Elgrew words than any other myrie. If she's commanded to do something, she will obey."

Yaklan rubs his thumb along the hollow of her throat as the boy crawls around, grabbing up his toy blocks with slobbery, mangled hands. Vera leans into Yaklan's touch, angling her neck for better access. Dressed in a simple long-sleeved gown, she shifts her legs, revealing dozens of dotted circular scars on her calves and thighs.

Yaklan lets go of the creature and she pouts.

"I give Vera whatever she wants within reason," he says,

patting her head. His knees pop as he rises from the ground. "I let her raise our children until they're four or five, then I send them away before they're old enough to remember her. Elves are much more docile when you let them keep their young. Treat them well enough and they'll spread their legs willingly—no need for drugs or force. She's never even seen the inside of a training house."

All I can do is stare at them and try to process what he's said—what I've seen.

My baby sister stirs in my arms just long enough to turn her head and smack her lips together. Adjusting the feverishly warm blanket, I peer at the closed curtain.

"I should go," I say. "It's a big day tomorrow, and this little one still needs to be fed."

Sighing, Yaklan removes the key from around his neck and unlocks the door. "Think about what I've said, Lyrick. This life is what you make it."

"You think I should take the appointment." It isn't a question.

"I shudder to think what elgrew will replace you should you refuse."

THE HUMID BREEZE tangles in my hair as I pace the abandoned city streets, forgoing my palanquin at the surgery center. My boots scrape across glimmering, silver-painted sidewalks as I pass between upscale apartment buildings that drip with ivy. At the bottom level, a handful of eateries have left their curtains open, casting dim yellow light onto the path ahead; Feron's Nursery is among them.

Tyla coos in my arms, her lumpy hands sneaking free of the baby blanket. Eyes closed, she presses a tiny palm to my cheek, and my chest tightens—those pesky paternal instincts kicking in, squirming around inside me like a festering disease. It's not that I don't want to be a father. It's that every conceivable scenario leading up to that outcome—and following it—is utterly abhorrent.

Tyla's cute now, but what will she be in twenty years? A Trainer like Sorso's daughter? Like Colette? Will she take after Azerin, beating her slaves into submission, scalping them the moment it becomes convenient?

I already know the answer. I've seen it with my other siblings.

A little line forms between Tyla's eyebrows as she frowns up at me. Gently, I smooth it away with my thumb then cross the street, climbing a small set of steps that lead to Feron's Nursery. A green awning stretches overhead, and flowers curl around a short iron fence that frames the apartment complex. Sweet orchids and purple *kissy lips* blow in the musty breeze. The rainforest is so fucking close, I could walk a mile and be hidden in it.

Juggling Tyla, I open the glass door instead. A golden bell rings overhead as I step into the brightly lit space. The entryway is barren, save for a lone hallway that leads deeper inside and a standing desk with frilly pink lace draped over the top—two male Trainers behind it. They smile in unison, straightening the fronts of their stuffy, three-piece suits. A mixture of purple and gray skin blots their features—lower middle class, by the looks of it.

"Your little one is so precious," the first one gushes, moving around the desk to get a better look at her. They don't need to know who I am to see that I'm important. Our gray skin screams privilege. That our pockets run deep enough to buy their entire establishment and every elf inside it.

"How old are they?" the second asks, approaching the other side.

I grunt. *Suck-ups.* "The Stitchers extracted her yesterday."

More noises. More fussing about how fantastic a job they did with replacing her skin.

I cut them off. "She needs to be fed."

"Are you looking to purchase a milk slave or is this—"

"A one-time thing," I say, cutting him off.

My father will have a slave at the estate, which he'll most certainly traumatize come morning. He prefers it when they don't know their roles beforehand, watching the shock and fear on their expressions as elgrew rather than elf babes latch onto their nipples for the first time, razor teeth digging in. It's fucking awful, just like everything he does.

I allow one of the Trainers to lead me into a back room, chattering away the whole time. I don't pretend to listen. My mind is half a world away—on Yaklan's surgery, Colette's training house, and the arena tomorrow. Half a dozen doors fill the hallway, all of them closed. Stained-glass chandeliers cast flecks of color in every direction, and soft yellow carpet squishes beneath our feet. The Trainer takes me to the last door, which is as unassuming as the rest. White painted. White knobbed. Ordinary.

He blocks the doorway. "The cost for feeding is—"

I hold up a hand. "I don't care. You can send the bill to Azerin's office."

His amethyst eyes glint at the revelation, gold coins flashing in them. Bowing, the Trainer opens the door for me and steps aside. "Yes, sir. Of course. Whatever we have is at your disposal."

"What I need is privacy," I grunt. Stepping around him, I enter the feeding room.

A soft lullaby fills my ears. In the corner, a Trainer plucks at silver harp strings, his purple fingers broken and crooked. Attention singularly focused, he doesn't pause or glance up when the door clicks shut.

Unlike the greeting area, this space is dark. The only light comes from a few flickering candles on low-rise glass tables.

Floral-printed couches fill the room—most are empty, but a few contain female elves that have been stripped bare. No chains pin them. No gags fill their mouths. But it doesn't matter. They're trapped here all the same.

Purple-skinned Butchers pace the aisles, cleavers in hand, a constant reminder that any misbehavior will be punished.

Thump-scrape.

Thump-scrape.

Thump—

Their shambling footfalls rumble past the music—legs uneven, backs hunched. Ignoring them, I hug Tyla closer and settle into the nearest couch. The plush cushions cave around me. The elf beside us stiffens, her engorged breasts hidden by long silver hair. If only she knew *this* facility was one of the kinder ones. Most milk-slaves get put into production lines, milked from sunup to sundown, with mechanical pumps that rub their nipples raw.

It's still torture here—I know that—but it's more ethical, at least. It's not as if we have a choice in the matter; our children have to eat sometime.

Another reason not to have one.

I think I'd have to truly hate whatever elf I bred. That's the only way they'd deserve the pregnancies, the surgeries, the forced lactation. It's a moot point, anyway. I'd have to *want* them too, and that's so fucking unrealistic it's not worth entertaining.

I don't fuck animals.

I'd sooner bash Colette's godsdamned skull in than let her drug me again.

"Sir?" The Trainer who led me inside approaches the couch, carrying a crocheted blanket and a porcelain teacup. The cup rattles on its saucer as he sets it on the nearest table, then drapes the blanket over my armrest. "Is there anything else I can bring you?"

"Do you have a pump?" I ask. "I prefer feeding her myself."

He bows his head. "Yes, sir. Right away, sir." Then, he scurries away.

The man returns a moment later with a clear glass bottle. On one end is a suction cup that adheres to the creature's nipple. On the other is glass tubing and a rubber ball affixed to the end. He tries to hand it to me, but I shake my head.

"Pumping bores me. I don't like the way it cramps my palm."

"Yes, sir." He sweeps the hair from the elf's shoulder, exposing her breasts. Scabbed-over bite marks circle her cracked nipples. I don't watch as he places or adjusts the pump, focusing instead on Tyla as I unfurl the crocheted blanket over us.

She makes this fussy sound, her cheeks blooming amethyst.

"Shhhh, I've got you," I say. "Food's almost ready." Her hand curls around my index finger, mouthing for milk that isn't there. I rock her as we wait, and eventually Tyla nestles into me—this small, helpless little monster. Warmth fills my chest, and for the thousandth time, I think having a child wouldn't be the worst thing imaginable. I could hunt with them. I could teach them my ways of thinking, the same as my uncle taught me.

And then I'd burn as a fanatic.

Shrieking cries.

Blazing heat.

I can still feel Morcai's meaty fingers digging into me, forcing me to watch as Korun burned my uncle alive. Skinning him wasn't enough. I should have gutted that bastard on the gambling hall floor—Conrin's feelings be damned.

Shaking my head, I push those desires down and force the images out.

Morcai isn't the problem; it's the whole damn system. Yaklan thinks I can change things, but that's what happens to the Hunters who try. Then again, the fanatics have never had the Politic on their side. Being a Karesai was my uncle's dream, not mine. All I ever wanted was to hunt, fuck, and mind my own damn business. But now?

Yaklan's words play on repeat, and the weight of my obligations and expectations drags me down.

It feels like an eternity before the Trainer passes me the warm bottle, a rubber nipple secured to it. Tyla's lips curl around the thing, her small, razor-like teeth digging in as she suckles. Adjusting the bottle, I tip it back and stare into her wide amethyst eyes, envisioning a world where I turn the appointment down.

If not me, then who? Conrin? Sarvenna? They're my friends and even *I* wouldn't want them in charge.

My freedom is so close I can practically taste it.

The rainforest is just outside those doors.

But I know deep down, when I leave this room, I'm leaving it in shackles.

XXVI. Lyrick

"In the year 941 A.T., the infamous Hunter, Talin of Kariss, was put to death by Korun, a newly appointed Karesai of Hunters. According to the ledger, Talin's crimes were extensive and included: unlawful communication with the A'sow Tribe, freeing and killing Marked elves, sabotaging four separate hunts, murdering six Hunters, kidnapping the Grand Overseer's son, and {redacted}—a crime so foul it has since been stricken from the record. Following Talin's execution, Korun was found dead in his home, his body ripped to shreds in an animal attack. While foul play was expected, no one could conclusively identify the animal or the elgrew who owned it."

—Eisel of Kariss
Master Historian

Bathed in moonlight, my verncat paces the gravel path at Azerin's estate. Red animal blood drips from his muddy orange fur, and his paws leave dirty imprints on the white walkways. All around him, purple elgrew buzz across gardens and walking trails—laying out carpets, stringing up blue glowfly lanterns, and pruning hedges—all last-minute preparations for my inauguration. They give Prowler a wide berth.

His pacing stops the instant he sees my palanquin. Then, the running starts.

No sooner am I out of the litter than he's rushing me, rubbing his cheek against my stomach and digging the sides of his sabreteeth into my upper thigh. The weight of him sends me stumbling back against the cart. Groaning, I cradle Tyla close in one hand and scratch his chin with the other.

Needy little asshole.

Purring vibrations rumble my palm. Dirt flakes off my skin when I pull my hand away from him. "Gentle," I warn, wiping my hand on my pants. "I'm carrying precious cargo."

Prowler scents the air, sitting on his haunches once he notices Tyla. His tail flicks from side to side as I straighten my clothing and push off the cart, crossing the remaining distance between us and Azerin's mansion. Yellow lamplight spills through open slats in the shuttered windows, alerting me that my father is still awake.

Prowler slinks beside me, eying the babe.

"You can't follow me inside," I say as if that'll stop him. The cat is quadruple my weight; if he wants to go through those doors, nothing and no one can stand in his way. Still, it'll put Azerin in a foul mood. Prowler frightens the slaves, and he'll no doubt track mud on our freshly polished floors.

No one speaks to us as we approach, gravel crunching under pad and foot. I don't expect them to. The servants are all illegitimates—elgrew sired without a breeding ceremony or witnesses—who aren't permitted to interact with grays, and in solidarity with Sorso, the Butchers guarding the estate despise me. I prefer their silence anyway. False pleasantries and small chat are barely tolerable in the daylight hours when I'm well rested. Now, it would be excruciating.

As I step onto the wraparound porch, two Butchers open the front door for me, revealing a multistory ladder that blocks the entry. On the upper rung, a servant stands on tiptoes, running a blue korkuran duster over a crystal chandelier. Servants carry flower bouquets and table skirts through the foyer, then out an open back door.

Turning to Prowler, I click my tongue and point at the ground. *Wait.*

He meows in protest. The sound is not nearly as frightening as he thinks it is.

"Most cats would be happy they *aren't* allowed inside," I say. "You're a spoiled asshole, you know that, right?"

In the city, Prowler would be forced into small animal care facilities where the closest thing to forests are garden rooftops and the occasional courtyard. He wouldn't be allowed to roam freely, but out here, he has full rein over the property and the jungle, only returning home when it suits him. The damn beast doesn't know how good he has it compared to the other Hunters' verncats, but he certainly knows how to complain.

Prowler meows louder, and I relent, gesturing him forward with a heavy sigh.

We're codependent, he and I. He's more friend than pet. More loyal than Conrin, Sarvenna, or Eleesy.

Eleesy. Gods, what have I done?

No one else can die for Arden—because of Arden. Once I become a Karesai—*if* I become a Karesai—it'll be *my* Hunters tracking her, and thanks to the bond, they'll know exactly where to look. Then, this thing between us will finally come to an end.

Dashing underneath the ladder, Prowler disappears somewhere out of eyeshot, tracking mud and blood over everything in his path. But that's the servants' problem, not mine. I step around the other elgrew, peering first into the kitchen, then into the dining room and library in search of my father, but he isn't there. Carefully, I climb the winding steps to Tyla's nursery—*my* nursery once—where the upper floors are blessedly silent.

Tyla stares at me the whole time, quiet but awake—complaisant and observant like Chalk.

Peeking into her bedroom, I find the lights off, the windows closed and barred for her protection, so a disgruntled slave can't snatch her. The room looks the exact same as it did when I was a boy—four walls painted with realistic bluewood trees, a carpet made from living moss, and at the center, a bassinet carved from dark wood, filled with blue downy bedding. A mobile hangs over the bed, and storm clouds made from cotton dangle from it.

Tyla's violet eyes widen in wonder as she takes the nursery in, breathing in the musty, rainlike scent.

"Maybe you *will* be a Hunter like me, huh?" I ask. Her small hand unroots itself from her baby blanket and curls around my index finger. My heart squeezes. "Some of the best trackers are those who know how to be quiet and observe. I think your . . . I think Chalk would have been very formidable in the wild. Maybe you inherited some of that."

The corners of my mouth tilt into a smile, imagining her as my apprentice seven years from now, running beside Prowler and me. It's wishful thinking. Azerin's children grow up to have cushy lives and prefer cushy jobs to go with them. I'm the odd one out.

Kissing Tyla's forehead, I place her in the bassinet then tuck her in, swaddling her back into her blue blanket. She continues staring as I tap on the mobile and spin it. "I'm going to go find our dad," I say, giving her one last look. Dried purple blood clings to the seams of her flesh, outlining the patchwork, but she doesn't appear to be in pain or distress. "Good night, Tyla."

Silently, I pad across the squishy damp moss, then ease the door shut. The latch clicks into place behind me, but that's not good enough. Azerin doesn't take any chances with his children.

Reaching into my pocket, I procure a set of key rings. Metal clicks against metal as I riffle through the keys for the correct one.

Once I find it, I lean my ear against the wooden door and listen for a cry or scream. A minute passes, then two. When she doesn't stir, I shove the key into the hole and turn it, locking her inside. Then, I resume my search for Azerin.

After everything that's happened, I don't *want* to speak to him, but he should know that Tyla's home safe. My father, for his many faults, loves his children.

I scour the estate, but he's nowhere in sight—neither is Prowler for that matter.

I'm about to say *screw it* when the ajar back door catches my eye, muddy pawprints leading up to it. Creaking it open, I pause and stare at my surroundings.

If the front of the estate looks luxurious, this is obscene.

Pavilion tents swarm the gardens, each of them made from soft blue fabrics that sway in the muggy floral breeze. Expensive beds and furniture fill the tents, and potted plants hang from the ceilings, spilling blue orchids and silver ivy onto ornate rugs. Dangling over the garden paths are blue glowfly orbs—clear, breathable crystals where little insects buzz around.

I swallow when I see the hexagonal gazebo in the center of the garden, the shadowy outline of five thrones within it. Yellow lamplight gleams from the building's archways, spilling over the low hill it's perched on and illuminating an elgrew's silhouette. *My father's.*

The servants have all but finished setting up, leaving only a handful to unfurl the remaining tablecloths and arrange ya'esen flutes. With the garden empty, the thudding of my bootsteps resonates across the moonstone walkways. Azerin must see me coming long before I reach him, but he doesn't move to greet me. Prowler, on the other hand, creeps out from behind a nearby tent and joins me on the walk, his warm body pressing into my side.

The closer I get, the more detailed the gazebo becomes. Blue kissy lips climb the cold-iron railings, and blue marble pillars support a stained-glass roof with turquoise, indigo, and cerulean panes. Carved into the marble are female elves adorned in netted brassieres and low-rise harem pants, kneeling in supplication with their hands bound behind their backs.

As a boy, I thought my father's obsession with the color was absurd. I didn't learn Azerin personally hunted and consumed the last of their subspecies until much later. It's not that he wants to fuck Arden—or rather, it's not *just* that. He views it as his moral obligation to bring them back, to breed her with every male elf in Kariss until there are enough blue children to start a captive population in the Butcher's Block and Agricultural District.

Chalk's fate, by comparison, was a fucking mercy.

Palm throbbing, I climb the blue mosaicked steps leading up to the gazebo. Blue and purple hydrangeas frame either side of the pathway and cover the hill, only broken up by kerosene lamp posts that jut from the ground in even intervals. Prowler darts in front of me, crossing under the gazebo's polished arches a moment before I do, then lies at my father's feet.

"How is she?" Azerin asks. He sits atop an enormous bed not meant for sleeping, with chains and cuffs hanging from the metal frame. A plain wooden trunk lies on the ground beside him. Unlike the rest of the estate, this place remains untouched by expensive decorations. The only furniture is practical—five thrones spaced evenly around the perimeter, the bed, and a sawhorse bench.

I may not have a choice in *whom* I breed, but it seems I'll have a choice in *how* I breed them.

How considerate.

"She's doing well," I say, leaning against the cold-iron railing. I shove my hands into my pockets, trying not to look at the bondage equipment intended for Brawler. "I fed Tyla and put her down in the nursery. She hasn't cried once since returning from Yaklan's surgery."

Azerin's shoulders sag in relief. "Of course, she hasn't. She must have inherited Chalk's disposition."

A tense silence settles between us. Prowler doesn't notice. He rolls from side to side and stretches his massive paws, rubbing his cheeks across the blue marble floor. His sabreteeth click on the stone. The wooden box groans as he jostles it.

Ignoring him, Azerin gazes past me, into the gardens and estate below. He has this glassy, faraway look to his eyes. "You were so fussy when I brought you home. I blame my myrie at the time. She'd been so strong-willed . . . just like you are."

My brows furrow. He's never spoken of my incubator before, and while it's not illegal, it is taboo. I swallow past the lump in my throat, forcing myself not to use Yaklan's word for it—*mother*. "What happened to her? Did you breed her again after?"

"Gods no." He chuckles, but it's humorless and dry. Patting the space beside him, Azerin motions me over.

I begrudgingly accept, pushing off the metal railing and stepping around Prowler to join him on the bed. The frame groans beneath me, the plush mattress squeaking as I settle into sleek blue sheets. Up above, loops have been welded into the wrought-iron frame—places to hook in wrist restraints, I realize.

My stomach churns at the sight.

"I was naive when I took her," Azerin says finally. "I gave her too much freedom and taught her too many words. That's something they don't tell you—how easy it is to bond with the elves once they're Marked and pregnant. I often doted on her the way Yaklan does his."

"What happened?"

How does someone go from *that* to scalping Chalk at Sorso's behest?

Azerin throws his arm around my shoulders. "One day—close to the end of the pregnancy—she was opening letters for me in my study and turned the blade on herself. Right into her stomach. I thought she'd killed you, but Yaklan got there quickly and worked fast. I had to euthanize her afterward, obviously."

"Obviously," I mumble.

It's no surprise she'd rather die than carry an elgrew child. There's a reason we keep them drugged and in chains, under constant supervision.

"At the training house, it was like reliving that day all over again," Azerin says. His throat bobs. When he speaks, his voice is low and thick with emotion. "I should have never let you apprentice under Talin. If I had known what he was going to teach you . . ."

My jaw clenches. "Talin was a good man."

"A good man who died for his ideals. I don't want you to burn like your uncle, Lyrick."

"I'm not—"

"You won't eat captive elves. You won't breed them or take them as slaves. If I don't lose you to becoming feral, then I'll lose you the way I lost him, whether you take the appointment or not." He waves his hand at the estate. "How long until your friends turn on you? What about your enemies?"

I try not to remember Sarvenna's parting words. Crossing my arms, I shrug out of reach.

"I know you don't want to take a myrie," Azerin says, "but it's the only way I know how to protect you. Like Yaklan, I need you to make a show of following tradition. The bare minimum will secure your future here."

I see it then. The desperation in my father's face. It's the same way he looked at me when he found me at the training house. For a brief moment, I wonder if he looked at Yaklan that way too. Were they friends before he became Karesai? Did Azerin save him from being burned as a fanatic?

There's so little I know about my father. So much he hides.

"Yaklan never had to breed Vera in front of an audience of ten thousand," I say finally.

"Yaklan doesn't have rumors circulating about him that he can't."

I peer over my shoulder to the turquoise lake behind us. In the moonlight, the water gleams a silvery black, the waves lapping at a rocky shore.

"I'm not your enemy, Lyrick. I waited five years for you to choose someone because I wanted it to be your choice. But the rumors have only gotten worse. It can't wait any longer." Azerin cups my shoulder. "They know you apprenticed under Talin. Half the city suspects you butchered the Karesai who put him to death. If you think hiding in the forest will save you from their prying eyes, you're wrong. It's best to face them head-on, from a position of strength."

"Do you think I killed Korun?" I ask. I'd only been fourteen at the time, too young for the other Karesai to suspect, too young for them to demand my head.

On the ground, Prowler stops rolling, staring up at us with his glowing orange eyes.

"What I know is that Korun took my brother and best friend from me, and someone did what I could not. I have always respected you for it."

Wiping at his inflamed eyes, my father jumps from the altar, and Prowler darts out of the way of his landing feet.

Azerin bends in front of the wooden box and unlatches the thick cold-iron buckles holding it together. It yawns open, groaning with age and use, to reveal piles of shining leather armor and a crown made from centuries-old vertebrate. The last time I held that crown, I was drenched in Korun's blood, bashing it into his thick fucking skull.

It was the best godsdamned moment of my life.

"This was my armor when I was a Hunter. I had Colette repair and resize it to fit your body." He places the armor beside me.

It's glossy and smooth—a dark shade of brown that almost looks black in the dull lighting. Intricate patterns decorate the pauldrons' and gorget's interlocking scales. When I pick them up, they're no heavier than linen and no thicker than my dress shirt.

"What's this made from?" I ask.

"Swamp dog hide." Azerin unfurls a shining, long-sleeved tunic. "It may feel insubstantial at first, but it's thick enough to stop an arrow from penetrating and flexible enough that you'll still be able to climb. Unlike normal leather, it's water resistant too, so you won't have to worry about shrinkage or smell."

I grab a pair of pants and tug, testing the resistance and flexibility. It's unlike anything I've ever worn before. I've never heard of an elgrew trapping swamp dogs for leather; few are willing to brave the Lycean Marshes.

"I'd like for you to wear it at your inauguration tomorrow." Azerin says, coughing to clear his throat.

That's when it finally hits. He's giving this to me. Not only is my father passing down his former title, but he's handing over the tools that helped him achieve it. Azerin killed his way to the top while wearing this. He became the greatest Hunter in Rayna while wearing this.

My eyes burn at the undeserved sentiment, but I force my face into a neutral expression.

Azerin retrieves the crown next, and when he places it on my head, I don't stop him.

XXVII. Arden

"An elf's sezin should only be utilized in dry, quiet conditions. Attempting to use them during a rainstorm event, near a loud water source, or inside a city could result in temporary or permanent hearing loss. Our sezins work best while sedentary. Moving and listening at the same time can make filtering noises more difficult. Before a soldier can be assigned scouting duties, they must first prove themselves proficient listeners."

—Ustas of the Ivory Forest, Starra'lee General
Leadership Correspondence

S*hink.*
Shink.
Shink.

Dagger in hand, I slide the blade across a whetstone balanced on my lap, sharpening the edges until even the shallowest graze could draw blood. I won't take any chances tomorrow. No risks. My favorite rusty dagger has been tucked away and replaced with a lighter, standard issue one that better conforms to my wrist—easier to wield, easier to throw, and, most importantly, easier to kill with. I finish sharpening the blade, then sheathe it at my thigh.

A pile of matching unsharpened daggers lies in the grasses at my feet. Maybe it's excessive. Then again, can there be such a thing as too many blades?

Shink.

Shink.

I grab the next one and get to work, ignoring Cheevy and Chest Wound, who sit on the moist ground beside me, half-hidden by purple coneflowers and orange grasses. Golden pollen dusts the landscape, the muggy air sweet and thick with its floral scent. Up above, yellow glowflies blink across the night sky and starlight stretches for infinity. It's so fucking beautiful. And distracting.

And there's no time to be distracted.

Shink.

Shink.

My squadmates chuckle, sipping spiced wine from their animal skin flasks. Useless as ever. Squinting through the blackness, I bite my tongue and keep my eyes on the blade, on the porous sharpening stone, and on the woven threads of sawgrass reeds that crisscross over my thighs. I could put a stop to it—*make them help*—but honestly, they'd do a shoddy job anyway. It's irritating as shit, but not worth the argument.

Shink.

Shink.

Cheevy strips his tunic free and chucks it somewhere in the darkened field, scooting closer to Chest Wound. Someone groans in what sounds like pleasure, and for the first time in my life, I'm so fucking thankful I don't have darkeyes to see what's going on. Their silhouettes are bad enough.

"How'd you get those scars?" Chest Wound asks. I don't need to see them to know what he's talking about. Like

Cheevy's face, his entire body is covered in deep, winding lumps that look like a child's nonsensical cave drawings.

"A pair of garden shears," Cheevy says, voice prideful. "Back when I was living in Kariss, I overheard my master say he was going to take me to the Stitchers for a transplant. Figured if I couldn't wear my skin, neither could they."

Chest Wound gasps. "You did this to yourself?"

Shink.

Shink.

"Yep." Cheevy tips his flask and takes a long swig, hissing in satisfaction. "Best decision of my fucking life. When the Stitcher saw what I'd done and realized he couldn't salvage it, he let me go. Pretty sure he wasn't supposed to, but I'm not complaining. Wanna see the rest?"

Not waiting for an answer, Cheevy fumbles with his belt. Metal jingles and clicks as he unhooks the buckle and threads the long leather strip free, tossing it into the grasses as well. Fabric rustles. Flowers shift. Cheevy peels his pants down his thighs, and my grip slips on the whetstone, wrist hitting a sharp edge.

How is anyone supposed to work in these fucking conditions?

Gritting my teeth, I close my eyes and take a deep breath. Then, I return my dagger to the stone and—

Cheevy moans as Chest Wound kneels between his thighs and reaches for his dick. "This looks fine to me," he says.

"Yeah, I left that bit alone."

Fucking kill me.

I clear my throat and fasten dagger number two to a matching sheathe on my other thigh. The blade's not as sharp as I'd like, but it's good enough to get the fuck out of here. "I'm going to run another patrol," I say. "Scout ahead for tomorrow. You guys good here?"

Cheevy's thumbs-up emerges from behind a wall of grasses. And then they're groping, kissing, exchanging spit and fluids and gods know what else—like sex isn't the most repulsive thing in the world. Like having to look at Cheevy's dick isn't a war crime.

Biologically, I get it. Physiologically, though, it's a mystery to me how anyone can find *that* pleasurable. Sticky. Messy. Gross. Everything about it is so fucking unappealing.

Trying not to look at them, trying not to gag, I check the tightness of my braids and the location of my twin daggers before taking off, heading south toward the Aegis River. Once we've crossed it tomorrow, it's only a two-hour hike to Azerin's estate. Normally, the proximity would make me nervous, but most of his lackeys will be in Kariss, preparing for their bullshit celebration, cramming themselves into the heart of the city for a good seat at the arena.

Yesterday, I couldn't shake the feeling of being watched. Today, I could probably shout at the top of my lungs and not a soul would hear me, save for my squadmates.

Still, I'm not about to take any chances.

I vibrate my sezin and cringe when the first thing I hear is skin slapping against skin—*no thank you.* It takes what feels like forever to tune them out, to focus on the other noises that surround me. Chittering rodents. Shrieking wind. A faint burble of water to my left. But no signs of any elgrew. I keep my hands near my daggers regardless, fingers sliding over the hilts, itching for another fight, another kill.

Number seventy-nine by my count.

As I walk, I continue straining my ears, vibrating my sezin. Each footfall lands like a chisel against stone, so fucking loud my knees threaten to buckle. Few elves can do this—walk and listen at the same time—but Julian taught me well, and on a mission this important, the throbbing headache seems like a cost worth paying.

Grasses crunch. Glowfly mandibles snap. The wind and water grow more deafening with each step. But I keep going. It isn't until the river is a roar inside my skull and the pressure on my eyes threatens to burst them that I relax my ears and let my feet guide me.

Slowly, the grasses thin, replaced by sedges and cattails. The moist dirt turns harder, sharper, the mud filling in with coarse gravel that digs into my calloused heels. By now, I can feel little sensation in my feet—the same as most adult elves who've spent their lives shoeless—but what I can feel fucking hurts. Hissing, I ignore the jabbing stones and press forward, where a row of spine trees forms a wall-like barrier between me and the rest of the riverbank.

I suck in my gut and squeeze past them, the thorny bark grazing and tugging at the layer of sawgrass reeds that cover my hide armor. My cuirass threatens to tear as I wrestle free of the trees, then stumble onto a gravel bar that's speckled with teal oo'ren moss and slimy orange algae. Rocks of every size and tangly mats of purple vines create the world's worst tripping hazard between the Aegis River and me. *And gods, that river. . .*

"Marr-dammit." My jaw drops as I take in the wide expanse of water keeping me from Lyrick.

Not Lyrick, I correct. *The mines.*

But my heart knots all the same, constricting me until it hurts to breathe. I'm so fucking close to him—to ridding myself of this bond once and for all—yet the river forms an impenetrable barrier between us. Because I can't swim.

In the moonlight, the jade-green water is so dark it looks black, with silver light bouncing and rippling in the current. Cool mist sprays the banks on both sides as water crashes and bursts against boulders as tall as I am. The current is fast and deep and impossible to cross—at least right here. But that's why I'm scouting. To find somewhere I'll make it through without admitting to Cheevy and Chest Wound that I *can't.* Gods, the thought of them realizing I'm too scared or too weak or too incompetent to cross a stupid river is unbearable.

Eyes on the Aegis, I pace the gravel banks, searching for a better spot. It never narrows. Occasionally, bedrock bursts through the surface, creating frothing rapids and sharp under-currents. A few spine trees lie uprooted near the water's edge, slowing the current down until it forms stagnant, reeking pools. A berserker like Julian might be strong enough to push the trees together and bridge the gap between one bank and the other, but neither my squadmates nor I have that kind of power. Even if we did, the trunk would be too sharp to walk across.

It's useless. It's—

The air catches in my lungs as I stumble forward, nearly falling flat on my face. Visceral rage has me balling my hands in frustration, but then I realize what tripped me. The purple vines are so thick here, it's hard to see the coarse gravel beneath them. *Of course.*

Smirking, I grab a fistful of vines and heave, yanking them from the surface into a wadded ball. I slide my dagger from its sheath and begin cutting through it until it forms long, uniform lines, red liquid oozing onto the ground below. In the darkness, the spatters almost resemble blood.

Avra vines. I haven't seen them since my tribe abandoned me. Since they used their juices to poison my tea. A small amount will help an elf sleep, but a large amount will ensure they never wake back up.

I grab one end of the vines and tie it around the largest boulder I can find. Then, I take the other and snake it around a smaller stone at my feet—this one is heavy in its own right, but not so heavy it's impossible to lift. I give the smaller stone a few test throws, tossing it high into the air and catching it in my outstretched palm. It fits snuggly there, the rough grooves solid and warm against my darkened skin.

This is going to work. It has to.

Across the riverbank, more spine trees line the way, their prickly silhouettes ill-defined in the pale light. One eye open, I squint and assess, then line my body up into the most advantageous position. Feet shoulder-width apart. Right foot forward. I take a deep breath and exhale, rotating my entire body as I chuck the stone at their branches. If I throw it hard enough, I should be able to catch it on the branches and form a rope-bridge to the other side.

Plop.

My stone splashes into the center of the river, flicking silver droplets in the air. As the current carries it downstream, the vine draws tight, and my boulder anchors it in place. Cursing under my breath, I trudge toward the boulder and begin pulling the vine's slack hand over hand, grunting at the strain of it. Sweat sticks to my forehead by the time that damn throwing rock is back in my hands.

A few more practice tosses. A few more real ones. Each attempt is more of the same. A failure.

My useless biceps ache with the effort. They're too small, too weak to get that stone across. *Julian could do it,* I think bitterly. *So could Cheevy and Chest Wound.*

Moping won't change reality, though. I'm small and so are my muscles. That's why I use daggers over sabers, why my fighting style leans more toward agility and stealth rather than charging elgrew head-on. I'm fucking useless when it comes to stuff like this.

Maybe I don't need strength, though. Maybe wit is enough.

Sitting on the hard gravel, I clutch the dripping rock to my chest, panting, thinking, my dagger discarded somewhere in the moist, tangled mat. If only I could throw my blade and use *it* to anchor me. The dagger is certainly small enough, light enough, and more aerodynamic. It could make it across the river, but could it catch between the branches? Could it dig into the bark deep enough to hold my weight?

Fuck it. I've come this far.

Too tired to search for my buried weapon, I unsheathe a new

one. My nails dig into the throwing stone, unknotting and reknotting the vines around my dagger's sleek black hilt. Groaning, I stand up one last time, line myself up to the nearest tree, and fling.

The dagger hits its mark, whistling through the air as fast as an arrow or throwing star. It dives between a set of dark branches, flipping horizontal to catch on either side. When I tug on the vine, the grip holds.

"Yes!" I pump my fist in victory, then yank a dozen more times for good measure. Once I'm certain it won't budge, I step into the chilly water, resisting a shiver as I grab the rope-vine and hold on tight, using it to anchor me even as the current lashes at my ankles, my calves, my thighs. The gravel shifts beneath my feet and I nearly fall, lungs seizing as the water splashes up to my cuirass.

Shit!

I jump to keep from falling in, swinging my legs around the vine like I'm a sloth. The makeshift rope bridge jiggles. The world flips upside down as I crawl hand over hand toward the other side of the bank, staring at the spine tree that holds my life in the balance. My dagger's dark hilt wobbles with each shimmy of my ankles, each tug of my hands. But it holds.

If the dagger slips, I can hug the rope and use the slack to pull myself to safety. I'm not in any real danger so long as I don't panic. Still, a pit of dread fills my stomach, and I fist the vine so hard my blue knuckles turn almost white. Goosebumps pebble every inch of me, and my teeth chatter as the chilly water mists my skin.

Halfway there.

Three quarters.

The deepest parts loom below, ready to swallow me whole. But I refuse to look down. I'm almost there. Just a few more feet and—

The vine snaps, and my body smashes into the icy river.

Cold seizes my chest as I slip under and drop the vine on reflex. Arms thrashing, lungs burning, I resurface long enough to cough up mouthfuls of water and gasp for breath. Water bobs around me, and my brows furrow when I see my dagger still wedged firmly in the tree. As I slip through the current, my head swivels to the other side of the bank where Sarvenna stands at my boulder, her longsword braced against it. The line lies cut at her feet.

And then I fall back under.

XXVIII. Arden

"Rylock and avra vines grow along partially submerged riparian corridors. Both purple in color, it can be challenging to distinguish between the two. While avra vines are poisonous if ingested in high enough quantities, small doses may prove a useful sleep aid. Rylock vines, however, serve no medicinal purpose. Even the smallest amounts can cause fever, nausea, breathlessness, skin rashes, suffocation, and death. It is for this reason, both vines should be avoided unless collected by a practiced healer."

—A Field Guide to Plants and Poisons Along the Aegis River

Icy darkness.

An intense need to draw breath.

Slimy gravel scrapes along the bottoms of my feet, and I use the riverbed as a launching pad, pushing off until my head breaks the surface. Starlight swirls up above me. Boulders jut from the river on all sides. I only have time to draw a single breath before the current drags me back under. And then I'm somersaulting so fast, I can't tell my ups from my downs until my feet hit the gravel again and I'm able to force myself back up.

I claw at the water, and it splashes up around me. Eyes burning, I grapple for something—anything—to latch onto. A boulder smashes into my chest with bruising force, knocking what little air I have from my lungs. Another springs up to my left and I reach for it, my fingers slipping through the orange algal film that's slicking its surface.

No, no, no. Come on.

The wilderness speeds past me. The river roars in my ears. A waterfall is approaching. If I don't drown to death, the drop will kill me.

I have to stay calm. I have to find something to stop my fall.

Another boulder races past, and my head slips back under. Icy water scorches my lungs as I reach behind me, grappling blindly for the giant stone. *There. A fingerhold.*

My biceps ache at the strain of holding onto the grooved edge. But I keep holding, keep pulling, keep sputtering up water and choking down air until both of my arms are wrapped around the boulder in a tight hug. Water whooshes past, but the hard, unforgiving rock takes the brunt of the force. For a moment, all I can do is press my forehead against the gray sandstone and pant, blinking droplets from my lashes.

The musty stench of algae and moss has never been so fucking appealing.

I'm alive. I fucking made it.

I haul myself up the stone and collapse onto it, staring at the starlight. Everything feels like jelly—bones, organs, joints. Movement seems an unlikely possibility. Chest heaving, I stare at the boulders that surround me in the center of the Aegis River and briefly consider how I'm supposed to reach the banks. The nearby boulders are too far apart to jump to or use as stepping stones. Maybe if I were taller, more muscular, longer legged.

Maybe if I were Julian or Giara.

Crushing hopelessness has me closing my eyes and resting them, ignoring the thunderous waterfall that's so close I can see it cresting the horizon. I have no weapons or rope. No way to do anything remotely productive. I'm stuck here—at least until the rains come and the water rises, the current dragging me back down.

"Lyrick, where are you?" I say the name like a prayer, but he doesn't answer. There's no throb in my palm—which is pretty unfair considering every other inch of my body is throbbing. "If you could take over and swim for me, that would be pretty fucking convenient."

Still, nothing.

I let my hand fall limply at my side, the coarse, uneven surface digging into flesh.

Minutes pass, maybe longer, and then something sharp digs into Lyrick's bite mark. My eyes snap open. I'm groggy and disoriented—*shit, I must've fallen asleep*—and Sarvenna's looming over me, straddling me as she pins me to the ground. Her waterlogged hair falls in snakelike tendrils over her shoulders. Silver threads glisten in the moonlight across her patchy gray skin.

"Who's your master?" She growls the words, speaking crudely in the Elvish tongue.

I try to buck her off. I thrash and kick, but she might as well be a boulder for all the good it does. Sarvenna is fucking strong. It's easy to see why Lyrick likes her. Hand to hand, I couldn't take her on the best of days. Half-drowned, the attempt is laughable. Still, that doesn't stop me from trying.

"Fuck off." I spit at her, and the glob lands on her jagged cheek.

She flashes her pointed teeth at me and digs her dagger into the soft skin of my palm until blue rivulets bead the surface. "Your master's name. Now."

Gritting my teeth, I glare at her with all the venom I possess, biting back a whimper when the blade sinks even deeper and my blood spills across the stone. *"Lyrick, please."*

But he isn't there.

"Fuck it. I don't care." Sarvenna drops the blade, and it clatters across the boulder's surface, *plunking* into the water. My brows furrow until she wraps her spindly fingers around my throat and squeezes—hard. "Your master can't save you here. You deserve to die for what you did to Eleesy."

I wheeze. Darkness dances at the edges of my vision, but she doesn't let up. With my free hand, I grab her wrist and tug. My grip slips on her wet skin and she smiles at me, tongue sliding across those razor-like teeth. Her violet eyes glimmer in the darkness, and my chest tightens as my nails dig white lines into her leather vambraces.

I need air. I need—

"Lyrick." I cough the name like it'll save me.

Her grip eases just enough for me to whistle an inhale. "What did you say?"

"Lyrick," I hiss. "My master's name is Lyrick."

A crease line forms between her brows. And then she stumbles back, that confused look still on her face. An arrow protrudes from her shoulder and another buzzes through the wind, puncturing her cuirass. Sarvenna tumbles over and *thunks* into the Aegis River, splashing water up around her. Blood seeps through her leather armor into the rippling current, where she thrashes at the surface before finally sinking below.

Her silver hair floats along the top of the water, then disappears when she crests the waterfall and plummets. It's a one-thousand-foot drop into sharp rocks and deep water. No one survives it.

I scan the horizon, searching for my savior. I half expect to find Lyrick standing there, but it's Cheevy and Chest Wound instead. My heart falls—just for a moment—and I try to convince myself it's not in disappointment.

Grinning, I cup my hands over my mouth and call out to them. "How'd you find me?"

Cheevy drops his thorny longbow into a cluster of cattails and holds up two fingers. "That's twice on the same mission. You owe me, Arden."

Glancing over my shoulders, I reassess my position. Water that's too deep. Boulders that are too far away. A bank that's impossible to reach on either side. Then, I do what I despise most. I swallow my fucking pride and ask for help. "Can you make it three? I can't swim."

***

TEETH CHATTERING, I hold the steaming wooden mug to my mouth and take a sip, letting the pale green tea soothe my aching throat. It's bitter and herby and reminds me of what the river tasted like. But gods, does it settle in my stomach like liquid warmth. A fire crackles and hisses in front of me, drying my armor while I sit crisscross in nothing but a hide breastwrap and matching shorts that barely reach mid-thigh. No sense being modest now—Cheevy and Chest Wound have already seen me at my weakest.

A dagger pile sits in front of me, blades still unsharpened, but I don't have the strength to deal with it right now. I barely have enough energy to hold myself upright. Splotchy, swollen skin covers every part of my weak and useless body, and I know tomorrow, I'll be bruised.

"You never answered how you found me," I say to Cheevy and Chest Wound, who sit on the other side of the campfire. Embers spark and snap between us, spitting high into the air.

"When you didn't turn back up, we used our sezins to track you," Cheevy explains. And I have to assume *we* means *he* because Chest Wound isn't trained for that. "We found your footprints and followed them to the river. That's when we heard *her* prowling around. I didn't think I'd make the shot—I'm not as good at archery as you are."

"But you did." I sniffle, wiping snot onto the back of my hand. "Thank you."

"We're just lucky her verncat wasn't around." Cheevy chuckles, but there's no humor there. "I wish I'd been paying better attention in the swamp. I should have seen that she'd gotten away."

No. I should have. I take another sip, shuddering at how Marr-damn good it feels. "We should put the fire out. It's too risky."

On the other side of the river, we're now firmly in elgrew territory—a short hike to Azerin's property. The spine trees along the riverbank offer minimal concealment for our rising smoke, and equally minimal concealment for us. It's not as though we can climb the thorny bark and hide in the trees if another Hunter comes along. This close to the water, we can't even use our sezins to monitor the environment.

"Not until you're dry," Cheevy says. "Hypothermia isn't any better."

I open my mouth, close it, then take another drink. It's selfish of me, but I really don't want to part with the warmth, not with water still dripping from my tightly braided hair, leaking trails down my collarbone and shoulders. Patting the ground, I reach for an avra vine then bite into it, the dark red liquid seeping into my mouth. I drip it into the tea—just enough to help me sleep, to forget about Sarvenna's fingers on my throat. The liquid turns a familiar shade of crimson, just as it did when Fenris used it to poison me.

Back then, I'd never think to consume it willingly.

"I wouldn't do that," Cheevy warns.

"I can't sleep without it," I say. "And I need to sleep if I'm going to be useful tomorrow."

He looks like he might object, but Chest Wound cuts him off. "What's wrong with it?"

"If it's an avra vine, nothing," Cheevy says. "If it's rylock, it'll fuck her up worse than that Hunter would have. Shit's toxic as fuck. Julian doesn't let us take the risk."

"But Julian isn't here," I say. "And I know how to identify between the two. I've used it before." I bring the liquid to my lips and pause, letting the now sweet steam into my nostrils. "If you need me to run more patrols, I won't drink it, but I'm not sure how helpful I'll be in a fight."

"If you're sure it's avra, take it," Cheevy says. "Torvin and I can handle patrols. We'll wake you in the morning."

I arch a brow. "You sure?"

They nod, and I down the rest of the drink in a single gulp, hissing in pleasure. Wooziness settles into the very marrow of my bones, and I let myself fall back, curling into the soft mat of vines, using them to cushion me against the coarse gravel below. The starlight blurs together as I trace the Great Three just like Dad taught me.

Corova.

Sarinya.

Precipi.

No longer do I dream of escaping there, to a world free of elgrew. Why dream of that when I can exterminate them here myself?

XXIX. Arden

"An elgrew's bite is a perversion of what the wood nymph's bite used to be. Prior to their extinction, it is believed the forest fae were monogamous and bit their mates to show possession. Little is known about the rituals associated with biting, or about their sexual selection in general, but it is widely believed mates were attracted to one another by a force outside their control—possibly pheromones."

—Yaklan of Kariss, Karesai of Stitchers
Classified Research Notes

I stand in a dark forest, the trees made of shadow, the dirt so black it looks like tar. There are no stars in the sky or traces of moonlight, despite the clouds being absent. Charred petals crunch beneath my bare feet, ash and soot staining them as I walk. Up ahead, a boy crouches over something, crying, sobbing. The despair is so great, it makes my heart clench in a way it hasn't since I lost Mom and Dad.

"Why are you crying?" I ask.

He doesn't answer. He doesn't hear me.

The boy's body is paler than most elves—and then I realize he's not *an elf at all. Thin silver thread connects his skin together. He's shirtless and bony, nearly starved by the looks of it. Long silver hair sweeps over his shoulders, concealing the thing he's leaning over. The boy doesn't notice me as I approach—too consumed in his grief.*

I kneel beside him and touch his shoulder. He jumps then stares at me through dark-rimmed violet eyes. I see it now. Cradled in his hands are the ashen remains of a corpse. A gust of wind comes and blows the ashes away, leaving his blackened hands empty.

"Who was it?" I ask. I can feel his pain as if it were my own, and it's unbearable.

"My uncle." The boy sniffles and wipes at his eyes. "They killed him and made me watch." He stares into the distance, where the shadows part to reveal a silver city made of stone and blood—my people's blood. "I'm scared I'm next. If they find out what I've done . . . If I can't perform tomorrow . . ."

The boy throws his arms around me, and I hug back, the warmth of his body spreading into mine. The bite mark on my hand throbs. "It's ok," I whisper. "I'm scared of them, too."

"Arden?" He pinches his brows together in confusion, blinking as he realizes who I am. "How are you here? Why—"

Our surroundings shift and suddenly we're in the underground, beneath the glowing opalescence of the Korring-Marr. Green glowflies blink around us, but the priests and priestesses are all gone. Everyone is. The only sound comes from the Great Tree, but I doubt the elgrew boy can hear its gentle hum, its soothing melody.

We stand in a nutrient pool, my back pressing against one of the Korring-Marr's nine trunks, our reflections rippling in the dark, steaming water. I look different now. My breasts are fuller, my legs longer. Freckles dot a face that's far too pretty to belong to me and yet . . .

"Gods, you're so fucking beautiful," the elgrew boy says.

His body morphs in front of me, becoming thicker, stronger, lithe and tall, and fuck, he has to be the most attractive fae I've ever seen, even with the stitchwork. A strong jawline frames his sharp-angled face. His lips are full, his violet eyes piercing. Every part of him commands authority, like he could put me in my place with a simple word, a single touch. A bone diadem sits atop the elgrew's long silver hair, and I know without asking it's made from the bones of my people.

A shiver cascades down my spine, but I don't pull away. Brain foggy, I can't remember why I'm supposed to. He feels safe to me. He feels like home.

"What happened?" the man asks, bending to look at me. His touch is gentle as he grabs my chin and tilts, exposing the bruised column of my neck. "Who did this to you?"

I open my mouth, then close it. I can't remember.

For the first time, alarm bells ring inside my head—we're not supposed to be here. He's not allowed to see the Tree—but it's quickly soothed when the man tucks a strand of hair behind my pointed eartip and leans forward. He smells like citrus and leather. Not the macabre stench of blood or rancid meat that follows most Hunters. I breathe him in, stomach fluttering in this strange, unfamiliar way. Like it's full of butterflies.

"I wish it were you tomorrow," he says, his voice a low growl. The man's breath is hot against my sensitive eartip, sending tingles down my spine. Something hard and warm presses into my thigh, and I try not to think about what it is, even as my body nudges closer, craving the friction, the heat.

"I can't wait to bite you again. To taste you." He grazes his teeth along the curve of my ear, and I melt into him, whimpering when his hands sink lower to squeeze my ass.

And then his lips are on mine.

My mouth parts as I take him in, head swirling. My pulse pounds in my chest, between my quivering thighs. The Hunter isn't gentle as he slides his tongue past my teeth, swallowing my moans, cupping my ass until all I can think about is . . .

More. I need more.

Sharp canines dig into my lower lip, and the taste of metal slicks our tongues, spills down my chin. The sting of it only makes it better, makes me weaker for him. My legs turn to jelly until I feel like I could melt into a puddle.

"Fuck, you taste even better than I remember." He licks into my mouth and groans in satisfaction. The man kisses with the full weight of his body, pushing me up against the Korring-Marr and pinning me there.

I never thought I'd like this, but gods, the way he's touching me . . .

"Don't stop," I say between jagged breaths. "Please."

"I don't intend to." He reaches for my palm, breaking the kiss long enough to find my pulsing, swollen bite mark. "Mine." Smirking, the Hunter brings my flesh to his lips and bites down hard, staring into my eyes as he pumps hot venom deep beneath the skin, marking me a second time just to prove he can.

I slide my fingers into his stolen, silky hair and moan his name. "Lyrick."

MY EYES SNAP OPEN.

Sweat drenches my body as I jolt from sleep, staring at the starry sky. I roll onto my belly and crawl over dewy vines and sharp stones to reach the Aegis River, barely registering the doused bonfire or the looks of apprehension Cheevy and Chest Wound shoot my way.

My mind is elsewhere.

I hugged him. I consoled him. I let him touch me.

Fuck, I think I'm going to be sick.

Sour bile climbs my throat and I lose my stomach at the water's edge, chunky red liquid spraying the coarse gravel, cool water soaking into my palms. My forearms tremble. My bite mark burns—the scar darker and more sensitive than it's ever been before. I can still feel his teeth on my skin, his wet tongue tangling with mine.

"What the fuck is wrong with me?" My face is pallid in the river's reflection—eyes sunken and cheeks flush with fever. But unlike in the dream, I still look like me. I've never been so Marr-damn relieved to see my small stature, even if moist hair clings to the back of my neck and every bone in my body fucking aches.

Stomach clenching, I heave again, remembering the way I *begged* him to keep going—like some horny new recruit. No better than Cheevy and Chest Wound. Worse than them because he's elgrew, because he thinks he *owns* me. More bile. The current carries some of it downstream, but the foul and bitter stench still fills the air.

My mind showed him the Korring-Marr. It put everything at risk.

The gravel crunches as Cheevy approaches, then kneels beside me. "Arden, are you alright?"

He rubs soothing circles into my upper back, holding my hair as I heave again and again until there's nothing left. I don't have the strength to tell him to fuck off, so I let him, moisture blurring my vision as everything inside me lies outside in a messy splatter.

"I'm fine," I croak, wiping my eyes. "It's nothing."

"Rylock vines," Cheevy whispers. "I knew it."

"It's not rylock." I start to argue, but then my head swims. I fall backward, vaguely aware of Cheevy lifting me, carrying me back to the unlit campfire. My head lolls, too Marr-damn heavy to lift, and the rest of me isn't any better. It's like weights have been tied to my ankles and wrists. Something cool and moist presses against my forehead as I drift in and out of consciousness.

"What do we do if she's like this tomorrow?" Chest Wound

asks, his voice fading as my eyelids flutter shut. "The plan hinges on her."

"We pray she's better by morning."

"And if she isn't?"

There's a long pause. "Then we pray she can work through the pain."

Letters

All government offices and private businesses are to close in conjunction with Kariss's annual Ring Day celebration. Any slaves who require supervision will be welcomed into our temporary storage facilities located at the Butcher's Block. All monetary transactions that occur outside of the arena will be met with a hefty fine.

—Holiday Proclamation: the Grand Overseer, City of Kariss

XXX. Lyrick

"A Karesai's appointment is not guaranteed. At the inauguration, if a member of their caste finds the candidate lacking, they may challenge them in combat. If the candidate wins, they join the Politic. If they fail, they die. Although this tradition is long-standing, it is rarely witnessed. Only four Karesai have been challenged before, and only one has failed."

—A Brief History of the Traditions and Customs in Kariss

I don't have to be here—in this glassy, sunlit palanquin that reeks of the feminine oils Chalk used to wear. I could be in the forest hunting Arden, sinking my teeth into her supple flesh like I did in last night's dream. Venom pools in the back of my throat at the prospect, my cock twitching to life. And I curse myself for it.

I'm not attracted to those creatures.

That dream meant nothing.

Our kiss wasn't real.

But I can still taste her tangy blood on my tongue, can feel her pulse flutter at my touch. *Mine.* Every inch of Arden belongs to me, and fuck, were I not a better man, I might take advantage of that. Use her. Breed her. Take her as the myrie my father's always wanted.

But I'm not a sadist. I'm not like him.

"What are you thinking about?" Azerin asks. He sits across from me in the palanquin, on soft blue cushions the same shade as Arden's flesh. The warm sunlight gleams in his silver-amethyst eyes, illuminating an indigo suit that's freshly pressed. Like me, he wears a crown atop his head, but this one is metallic and blue, made from cold iron, extracted by the slaves he keeps.

We're too close to one another. Sitting crisscross and face-to-face, our knees nearly brush.

"I'm thinking about the inauguration," I lie.

He sees right through me. "Not the breeding ceremony after?"

Azerin arches a brow, and I lean back, folding my arms over my swamp dog armor—the tunic clinging to me like a second skin. "I'll do what needs to be done."

Thankfully, I sound more confident than I feel.

"Brawler is a good match for you," he says. "And it's just for tonight. Once she's pregnant, you won't have to touch her again."

"I know." My lips form a hard line, a vein pulsing in my jaw. Outside, orangeleaf trees rustle in the breeze. Grasses bend and flatten as Prowler weaves through them, following at our side— he'll give up soon. My verncat never crosses the city walls.

Our palanquin dips and bobs with the slaves' choppy movements, and I half-expect Azerin to lecture them, but he's thoroughly distracted, staring out the glassy panes as well.

"What are *you* thinking about?" I counter. It's rare to speak with him alone—no babes, or myrie, or Karesai to intrude. When I was a child, he'd always make time for me—the way he'll no doubt make time for Tyla now—but it's been years since we had any extended privacy.

For a long while, Azerin says nothing—the silence punctuated by the slaves' thudding footsteps and the palanquin's groaning metal frame.

"Sorso. He's going to be a problem for us." Azerin strokes his chin in the glass's reflection, not turning to face me as we approach the city's towering silver walls. Half as many Butchers as normal pace the ramparts, their arrows fixed on the forest. As predicted, my verncat halts at the portcullis, resting on his haunches as we pass through the darkened tunnel.

"Giving him Chalk was a bandage, not a solution," Azerin adds.

"I don't get it," I say. "I didn't rape his myrie—he has to know that by now." Much to my annoyance, Colette's made a point of telling every Karesai what happened at the training house. "Fuck, when Conrin tried to put his hands on her, I'm the one who stopped it. Sorso's a lunatic."

We emerge on the other side of the glittering, bloodstained walls into a city half-abandoned. Empty storefronts. Deserted sidewalks. By now, almost everyone will be in the arena, finding seats and placing bets with Bracers.

"Do you know how our species came to be?" Azerin asks.

My brows furrow. "Where are you going with this?"

"Answer the question."

"We were originally the offspring of wood nymphs and elves. Why?"

"Because we inherited traits from both species. The bite, for example—that's a wood nymph trait. We use it to keep tabs on our pets, but to wood nymphs, biting was seen as an intimate act between monogamous pairs—mates, they called it."

"And what does this have to do with Sorso?"

My father lifts his hand, silencing me. "Mating pairs were incredibly rare. Yaklan's research suggests they were drawn together like magnets. The bite could link them emotionally, mentally, and physically. Sometimes, we experience that too.

Yaklan with Vera. Me with your incubator. Sorso with Spirit. It's not romantic. It's possessive and consuming and clouds our judgment."

I swallow. *Mate. Arden. Mine.*

It feels so right. Like an answer to a question that I didn't know to ask.

The words threaten to flow out of me, but I hold them back and wait for my father to finish parsing through his thoughts. No one ever speaks of the wood nymphs—not since we exterminated them a millennium ago. And I know, without him ever having to say it, this is a conversation that can't be repeated outside of the Politic. Somehow, for some reason, they've managed to hide the existence of these bonds from the general public.

"It's difficult to explain a mate to someone who hasn't had one before, but when someone else touches them—marks them —it's unforgivable. Sorso will keep coming for you, and you need to be prepared for that. I'm concerned he'll have something planned for the inauguration."

I snort. "Sorso's not a Hunter. He can't challenge me in the arena. And he's not stupid enough to plot an assassination."

"Don't underestimate him, Lyrick. He's a dangerous enemy to have."

"Yeah, well, so am I."

THE UNWASHED MASSES gather outside the arena for blocks, the crowds overflowing onto rooftops, alleyways, and the main thoroughfare. Most are purple skinned, but a few grays try to elbow their way to the entrances and get shoved back like anybody else. On Ring Day, arena seats are first come, first serve —no longer divvied up by caste.

Unlike the Gambling Block, the crowd parts for our palanquin—for the Grand Overseer. My father basks in the attention, waving to his subjects and grinning wide. They cheer for him, perhaps for me as well, and a nervous lump settles in my gut. Still, I force the obligatory smile to my face and mirror my father. They're my subjects too, whether I want it or not.

Dirty, deformed faces smush against the glass, trying to get a better look at us. Children's lumpy hands press up to mine, smudging the panes in snot and gods know what else. All around us, green confetti floats from the sky—remnants of betting slips that land on the litter, on the pavement, and on the slaves who carry our palanquin. Our elves are the only elves in sight—all the others will be in daycare centers at the Butcher's Block, so spectators can take the day off without risking an uprising.

We keep a slow but steady pace toward the arena's entrances, giving everyone a chance to greet us. Mixed-skinned Bracers pace along the perimeter, clad in fighting leathers, hefting wicker baskets filled to the brim with betting slips. Peasants approach them, shoving more in, losing even more money to my father's rigged game.

Idiots.

"You should enjoy this," Azerin says through his smile—serrated teeth on full display. "This is the perk of being a leader. They worship you."

But I don't want to be worshipped. I want to be free.

I keep those thoughts to myself as we pass beneath one of the arena's grand arches. The Butchers guarding it, holding back the crowd, part for us without so much as a command. My father rarely needs to order anything. They anticipate his movements. They exalt him as if he were a god. Three hundred years of leadership and he might as well be one. Generations of elgrew have come and gone, but my father remains as young and powerful as ever, thanks to the Stitchers. The purples will be lucky to survive to forty. A consequence of their malformed bodies and failing organs.

"Talin would be proud of you," Azerin whispers, low enough to be unheard above the roar of the crowd. "I wish he could be here to see it."

I try to swallow the ball of emotion wedged inside my throat but can't. *Me too.*

Head held high, I remind myself of the crown I'm wearing and who I took it from. Korun is dead, and now I'm in charge. A fanatic. A heretic. For the first time all morning, a genuine smile spreads from ear to ear. Talin *would* be proud—of that, I'm absolutely certain.

"A-zer-in! A-zer-in! A-zer-in!" The arena booms with the force of our people's chanting.

Eighty thousand elgrew fill every seat, the heat of the afternoon sun boring down on them, baking their skins until they're sheeny with sweat. Malformed children wave sports paraphernalia high into the air—plushies shaped like biceps, flower crowns made from kissy lips, ceramic teeth, and a dozen other objects to represent their favorite fighters. There are so many purples, I have to squint to find the grays.

Our slaves carry us to the heart of the arena through a cold-iron gate that has their muscles quivering and the box rattling, but they don't let us drop—not even when their eyes bleed. Well trained, just like all my father's pets. I don't want to think about what would happen to them if they failed him, especially in public like this.

Five thrones sit in the center of the arena's dusty field—each one filled with members of the Politic. In front of them lies a silver ceremonial altar, a blue velvet box atop it. Yaklan smiles at me, waving as we approach, but the other Karesai look on, their gazes fixed on the crowd. The corner of Sorso's lumpy, calloused mouth twitches up into a smirk—or maybe it doesn't—the look is there and gone so fast, I can barely register it.

Still, it has my palms sweating, my spine tensing. *Mate.*

How would I feel if our roles were reversed? If *he* bit Arden? Sunk his filthy canines beneath her flesh and pinned her to the ground while she begged him to stop?

Every inch of me screams in protest, nostrils flaring, jaw clenching. And I know then, my father is right. There can be no peace between us—not as long as my mark mars his myrie's flesh. A myrie who's notably absent.

The palanquin dips and groans as the slaves lower it onto the ground, opening the door to the litter with bulging, bloodshot eyes. Glittering silver liquid streams down their cheeks, mouths, and ears, but they don't show any outward signs of pain. The slaves avert their gazes as they offer hands to Azerin and assist him from the box. As he exits, he makes a show of licking the blood from one of their faces, which gains a fresh wave of applause from our spectators.

My still-full stomach convulses.

This place is fucked. These people and their morals are beyond saving.

A slave offers me their hand, but I slap it away. "Don't touch me," I hiss, climbing out on my own. The dust and dirt swirl up around me, and my military boots slip on the shifting ground. Blinking the grit from my eyes, I fight the urge to slink beside Yaklan and straighten my shoulders instead, joining my father at the gleaming silver altar.

Wordlessly, Azerin holds out his hand, and a Bracer scurries onto the field, passing him a sound amplification mask. With a bow, she exits, taking the slaves with her.

"Welcome to our nine hundred and twenty-seventh Ring Day celebration!" Azerin booms, affixing the brightly painted wooden mask to his face. It resembles a verncat head, its sabre-tooth jaws opened wide. Sharp whistles and a round of thunderous applause pierce my ears from every direction. Azerin waits for the crowd to settle before continuing.

"Before the games begin, you all have the honor of witnessing the inauguration of our newest Karesai of Hunters," he says, voice radiating authority. "I give you Lyrick of Kariss, my eldest son. Four hundred and thirteen captures. Over two hundred kills. He has led dozens of successful hunting parties. I can think of no one more qualified—and the Politic agrees."

Behind me, someone snorts. I can only guess it's Sorso, but the clapping drowns him out—the crowd oblivious to the inner turmoil within my father's council.

Azerin clasps both of my shoulders and pulls me close. For a moment, there is no arena, no crowd, no Karesai. Just us. "This is the happiest day of my life," he whispers, throat bobbing, eyes glassy. "It's everything I've ever wanted for you."

He smiles at me like I'm not a disgrace to my species. Like I'm *worthy*. And for the first time in my life, I start to believe it.

"Lyrick, do you swear allegiance to Kariss and to all the elgrew within it?" he asks, projecting his voice once more.

"I do."

"Do you swear to—"

"You're getting ahead of yourself," Sorso says.

A shiver runs down my spine despite the heat.

Slowly, the Karesai of Butchers rises from his cold-iron throne—blue metal creaking. His lumpy thighs jiggle with each step toward the altar and the ground quakes beneath him. The crowd goes deadly silent—so silent we could hear a pin drop as Sorso leans over the altar, black apron fluttering in the breeze, black suit dusty brown from the arena's floor.

And then that smirk is back. Bigger this time. Bolder. His clubbed lip looks like it's trying to tear free of his mouth.

Rifling through his apron pockets, Sorso procures his own amplification mask—the face of a screaming elf, silver blood-stains streaming from its eyeholes. He straps it to his face and clears his throat. "Tradition dictates before an inauguration, the candidate's worthiness must be tested against the opinions of his peers. Hunters, I ask, do *you* find him worthy? Lyrick of Kariss is Talin's sole apprentice—put to death for treason. Will you follow the orders of a traitor's pupil?"

Beside me, my father's hands curl into fists. "This is highly inappropriate," he hisses. "No one has challenged an appointment in almost a century."

"There's a first time for everything," Sorso murmurs.

Everyone in the arena glances back and forth at one another, waiting, watching. It's too crowded to recognize anyone from my caste, but I know they're there. Hundreds of them. Maybe thousands.

My stomach drops when the arena gate yawns open and a familiar face steps forward. "I watched your uncle burn. Now, I'll watch you too. I will challenge the appointment."

Standing in front of me is Morcai, and behind him, his son— *Conrin.*

XXXI. Lyrick

**"In the year 119 A.T. (After Takeover), the Politic was unable
to agree upon a Karesai of Bracers. Two selections were made,
and rather than debate the merits of each candidate, the Grand
Overseer allowed them to challenge one another in the
fighting pits—winner take the crown. Praig of Kariss emerged
victorious; now his granddaughter, Ryla, holds the seat."**

—A Brief History of the Traditions and Customs in Kariss:
An Addendum.

uck. Me.

I gaze up, and up, and up at the behemoth of a man in front of me. Morcai is all but unrecognizable save for his face. Muscles stack on top of muscles until he more closely resembles a mountain than a gray. But he *is* gray. No purple scars. No missing flesh. Someone's surgically enhanced him into this . . . *thing.*

Shirtless, Morcai's biceps ripple as he folds his arms over his chest, smirking down at me like I'm a puny insect about to be squashed. Conrin mirrors his father's movements and peers out from behind him—arms crossed, jaw set, choice made. Whatever remained of our friendship is no more.

"I see you visited the Stitchers," I say, swallowing to keep my voice steady. A Karesai shows no fear, especially not to lowlife scum like Morcai. "Shame you couldn't pay me when I came to collect."

Morcai's grin widens, exposing his serrated teeth. Sharp cold-iron caps cover them, barbs protruding from the surface. "Shame you couldn't burn with your uncle."

Fingers flexing, I narrow my eyes at him, and my father steps between us. If Azerin's worried for me, his expression doesn't show it. He remains the ever-confident leader, the unflappable, untouchable god our people know him to be. Smoothing down his suit jacket, he turns to Morcai, his wooden amplification mask still intact. "As tradition dictates, all challenges are to the death. Lyrick is armed and armored. We can provide you with—"

"I don't need shit." Morcai makes a point to crack each of his knuckles, then his neck. His newly bald scalp gleams with sweat. No hair to latch onto, to yank back. Mine blows in the wind, unbound, and it feels like a godsdamned death sentence. A set of ceremonial daggers and a thin layer of swamp dog hide isn't going to protect me against him, and we both know it.

My father clasps his hands behind his back. "Very well. We'll clear the field."

On cue, the Karesai exit the arena single file. Colette doesn't speak to me; she *humphs* instead, holding her nose in the air like this is all beneath her. Yaklan clasps my shoulder and wishes me luck, but luck won't save me here. I'm not sure anything will. How the Stitchers did this is beyond me. They must've found the strongest elves in all of Kariss to dissect, perhaps arena champions themselves. It would have cost a fortune—more than anything Conrin or Morcai or any Hunter could afford.

"Do you like it?" Sorso whispers, lifting his mask so we're

staring face-to-face. His breath is rancid, and I nearly vomit at the stench of rotting meat. "After your little stunt at the gambling hall, Morcai was more than happy to let my friends experiment with him. Yaklan may command the Stitchers, but I control their debts."

Of course.

Scrunching my nose, I stare him down. "Morcai's out of shape, Sorso. He hasn't hunted anything in almost two decades. You can't replace skill with brawn."

It sounds like false bravado because it is.

"See his knuckles?" Sorso asks. "Those are cold-iron spikes fused to his bones. One punch is all it'll take. I like my odds."

My gaze shifts to Morcai's hands and nausea knots my stomach. Sure enough, blue metal protrudes from the skin—barbed just like his tooth caps. Now that I'm looking for it, small metal spikes jut from other places as well. Forearms. Clavicles. Back. Most of them are needle-thin—almost invisible if they didn't glint in the afternoon sun. Touching him anywhere will shred my skin. It's an impossible fucking fight.

"Seems your appointment will be even shorter lived than Korun or Tenok's." And with that, Sorso joins Colette, linking arms with her just outside the cold-iron gate. Conrin marches after them, kicking up dust and dirt with every step. His eyes are steely, his thin lips pressed into a hard line as he leans over the railing in rapt attention.

In full sight of the crowd, Azerin pulls me to the side and cups my cheeks. The face mask hangs from a belt at his hips. "You will not die today. Do you understand me?"

"Dad, I can't—"

"You can," he growls. "Figure it out. You're smarter than Morcai and Sorso. If anyone can best them, it's you."

And then he shakes my hand, squeezing my palm and wrist in a two-handed embrace—the closest form of affection a man like him can offer me in public. He leans in close and whispers so lowly, I have to strain my ears to hear, "You're all I have left of her."

Before I can interpret what he said, let alone summon a response, Azerin separates himself from me and joins the others at the railing, leaving me alone in the arena with Morcai and Ryla—the Karesai of Bracers. This is *her* domain, not my father's. She alone commands the fighting pits. I've never spoken to Ryla one-on-one. Fuck, I've never even seen her without Colette at her side, so I can only guess who she's rooting for here.

Unlike the other Bracers, Ryla dresses in purple fighting leathers, not brown. Strapped to her back is a pair of throwing axes ready to be wielded at a moment's notice. Though her skin is mottled gray like Sarvenna's, her hair is a natural shade of lilac—pin straight and shiny in the sun. It's barely long enough to brush her shoulders.

She walks to the center of the field—or perhaps swagger is a better word for it. Ryla is all confidence as she fastens an amplification mask to her face and addresses the crowd. The mask is bright white, covered in charcoal glyphs that only Bracers can understand. "You're in for a rare treat today," she says. "Our candidate for Karesai has been challenged. In the aisles, my Bracers will be coming around with betting slips. Make sure you flag them before the fight begins."

A fucking money grab. For the love of—

"There will be a single round of combat. As always, biting remains a capital offense. All else is fair game. The fight ends only when one of you is dead. Try not to die." Ryla winks at me in this flirty, almost playful way, like my life doesn't hang in the fucking balance. I want to rip that eye from her skull and shove it down her fucking throat.

I grit my teeth instead.

"Both of you, come to the center of the field."

The ground shudders with Morcai's movements, his bare

feet leaving imprints in the dust. Wind whips my long hair into my eyes, my mouth, and I have to spit it out. Dry dirt sticks to my tongue as I sweep my hair back, then tilt my head to stare into the violet eyes of my opponent.

Something slips into my palm.

When I glance down, I see that Ryla has offered me a leather thong. She acts oblivious as I tie my hair into a bun—it's not much, but at least it'll keep me from getting blinded in the fight. I'm not stupid enough to thank her—to draw attention to her act of kindness. The last thing she needs is Sorso as an enemy too. But I nod in appreciation and she nods back, the action infinitesimally small. Unnoticeable to anyone not looking for it.

"Wait until I've exited the field. You'll begin when you hear my death whistle." Ryla rummages through her cuirass and procures the skull-shaped whistle, then she backs away—but not before snatching the crown from my head and taking it with her.

More dust billows around us, stinging my eyes, but I don't blink. Looking away, losing focus for just a second, is all it'll take to get me killed. But I'm fucked regardless. A million fighting strategies and sparring sessions roll through my head, each one nonviable. He's too big. It's too easy for him to rip me apart.

I'm going to die before I ever get to see her again.

Arden. Mine.

Suddenly, I'm back beneath that glowing tree, her lips parting for me. *Don't stop.*

Maybe it's better this way. I don't know if I *could* stop if I found her in person. After all, my morals meant nothing last night when I saw her for the first time in years, felt her softness, smelled her heat. I've never been attracted to elves before, but Arden—

The death whistle shrieks—shrill and sharp—catching me off guard. I roll out of the way of Morcai as he barrels toward me, then I dive for the metal altar. His fists are a blur as they fly through the air. Back flush against the hard, unforgiving frame, I shift a second before he slams home. Metal groans. A giant head-shaped indent appears on the altar's surface where my body was just moments before.

Shit.

Fuck.

Too godsdamned close.

Pushing Arden from my mind, I reassess. He's big but slow, weighed down by muscles he doesn't know how to use yet. I can gut him if I can get close enough. Unsheathing a blade at my hip, I charge forward, angling it toward his thick abdominals. The man catches me by the wrist and squeezes. Something crunches. The dagger clatters to the ground as I hiss in pain, clutching at a wrist that's bent at an unnatural angle.

Morcai throws his head back and laughs, deep and throaty. Then, he kicks my dagger out of the way. It goes sliding toward the railing, lost somewhere in the dust piles. My boots slip as I scurry away from another hit, barely dodging it in time. I unsheathe my other dagger, switching to my offhand, letting the broken one dangle uselessly at my side.

Block the pain. Focus on the fight.

It's easier said than done, but I manage to avoid two more blows.

Morcai rips a throne from the ground and flings it at me. It whizzes through the air and thumps to the ground less than a foot away. Heart hammering, I rush toward him again, readying my knife. I need to end him before he has time to land a hit. A single one will be fatal.

My palm burns in the same place I bit Arden. *Now's not the time.*

Ignoring the bond, I lunge. The blade slicks flesh, and purple blood beads to the surface, but Morcai shifts and I miss my mark, slicing through his forearm rather than something fatal. He reaches for my face, fingers smushing into both sides until it feels like my skull might burst. Sticky liquid runs down my skull. Blood spatters the dusty arena.

My body lifts from the ground, and I kick out with my feet, Morcai laughing the entire time. My boots make purchase with his stomach, but it's not enough. I slice at his already bleeding forearm, but it's still not enough.

My skull's going to cave in. It's —

"Throw the dagger," Arden hisses.

"But then I'll be weaponless."

"Marr-dammit, listen to me!"

Blindly, I fling my blade in the general direction of his body and Morcai drops me. Tinnitus has me gripping my ears, panting on all fours as my vision blurs. The pain in my skull is crippling. I barely have time to glance up, to watch Morcai pull the blade from his oozing side before he's readying another blow. Coughing, I clutch my aching head and stumble back to my feet, body swaying, legs wobbling. In the distance, the crowd cheers.

I prepare to strike again, knowing if I can't get to my dagger before he throws it, this is all for nothing. Weaponless, I don't stand a chance.

"Stop!" Arden's voice rings in my head—a loud plea that has me freezing in place. Morcai uses the time to chuck my weapon alongside the other one, removing it from combat.

"Fuck," I hiss. *"Get out of my head. You're going to get me killed."*

"Do you remember when I hunted that swamp dog?" she asks. Arden doesn't wait for me to answer. *"When you're outmatched physically, you have to wear them down first. Stop going on offense. Tire him out, then go for the kill when he's not expecting it."*

It's sage advice. Plus, I'm out of options.

When Morcai comes for me, I let it happen, ducking and dodging each hit. Lungs burning, I dance with him—meeting his movements with an opposite, defensive one. It's nothing like my normal fighting style, but it works. I'm in better shape, and his movements are clumsy. The more he strikes, the slower he gets, the more labored his breaths become until we're both slippery with sweat, both struggling for air.

But I know how to work while exhausted. I've been doing it for years.

Body swaying, eyes drooping, Morcai looks like he's about to pass out. That's when I headbutt the bastard. Growling, I slam myself against him as hard as I physically can, and he stumbles back, landing ass first on the arena ground. The dust plumes up around him, and I climb on top, grappling him, aiming for his neck. My good hand slips on his body, struggling to find purchase. Metal barbs sink into my skin and shred it, lodging splinters deep inside tissue and flesh, but I don't let up.

Morcai reaches for my bun; it's all too easy to evade. Ignoring the blood, the broken bones, the fucking splinters in my skin, I shove my forearm against his throat and push. He sputters for breath. His meaty fist strikes my side and more bones crunch, but the armor stops the spikes from killing me. His face turns lilac, then dark purple. His cheeks puff up and eyes bulge.

When he's too exhausted to fight me, I lean down and lower my voice. "You were right," I whisper. "All those years ago when you accused me of killing your lover."

He whimpers in pain, and the sound fills me with euphoric bliss.

"You think Talin was bad? I promise you, I'm much worse."

Mouth open, he snaps at me with those metal jaws in a desperate ploy to win. But we're well past that. "I'm going to skin you again—not because I have to, but because I can."

I wait for the bastard to pass out before I find my ceremonial blade, scooping it from the dirt. Then, I lean over him, grinning at the crowd as I carve every bit of skin from his body—this time starting at the scalp. The spectators chant my name, "Lye-rick,

Lye-rick, Lye-rick," as I slice through connective tissue and tendon, drowning out his pleas. Sticky blood saturates the ground, clumping in the dirt. It sprays into my eyes and stains my armor. Muscles aching, hands shaking, I keep going, spurred by adrenaline to finish the job.

No one fucks with me or my family.

Groaning, I finally yank the last bit of flesh free from his muscles, then bundle it into my sweat-slicked arms. By now, Morcai's long stopped breathing and the crowd's gone quiet. Everyone stares at me in horror—eyes wide, mouths open, whispers floating through the arena aisles. Ignoring the other Kare-sai, I drop the flesh at Sorso's feet where it lands with a heavy splat.

Chest heaving, I sneer up at him. "I believe this belongs to you."

And then I limp to my godsdamned throne and take my seat.

XXXII. Lyrick

"All Karesai are imbued with the *ichor of life*, separating and elevating them from the rest of their caste. Origins unknown, the substance interferes with our species' senses, stripping the Karesai of their chemical cues and heat signatures. Additionally, it is known to heighten the potency of their venom, creating a temporary but often euphoric effect in the elves they Claim. To be bestowed the ichor is a great honor—one that comes with a lifetime promise to serve and protect our city. Those who abandon their posts are swiftly executed."

—A BRIEF HISTORY OF THE TRADITIONS AND CUSTOMS OF KARISS

"This might hurt a bit." Yaklan grabs my wrist and twists, resetting the bone with a nasty crunch. I grit my teeth to keep from crying out, but a groan still slips free. "It should be functional by the party tonight, but be gentle with it over the next few days. Keep it in a sling if you can."

I know how broken bones work. I bite back the retort, knowing

Yaklan is neither the cause of my ire nor does he deserve to be a recipient of it.

Bent over me, he fastens a silk sling around my shoulder and tightens it, securing the broken bone to my chest. We're not like elves—they take weeks, sometimes months to recover from an injury like this. So long as I don't do anything stupid, I'll be back to full fighting shape by the end of the week. Maybe sooner.

From his white apron pocket, Yaklan procures a needle and spool of silver thread. "I'll fix the minor injuries before any scar tissue can form, but you'll need to visit me later to skin graft the rest."

With nimble fingers, he gets to work, shoving that needle deep beneath the flesh. I wince but say nothing as he tugs the skin back into place—first at my temples, then my hands. In my periphery, Azerin's slaves struggle to clean up Morcai's body—rather, what remains of it. They roll the muscly, oozing lump onto an ornate blanket far nicer than anything that bastard deserves and scoop the blood-dirt slurry from the ground with a duster and a broom. Plumes of dirt conceal Azerin's and Sorso's faces from view as they whisper-argue with one another, too quiet to be heard above the chattering buzz of arena spectators.

Yaklan pauses, following my line of sight to the both of them. "You'll still be initiated," he says. "Sorso is a man of his word—I'm going to treat the bigger wounds as best I can. I'm sorry it'll look so crude, but my skills are limited outside of the surgery centers."

He stuffs the spool away and switches it for a pouch of ossi dust. Touch gentle, Yaklan smooths the ashy substance over my face, palms, and neck—any part of exposed flesh Morcai's metal spurs shredded. The smaller cuts—the ones he managed to stitch—tighten into the seamless patchwork that covers the rest of me. The larger ones don't. Purple skin sprouts from gaping sections of exposed muscle, and I curl my lip at how fucking hideous it is.

I look no better than the peasants.

Yaklan apologizes again—like he's the cause of these disgusting fucking injuries. "I'll get you into the center tomorrow. I'm certain I can find an elf that matches the rest."

I sigh—long and deep. Tomorrow is a long fucking time to look like this. Any length of time is. I haven't had to see my natural flesh in years, and it makes my hackles rise. Pushing down my anger, I shoo him away. "It's fine."

Standing, he dusts his apron off, but it does no good. Both it and his matching white suit are speckled with amethyst blood. As if realizing this himself, Yaklan frowns down at the outfit before claiming his throne beside me—made of cold iron like all the others. Colette and Ryla lean over their armrests, chattering away to one another, making grand gestures with their hands and smiling, completely oblivious to the argument Sorso and Azerin are locked in.

As the slaves heft Morcai's corpse from the ground, a dozen Bracers follow them out of the arena gate, toward the exit. Conrin's no longer standing at the railing, though I never saw him leave.

"We continue as planned," Azerin says, returning to the four of us. Sorso's nostrils flare, the metal throne groaning as he plants himself atop it. But he doesn't argue, just glares at me with those dark violet eyes, as if doing so could turn me to dust.

I flash him a toothy grin and a crude gesture. "Your myrie put up a bigger fight against me."

My father pinches the bridge of his nose and groans. He doesn't need to say anything for me to guess what he's thinking. *Why are you like this?*

I repress the chuckle bubbling up my throat and lean back in my seat as Sorso dark-knuckles his armrests. Reaching into his suit jacket, Azerin retrieves the small blue-velvet box that had been on the altar before my challenge. He returns it there—though it lies unevenly on the fist-sized dent Morcai left behind.

Returning the amplification mask to his face, my father addresses the crowd once more, facing away from us.

"Does anyone else wish to challenge Lyrick of Kariss?"

The arena falls deadly silent.

A moment passes.

Two.

No one looks at one another this time. They're all afraid of me.

As they should be.

I can't stop the smug smirk from curling my face, the pride burgeoning in my chest. It'll take more than a few hundred pounds of muscle to take me out. And now anyone who tries knows what consequences they risk.

"Very well," Azerin says. "Lyrick, please join me once more at the altar."

I stand from my seat, my sweat-soaked clothing crunching in the spots it dried. Exhausted, my knees threaten to buckle, but I force myself forward, head held high. Once again, Azerin clasps my shoulders, and once again we begin reciting the vows.

"Do you swear allegiance to Kariss and to all the elgrew within it?"

"I do."

"Do you swear to represent your caste fairly and honestly? To uphold the traditions of the Karesai who have come before you?"

"I do."

Azerin glances to the crowd then back to me, his silver-violet eyes as serious as they've ever been. "Are you aware that this is a lifetime appointment and that the punishment for abandoning your duties or breaking your oaths is death?"

For the first time today, a wave of unease, *uncertainty*, washes over me. But this is what Talin would have wanted. It's what my father and Yaklan want. It's the only way to right the wrongs of my caste. Saying I have no choice—while it wouldn't be correct

—certainly feels that way. I was born to rule, trained for it because I'm the only one strong enough, brave enough, and smart enough to fix things.

"I am." My mouth turns to sandpaper, the finality of my decision creeping in. Swallowing, I rub my slick palms against my swamp dog slacks. The action stings, and I'm all but certain there's metal splinters still wedged beneath the skin. It'll take weeks for my pores to excise them, and until then, everything's going to be painfully sore.

Azerin smiles at me. "Very well."

He reaches for the velvet box and unhooks the latch, throwing it open to reveal a glass syringe filled with metallic black liquid. The substance swirls. Faint tints of purple and green then blue and red appear, then vanish into the mix. Azerin lifts the syringe from the box and flashes it to the crowd. "This is the *ichor of the gods*. With it, we shall initiate him into the Politic. Lyrick, please take a seat."

He pats the altar, and I struggle atop it, my broken ribs aching in protest. I stare at the strange liquid, transfixed. Its origins are as much a mystery to me as they are to the spectators. Perhaps the only one who knows what it is and where it comes from is Azerin himself.

"This will sting," he warns.

Azerin rolls my flexible, long-sleeved armor up to the bicep. Withdrawing a rubber string from his pocket, he ties it around my upper arm and pulls tight, pinching the skin until my pulse throbs. Then he grabs the syringe, points the giant fucking needle in the air, and flicks the sides of the glass to check for air bubbles. Once he's certain there are none, he depresses the plunger until a small amount of that viscous black liquid oozes out.

It smells like liquid smoke, except sweeter—with hidden notes of sour fruit and decaying tree bark. Under normal circumstances, putting *that* inside me would be a nonstarter. But all Karesai undergo the ritual, and I'm all too aware of the power it bestows. No heat signatures. No chemical cues. The ability to slip through the night, unseen by our species' pit organs.

A thick purple vein throbs at the juncture of my forearm. Azerin jabs the needle in and pours the liquid inside me. There's a sharp pinch, followed by the sensation of heavy sludge crawling through my veins. It's uncomfortable, but not as bad as I thought it would—

Shit.

Icy heat spreads everywhere.

It scorches everything.

I stave off a scream as fire licks through my ribcage and curls around my heart, squeezing, burning. Black dots flicker at the edges of my vision and salty liquid rolls down my cheeks. As Azerin removes the syringe and sets it on the altar beside me, he whispers low in my ear, "Do not cry out. You are a Hunter. You will endure."

"Lyrick? What's happening?" Arden's voice again. I push her out, unable to answer, unable to explain. Clenching my hands into tight fists, I writhe in silence as the white-hot pain consumes me. Everything that I am is being stripped away, replaced with something else, something *other.* There's not enough ya'esen in the world to drown this feeling out.

My teeth vibrate as venom drains to the back of my throat— the taste sweeter than normal, the texture thicker. My muscles spasm involuntarily, twitching with an unseen electric current. Minutes pass—or maybe it's seconds—but it feels like an eternity before the intensity ebbs, leaving behind veins and muscle and sinew that have been stripped raw.

It's all I can do to hold my head up, to keep it from lolling.

"How do you feel?" Azerin asks, still too low for the spectators to hear.

"Like someone pulled all the veins from my body and made me jump rope with them."

He chuckles. "Focus. Breathe."

I wipe the moisture from my eyes and do as he says, breathing slowly, deeply. When I glance out into the arena, everything looks . . . *Fuck. It's so godsdamned beautiful.*

The world is sharper, clearer. I can smell everything. Wet ink from the Bracers' betting slips. The crisp paper it's written on. Smoked meats from food carts just outside the arena—savory and sweet, covered in a creamy curry sauce. A block away, a sharp chemical stench lingers outside what can only be the surgery center. Miles from that, must and rain crawl from the rainforest as if the orangeleaf trees press right against my nose. It's . . . incredible. It's overwhelming.

"Now, open your pit organs," Azerin commands.

I hesitate. There's a reason we don't use our pit organs during the day. They don't work—at least, not very well. The ambient air is too hot, making everything appear the same shade of bright white. It's a fucking tripping hazard.

Still, I oblige him.

The tiny pores near my tear ducts expand, and like usual, the stadium, the sky, the dirt in front of me become indistinguishably pale—almost invisible. But then I see what he's talking about. In place of the arena spectators are glowing auras—all different, all unique—with shades of color I've never seen before. Without ever having to bite them, I can distinguish each person from the next in a way that goes beyond sight or smell or temperature.

The only elgrew who remain a blank slate are the other members of the Politic.

My skull throbs at the sensory overload, and I force my pit organs shut, head drooping, sweat sticking the hair to my face. When Azerin offers me his hand, I take it. No sooner does he yank me to my feet that his arm's slung over my shoulders as he addresses the crowd. "Citizens of Kariss, I present to you your Karesai of Hunters!"

In the stands, the Bracers, Trainers, and Stitchers bow in unison. But the Hunters raise their blades and slash them across their palms in a show of respect. It's an ancient custom to signal that they would do anything for me—bleed for me, die for me— I need only say the word.

It's a giddy feeling, having so much power.

A broad smile spreads across my cheeks. I unsheathe the ceremonial dagger at my side and repeat the gesture back to my people. Because they *are* my people, flaws and all, and I meant my oaths. Most of them, anyway.

Cheering breaks out amongst the crowd. They shred green betting slips into tiny squares and toss them into the air, littering the aisles with confetti. And for the first time in my life, I feel like I belong.

XXXIII

The Championship

"Kariss's cold-iron reserves were discovered in the year 114 B.T. (Before Takeover) and have been largely attributed to our species' success. As the oldest, largest mine in Rayna, it has been expanded and maintained for nearly a millennium via the construction of underground dams. Flooding in the region is channeled to the Turquoise Lake, and excess water is pumped out manually every day. In 609 A.T., the dams were reinforced after a flooding event killed seventeen Butchers and one hundred and thirteen slaves."

—A Brief History of the Settlement of Kariss, Mining Production

Stolen by General Ustas at the failed invasion of Visha.

ARDEN

A crowd of elgrew swarm me, and someone places a bony diadem atop my head—not mine, *his*. They set him on a throne of cold iron that has my teeth chattering, my bones aching. Or maybe that's the poison. I can't tell what's real anymore—what's happening to Lyrick versus what's happening to me. Orange leaves flutter around me, then green confetti, then orange leaves again. The forest whirls as lumpy and twisted elgrew flash their razor-like smiles in my direction.

"Arden?" The sound of Cheevy's voice pulls me into the moment. Groaning, I force my million-pound head to rise from the itchy grasses—or maybe it's the dusty ground. A crease line forms between his brows, his hand brushing against my too-hot forehead. "Shit, you're burning up."

I saved Lyrick. I had the chance to watch him die and I intervened. Why?

Was that even real?

Is anything?

I shake so hard I brush up against Cheevy. But as I claw my way into a crawling position, the only thing I can think about is those stupid fucking vines. "It wasn't rylock," I rasp, my throat burning, the taste of sweet venom washing over it. "I know my poisons."

He doesn't believe me. I'm not sure *I* believe me either. Breathlessness. Fever. Nausea. All classic symptoms of rylock poisoning. But Cheevy at least has the grace—or maybe it's the common sense—not to say I told you so. Instead, he runs a cool compress over my forehead, my cheeks, the back of my neck. But the cool water offers little relief, heating as soon as it touches my skin.

In Lyrick's cold-iron throne, elvish slaves carry us up dozens of steps that lead to a balcony overlook, the dusty arena spraying dirt everywhere. Silver blood drains from the elves' eyes, ears, and mouths. Their muscles wobble.

Eyes watering, I cough, hacking up blue bile onto Cheevy's lap.

A high-pitched whistle threatens to burst my eardrums. *Fuck, it hurts.*

"It doesn't matter what it was," Cheevy says. He runs the

compress underneath my eyes and it comes back splotchy blue. "Tell me what to do. Giara taught you how to forage. Tell me what Torvin and I can find that'll help."

Nothing. If it's rylock, I'm fucked.

But it won't kill me right away. I can still complete the mission so long as I can block out the pain. "You keep a stash of lavender oil," I say. It isn't a question. Everyone knows Sora's supply runs out faster than all the other healers. It's not a mystery as to why.

"Arden, that's—"

"A painkiller," I snap. For a moment, it's not Cheevy staring at me, but a gray-eyed Stitcher dressed in all white, his expression kind, almost soft. That blue metal throne beneath him makes my brain feel tacky, slow.

"It's an aphrodisiac," Cheevy corrects. His face is his own again. All broken and scarred and missing a nose.

Sniffling, I make it into a sitting position and lean against an orangeleaf tree. We aren't near the riverbank anymore. There are no spine trees, no gravel, no tangly vines. My cheeks heat with embarrassment when I realize either he or Chest Wound must've carried me for gods know how long. "It doesn't work like that for me," I tell him. "I don't have those parts, remember?"

"You're sure?" he asks.

"Of my anatomy?" I arch a brow. "I think I'd know."

Uncertainty flickers in his mercury-shaded eyes, but he nods. Unhooking one of two go-bags from his shoulder, he digs through it, procuring a thumb-sized vial of pale-yellow liquid that resembles piss. "A drop or two won't get you high, but I'm not sure how well it'll treat pain, either. When we were digging the cold iron from Torvin, we used half the bottle."

Uncorking the stopper, Cheevy hands the vial to me, then rummages through his bag for a glass dropper. *Just enough to get me through this.* One drop. Two. For half a second, I consider risking a third, but the last thing any of us needs is an incoherent asshole trying to plant explosives.

The smell is potent. The flavor is worse. Floral, minty, soap. It's like taking a bar of lye to the inside of my tongue. I make a face, coughing at how fucking foul it is, and more blue bile sprays the grass in front of me. But it isn't bile; it's blood.

"Here. Take the rest," I say, passing it back. "I'll re-dose later if I have to."

I wipe the slick, sheeny oil from my lips and wait for it to take effect.

"Purples, grays, members of the Politic, allow me to present to you our champions for this year's Ring Day celebration." A leather-clad Bracer stands in the center of the arena, her purple hair so out of place on a body otherwise gray. At her announcement, eight cold-iron gates yawn open and eight elvish slaves emerge from somewhere deep beneath the stadium. My heart clenches.

Giara.

Fenris.

They're both there, fighting for the elgrews' entertainment. And gods, how I want to make Azerin suffer for it. A sharp pain spears my stomach when I stand, bark digging into my palms as I use the tree to prop myself up. I sweep the moist hair from my face, my breathing rapid, and a fresh wave of dizziness threatens to send me toppling. "How far are we from the Grand Overseer's estate?"

"Two clicks. Maybe closer," Cheevy says.

I glance down at my unarmored body, not sure I have the strength to put on the hide cuirass or vambraces, let alone carry the extra weight that far. "My sawgrass overlayer. I need it."

He shakes his head. "It's in the bag but . . . I can't carry you with it on."

"I don't need you to—" But that isn't true, as much as I despise it. Reluctantly, I nod. "Okay. Just the daggers, then."

He shrugs the other bag off—my duffle, I realize—and

begins tossing blades onto the forest floor. Metal clangs and clanks until all fifteen daggers lay in a glinting pile. Bandoliers join them, then thigh straps and sheathes. I try to put them on, but my hands and fingers shake, cramping up like there's something wrong with the joints.

"I've got you," Cheevy says, buckling me in. Straps click and tighten across my chest, my thighs, the leather digging into bare skin. A hide breastwrap and thin shorts offer little protection in a fight, but shit, if I have to fight someone like this, we're all fucked, anyway.

I rub my hands against my biceps, shivering harder than leaves in the wind. Salty water drips from my brow and stings my eyes. I clamp them shut as if doing so can will this sickness away. *It's not rylock. I'm not that fucking incompetent.*

"Kill him!"

"Go left!"

Elgrew roar inside my ears. I blink and the Grand Overseer cups my shoulder, every bit as terrifying as he was the first time I saw him, when he had Tenok executed. He's gone in a blur of colors, the world flipping upside down as Cheevy swings me over his shoulder like a sack of grain. I open my mouth to protest, then whimper instead. The bones in my body throb as if trying to break free of my flesh. Behind us, Chest Wound now holds all three bags, his face pallid with . . . Fear? Anxiety?

For a moment, we just stare at one another, and then the lavender oil washes over me, turning my legs comfortably leaden. The pain ebbs ever-so-slightly, and the forest disintegrates into silver-stained concrete and eighty-thousand monsters all cheering for my oldest and longest friends to slaughter one another.

LYRICK

It feels surreal—sitting amongst the Politic, being one of them. Platters of meat lay in a spread before us, carried up by the city's Butchers who refuse to meet my gaze. Each of us has food befitting our castes' preferences: cooked cubes for Yaklan and Colette, covered in sweet spices and drizzled in honey, skinned but not deboned cuts of meat for Azerin, with a tray of curry sauces in varying shades of red, yellow, and orange, still bleeding thigh quarters for Ryla and me—though the sight makes my stomach queasy. Sorso's section of the buffet table is the only one that remains empty because he's nowhere to be found.

He left after the inauguration. No doubt to sulk.

With my good arm, I reach past the meats for one of the many, many chalices of ya'esen on the table and take a swig, leaning back in my throne to watch the match. Alcohol makes the "entertainment" tolerable—albeit barely—and numbs the pain of my injuries. A few seats down, Ryla excuses herself from the balcony to announce the grand finale, and I drink deeper—not quite drunk enough to convince myself that breeding one of those creatures won't be that bad.

As soon as Ryla leaves, Colette glares at me from two thrones over, her lilac eyes narrowed into thin slits.

"She'll come around," Yaklan whispers, placing a hand on my armrest. "Colette pulled you off her elves before you could damage the bodies. My Stitchers tell me she recuperated most of the training fees by selling them at the surgery centers."

Because that's what matters. The cost.

I grunt a response, careful not to watch as Yaklan pops the meat squares into his mouth. The girls' blood is on Colette's hands as much as it's on mine. If I could kill her, I would. Not just for the drugs or the attempted rape, but for putting me in a situation where I had to . . . where Azerin made me . . .

The table's meaty smells wash over me and bile rises to my throat, my still-full belly squirming in protest. Decades of control gone in an instant. All my morals, all my grandstanding rendered moot by that bitch. Death would be too good for her. Perhaps skinning her like I did Morcai would be the justice she deserves.

I force myself to grab a thigh quarter from the buffet and bite down, determined to prevent a repeat of the training house, ignoring the way it squishes beneath my teeth. Silver blood and fatty oils slick my lips and chin, but I do my best not to taste them. It doesn't matter what I want anymore, not when I've seen the consequences—no, the futility—of ignoring my hunger. At least this way, I have some semblance of control of what and who I eat.

In the arena, a team of Bracers carries an unconscious fighter away on a stretcher, the female elf's leg twisted at a wrong angle. As they remove her from the ring, my father's slaves enter the dusty field, spraying it with water hoses until the ground becomes a slurry, mucky mess. More Bracers arrive, rolling out rock walls and makeshift structures, providing hide-outs to make the grand finale more challenging. They assemble them in the shape of a labyrinth, pulling out the rolling plat-forms once they're in place.

And then Ryla enters the ring for the fourth and final time, all smiles.

Mud and dirt cover her underlings, but Ryla's purple leather armor is spotless. Atop her head sits a bronze diadem that glints in the light. She straps an amplification mask to her face and addresses the chattering spectators, all watching in rapt atten-tion, asses slid to the edges of their seats. "Allow me to intro-duce to you our two finalists. I give you, Brawler, pet to the Bracer Trinth of Kariss."

A metal gate rattles open at the far-right side of the arena, and my soon-to-be myrie steps through with a red sash around her waist. Dried silver blood and splotchy dark gray bruises coat almost every inch of her naked, muscular form. The last rounds of the game are always the most barbaric. No weapons. No armor. Single combatants.

The unwashed masses whistle and clap for her, waving betting slips high into the air.

Ryla lets them carry on for a small eternity before indicating to her Bracers to open the other gate. "And our challenger, Big Arms, pet to the Bracer Amreth of Vishi."

On the opposite side of the arena, Big Arms emerges—a hulking male elf with biceps as large as Brawler's face and an even larger ego. The elf is equally nude, equally battered, his red sash fluttering in the soft breeze.

"I think our Bracers are getting lazy with their names," I remark.

Yaklan snorts. "You should have seen the preliminaries. Three Fingers was all the rage."

I start to respond, but the roar of the crowd cuts me off.

They leap from their seats, fists pumping the air, throwing plushy biceps into the arena. One of the plushies bounces off a stone wall and lands at Big Arms's feet. Bending, he picks it up and kisses it, then tosses it back into the stands. A small purple boy catches the toy and hugs it tight to his lumpy chest, grinning wide. I roll my eyes, knowing this kind of crowd work is beaten into elves—not something they'd ever willingly do.

They're fucking delusional to think he likes them.

Still, Big Arms basks in the praise. He spins in a slow circle, blowing kisses to the people that enslaved him. It's no wonder he's a crowd favorite. Brawler, by comparison, is practically belligerent, glaring up at our balcony—at me—with nothing but contempt.

I much prefer the honesty.

"On my whistle," Ryla says, "let the games begin."

She and her lackeys exit the outskirts of the labyrinth,

clearing the cold-iron gate entirely before she presses the clay death whistle to her lips and blows. A shrill, pained screech silences the spectators. Palpable tension fills the air—the purples unblinking, unmoving as they watch the fight, unaware that it was fixed by my father. That they're about to lose what little remains of their savings.

It's hard to feel sorry for them.

Brawler peers through a crevice in the rock wall nearest her, trying to figure out how to approach Big Arms as the sun sinks lower along the horizon. The first stars appear in the moss-green sky, and both their pupils dilate to saucers, giving them this otherworldly, creepy look that sets my teeth on edge. I'm not sure how my cock's supposed to stay hard staring into that.

There's not enough ya'esen in the world.

I lean toward Yaklan, face sunk into my cup. "Do you think the breeding ceremony can be renegotiated?" I ask, voice low. "I'm already a Karesai. It's not like Azerin can take it back."

He quirks a brow. "Do you have someone else in mind?"

"Yes. No." I shake my head. "It's complicated."

But it isn't.

No one deserves to be imprisoned here. Forced to carry our spawn and service us on command. With Brawler, there's comfort in knowing I'll only touch her once, and then she'll never have to see me again. With Arden, were she in this city, I'm not sure I'd have the strength to let her leave—to keep my fucking hands off her—whether she wanted it or not. And I don't want to do that to her.

I don't want to become my father. Or worse, Sorso.

I wish I'd never seen her fucking face. Things had been so much simpler when I thought of her as that tiny, pathetic thing I released all those years ago. Now everything is messy. "Maybe Brawler will lose and Big Arms will kill her." I take a long swig of the bitter liquid, draining it, savoring the way it burns my throat. "Then I won't have to breed anyone."

Yaklan says nothing. He doesn't need to. The man knows as well as I that Azerin never loses.

Brawler and Big Arms press their backs to the walls as they approach one another, slinking through the muddy corridors. Ears twitching, Brawler moves twice as fast as the brute with a feline grace that reminds me of Prowler. By comparison, Big Arms all but stomps, feet splattering muck with every step. Closer and closer they get.

The sun sinks lower, then disappears. Like every other elgrew in the stands, I open my pit organs and cast the world into darkness. The walls and ground turn a blurry dark gray—barely warmer than the air temperature, barely lighter than the black of the night sky. It's a sharp contrast to the thousands of flashing auras in the stadium. With great strain, I narrow the scope of my vision to our two combatants, whose silhouettes shimmer with gray light. Their bodies are brightest at the groins, armpits, and heads, where the gray brightens to a hot white. Every vein in their bodies light up too, pulsing, throbbing, exposing their weak points.

It doesn't matter that my belly's full or that I'm surrounded by putrid meats. The sight of those beautiful fucking veins has my stomach rumbling. Of their own accord, my pit organs flare wider, venom pooling in the back of my throat. I lick my lips and clench my throne's armrests so tight my fingers ache.

Gods, how I miss the hunt, especially at night. Watching those veins flair and gush as I sink my teeth inside them.

Brawler rounds a corner, and I see the bite mark on her collarbone—chartreuse and bright against her blurry silhouette. A burgundy one flares at the back of Big Arms's thigh. If I tried hard enough, I could find the elgrew in the stands whose auras match them.

As Big Arms nears the middle of the labyrinth, Brawler ducks, her body disappearing behind a rock wall. A moment passes. Two. And then Big Arms walks by her hiding spot. She kicks out, foot slamming into the backs of his knees, and he crumples to the ground. Black water mists the air as he splats into a mud puddle.

"Yes!" someone in the crowd screams. "Kill him!"

More join in the sentiment.

Brawler climbs atop him, straddling his naked form, and they grapple for dominance. Dark gray fingers slip and slide across lighter gray silhouettes. Fists fly and heat rises at the epicenter of each hit until their bodies are a blur of splotchy bright white. It's hard to tell where one torso begins and another ends.

The brute leans forward, and for half a second their heads merge into one. He's whispering something in her ear.

My pit organs snap shut and color returns to the world. An elgrew wouldn't be able to see them in this darkness or hear them above the cheering crowd. But I'm not an elgrew anymore. I'm a Karesai. Concentrating on his lips, I watch the way they move and my mind supplies me with sound. It's not quite lipreading, not quite hearing either, but something between the two.

"You don't have to do this," he says. "Let me win." Brawler shakes her head, and he rams his skull into hers, knocking her onto her back. In seconds, Big Arms pins her beneath his hulking frame. "Yield."

My father jolts from his throne, pit organs flaring. This isn't part of the practiced choreography. "What the fuck is he doing?"

Winning, I hope.

Silver blood shimmers through the dirt-caked layers of their flesh. Brawler claws and kicks at Big Arms, but he might as well be a statue for as much as it moves him. "Yield," he hisses.

"Your father is going to kill Ryla," Yaklan says, lips curled in amusement. He sips from his chalice, legs crossed as he leans back in his throne—clearly unbothered.

"Looks like the Karesai of Bracers can't control her fighters after all," I add.

Azerin glares at both of us. "There are worse myries I could pick for you, Lyrick. And as for you, Yaklan, you have as much money invested in this match as I do."

Yaklan's smile falters. But there's no need.

Down below, Brawler knees Big Arms in the testicles once, twice, three times before he finally relents. The male elf collapses in on himself, sucking in air and wincing in pain, and Brawler wastes no time getting the upper hand. She hops to her feet and smiles wide, her sharp, serrated teeth flashing in the pale moonlight. They've been filed to look like ours—by Bracers or herself, I have no idea. I half expect the creature to bite through his throat, but she stomps on him instead.

Bone crunches.

Cartilage splits as she thrusts her heel into his nose.

"Yield!" Brawler spits. He doesn't and she stomps again, his jaw cracking, his face a gory mess on the ground. "Give up!"

But the man's determined.

She shifts her foot to his esophagus and grinds until he's sputtering. "Please, Fenris. I promised I'd get you home." There's a desperate edge to her expression. Warm tears leak down her face, creating streaks in the caked on mud.

Eyes swollen shut, Big Arms—*Fenris*—shudders in defeat. He reaches for the red sash around his waist and waves it in the air, surrendering to her. And then his entire body goes limp with exhaustion.

Shouts ripple through the crowd, cheering Brawler on, chanting her name. They toss green confetti and sports paraphernalia into the ring—plushie arms, flower crowns, crochet dolls, kissy lips and coins, and at least a dozen other things I don't recognize. The way the spectators carry on—the fucking volume of it—makes my ears throb.

And then the sharp cry of Ryla's death whistle pierces the air.

In an instant, everyone falls silent.

Weaving through the rock walls, Ryla arrives at Brawler's location within seconds—a master of her own maze. The Karesai of Bracers offers the champion her hand, which she hesitates before accepting, stepping over Fenris's unconscious form.

"Citizens of Kariss," Ryla says—readjusting her amplification mask. "I give you our nine-hundred and twenty seventh Ring Day champion!" She intertwines their fingers and raises their joined hands in the air.

The crowd leaps to their feet—all eighty thousand of them fist-pumping and waving at the sky. Covered in blood, Brawler's chest heaves as she squares her shoulders and grins at them, the gesture cracking open a split, swollen lip.

Once the noises settle, Ryla removes the diadem from her head and places it onto the elf's, congratulating her on her win. "Tradition dictates our victor be given two choices," Ryla says, facing Brawler. Although their gazes remain locked, she projects her voice loud enough for the entire crowd to hear. "Name an elgrew to fight or an elf to free; it cannot be yourself."

"Fight!" someone screams.

"Yeah! Name me! Varish of Asai."

"Call Revin of Drannel!"

Giggles bubble up as more elgrew join in, calling out their names and the names of their friends to fight her. In good condition, Brawler could kick their asses, but as beat up as she is, almost anyone could best her. It's why our champions never choose that option.

Brawler whispers her response, and Ryla nods.

Frowning, the Karesai of Bracers returns her attention to the crowd. "Big Arms will be released!"

Everyone boos, but it's fucking irrelevant. No matter how our people may feel about losing one of their best fighters, Brawler's choice will be honored. It's perhaps the one thing my father can't influence. Come tomorrow, the betting fees will be used to compensate Big Arms's—Fenris's—owner for their loss, and they'll become one of the wealthiest elgrew in the city.

Ryla jams her thumb and forefinger into her mouth. Whistling sharp and loud, she summons two leather-clad Bracers into the arena. Scurrying past her, they toss Big Arms over their shoulders and drag him through the muck, past one of eight doorways leading into the stadium's underbelly. Once they're gone, Ryla throws her arm over Brawler's shoulder.

"As always, our victor's celebration will be held at the Grand Overseer's estate," she announces. "To honor our newest Kare-sai, Hunters will be given priority entry. Our champions and I look forward to seeing you there!"

The ground shakes with the force of the crowd's applause. Clapping and stomping echo in the stands, reverberating in my eardrums as Ryla exits the arena flanked by her Bracers. Azerin says something, but I can't quite hear it.

"What?" I ask.

He raises his voice. "Go find Ryla. She's waiting for you in the underbelly."

I arch a brow. Every year, the Karesai lead a parade from the stadium to the estate—champions in tow. I assumed I'd be at the front with the Hunters, not in the back, with Ryla and the other Bracers.

"I want you with your myrie," Azerin says. "Go. I'll meet you at the estate."

My myrie. The words alone are enough to make me gag.

Something smooth slides into my arm sling. Brows furrowed, I pull it out and find an unlabeled vial of red liquid. Beside me, Colette peers into the stadium below, careful not to meet my gaze. She lowers her voice. "The last one wasn't meant to act as a paralytic, but everyone responds differently. I've modified this one."

I clench my fist and the glass crunches. Sticky liquid and

blood dribbles onto the balcony, but I barely feel it through my white-hot rage. "You can take your potions and—"

On the other side of me, Azerin cups my shoulder. "Go find Ryla."

I clench my jaw, a vein throbbing near my temple. The overwhelming urge to curse at both of them nearly wins out, but I hold my tongue at the last second. I *chose* this. I'm here because I want to be, and that means behaving. Enduring. Making friends.

I can do this.

"I'll see you at home," I grind out. Then I exit into the crowd.

ARDEN

Fenris. Giara. My heart squeezes for them as I work to separate my thoughts from Lyrick's. Orange leaves smack against my face and tangle in my hair. Elsewhere, mud squelches beneath the thick soles of my military boots, and the arena's metallic gates click open. Groaning, I clutch the sides of my head, my thoughts and his a discombobulated jumble.

"We can't send her down there," Cheevy says.

"We have to," Chest Wound snaps. "It's the only night—"

"We're out of time and she's too fucking sick. What's your Marr-damn problem?"

They're talking about me.

I blink. For the first time in hours, the brain fog clears long enough for me to realize where we are—the canopy near Azerin's estate. Glittering silver ramparts peek through the orange foliage. The walls are at least sixty feet tall, with lookout towers posted in even intervals. I cough my throat to clear it, and it feels like daggers slashing through my esophagus.

"I need my binoculars," I croak.

A branch below me, Cheevy and Chest Wound whisper-argue. They stop mid-conversation to peer up at me. "You're awake." Chest Wound rummages through my go-bag and passes me a pair of bronze binoculars. Twine attaches to the ends of it, letting it serve as a rudimentary necklace when not in use.

I pull them over my head and peer at the parapet, clammy sweat dripping from my brow. Magnified, the cracks in the wall become apparent. They're not made from metal, but sandstone painted in elves' blood. I think of Giara and Fenris, the arena, the fucking breeding ceremony Lyrick has planned, and rage hazes my vision.

The need to kill every last one of them is so overpowering, my hands shake. The elgrew deserve everything that's coming to them—Azerin, Lyrick, Ryla—*all* of them. Some creatures are born evil, and the only cure is extermination.

I concentrate on my still-throbbing bite mark, vision flitting between a dank metal cell and the musty rainforest. Digging deep within myself, I cut the connection to Lyrick, bury it, and focus on the task at hand. Cheevy's right about one thing—*we're out of fucking time.*

Shivering, I aim my binoculars at the guard towers. They're empty. A single Butcher paces the walkways, the silver moonlight glinting off his dark purple skin. He's not watching the jungle, but staring at his feet—bored. In the history of Kariss, no elf has ever attacked here. He probably thinks this is a waste of time. That he should be out with the others, celebrating.

If we don't kill him, Azerin will for his incompetence.

"Bow," I demand, holding out my hand. Cheevy stares at me, brows pinched together like I'm some kind of psychopath. "Bow," I repeat, more insistent this time, snapping my fingers.

Chest Wound unhooks his from his back and hands it up, careful to avoid the spiny tips that protrude from its limbs. My hands curl around it, and Marr-damn, it weighs so much more than I remember. I collapse face-first onto the branch, cheek smushing against rough bark. Panic blossoms in my chest, heart thundering.

Why can't I lift it?

"Here, I'll take it back." Cheevy offers his hand, and I see the pity there.

Fuck him. "I'm fine."

Gripping the wood tighter, I force myself back to an upright position, my muscles straining in protest, weaker than they've ever been before—not that I was strong to begin with. With sheer determination, I lift the bow and hold it steady. "Arrow."

One appears in my outstretched hand, and I line it up to the sight, my biceps burning from the strain. Sweat trails down my neck, soaking through my breastwrap, catching in my dripping hair. "I did not poison myself," I say. "I'm not sick."

The Butcher stares up into the sky. Too easy. I draw my bowstring and—

And nothing. If I shoot him and he falls, someone nearby might see. If I miss, the arrow could land anywhere, giving away our presence. Proving to Cheevy and Chest Wound that I'm strong enough to shoot him isn't worth the risk. Sighing, I let the bow fall and hand it back to them.

Stay on mission. The stealthier we are, the better our chances of survival. Lyrick's coming—that's an unforeseen and unfortunate obstacle—but he's not here yet. We still have time to plant the explosives and escape unnoticed if we move quickly.

"Chest Wound, do you know where we're going? How far away—"

"You can't be serious," Cheevy says. "Arden, look at you. You've been vomiting all night, sleeping all day. Your skin—fuck —have you even seen yourself?"

I glance down. My blue skin is rashy, patchy, glossy. I poke a particularly offensive blotch on my lower abdominals and bite back a whimper. It's so fucking sensitive, like a wound freshly healed. Skin rashes. Another telltale symptom of rylock poisoning. *Marr-fucking-dammit.*

Without the lavender, I'd no doubt be a writhing mess on the forest floor. If my sickness worsens and the drugs stop working, we're all fucked. But it's too late to turn back now. Starra'lee hasn't had a victory like this in centuries—maybe ever.

"I can do this," I hiss. Pivoting on the branch, I run my fingers down the bandoliers strapped to my chest, confirming they're still there. Then, I address Chest Wound. "Where's the vent?"

He glances between Cheevy and me, fidgeting with the go-bags. "A-a couple minutes that way, past the road," he stutters, pointing to the dirty, blue-tiled road that leads between Kariss and the Grand Overseer's estate. Lanterns line the path, casting it in pale yellow light. It's in clear sight of the Butcher on the rampart, but he's not watching it.

Tree canopy covers the pathway—thick enough we might be able to climb and hop between branches without being seen. Risky, but safer than sprinting in the grasses. "Okay, on my mark, we start jumping. Keep your eyes on the ground. There could be more Butchers on the forest floor. If we get separated, I'll make this sound."

I clear my throat, curl my tongue, and form a puckered O with my lips. The resulting noise is this high-pitched screeching that mimics the korkuran's mating call. They're nocturnal; it won't draw any attention. As expected, the Butcher guarding the rampart doesn't acknowledge it.

"Got it." Chest Wound flashes me a thumbs-up and Cheevy glares.

"Julian wouldn't want—"

"I don't care what Julian wants," I whisper-shout. "I'm not failing this mission because of something stupid *I* did."

"And what happens when the Grand Overseer finds you?" Cheevy asks, folding his arms across his chest. "Does he keep you for himself or give you to his son? Is that what you want—to be Lyrick's pet?"

My cheeks burn with unmitigated rage. *How dare he?*

"Fuck you," I spit. "Either help me finish the job or fuck off. I don't care which."

I flash him a vulgar gesture then force myself onto wobbly legs, rushing headfirst into the nearest tree. The branch I land on groans beneath me. My knees threaten to buckle, but I flex my lamellae and throw my hands out, bracing myself against the trunk. My finger and toepads stick to the knotted bark, stabilizing me before I can lose my balance. A moment later, the branches above and below me tremble, too.

I guess Cheevy's coming after all.

I don't acknowledge either of them. Instead, I wiggle my ears and activate my sezin. The bones vibrate to life and the noises around us amplify. Breezeless, the forest is all too easy to hear. Termites crawl through a nest to my right. Muffled water whooshes underground, smacking up against something hard and metal—the dam that keeps the mine from flooding, that creates the turquoise lake on Azerin's estate. Across the dusty road tiles, a lone rodent scurries out of eyesight.

Straining my ears, I jump to the next tree then the next, crossing over the pathway. Sweat rolls down my forehead, the clammy chill replaced by volcanic heat. With my sezin in use, each breath becomes a cyclone, each thud of my feet a thunderclap. The leaves rustle so loudly, they could be musical instruments. For a moment, I fear the Butcher might hear us or see something strange in the foliage, but when I bring the binoculars to my face, he's sitting on his ass—feet dangling over the rampart. A silver flask shines in his clubbed hand.

Azerin's definitely going to kill him.

I let the binoculars drop and keep going—afraid to stop. If I rest now, I might not be able to start again. A dull ache radiates through my bones, and a light sting pierces my joints with every jump. The lavender is wearing off. I'll need to re-dose once we reach the vent and pray the treatment works.

To my left comes the steady stream of liquid hitting wood, followed by the sharp stench of ammonia. As Chest Wound and Cheevy land behind me, I disconnect my sezin and press a finger to my lips, then gesture for them to stay put. I jump twice more, following the sound to its source. Down below, a Butcher faces away from me, toward another orangeleaf tree, his pants lowered to expose a lumpy purple ass.

Not a Butcher, I realize. He's too young and too short to be anything more than an apprentice. Still a problem if the kid sees us, though. Dick in hand, he pisses against the tree. It splashes as it hits, wetness oozing down the bark and into the orange grass. Without thinking, I reach for two throwing daggers and fling them into the elgrew's back, my muscles quivering with the strain of it.

They hit their marks in short succession—one to his nape, the other to his kidney. Grunting, he topples over into the piss puddle, bleeding out onto the forest floor. Blood gurgles past his open mouth, but with the blade lodged through his throat, no sound comes out. Within seconds, his lilac eyes glaze over— dead.

The logical part of me knows it's insane to mark my kill. I don't have any paper, I'm on a time crunch, and the dull ache in my bones is starting to become an all-encompassing, debilitating pain. But I almost always mark them.

Lamellae extended, I descend the tree—vision swimming, body so hot I can barely breathe. My clothing clings to me as badly as when Cheevy carried me from the river. Hands on my knees, I take several panting breaths before approaching the corpse, stepping around wet grasses to retrieve my blades. Soft, damp soil clings to my soles. The stench of it gags me.

Fucking disgusting.

Crinkling my nose, I wiggle my weapons free of the

monster's thick, deformed skin then carve the number seventy-nine into his palm—Sarvenna wasn't my kill after all. It was Cheevy's. Amethyst blood slicks the blades. I wipe them on my sopping leather shorts before re-sheathing them in my bandoliers.

"Arden?" Cheevy and Chest Wound appear beside me, apparently unable to take directions. "Are you alright?" Cheevy asks.

"Of course I am. Why—"

I glance down and see that glossy, patchy rash has spread. My entire body shines like it's made of marble. I brush my fingertips against it and wince. "Lavender," I say, extending my palm. Cheevy doesn't object. He passes the vial to me, and I swallow down three more drops of that soapy, floral goo. It's not enough. I know that already, but I can't risk anything more.

"Are we close to the vent?" I ask Chest Wound, stashing the rest of the vial into my pocket.

He nods. "It's just around those trees. That's probably why they stationed the guard here."

Taking the lead, Chest Wound weaves us through a worn dirt path—easy to miss if someone didn't know to look for it. He stops over a patch of grasses and swipes at the nearby ground, clearing it of twiggy underbrush and fallen leaf litter. A shimmering silver net appears, staked to the dirt in a half dozen places.

I sit beside him and unsheathe a dagger strapped to my thigh, then saw through the netting. It's thicker than it looks and impossible to break through via hands alone. A perfect safeguard to keep the slaves in their place.

"Go-bag?" I glance to Chest Wound, but he doesn't have it. Peering behind me, I find Cheevy staring at us with his lips pursed, his forehead crinkled with worry lines. "Go-bag. Now."

Slipping it from his shoulder, he sets it in the grass beside us. "Do you remember where you're going?" he asks.

"I've memorized the maps." A lump of emotion wedges in my throat, but I swallow it back down. I will not die here tonight. I will not get caught. These assholes' faces won't be the last ones I see. *But what if they are?* Doubt creeps in, but I square my shoulders and steel my jaw. Soldiers who panic die, and that isn't me.

"Do you remember where the rendezvous point is?" Cheevy asks.

I nod. "At that spot by the river."

Cheevy lowers himself to the forest floor and cups my shoulder. There's a comradery here I've never seen before—not with him. And it makes my eyes burn. He reaches into a sheathe at his thigh and pulls out a small, rusty dagger—*mine*. It's banged up, the dull and dented edges magnified in the moonlight, all but useless for a mission like this. "For luck. Even if you don't use it, it's never let you down."

He places the familiar, shoddy hilt in my hand and curls my fingers around it. Then, he repeats the exact same words the spotter said to me all those years ago—words I told him once when I first joined the squad. "Don't let yourself get taken. If you can't get out . . . don't let those assholes have you, Arden."

There's no animosity there—not like there was with the Lok'owe Tribe. Just pity.

I refuse to meet his gaze, though my heart twists at the weight of the dagger against my scarred palm. If I can't escape, both he and the spotter are right. It's better to end things by my hand than let Lyrick or his father find me. But I'm not thinking about that because failure isn't an option.

"Once the bombs go off, the Butchers stationed here will be too distracted to see me slipping away," I say, sheathing the dagger in one of my bandoliers. "I'll be fine."

I roll onto my stomach and stare into the dark, unlit tunnel that stretches far into the ground. The opening is narrow, but I've climbed through worse. Ignoring Cheevy and Chest

Wound, I crawl forward, brain throbbing, breaths rapid. My sensitive skin stings as it rubs against the itchy grass like I have the world's worst sunburn.

This is not how I envisioned things.

I debate the validity of sending my go-bag in first. From Chest Wound's blueprints, I know the tunnel runs at a mostly acute angle. So, it's not in danger of any hard drops. But I also dislike the idea of not being able to see what's in front of me. Then again—

Fuck it. My temples hurt too much for higher-level thought. I'll make it work.

I shove the go-bag into the hole.

"See you on the other side," I say. And then I plunge face-first into darkness.

XXXIV. Lyrick

"Ring Day was founded in the year 11 A.T. (After Takeover) by the Bracer Lenis of Eldwood. In addition to being a master tactician during the Great War, Lenis funded the construction of Kariss's arena, allowing the popularization of the fighting pits. Today, Bracers are not only responsible for training our champions in combat, but for training our Butchers and Hunters as well."

—On Elgrew History, The Emergence of Castes: Volume 1

Skin sizzles as the Karesai of Bracers drives a hexagonal brand into Big Arm's—Fenris's—chest, directly over his heart. The elf groans in agony but otherwise remains perfectly still as she pulls the glowing orange rod away. Steam fills the arena's armory, and water hisses as Ryla plunges the rod into a metal bucket near her feet.

The room is small and empty save for the three of us. It reminds me of a prison cell, with barred iron doors on either side—one leading into the stadium's underbelly, the other leading up to the fighting pit. Stone benches line the walls. Fenris sits on one of them, head lolling.

"Have you ever found a freed elf before?" Ryla asks, taking a step back to admire her handiwork. Covered in blood and dirt, I can't make out anything besides the elf's bubbling scorch marks. Silver liquid gushes from Big Arm's mushy, broken nose, and each breath comes out a whistle. It's a wonder he's still conscious.

"I've caught them a few times," I admit, "but it's rare."

Ryla hums a response. Rummaging through her pockets, she procures a metal implement that's shaped a bit like a mouth, with screws attached to the hinges. She grabs a fistful of Fenris's short silver hair and yanks, dragging his gaze to the ceiling.

"Open up," Ryla says, wedging the implement between his teeth.

His mouth stretches, a split lip cracking open.

"Lyrick, would you hold his head for me? It'll go easier with help."

A lead ball settles in my gut. It would do no good to refuse her—whatever she's about to do will be done with or without me, and I can't risk alienating another member of the Politic. Not if I have to work with her for the next few centuries. Throat dry, I nod, wedging myself between them.

"One hand on either side of his temples," she says. "He'll jerk, so you'll need to keep a firm grip."

Tears leak from the elf's swollen eyes. He moans, drool seeping down his chin as Ryla tightens the screws on either side of the implement, stretching his mouth as wide as it'll go. I shimmy my wrist from its sling and rotate it, checking the bone's in one piece before placing my hands where instructed.

Warm, sticky blood coats my fingers; my stomach growls and churns in equal measure.

Ryla retrieves the blade sheathed to her thigh and sprinkles powder on it until it glows fiery orange. Then she reaches into Fenris's mouth and withdraws his wet tongue. His eyes flash in realization. Screaming, he bucks against us, and my grip tightens to hold him in place, the bones in my wrist grinding together.

The knife slices through dark gray flesh, and his tongue tumbles to the floor, landing in a pool of drool and blood.

Unintelligible words spill from Fenris's mouth. Full-bodied sobs shake him.

I close my eyes and avert my head as Ryla unscrews the implements and plops her knife into the hissing water bucket.

"We've started removing their tongues if they speak too much Elgrew or belong to grays," Ryla explains. "It's a liability not to."

She whistles, and a pair of Bracers emerge from the hallway —the same ones who carted Fenris in after the final match. The metal door creaks as they unlock and open it.

"Set it loose near the Aegis," she tells them.

"Aren't you going to heal him first?" I ask.

"Why waste the ossi dust? He's free. Not my problem anymore." Ryla wipes her hands on her thighs, smearing silver blood over the well-worn leather. White lines and patched knife holes mar almost every part of it. I wonder how many of those tears were caused by elgrew or elves. She's spent her life training both.

It's a shame none of them pierced all the way through.

The Bracers say nothing as they heave Fenris from the bench, draping his arms over their shoulders. They drag him down a darkened staircase—the sound of his moaning and their receding bootsteps echoing off the stonework.

"Do you ever wonder where they go?" Ryla asks, staring down the corridor, her tone pensive.

"I don't follow." My mind feels sluggish. I barely remember

what we'd been talking about before the cutting. "The freed elves," she clarifies. "Aren't you curious?"

"Not really." I lean against the wall and return my wrist to its sling, letting it rest a bit more before the party. "Hunters can't sell them, so it's hardly worth our time."

The law dictates a freed elf can't be bought—not as food *or* as pets—and the punishments for breaking it are severe. Since we make our livelihoods trading elves, it's never made sense to care about what the freed ones did.

"Shame." Ryla sits on the bloody bench, toying with the metal implement that had been in Big Arm's mouth. Drool glimmers on her fingertips. "Everyone says you're the best tracker in Kariss. Maybe next year you can find them for me. Tail the one we let loose."

I arch a brow. "Why?"

There's an awkward pause as she considers her words, flipping the implement over and turning the screws. "You may not be curious, but I am. I want to know where they vanish to."

"It's hardly a mystery," I say, voice flippant. "The tribes don't like to harbor marked elves, but they will when it suits them. Look at Sorso's myrie. She took refuge with the A'sow Tribe."

"Did she?" Ryla hums, and I press my lips together, considering.

"You think she was living somewhere else?"

Ryla sets her toy aside. "I think she escaped, barely knowing the words *bend over* and *spread your legs*. Now she tracks our conversations. Someone taught her Elgrew and a lot of it—hence the new precautions."

Doubling over, she dunks her hand into the water bucket and retrieves her knife—the metal now faded to black. It clanks as she sets it on the bench. "I checked with the hunting party who exterminated the A'sow Tribe. There were no freed elves amongst them, which means our language has either become so prevalent any elf can speak it or . . ."

"Or she was staying somewhere else."

I can't help but think of Arden, who spoke to me in fluent Elgrew as well. But I keep those thoughts to myself, not knowing how she connects to all this. Not wanting to give our history or bond away. Still, it *is* peculiar. In my entire life, only a handful of wild elves have ever been intelligent enough to communicate with me.

Why is she so good at it?

"Perhaps it's not my place to tell you, but there are rumors of a militia gathering in the jungle," Ryla says. "There have been attacks. Losses. I'm certain your father will fill you in on the details tomorrow once your official duties start."

"That's not possible."

Hunters know every section of the rainforest. We keep tabs on the tribes, razing their canopies when the communities get too large. To organize anything bigger than a handful of insurgents would require secrecy, privacy, a place to train where we aren't—and we're everywhere. Elves aren't clever enough to pull that off. Excluding Arden, they're barely smarter than our verncats.

But then I remember that dream. That tree. The underground cave.

Even if those images were a product of our combined imaginations, Arden showered once surrounded by rock walls, and that's a fact. I caught glimpses of it in the apartment.

They could be hiding below the dirt and we'd never know it.

I'm about to say as much when the crowd outside whistles and applauds, effectively cutting off our conversation. I squint past the barred doors into the blinding torchlight where a pair of fighters enter the arena, clubs in hand. They'll fight like this until morning—in smaller, lower-stakes matches that'll give the illegitimates and purples a way to occupy their time that isn't at Azerin's estate.

"We should go," Ryla says. "The parade will start soon, and

by now the Stitchers should be done patching up your myrie. We'll talk more about this at breakfast tomorrow."

She pats her knees and stands. Halfway to the door, Ryla's attention catches on Fenris's swollen tongue. She plucks it off the ground and plops it into her mouth, moaning as she chews. Smacking her lips together, Ryla sucks the blood from her fingers, then flashes me a serrated smile.

"Wouldn't want it to go to waste."

UNDERNEATH THE STADIUM, Ryla leads me single file through a series of interconnected tunnels. A contiguous mural decorates the walls, depicting a thousand years of champions mid-combat. The colors are vibrant and bright—emerald skies, golden sunlight, and silver blood dripping from axes and knives. To my right, one of the immortalized elves stands on her opponent's headless carcass, grinning as she holds the missing head like a trophy.

"We're almost there," Ryla says, not bothering to glance at me. I have no idea where *there* is.

Above us, the crowd stomps, and the ceiling shakes with the force of it, swaying kerosene chandeliers. Debris rains and pale light scatters in every direction, the floor quaking so hard it vibrates my bones.

"Is it always like this?" I ask.

She chuckles. "You should have seen it during the final match. My Bracers thought the roof was going to collapse. The arena desperately needs to be reinforced."

A pair of Stitchers dart past us, carrying medical bags, buckets, and spools of gauze—their nervous energy palpable. We pass several palatial bedrooms with the doors wide open. Inside, elven occupants bleed out onto plush carpets and fine linen. Elgrew buzz around the injured, silver staining their white aprons as they perform impromptu surgeries.

"I didn't realize your pets lived down here," I say.

"Only the champions."

More Stitchers rush past. A moan echoes off the walls.

"They're spoiled assholes, too," she adds. "One of them sprains an ankle and suddenly, it's the end of the godsdamned world. It'll be nice to see Brawler humbled for a change."

My brows furrow. I've seen the way our fighters live inside the city—in cramped, bedless slums that harbor disease. The Bracers I've met are more likely to scrap their pets' bodies for parts than pay a Stitcher to mend anything. Complaining about an injury is as good as asking to be cooked.

"By the time they earn their way here, they think they're invincible," Ryla explains. "The crowds love them and pay a fortune to see them fight, so we can't exactly threaten them with being eaten. We're left with *positive reinforcement*." She spits the words like they're a slur. "That means expensive lodging. Round-the-clock Stitchers. Half of them have their own pleasure slaves—fucking gag me. Ungrateful animals, the lot of them."

We stop in front of an ornate door carved from wrought iron. Golden swirls and frosted glass panels decorate the front, and a purple-skinned Butcher guards the entryway, gripping a cleaver in his fist. He inclines his head to Ryla but glares at me.

"Has there been any trouble?" Ryla asks him, glancing down the corridors.

The Butcher drops his cleaver into a black apron pocket. He runs his mangled fingers through his wispy lavender hair. "No, ma'am. Everything is on schedule."

The corners of her lips twitch into a smug smirk. "And Brawler?"

"Inside with the Stitcher. As requested, a Trainer stopped by earlier this morning and delivered her outfit." The Butcher returns her smile, although his cleft lip dulls the effect. Droopy, lumpy skin covers the space where his left eye should be. A hunchback prevents him from standing straight. Still, he tries. Shambling, the elgrew opens the door for us, and sweet purple smoke rushes into the hallway.

Coughing, I fan the air in front of me.

Hazy golden light burns my eyes as Ryla pulls me through the entryway into debauchery.

Everywhere, elves grunt and moan. Skin slaps against skin as dozens of animals straddle and mount each other, totally ambivalent about who's watching. It's exactly how I imagined Colette's training house would be—a large, opulent room filled with pillows, rugs, and expensive bedding, sectioned off by diaphanous curtains that offer little in the form of privacy.

Floral incense fills the air. Purple smoke pours from bronze burners that hang from the ceiling, the scent mixing with sweat and sex and arousal. At the room's center, water trickles from a bathing pool where two female elves giggle, splashing about as Stitchers check them over for injuries.

"What is this place?" I ask, my nose burning from the stench.

"The Room of Champions," Ryla says. "It's where our pets go to wind down and where we store our pleasure slaves. We have to restrict access or else nothing would ever get done."

That's when I notice it.

Underneath the sloppy sex noises come muffled sobs and jingling chains. Behind a sheer golden curtain, a male elf pins a female to the floor and drives his cock into her ass. Hands cuffed, she can't do anything but lie there and let him. Her choked pleas come out in ragged gasps.

"Stop, it hurts!"

"Slow down."

"*Please.*"

A dozen similar scenes play out all throughout the chamber —a male elf force-feeding another male his cock, a chained female being passed around a large group. I turn away.

It's not my business.

Not my problem.

But my stomach knots all the same.

"Your uncle believed elves were these stupid, innocent creatures that deserved to be handled with compassion." Ryla chuckles, but it's dry and humorless. "I'm sure when you were apprenticing under Talin, he filled your head with all sorts of silly thoughts. Allow me to correct the record. When given the opportunity, elves are every bit as sadistic as we are."

She offers me her arm, which I begrudgingly accept. As we step deeper into the chamber—over blankets and around furniture—my gaze returns unbidden to the golden curtain. To the male elf pounding into the female's ass, her body prone beneath him. Silver slicks her thighs and stains the pillows. Tears leak from her now closed eyes.

"As Karesai, it's our job to put them in their place," Ryla says. "The strong rule over the weak, Lyrick; if we don't break and tame them, *this* is the result—except it would be *us* underneath them. It's our species or theirs, and there's no room for niceness."

The male elf quickens his thrusts, grunting as he spills himself inside her. Then he leaves her bloody and broken on the floor while he trots off to the bathing area, whistling an upbeat jig.

Maybe some elves *do* deserve to be tortured and bred. I certainly wouldn't mind seeing these ones in the mess hall. Fuck, I'd take a cleaver to them myself. And if my father selected a myrie who had raped others, well . . . it's hard to pity them.

"Does Brawler have pleasure slaves?" I ask, looking to ease my conscience.

Ryla shakes her head. "No. She and Big Arms are—*were*—together. I knew she'd free him today, which is . . . *annoying*. But it was the easiest way to rig the match in her favor. He always pulls his punches in their practice matches. They think I don't notice, but I do."

"Does she know what's going to happen tonight?"

I can already guess the answer.

Ryla snorts. "Of course not. That would have affected her performance in the ring. Speaking of which . . ."

We come to a stop in front of a sheer red curtain.

Behind it, Brawler lies naked on a mountain of silk pillows, sipping ya'esen from a golden chalice. At her feet, a Stitcher gingerly, slowly, rubs ossi dust into her cracked and bleeding soles. Her eyelids flutter shut, and she moans as if *enjoying* his touch.

Beside her, a red chaise is littered with piles of folded silk and pieces of leather armor. A chain-mail corset hangs off the armrest—the laces little more than delicate crisscrossing chains down the front, designed to expose everything. Ryla's crown— the victor's crown on Ring Day—glitters atop a velvety red cushion.

Ryla brushes the curtain aside, and we duck beneath it. "Are you mending her or giving her a foot massage?" she asks the Stitcher.

His cheeks flush dark gray. He stops rubbing and wipes his hands on his white apron, staining it black with ossi dust. "Sorry, ma'am. All finished." Standing, he retrieves his medical bag from beneath a pile of orange and red pillows. "Do you need help dressing her?"

Ryla rolls her eyes. "I think we've got it covered. You're dismissed."

As the Stitcher passes us, I can't help but notice the dilation in his pupils—they're more black than amethyst. Brawler's pupils are blown too. Her head lolls, a sleepy smile spreading across her cheeks; I doubt she has the energy to move, let alone speak. She certainly isn't listening to our conversation.

My gaze darts toward the ceiling, where smoke continuously

pours down on us, bathing everything in a purple haze. The floral fumes are so thick now, I almost choke on them. My lungs and eyes burn with each breath I take.

"Did you bring me here to get me high?" I hiss, my nose crinkling.

"Don't be angry, Lyrick," Ryla says. "It isn't anything like Colette's potions. Lavender relaxes your muscles and makes sensations stronger. It's meant to loosen you up, not get you hard—although the two often go hand in hand."

My jaw clenches.

I'm surrounded by bitches and assholes who think they know how to manage me. Frankly, it's insulting.

"Gossiping busybodies," I spit. My boots squeak on the marble floor as I spin on my heels to leave.

Ryla grasps my shoulder before I can, staring up at me with glowing amethyst eyes. "I took lavender before *my* inauguration party. It's overwhelming the first time—being fawned over by so many people—and I didn't have the added pressure of taking a myrie either. Tonight doesn't have to be miserable for you. It certainly won't be for her."

She cocks her head, gesturing to Brawler, who rolls onto her stomach, giggling. Ya'esin sloshes from her chalice, spilling everywhere as she goes to drink it and misses her mouth by a full inch.

"Let me alleviate some of the guilt you've been feeling," Ryla says, lowering her voice to a whisper. "Between the ya'esen, rowan berries, and lavender, Brawler won't remember a damn thing you do to her tonight."

She'll remember a year of pregnancy, though—a cesarean section, dietary restrictions, being milked until her nipples crack, and dragged around as my pet. I wish she were a monster like the other elves in this room; it would be so much easier to live with myself then.

Disgust and regret form a tight constriction around my chest, but it's too late to retract my decision, and even if I could, I wouldn't. It's my duty to rein my people in—to control them as Yaklan does. Brawler is just collateral damage. So is my soul.

I inhale long and deep, letting the smoke fill my lungs, banishing with it the last of my inhibitions.

XXXV. Cheevy

"Most of the high priests' and priestesses' work is done in secret, behind hidden doors inaccessible to the layman or foot soldier. Only leadership is privy to what happens there, and only leadership knows why Clara, our High Priestess Supreme's prized pupil, left."

—ELIAS OF THE DRIFT, STARRA'LEE COMBAT MEDIC
PERSONAL COMMUNICATION

"Where are you going?" I duck beneath a spiny death tree, keeping pace with Torvin. Icy water and sharp gravel dig into the soles of my calloused feet. Up ahead, the Aegis River sprays mist into the air, water tumbling over rapids, crashing over boulders. We've just passed our meeting spot with Arden, but he seems damned determined to reach the mossy banks. "Slow down."

Torvin doesn't listen. Feet planted in the dark water, he sizes up the river, quirking his head as if trying to find the best place to cross. But we can't cross yet. She wouldn't have had time to plant the bombs, let alone escape their blast radius.

"Torvin, we need to set up camp."

"There's no point. She's not coming back."

I snort. "You don't know her very well if you think that. She's tiny, but vicious. Being sick isn't going to stop her—"

"She isn't sick." He wades deeper into the river, the current slamming into his calves. The hairs rise on the back of my neck as I stomp after him, grabbing him by the collar of his tunic. I barely feel the icy chill, though my calves strain with the effort of standing in one place.

"What do you mean, she isn't sick?" I ask through gritted teeth. My voice is as cold and unforgiving as the water below. "Answer me right fucking now."

He struggles to free himself from my grasp, but I pull tighter, twisting the fabric in my fist. "She's going through her Age of Majority, okay? Elder Risha saw it in a vision."

I can feel the color leech from my face. *No, that isn't possible.*

But then I think of the symptoms—fever, breathlessness, nausea, joint pain, skin rashes, and growth—and my stomach sinks into my ass. The fact that she's able to move at all is nothing short of a Marr-damn miracle.

What have we done?

"You knew and you let her go down there?" I hiss. Dropping my hold on him, I shove him into the river, and he lands with a heavy splash. Torvin scrabbles through the current on hands and knees, sputtering water as it drips from his hair, down his flushed face. A day ago, I might've helped him up. A day ago, I might've called him my friend. "How is she supposed to escape if she's twice her regular size?"

"She isn't." Torvin stands on unsteady legs, flinging the water from his hands. "She was never coming back. I didn't give her functional schematics. She'll get stuck in one of the vents and the workers will find her on routine cleaning tomorrow. They'll dig her out come morning."

"What the fuck is wrong with you? She's our squadmate. Do

you know how many times I'd be dead if it wasn't for her?" Fury settles in every bone, every tendon. Arden and I have never been close, but fuck, she doesn't deserve *that*. "Do you have any idea what Lyrick and Azerin will do if they capture her? Why would you put her through that?"

The traitor looks nonplussed. Shrugging, he wades a little deeper. "The Kor—the *you know what* demanded it. She's more useful to Starra'lee as a spy in their beds than as a foot soldier. Besides, Elder Risha said—"

And there it is. That fucking bitch of a priestess. She's always despised Arden—ever since her parents abandoned the cause. Cursing, I throw my hands in the air and storm the other direction. Torvin can get himself home. I'm through caring about what the fuck happens to him.

"Where are you going?" he calls out, cupping his hand over his mouth.

"To wait for her," I growl. "She's coming back."

Water splashes as he rushes to catch up to me. "She isn't, Cheevy. Have you ever been around that much cold iron?" Torvin peers into my eyes, expression deadly serious. "If Arden makes it into the mine, she won't even remember who she is."

XXXVI. Arden

"Reaching one's Age of Majority is the most excruciating experience in an elf's life. It is a blessing that most of us undergo it while unconscious. Those who wake in the middle of their transformation should be quickly sedated. To not do so is an act of cruelty only befitting the elgrew."

—Rikkon of Ashwood, Starra'lee Medic
Personal Medical Journal

Fucking rylock vines.

I crawl deeper into the tunnel, blindly pushing my go-bag in front of me. How could I be so fucking stupid? Dying in enemy territory—not in combat but via accidental food poisoning—has to be the single dumbest thing I've ever heard of. Except, I can't die. I *won't*. I have Nirissa to get back to, a mine to explode, and Julian to prove wrong. I've defeated swamp dogs and mudsnakes and more than six dozen elgrew. A stupid plant won't do me in.

With that in mind, I force myself deeper.

Sweat drenches my body, dripping onto the slick rocks

below. Eyes burning, heart hammering, I push myself even deeper, but my grip slips on the moistened stones—again and again and again—sending me falling chest first into rubble. Skin rips. I can't see it, but I can feel it—the sticky blood that oozes from my palms and knees. But I'm almost there. Left. Left. According to the schematics, one more turn and—

My brows furrow.

The go-bag's hit a wall, but that can't be right. The maps clearly said the exit would be here—unless I read them wrong? Panic constricts my chest, turns my breathing ragged, but I block it out and do the only logical thing. I retrace my steps.

Carefully, slowly, I crawl backwards through the vent, dragging my go-bag with me. The duffel snags on the rocks, straps and flaps fighting me with each pull. Cursing under my breath, I get us both close enough to the opening to see the moonlight above. Then, I try again.

My bag hits the same unyielding stone in front of me, and I growl in frustration. Chest Wound, that fucking idiot, got the maps wrong. Either that or the tunnel collapsed. I pull my hair and yank, staring at the dark tunnels that surround me. I'm so fucking close. Marr-dammit, I've come too far to fail at the final stretch.

As long as this mine is in operation, there will always be more elves to put in the arena, to collar as myrie, to kill in the mess halls. Giving up means letting everyone down. Failing them.

Steeling my resolve, I backtrack to the opening one more time. Back in Starra'lee, Chest Wound and I discussed other routes—I don't remember them as clearly, but I'll make do. Panting, my lungs struggle to keep pace with my body, pumping in dusty air that burns worse than inhaling smoke. My nose runs. An ashy paste coats my tongue—metallic and sharp.

I turn right near the vent's opening instead of left, crawling forward until rocks surround me on all sides. They press against my spine, my chest. They snag on my leather breastwrap despite Chest Wound's assurances that the vents would be narrowest near the opening.

I'm not small enough to clear it.

A headache pulses low at the center of my temples, but I push through it. With a heavy sigh, I turn around for the third fucking time until the vent is wide enough for me to roll over. I flip onto my back, pin my arms to my sides, and crawl back to the squeeze point. The rugged sandstone grips me like a mudsnake. Blue dust shimmers all around me, plastering to my moist flesh. But I keep squirming forward, kicking my feet and wriggling my hips to propel me deeper into the air duct. My oversensitive, rashy skin screams in protest. Something sharp stabs into my stomach.

Almost there.

Almost—

With a pop, my body and my duffel squeeze into a space barely any larger than either one. And then that panic I've been working through worms its way back. I can't turn around. It's physically impossible for me to propel my hands and feet any direction but forward. Even then . . .

I twist my body from side to side but can't make enough space to use my arms.

I'm not going to fit.

I'm going to die down here, alone and in the dark.

Terrified, angry tears leak down my cheeks. I choke and cough on that metallic dust, unable to move, unable to breathe. My legs feel like they're made of lead. And although the air is cool around me, my veins feel like they're pumping magma rather than blood.

Colorful dots flicker at the edges of my vision. I'm hyperventilating, but I don't know how to stop it.

The balls of my feet slide across a patch of glossy bedrock, the texture too flat to gain any traction. A fingernail splinters as I claw at the unforgiving, unyielding stone. Then another. I cry out in pain, my entire body throbbing—the bones, the flesh, the joints, they're all so fucking tender. I'm suffocating underneath layers of skin and clothing and dirt.

These vents aren't just narrow; they're impossible.

More colorful dots appear—my head so woozy I know I'm minutes, maybe seconds from passing out. And then the walls get even tighter. Impossibly so. But that doesn't make sense because I'm no longer moving. Maybe it's my imagination, or maybe I'm . . .

"No." I shake my head, unable, unwilling to believe the truth. The tunnel isn't shrinking; I'm growing. I'm not sick—I'm transforming. "No, no, no. Not here. Not now. Please let it be rylock," I croak.

"I wish it were you tomorrow." Lyrick's words from last night's dream are a low purr inside my ears. And now I understand what they mean. The breeding ceremony. Giara.

I kick and thrash as hard as I possibly can and move a handful of inches. Cold liquid percolates down the stone, seeping onto my burning face. It's the water from Azerin's damned lake. I'm getting close. I must be.

To my left, a gust of air tangles with my soaked hair. A branching path wasn't on the map, but I take it anyway, desperate for an escape. Through sheer fucking will, I force myself past an opening I shouldn't be able to fit through and stones scrape against every part of me.

For a moment, I'm in free fall. Then my bag and I thump to the floor.

Dim glowfly lanterns bathe the mine in blue light, but I barely notice the stockpile of cold iron that surrounds me. My blurry, tear-filled gaze is focused on my body. Lumps that didn't exist before press up against my breastwrap. Curvy hips and long legs cause my shorts to hug painfully tight. The fresh skin —*new* skin—looks glossy in the lighting.

"Don't stop. Please."

My words send a fresh wave of horror through me, as I remember just how much I wanted him to touch me. Darkness creeps along the edges of my vision—a combination of panic and growth dragging me toward unconsciousness.

"Do you know what my people want to do to you, Blue? Are you old enough to have been told?"

All my life, I've worked hard to avoid that fate. And now I've delivered myself right into their stronghold.

XXXVII. Lyrick

"Verncats domesticated themselves. Following the Great Takeover, they began lingering outside our cities—likely lured by the scent of cooked elves and animal feed. Social by nature, their species developed a close bond with our Hunters, who have since utilized them for a variety of purposes, including elf trapping. While elgrew have always struggled to follow our prey into the canopy, verncats possess no such limitations. Equipped with sharp claws built for tree-climbing, they are largely responsible for the success of our hunts."

—Modern Hunting: Chapter Seven, A Hunter's Greatest Tool

I barely remember exiting the arena. I *don't* remember how Brawler got into my lap, my arms pulled tight around her waist.

On top of a parade float, our Ring Day champion sits not as a fighter, but as my myrie, dressed in low-rise harem pants with a brassy chain-mail corset that exposes everything. The victor's crown glitters atop her shaved head—mocking her while simultaneously reminding every elf in the city that even their most powerful fighters can be laid low. It's the exact reason Azerin picked her.

And for once, I don't care.

My father can have his machinations, as long as I don't have to think about them.

Reaching between Brawler's teeth, I pluck the blunt from her glossy purple lips and take a long draw. The floral fumes burn my nostrils. The sweet smoke rolls over my tongue. Eyes heavy, I slump in the gilded throne we're sitting on and inhale again, feeling the sweet relief of brain cells departing my body.

Hug-like warmth floods my veins, and the tension in my muscles eases, turning my bones liquid. I can't feel my injuries anymore—not the bruises, or metal splinters, or the still-healing wrist that's no longer in its sling. Lavender's taken all the pain away. My greatest regret in life is not seeking Ryla sooner. Fuck ya'esen; this stuff is so much stronger.

I pull Brawler close and nuzzle into her neck, putting on a show for Kariss's peasants. The spectators whoop as I lick a trail up her throat, lapping at the lavender oil Ryla so kindly lathered there. Brawler's body is slick with it, and the fumes are more than strong enough to keep us both complacent.

Mouth salivating, I moan at the salty sweetness of her skin, at the *thump-thump* of her steady pulse. She stiffens against me but doesn't struggle when I press my lips to her carotid artery. I can do whatever I want to her and none of these assholes would care.

Venom floods my mouth, but I yank my head away before I accidentally bite down. She's a rental—not for keeps. Biting her means Claiming her, and Claiming her means keeping her long after the pregnancy ends. While my father would gladly pay the wholesale cost, it's not something I'm keen on, even high as I am.

Besides, there's only one elf I care to own—and it's not her.

Staving off my instincts, I set my sights on the crowd instead.

Gray and purple elgrew amass in the Butcher's Block, roaring as we pass, nudging and shoving at one another to get a closer look at our procession. On either side of the congested roadway, elves stand in multistory metal cages that are as large as buildings—*daycare centers,* my father calls them. They're free to the purples who can't afford a proper observation facility for their pets.

Thousands of dirty elven faces smush up against the centers' rusty iron bars—all of them crammed together so tightly, there's no space to turn, let alone sit. Black-aproned Butchers pace beside the cages, smacking canes against the bars any time a pet tries to speak.

The clanging of metal is constant.

When we're gone, dozens of elves will no doubt be pulled out and whipped for their transgressions. Repeat offenders might lose their tongues, same as Fenris.

Talin always hated *here* the most—where the abuse is most prominent. It's hard to disagree, though the lavender makes it a bit easier. It's not my caste, not my problem. This is Sorso's territory, and nothing I can say or do will ever make a difference here.

"Congratulations on the match," a purple boy says, forcing my gaze away from those eyesore cages. He stumbles up to the float, a yellow coneflower in hand. Dressed in Butcher's black, the boy is barely old enough to be an apprentice, but not old enough to despise me. Yet.

The oxen pulling Brawler and I move at a slow crawl. Still, he struggles to keep pace.

"I hope I can fight as good as you someday," the boy wheezes. "Both of you." Warts cover his bulbous nose and a pulsing tumor grows from the side of his neck. He may not survive long enough to become one of those assholes manning the daycare centers. Or he might outlive them all. It's hard to tell.

Beaming up at us, the boy sets the flower down at our feet, then disappears into the crowd. We turn a corner, exiting the last parts of the Butcher's Block, where an adult elgrew replaces him, this one wearing dull leather armor that's fraying at the seams. His skin is mottled gray, and when he smiles, he exposes several shattered and missing front teeth.

"It will be an honor to hunt with you," he says to me, depositing a wreath made of white ivy.

The man withdraws a blade from his belt and slashes it across his palm, sending purple blood beading to the surface. He places his wounded hand over his heart and recites the motto we all learn as children. *"Hunters do not bow. We bleed."* Then he leans in close. "Talin was a good friend of mine. It's time everyone learned the truth."

"What truth?" I ask.

A throng of people shove the Hunter aside before he can answer. I blink and then he's gone, replaced by an endless stream of visitors who either congratulate us on our matches or make crude remarks about what it'll be like to have Brawler in my bed.

It's probably nothing.

I shrug the man's words off and take another draw from my blunt. Then offer it back to Brawler, who inhales as well. She doesn't acknowledge any of the elgrew who greet us, but her pointed ears twitch to let me know she's listening. And that simply won't do. If she's sober enough to listen, then she's sober enough to remember, and I don't want her remembering any of this abject humiliation.

By the time we near the city's outer walls, the flowers on our float are inches deep and we've smoked the blunt to near termination. Head reeling, I hear the crowd's words meld into gibberish. If I concentrate hard enough, I can keep a straight face and nod along like I care what they're saying, but I'm not concentrating. I'm imagining Arden in my lap. That it's her body, not Brawler's, that's sluggish and warm from lavender oil. That it's her arousal I can smell.

I'm too far gone to be ashamed that I *want* her. The only thing keeping me on this float, and not rushing into the godsdamned jungle, are the morals Talin ingrained into me. But they're hanging by a thread.

As our float exits the portcullis, my pit organs open and I scan the trees for her on instinct. The silhouettes of light gray trees and a dozen parade floats come into focus, followed by the glowing auras of the elgrew that surround us. I revert to sight—disappointed but not surprised. At least the crowd has dissipated. Out here, anyone with purple skin has vanished—all the Butchers and their children and any of the lower-class Bracers, Trainers, and illegitimates—leaving only the elite. Even the elgrew guiding our oxen are gray.

Orangeleaf canopy blots out the moonlight, casting the blue pathway into shadow. Thunder rumbles in the distance, and white smoke climbs into the sky, carrying with it the stench of savory meats and cooking oils. At Azerin's estate, dozens of food carts will be setting up for the event—hundreds of pleasure slaves too. Everyone important in Kariss is expected to attend, and my father has spared no expense.

He's the best showman in the city. I just wish *I* weren't the main act.

I take one last draw from the blunt then flick it into the forest. The fiery-orange cherry vanishes behind tall grasses before fizzling out.

Rhythmic drumbeats reverberate through the air, pounding through my blood as we near the last stretch between Kariss and the estate. Somewhere to my left, the grasses rustle, and a moment later Prowler emerges, bounding onto the float, knocking off dozens of flowers in the process. Brawler curls in on me like I'm her fucking protector, not her soon-to-be rapist, and I sigh in frustration.

"Sit." I point to the float, and Prowler meows at me, brushing up against mine and Brawler's calves. The elf trembles so hard, it shakes the armrest. I stroke her back until she settles, soothing her the way I'd soothe a frightened animal because that's all she is—a frightened animal.

"I said, sit." I snap at my verncat, but the beast meows louder, nudges harder. His saberteeth clack against the throne, and Brawler digs her sharp fingernails into my forearm. She opens her mouth, closes it, then tugs on my swamp-dog tunic instead. At the same time, Prowler drools onto her harem pants.

I pinch the bridge of my nose. "Message-fucking-received. I'm getting up."

Groaning, I pry Brawler's fingers off me one at a time and stand from the throne, knocking her on her ass. She tumbles into the pile of soft flowers, and I step over her before jumping off the cart. Engaging with Prowler only encourages his inappropriate behavior, but I've had terrified elves piss on me before and I have no interest in repeating the experience.

Prowler leaps after me and headbutts my stomach, almost knocking me over. The elgrew guiding our oxen peer over their shoulders, but I wave them on. "We'll catch up. Send for someone to watch the elf."

"What do you want?" I ask, growling at him.

On his haunches, he meows at me and turns his head toward the forest.

"I don't have time for a hunt," I say.

His golden eyes blink. He jerks his head again and taps me with his muzzle.

"Fine." I rub my temples, my vision whirling as I stumble off in that general direction. Twigs snap beneath my military boots. Orange grasses swat at my stomach, obscuring my surroundings. For a moment, I half-forget why I'm trudging through the forest, when Prowler pushes me again and meows into the back of my knee. *Annoying little ass—*

And then I see it.

Half-hidden by the bramble, a purple elgrew boy lies belly up beside a tree. My cat slinks toward him and nudges his hand, but the guard-in-training doesn't move. From this angle, I can't see his glassy eyes, nor the purple blood that would no doubt blend into his black Butcher's apron. But I feel it in my bones. The boy is dead.

When Prowler steps away, the child's hand flips. Carved into his flesh is the number seventy-nine. And there's only one elf who marks her kills.

Arden. *She's here.*

XXXVIII. Arden

"Upon reaching their Age of Majority, an elf's body is inundated with sex hormones, leading to hypersexuality that can last for months or even years. Little can be done to minimize the effect. Thank Marr an elf cannot be impregnated without rowan berries."

—ANYA OF THE DRIFT, HEALER OF THE SELENQUIN TRIBE

Something sweet and floral coats my tongue.

I come to with a vial in one hand and a knife in the other, with no recollection as to how either got there. Lowered onto all fours, I've wedged the blade between my hip bone and waistband, which is several inches too tight—the inseam digging painfully into my crotch. I finish what I apparently started, dropping the vial so I can saw myself free.

The glass clinks as it hits the floor and rolls away, but I pay it no heed, slicing loose the sweat-soaked fabric from my upper thighs. A hide breastwrap constricts my chest in an equally unpleasant way, so I cut myself out of that as well, throwing both it and the shorts into a shallow pool of icy water.

Marr-damn, the relief is instantaneous.

Sighing, I stare down at the pair of bandoliers that lay beneath me on the gritty sandstone—the straps severed in half, a dozen or more daggers gleaming in the room's dim blue light. I must've rid myself of them earlier.

A quick scan of my body shows dark lines cut into my shoulders, ribcage, and abdominals—some of them deep enough to draw blood. I check myself for other injuries, trying to conjure up memories of where I am, *who* I am, but the answers remain elusive. Dried blood flakes off my earlobes and even more runs down my nose, but neither hurt. Aside from a low-grade headache, I'm not in any pain at all.

My gaze snaps back to the vial of clear liquid—*no, oil*—now lying next to my discarded clothing.

Medicine? A painkiller?

Whatever it is, it's nearly full.

I ignore the dull pin pricks behind my eyes and crawl to it, scooping the vial into my hands. When I shake the container, viscous oil clings to its sides, but it doesn't elicit any new memories. So I keep scanning, assessing, searching for answers.

Azure light flickers all around me; I'm not in a room, but a cave. Metallic blue dust sparkles in the nearby distance, down a darkened tunnel where a go-bag lies discarded in the center of the walkway. *My bag*, I realize. With a grunt, I force myself to my feet and stumble toward it. And that dull pricking in my skull becomes a steady throb. With each step, my legs wobble beneath me like a freshly birthed calf and I have to brace myself against the jagged stone walls to keep from falling.

Everything feels . . . strange. Wrong. Soft feminine curves frame a pair of too-long legs that make my gait awkward and clumsy. Unbound hair brushes against the tips of my breasts, which are abnormally heavy and ache at their peaks. And my pussy . . . I refuse to acknowledge how swollen and puffy it looks, how it throbs, not with pain but with *need*.

Atop my go-bag lies a set of blueprints with red ink scribbled across them. Sloppy handwriting—*my handwriting*—overlays images of scratched out tunnels and air pockets with the words *"this map isn't accurate, use your sezin"* written in bold.

My sezin?

My sezin.

I wiggle my ears and they pop, the inner bone vibrating to life. Water *drip-plinks* down the hallway, condensing on the ceiling before hitting the stony floor. Somewhere much deeper and to my right, a heavy current slams against a stone barrier, threatening to burst my eardrums. I cut the sezin off before the noise can deafen me, but not before my once manageable headache intensifies into what might as well be a javelin spearing my frontal lobe.

More painkiller. Now!

Returning to my earlier spot, I retrieve the vial and down a quarter of it. That pain dulls to nothing, but the ache between my thighs grows worse. I ignore it, snatching up my bandoliers and blades and swinging them 'round my shoulders, holding onto the vial in my clenched fist.

I'm here for a reason, I think.

Something about a lake? A dam?

Something involving that stone barrier that must be almost a mile away.

Scooping up my go-bag, I proceed down the darkened hallway, sparsely lit by glowfly lanterns strung up on either side. My vision blurs with liquid as I near a mining cart full of blue metallic ore. I blink the liquid away, but not before more replaces it then spills down my nose. Sniffling, I wipe my face with the back of my hand, and it comes back not wet with tears or snot, but bloody.

The closer I get to the cart, the more my nostrils and tear ducts gush and the more my vision blurs. I pinch the bridge of my nose as blood drains into my throat, choking me on its tangy, metallic taste. But I don't slow.

A sense of urgency propels me farther, allowing me to push everything aside and focus on the mission. Even though I can't remember what that mission is—just that I need to hurry.

The farther I travel, the more ore appears in the walls in front of me, jutting out in a way I'm forced to touch them. Zinging pain shoots through my nerve endings, frying them like a bolt of lightning. I take another swig of oil—*lavender oil,* I remember now—but even it isn't enough to abate the spasms rocking through my arms and legs, turning them to gelatin.

Blue dust glimmers in the air around me, making it hazy and thick. Each breath splinters my lungs until I'm coughing up blood onto the sandstone floor.

With a gasp, I fall to all fours and drain what little remains of that vial. The sickly-sweet taste of the lavender oil is missing this time, drowned out by the thick tang of my blood. I swipe the sweat-soaked hair from the back of my fevered neck and try to think beyond the pain, the crippling headache.

The vial slips from my hand and rolls across the floor, hitting a jagged wall. And suddenly I can't remember what was in it.

Where am I?

Who am I?

What the fuck am I doing here?

Absolutely nothing comes to mind.

My arms and legs give out—elbows and knees smashing into rough stone. But I can't feel it. I can't feel anything past the tingling between my thighs. My eyes snap shut. My vision shifts. And then I'm somewhere else, seeing the world through someone else's eyes as they elbow their way through a crowded garden.

Elves writhe in front of me, grinding up against each other, dancing to a heavy drumbeat. Some of them wear formal clothing, and others dress in combat gear; nearly a fifth wear nothing at all. All around me, flames flicker from at least a dozen firepits, casting their spindly silhouettes across canvas tents and food carts.

Pleasured cries fill the muggy air, and I watch in morbid fascination as a male elf in hunting leathers slips his hands between a naked female's thighs. She parts her legs for him, granting him easier access, and I cup my own pussy in return, grinding my palm into something small and achy—that little bundle of nerves adult females have that makes sex pleasurable. The woman throws her head back as he pumps her, and I do too, a fire burning inside me until it feels like I might combust.

Another elf—a woman in a glittering teal suit—shoves a naked man to his knees and unhooks her pants, shimmying them down her thighs. She tugs his face to her crotch then bucks into his mouth, the grasses crumpling around them. He grunts beneath her, hugging her knees for support as he licks her.

Similar scenes seem to stretch out for infinity. Everywhere is a sea of debauchery that I can't stop watching. And the more I watch, the hotter I burn. The tension in my lower stomach coils tighter and tighter, driving me toward the edge of something that I can't quite reach.

Farther into the garden, I—*he*—walks. On a bed inside one of the tents, two suited men pin a woman between them—one rutting into her throat, the other between her thighs. Tears and kohl stream down her cheeks. The bed squeaks from the force of their thrusting. And I'm acutely aware of how empty I am—how much I crave not to be . . . until one of the men smiles, exposing his sharp, serrated teeth.

Not men—*elgrew*.

In the darkness, their silver threads are all but invisible. But now that I'm looking for it, I can see the edges of their patchwork skin shimmering in the firelight. All the naked ones are pleasure slaves, and all the dressed ones, their masters. Bile rises to the back of my throat, my hand jerking free of my clit like I burned it on a stove. The moisture pooling between my thighs quickly dries up, replaced by guilt that I'd been pleasuring myself to *that*.

With concentration, I yank myself free of the vision and return to my spot on the floor. For one brief moment, I remember exactly why I'm here—to destroy their cold-iron production, to stop any more elves from ending up exactly like those ones.

Nirissa. Me. Giara. Fenris.

I can't save the ones in Kariss, but I can save the ones back home.

An unfamiliar bag lies beside me, and a set of daggered bandoliers drapes atop it—a rusty dagger standing out amongst the other, more uniform blades. Peering over my shoulder, I see a hallway where the dust isn't quite so thick and the ore isn't quite so dominant. In front of me, it continues in a curtain.

Every instinct begs me to turn back, but I've come too far, and I won't stop now. I'm almost there—wherever *there* is. I give the safer tunnel a longing glance before tossing the duffle around my shoulders and neck, crawling forward one hand, one foot at a time. It's too hard to see past the blood draining down my eyes and nose, so I rely on feeling alone.

Wet rock scrapes against my raw and bloodied knees.

Grit and metal shards dig into my palms.

The deeper I go, the wetter and sharper the ground gets, until I'm splashing through a thin film of icy blue-green water. Even without my sezin, the roar of an unseen current grows painfully loud, whooshing through my bloodied ears. Sharp ringing pierces my skull, and I follow the pain, letting it guide me where I need to go—to a room made entirely of cold iron. To an underground dam that keeps the Aegis River from reaching the mines, creating the turquoise lake on Azerin's estate. Because that's why I'm here.

To plant bombs.

To collapse the tunnels beneath his property.

Brain fog threatens to return, but I shake it away, then wipe the blood draining down my tear ducts, and crawl to the stone dam that's keeping this place intact. Mortar infused with blue dust forms a thick line between each pink sandstone brick; if I touch it, it'll be no different from touching the ore. Careful not to, I toss the go-bag from my neck and fumble past buckles and straps to reach the folded wad of animal furs at the bottom. Children's clothing, first-aid supplies, and a jar of *survival glue*—a sticky black substance made from boiled orangeleaf resin and charcoal—spills out onto the floor.

My fingers curl around the soft furs, gently unfurling them to expose the modified firecaps inside. Long silver strings have been glued to the pull tabs, then wrapped around a thick spool that will allow me to pull and detonate them from afar. Through teary, bloody eyes, I pop open my jar of survival glue, then dunk my fingers into the sticky, gummy mix, slathering it onto the caps. Crawling parallel to the dam, I check for weak points—cracks in the foundation—that I can stick the bombs to.

Something warm and tingly tugs on my palm. *Lyrick.*

A pit of dread settles in my gut.

He's here. He's coming for me. And if he catches me, I could very well be one of those elves in the garden, forced to pleasure him, his father, and all the elves in Kariss until they've bred me with half the city. *But that's not going to happen; I'd sooner die.*

Gritting my teeth, I slap the glue then firecaps onto Azerin's dam. As I search for an exit, I grab the strings that dangle from the bombs' pull tabs, unspooling them a little bit more with each step. There are no air ducts in sight—just the surface entrance Butchers use to service the dam's pumps. If I escape through that, I'm caught. If I stay in the tunnels—gods know how long it'll be until the lavender oil stops helping and my brain turns to mush.

I'm fucked.

"*I own you.*" Lyrick's words echo in my head. I can still taste his lips on mine—and damn it all, thanks to the lavender oil, my stomach flutters at the memory. The only thing worse than being trapped in that garden would be my traitorous body wanting to be there.

In the corner of my eye, I spot my discarded bandoliers—my favorite rusty dagger amongst them. If I can't escape . . . well, I won't let myself get caught. I unsheathe it, ready to end it all if it comes to that, and toss the rest of the blades into my bag.

Then, I find the cold-iron elevator leading to the surface and step inside.

XIL. Lyrick

"To wood nymphs, losing one's mate was a fate worse than death. To kill them was unthinkable. Elgrew are not entirely dissimilar in this way. Euthanizing Orella changed Azerin forever. When we were young, he, Talin, and I used to dream of a better world. Now I fear he dreams of nothing at all."

—Yaklan of Kariss, Karesai of Stitchers
Classified and Personal Journal

Opening my pit organs, I push through the crowded garden and scan for Arden's silhouette.

Killing her is the morally responsible thing to do —*I know that*—yet I chafe against the decision.

It doesn't matter that I want her, that I've *saved* her once before. She's murdering children now—a line I'd never cross. Stabbing that elgrew boy from behind, carving numbers into his flesh, those are the actions of a coward and a sadist. A rabid animal who needs to be put down. As her owner, it's my job to stop her, desires be damned.

So, I'll hunt her like I planned, eat her like I planned, and be rid of this pesky bond once and for all.

Mate. It's just a word, and I'm a godsdamned force of nature.

I growl in frustration, the sound lost amongst the ground-vibrating drumbeats and sloppy sex noises now filling the garden. She isn't here. Given the crowd size and lack of tree cover, I didn't think she would be, but it's still annoying. I've already paced the ramparts and peered into the forest. I've checked the perimeter, the lake, and a dozen other hiding spots in the blueleaf canopy, but her iridescent silhouette is nowhere in sight. It's hard enough tracking someone while sober. Doing it while high is fucking impossible.

"Why are you here?" I hiss, staring at my palm and willing her to hear me. There's no response.

What could she hope to gain from this?

Sneaking onto my father's property is the single stupidest thing an elf could do, especially on a night like tonight. With over ten-thousand armed elgrew in attendance, there's no chance of escape. She should fucking hope I catch her first. I'll eat her; Azerin will do much worse.

"Where are you?"

Still no answer.

Prowler slinks behind me through rows of white bellflowers that jingle when his orange fur brushes up against them. The crowd gives him a wide berth, guiding their pleasure slaves and dance partners away from his massive, muscular body. His tail flicks from side to side, nostrils flaring as my beast tries and fails to track her scent again.

It's not his fault. Wood smoke and cooking meats congest the air around us. Colette's brought all her best and most expensive pleasure slaves to the party, and they reek of vanilla, cinnamon, fruits, and a dozen other overpowering sweet things. Then there's the sex itself. Musky arousal, soury blood, semen, and lubricant—it's an assault on my own nostrils, so I can't imagine what it must be like for him.

In the forest, finding elves is easy. Their smells, sounds, footprints, and fallen leaf patterns are traceable. Predictable. But here, the ground is well trodden, the smells and sounds are a headache-inducing nightmare, and now that I'm a Karesai and everyone's heat signatures look unique, it's challenging to weed through their flickering auras.

Overwhelmed by the coloration, I shut my pit organs for the dozenth time and return to eyesight alone. The crescent moon hangs high in the sky, half-hidden by heavy rain clouds, puffy and threatening to burst. It's almost time for the breeding ceremony and I'm still no closer to finding her. *So. Godsdamned. Frustrating.*

"Lyrick?" Fingers coil around my shoulder, and I resist the urge to recoil. "Why are you here? You should be with Brawler."

Ryla steps in my path and gestures to the estate. Near the entryway, all the Ring Day competitors stand in a single-file line —flowers, wreaths, and other tokens piled high around them. Naked, they look no different from the pleasure slaves save for the added bruises and cuts that mar their skin. A combination of Bracers and Butchers pace the area behind them, wielding cleavers and whips, ready to put them in their place if they act out.

Brawler is the only one who's clothed—seated on the gleaming bronze throne I left her in.

Gray elgrew dressed in fighting leathers take turns greeting the competitors—although greeting might be too generous a term. They make circles around them, taking measurements of various body parts, opening their mouths to examine their teeth, poking and prodding at tender nerve endings while timing their reflexes on dangling pocket watches. Some of the elgrew might be looking to own them, others to eat them, but most will be vying for a chance to wear their muscles and skin. Because it's easier to buy the damned things than hunt one themselves.

Useless sacks of shit. Barely better than the peasants.

The one good thing about Brawler being rented out to me, though, is that she's not exposed to this barbarity. No one touches her; they don't even look her way.

"I'm . . ." I try to explain my absence to Ryla, but the lavender makes it hard to conjure a suitable response. So, I pivot instead. "Do you know where Azerin is?"

She cocks her head toward the estate. "The nursery with Tyla. He wanted to check on her before the ceremony. You look tense. Is everything alright?"

"It's fine," I grunt, stepping out of reach. "I need to speak with him."

Because he's the only one with the authority to dismiss me.

Surely a security breach means I'll have his permission to track the culprit. We can delay the ceremony . . . or cancel it altogether.

Not wanting to engage with the competitors or the elgrew fawning over them, I take the back entrance, weaving through writhing masses of flesh. Ryla doesn't follow. Neither does Prowler, choosing instead to track and hunt Arden on his own. It'll be more effective this way. Separately, we can cover more ground.

What started as erotic dancing has shifted to fucking, to Colette's pleasure slaves being passed around to whoever wants them. No breaks. No mercy. To their credit, most of them pretend they enjoy it—perhaps some even do—riding their patrons inside canvas tents, on plush beds Azerin imported. Unlike the Room of Champions, none of them wear chains; there's no need. We're stronger than them, faster, and they have nowhere to run.

My footfalls land clumsily. Through half-lidded eyes, I watch a Hunter bend one of the slaves over mid-dance and smack her ass, belt jingling as he frees himself. For a moment, my mind scatters, and I imagine it's Arden and me in their place—my cock instantly hard, pushing up against my form-fitting leathers. Through the drugs, it's hard to remember why it *can't* be Arden and me. She's here. She's mine. I just have to find her and . . .

No. I'm better than that.

Breeding Brawler is one thing. It's necessary for my leadership—my survival. Keeping Arden as a pet and using her to pleasure me on command is altogether different. She might be a rabid animal, but she's done nothing so evil as to warrant *that.*

Still, I can't pull my eyes away from them, can't stop wondering what her blue pussy looks like all swollen and exposed to me. And it makes me a terrible person, but fuck if I care. I send the mental image down our bond—or at least I try to —but she doesn't respond to that either.

It takes longer than it should to reach my father's house. Dozens of elgrew stop me along the way, congratulating me on my position, sucking up so they're in my good graces. It's annoying as fuck, but I fake a smile and pretend to listen. All the while, my attention lingers on my palm, which burns hotter than ever before.

Opening the back door to the estate, I stumble toward the familiar steps leading to Tyla's nursery. Elgrew sit on couches in the parlor room, sipping ya'esen and eating curried meats. Elves wind arms around their necks, bounce on their laps, kneel at their feet. Besides giving the group a cursory wave, I ignore them—my goals singularly focused. When I reach the upstairs, my sister's nursery door is open and Azerin is holding Tyla, shushing her to sleep.

"Dad?" Water seeps over my leather boots, through the damp moss-covered floor as I cross the threshold. Relief floods through me at how fucking comfortable it is up here. No loud sounds. No unwanted scents. Even the humid air is less sticky, its moisture absorbed by the living moss.

Azerin doesn't look at me as he sets a snoring Tyla in her crib, tucking in the sides of her dark blue baby blanket. "You should be celebrating with the others. Not up here with me." He smooths his thumb over her patchwork cheek then spins the mobile above her crib. "Is there something you need?"

I clear my throat, not sure how to explain Arden without mentioning her by name. "I found a dead guard outside the walls. I'd like permission to track the elf who did it."

"No," Azerin says plainly. He crosses the room and ushers me outside. "We have people for that. Greet your new subjects and I'll send Hunters out to look."

"But—"

"The breeding ceremony is nonnegotiable, Lyrick. There are thousands of elgrew on the premises. If it's still here, my people will find it. Go. Enjoy your party."

I grind my teeth and resist the urge to remind him the Hunters are *my* people now. "If it's found, I want to be the first to hear of it."

Quietly, Azerin shuts the door and locks it, his key ring jingling as he clips it onto his belt. "Fine. Now return to your myrie. It's uncouth to leave her alone."

The tone in his voice is final. But the thought of anyone else catching her, pinning her, biting her, doing to Arden what I did to Sorso's mate sends fire coursing through my veins. But how can I admit to Azerin who she is to me and what I've done? There are seventy-nine deaths on my hands, including that of a child, because I foolishly released her all those years ago. I'm culpable—legally and morally.

"You can't let them catch you," I whisper to her. *"Do you understand?"*

She doesn't answer.

I PRESS another blunt between my lips and try to soothe my jittery nerves. If the guards find Arden, I'm fucked—unless Azerin chooses to cover up my crime. I take a deep breath and let the sweetened smoke roll over my tongue, then hold it there before puffing it out in concentric circles. Surely, he won't let them burn me. *Right?*

Up above, rain tinks against the blue stained-glass roof that covers Azerin's gazebo. It's little more than a drizzle, but thunder rumbles in the distance, threatening to crack open the sky. Brawler and I wait alone for the breeding ceremony—me from my throne, her from the enormous bed at the gazebo's center. She sits crisscross in the middle of it, unchained and uncuffed, staring out into the flower gardens where bonfires flicker, illuminating the ongoing orgy in red light.

I don't want to fuck her.

I don't know if I *can.*

Despite the lavender, my cock revolts at the idea of touching anyone but my mate. Even Sarvenna's lost her appeal, and I fucking hate Arden for that. I blow out more smoke rings—this time toward Brawler's cheek. She doesn't flinch. Her blown pupils are locked somewhere deep within the crowd—perhaps hoping someone will save her. Or maybe she's too high to care.

Footsteps shuffle up the gazebo's blue-tiled steps, and my gaze swivels to the entryway where Yaklan opens the creaky gate, pulling Vera on a leash behind him. Around her throat, a golden collar gleams in the torchlight—covered in pink topaz and glittering diamonds. Matching gemstones peek out from her pierced nipples—her breasts exposed for everyone to see. Sheer, blush-colored harem pants hang low on her hips and there's nothing beneath them.

I try not to stare at the hundreds of bites that scar her body from toe to neck, all belonging to Yaklan. She doesn't acknowledge me. Like a good pet, she keeps her head hung low, her gaze on the floor. If I didn't know better, I'd never suspect the creature means something to him.

Yaklan offers me a gentle smile and walks to his throne beside mine, softly tugging on Vera's leather leash—not metal because Yaklan knows she won't run. The outfit, the collar, it's all for show. And it's a damn good one.

I'd like to see Arden in my collar, covered in my marks.

The thought catches me off guard. It's not something I've ever yearned for before, but gods, do I want it now, and I'm horrified by it. Terrified that I might be no better than the others. But then I take another draw from my blunt, and suddenly I care just a little less. It's not like Talin's around to be disappointed in me, and it's not like I'm going to act on it. She's nothing but an animal—*food*—no matter what our bond would have me believe.

Still, all sorts of violent, possessive thoughts run rampant through my drug-addled mind, blurring together. I'm lost to them—my heavy head lolling, my muscles relaxing into the chair—by the time I hear Yaklan clear his throat.

Who knows how long he's been trying to speak to me.

"I'm sorry," I say. "Too much lavender."

I offer him the blunt, but he motions me away. "I've never cared for the stuff."

Yaklan lowers himself onto his throne and commands Vera to her knees beside him, where she seats herself between his thighs and stares at his cock—the way all trained elves are taught to. For a moment, I wonder if she'll take him out, if he'll make her. And then I imagine Arden the same way, and sweet venom gushes into my throat.

"I didn't see you at the greeting ceremony earlier," he says, shredding my daydream. "Where were you?"

My vision swims when I shift in my seat to better meet his gaze. I consider a real explanation, but I'm not sure how many words I can speak without slurring, and I might say something damning by accident. So, I settle for, "Security issue." And then, "Why is Vera here? I thought you didn't take her out in public."

"Azerin sent for her," he says sourly. "For big events like these, he likes that I bring her out and remind our subjects she exists."

More Karesai enter the gazebo, interrupting our conversation —first Colette then Ryla, claiming their seats around the mattress.

Three witnesses down, two more to go.

A small, female Butcher prances through the gate—not in the traditional suit, but in a frilly black dress with a matching apron to cover it. Her cleaver barely fits inside its tiny pockets. She's less deformed than most purples, with scars running down her body where the Stitchers have cut lumps and bone spurs out. Wealthy Butchers don't replace their skin and muscle the way grays do; they use elgrew donors instead—criminals sentenced to death. I've never met the woman before, but I don't need to to know she's Sorso's eldest daughter, next in line for his position when he dies.

"Your father couldn't make it?" Yaklan asks as the Butcher takes her seat on Sorso's throne. She practically drowns in it— her body so much smaller, so much more petite than its normal occupant. Dark purple hair cascades down her shoulders, shifting as she shakes her head.

"His myrie is in delivery," she says in this wispy, airy voice.

Yaklan's brows pinch together. "She's having an emergency cesarean? I wasn't aware."

"No." The woman rolls her eyes at him. Her purple lips twist into a wicked smile. *"She's in delivery."*

I nearly choke on my smoke. The other Karesai blanch, their faces going several shades paler. That bastard is going to force her to give birth the natural way. I open my mouth—a dozen insults burning a hole through my tongue—but the sound of dress shoes clacking against the mosaicked tiles cut me off, and we all turn our heads.

Azerin crosses the gazebo's threshold with a death whistle in hand. Before I can ask him if the guards have found our intruder, he subtly shakes his head. And then he blows the shrieking whistle and the drumbeats stop.

Silence.

No grunts, moans, or giggling laughter from the crowd. Just the sounds of our own breathing.

Thunder booms and lightning streaks across the dark horizon, illuminating the gardens in a silver flash. Thousands of gray bodies extend from one side of the property to the other—some on blankets, others in open-flapped tents—all joined in pleasure. But they stop fucking to stare at me. To either celebrate with me or watch me fail.

Either way, it'll be a damn good show.

I take a final pull from my blunt before tossing it behind me, over the gazebo's railing where the moist flowers consume its glowing embers. As I work up the courage to stand, Azerin tightens an amplification mask to his face and addresses the crowd. "As you all know, Lyrick has decided to take his first myrie tonight, and you're all invited to bear witness."

The drumbeats resume but change in tempo to something that sounds more akin to a death march—which is exactly what'll happen if I can't perform tonight. But I'm not thinking about Brawler. I'm thinking about Arden, wishing she'd find a way to save me from this godsdamned nightmare.

"Where are you?" I ask.

My palm aches from how close she is, and it's so fucking irritating that she won't respond. It doesn't matter though; there's nothing she can do to stop this.

Metal groans as I stand from my chair, and Colette joins me at the mattress, her puffy red dress bouncing with each step. From deep pockets within her crinoline skirts, she procures an ink pen and a crisp sheet of parchment made from elf skin, bleached to appear white. She unfolds the parchment then passes it to me, revealing a standard breeding contract with mine and Brawler's names at the top. Underneath it is the name of Brawler's Bracer, granting me temporary ownership for the duration of the pregnancy.

Eyes narrowed in concentration, I try to read the several paragraphs of text below, but the words shift and blur in and out of focus, forming an incoherent jumble in my mind. It doesn't matter though—Colette's not fool enough to bamboozle another Karesai with hidden loopholes or secret texts, and I know the process well enough.

After I sign the papers, a witness from each caste will certify the union by signing below mine, and then Colette will give me rowan berries to feed to Brawler in front of everyone.

I snatch the pen from her, my sweaty palms shaking. But I manage to scribble my name on the dotted line. Colette's puffy, red-stained lips take on this smug expression, though she says nothing as she collects the parchment and pen, then passes it to Azerin and the others.

My stomach knots as I watch each of them sign it, their expressions uncaring or, worse, *pleased.*

Fuck. They're really going to make me do this.

Colette returns the contract to her pocket, exchanging it for a small vial of glittering silver berries. One is enough to make Brawler ovulate, but there are several inside. I take it from her— the glass warm to the touch—and she returns to her seat.

Brawler still isn't looking at me. Her gaze is on the horizon.

Thunder rumbles close enough to shake the gazebo, and another flash of lightning brightens the landscape, revealing what she's staring at—the turquoise lake. More specifically, the small building leading to its service elevator and underground dam.

Strange. Still, it's better to have her look at that than me.

Dark water churns, lapping against the lakeshore as more and more lightning streaks the sky. Rain pelts the glass above us in a steady downpour, and the flickering bonfires that surround the gazebo hiss, sputtering to stay alive.

I ignore it all, the bed creaking as I climb onto it and kneel before Brawler. Stomach knotting, I uncork the vial and shake a rowan berry loose, where it rolls onto my palm, dusting my skin in a thin silver coating that resembles elf's blood. "I'm sorry," I whisper, low enough that only she can hear me. I refuse to look at her as I stopper the vial and return the remaining berries to my swamp-dog tunic.

Brawler doesn't fight me when I grab her cheeks and squeeze, forcing her mouth open. Her lips pop into an O and I shove the berry down her throat, past teeth every bit as sharp as mine. A full body shudder ripples through her, and then every muscle, every bone practically turns to liquid. She gags on my fingers then slumps, her irises shifting from dull gray to bright silver. It's strange to find her so pliable after watching what she did to Big Arms in the arena.

Saliva slicks my fingers, but I wipe them off on the mattress before repositioning her. I don't want to see Brawler's face. *I can't.* Even the lavender isn't strong enough to let me take her in such a personal way. I'm acutely aware of all ten-thousand eyes on us as I move behind her and push her face into the plush bedding. Over my shoulder, Azerin nods in encouragement.

It should be easy. But it isn't.

Every part of me revolts as I slip my fingers into her waistband and yank down, exposing her ass to me. Arousal glistens between Brawler's thighs, and she's just as agreeable as Ryla promised she'd be. I could be done with it in a matter of minutes. The creature won't even remember.

Swallowing, I pull myself out and jerk myself to hardness. Despite my worries, the lavender amplifies the sensation and my purple cock springs to life. It's nothing like the male elves' reproductive organs—it's thick and grooved, with bumps that span from base to tip. Stretching elves before sex isn't just a kindness, it's a necessity to make it fit without tearing.

But I don't want to touch her.

I *can't*. It would be no better than fucking an ox or a snake. She's innocent in all this—undeserving.

As if sensing my thoughts, Azerin appears beside me. He flashes open his suit jacket, revealing a cold-iron knife that gleams when the lightning strikes, branching out above us. I'm no longer fool enough to believe Azerin would stab me himself, but that wouldn't stop Ryla or Colette or any of the other onlookers who already doubt my loyalties. The message is clear enough. *Do it or die.*

My gaze swivels around the gazebo, looking for someone—*anyone*—to stop me. But no one does.

Brawler lifts her head, and her gaze returns to that spot on the horizon. My pit organs open on reflex to find a light gray silhouette creeping from the dam's service entrance. It's not colorful or iridescent, but I'm drawn to it regardless. My vision reverts to normal, and I squint into the darkness as that figure drags something behind her—a spool of silver threads with strings leading back to the building.

"Get on with it," Azerin growls, too low to be heard above the rain. But I'm not listening to him. I'm staring at the creature, my palm burning in recognition even though the bite isn't visible.

Lightning bursts across the sky, and then I see it.

Blue hair. Blue skin. *Mine.*

"Arden?"

She lifts her chin and our gazes lock. Then she jerks the strings, and the world collapses out from underneath me.

XL

Run

LYRICK

Azerin grabs my wrist and pulls me from the exposed mining tunnel before it can suck me in. I collapse onto my hands and knees, coughing up icy water, my nostrils burning. Rainfall pelts me freely, and when I glance back up, the glass ceiling is gone.

The gazebo is gone.

Azerin and I stand on what remains of the mosaic tiles, but the rest have fallen into a flooded mining tunnel. Wiping my nose, I pull my hair into a bun and try to make sense of the wreckage in front of me. Through a curtain of rain, elgrew fall into the ground, clawing at dirt and moss to reach the surface as millions of gallons of water flood the property, collapsing every support structure beneath.

Something groans and mine and Azerin's attention pivots toward the sound. *The estate.* Its cracked foundation is falling into the wreckage, and the cold-iron mines are deep enough to consume it all. We glance at each other at the exact same time, sharing the exact same thought.

Tyla.

"Help the others," Azerin commands. "I have to go back for her."

Open-mouthed, I stare at the gardens that stand between us and the estate. They're all gone, with no way to cross them and no way to reach her.

"Dad—" My throat bobs.

"Help the others."

And he takes off, disappearing behind rainfall and scrabbling bodies, trying not to fall in. The lake might as well be the entire godsdamned property. A slushy, muddy mess squishes beside me, threatening to collapse when I put any weight on it. I re-button my pants and search for my peers. Colette, Ryla, Sorso's daughter—they're nowhere in sight. Yaklan kneels beside a nearby tunnel, staring at the muddy depths.

"She's gone," he whispers. And it's the sound of a broken man. I don't need to ask to know who he's speaking about. *Vera. His mate.* "I . . . She just slipped through my fingers."

A million emotions flicker across his face, and I can see him contemplating jumping in too, going after her. But it's a death sentence. The water could have carried her anywhere. She's likely trapped beneath the dirt or dead on impact. "You can't," I tell him. "Yaklan, you can't get her back."

Reaching under his armpits, I yank him to his feet.

Then, I realize what my father didn't. There's no one left to help. In the time it's taken me to speak with Yaklan, those scrabbling at the surface have either pulled themselves up or fallen down. And once they're down . . .

Something cracks, and the estate tilts onto its side, smashing into the dirt as it sinks. I can't see my father—if he's reached it or not—but shattered glass covers the mucky dirt and uprooted trees drag against the current.

In the collapsed tunnel nearest to me, a mattress lies half in the water, half on the ground, but Brawler's not on it. The initial burst must've taken her too. Fury and hatred wind their way through every fiber of my being. That fucking bitch killed her own people just to spite us.

And now she'll suffer for it.

I peer into the rain and darkness where the service elevator had been. There Arden stands, naked and smiling, like she's proud of this. I snarl at her and then I give chase.

ARDEN

I did it. I fucking did it!

Icy rain pelts my skin as I take in the destruction my bombs have wrought. The estate was supposed to be empty when I attacked, but this is so much better—thousands of Hunters dead in a single, sweeping blow, their screams a Marr-damn symphony as they struggle to climb from the collapsed mining tunnels and fail.

Grinning, I watch Azerin's house fall into the murky water and full-body laugh, doubling over with it. Free of cold iron, my mind clears for the first time in hours, the rain washing sweat and metallic dust away until I can finally breathe again.

I should either be trapped or dead, but I'm not. I'm—

A dark silhouette appears on the other side of the flooded tunnel closest to me, and my palm burns. Glancing down at my body, I stare in horror at my too-long arms and legs, my full breasts that weren't there before, and swallow. I'm totally and completely fucked.

Lyrick's face emerges through the downpour, serrated teeth flashing.

And I bolt.

I don't search for an escape route—there's no time. Heart pounding, lungs screaming, I take off toward the ramparts and hope a path will reveal itself. I have minutes until other Hunters spot me and come to Lyrick's aid. The chaos helps, but not enough to save my life.

Bluewood trees block my path. I weave through them, twigs snapping, mud squishing underfoot, stumbling and tripping over my newfound legs. My gait is too long, my weight too awkward. I don't know how to move in this new body, and it's so fucking inconvenient.

Through the rain, I can't hear him, but I can see him—his dark silhouette getting closer with each of my missteps.

My foot lands in mud that's too squishy and I sink up to my ankle. "Come on," I shout, tugging on my calf, trying to wedge it free. Lyrick's glowing violet eyes appear in my periphery, him nearly close enough to touch me. But I tug harder, frustrated tears burning my eyes. I didn't come all this way to fail at the finish line.

My foot *shloops* free and I trip backwards, slipping in the muck. Bark scrapes against my back and branches tangle in my soaking hair as I collide with one of the bluewood trees. I grit my teeth and keep going. Thunder booms, vibrating the ground, and lightning flashes, igniting the entire skyline in silver.

There.

The brightness lasts just long enough to expose a gap in the northwest rampart, where a collapsed tunnel cracked and sank the bricks. If I can make it past the bluewood trees, then clear the sunken dirt, I'm free. My scar burns so hotly, it feels like my palm is on fire.

"You'll never be free," Lyrick hisses. *"I will make you pay for what you've done."*

An icy chill spreads through me. But I'm almost there.

Chest heaving, I race toward that single spot on the rampart, through wet grasses that scratch at my calves and thighs. My feet slip and I go sliding on my ass, smacking into flowers and mud. Wet tendrils of hair cling to my cheeks, stabbing into my eyes as he approaches, looming over me like some kind of dark and vengeful god.

A pair of twin daggers are sheathed at his sides. He removes them faster than I can blink and climbs atop me. *He* isn't out of breath. *He* isn't covered in muck or grime. And I realize then he's been toying with me, letting me run myself to exhaustion. Like Morcai. Like the swamp dog. Using my own fucking tactics against me.

I buck against him, but his weight is substantial.

One of Lyrick's daggers slides to my neck and pauses there— so fucking close to killing me. The other hovers at my liver, poking but not spearing through. Yet.

"What are you waiting for?" I hiss.

Lyrick glares at me—those amethyst eyes colder than the rain. "Death is too good for you," he says. "I spent years deluding myself into believing your kind were innocent. That we should be better. But I don't want to be better. Not with you."

The pressure on my liver eases as he re-sheathes the blade and withdraws something from his leather tunic. A glass vial filled with silver berries. *Rowan berries.* My heart stutters, thudding against my ribcage so hard I fear it might crack.

"Lyrick, no." I shake my head, but the blade on my throat only digs in deeper when he un-stoppers the vial with his teeth and shoves it to my lips.

"Open your mouth."

"Please." Tears burn my eyes. I pat the ground beside me, looking for something that can help, that can stop him, but there's nothing. The glass digs past my lips, clicking against my gritted teeth, and my throat turns achingly dry.

Rain drips down his eyes, his cheeks, his chin, but he doesn't blink. His pupils are blown to saucers, breath reeking of floral oil. "Swallow."

I obey, having no other choice. My whole body trembles as the berries slip into my mouth—spicy and metallic, like blood soaked in chili powder. They burn all the way down, settling in my stomach like lead balls. I narrow my eyes at him as he pulls the vial out and pockets it.

"Fuck you," I spit.

"That's the plan."

The warmth of the berries spreads outward, from my stomach to my chest to the tips of my fingers. I shudder at the sensation, my limbs so heavy they can barely twitch, let alone move. I'm at his mercy, my tongue too swollen to form words.

The dagger slides away from my neck and Lyrick moves to spread my thighs apart, flipping the weapon so he's holding it by the blade. The grooved pommel taps against my most sensitive part—that little bundle of nerves I didn't have before today—and I jolt at the icy hardness.

"Your pussy looks exactly as I imagined it," Lyrick says. He grinds the pommel into me, moving it in slow, agonizing circles around my clit. The grooved edges bite into my flesh, turning it swollen. Despite the pain—maybe because of it—moisture pools between my thighs, getting me slick for him.

It's not my fault it feels good. It's the berries. The lavender. The Marr-damn bond between us. But I hate myself regardless. Each twist of the pommel, each flick of his wrist has my brain turning mushy at the edges, tension coiling in my lower stomach, until he removes the dagger and slides it lower.

Its hard length presses against my wet center, poised and ready, and I stiffen beneath him.

I can't speak, but I can still think. I can still make him hear me. *"Lyrick, please don't do this."*

"It'll hurt worse if I take you without it, but if that's what you

want . . ." Lyrick reaches for his belt buckle, and I shake my head emphatically. *"That's what I thought."*

A moment passes between us—us staring into each other's eyes. The anger in his dulls to a simmer as I tremble beneath him, more scared than I've ever been. *"Don't pretend you don't want this,"* he says. *"I'm in your thoughts, Arden. I can see every-thing—feel everything you feel. Gods, you're so fucking wet for me already."*

As if to prove his point, Lyrick shoves the mental image of me spread before him into my mind, soaked and moaning, body flush with fever and desire. My irises glimmer like mercury in the darkness and silver dusts my cheeks. Through his mind's eye, I watch him sink the metal hilt inside me inch by arduous inch, stretching me for him, and I feel the excitement surging through his cock. It hurts so fucking good, burning as he opens me, and I'm so ashamed I can't stand it.

He's going to breed me.

And I'm going to let him.

I'm going to *want* it.

Horror strikes me at the revelation.

"Of course you want it. You belong to me."

Our minds separate as he plunges the dagger in and out of me in shallow strokes. I claw at the grasses—mud wedging between my fingernails, grasses crumpling beneath my fists as those strokes become slower, deeper. The pommel pushes against that thin line of skin protecting my maidenhead and I feel it rip apart. Sticky, warm blood oozes onto the hilt, and Lyrick stills. His pit organs flare, taking in the sight.

"You're a virgin?" he asks, face uncharacteristically pale. *"Fuck."*

For a moment, I think he might stop and let me go, but then those pit organs flare again and he brings the hilt to his mouth. Serrated teeth flash in the darkness as he wraps his tongue around the blade and licks it clean. The groan Lyrick makes is bestial, his eyes darkening with hunger.

When he's done swallowing my blood, Lyrick casts the blade aside, dropping it somewhere in the tall grasses. "Mine," he says in a throaty growl that's more monster than man.

A shiver rolls down my spine, and it has nothing to do with the rain pelting us or the chilly wind rustling the canopy above. *His.*

I shake my head when he presses his thumb against my clit, massaging it in slow, languid strokes. He's softer this time— gentler—as if that'll make it okay. Determined not to enjoy it, I grit my teeth and close my eyes. But the man is like a musician with an instrument. Or like an asshole with a mental link to my pleasure center.

He spits onto my pussy and shoves a finger deep inside me, then two, pumping me in a way that has my toes curling, my insides clenching. In my periphery, Lyrick's dagger gleams in the mud and leaves—close enough I can almost reach it. With great effort, I force my hands to work. Lyrick doesn't notice me stretching for the blade, patting around the leaf litter until I brush against its metal hilt. He doesn't see me wrap my fingers around it, knuckles gripping it so tightly they turn white.

One good hit is all I need . . .

But then he curls those fingers deep inside me and I see stars.

Up and up and up, my pleasure climbs, pushing me toward a peak I've never reached before. I could stop him—at the very least I could try—but I *want* to know what my body's building toward. Maybe that makes me sick, but if I'm sick, he is too.

Lyrick increases the friction on my clit until my muscles tighten, hips lifting off the ground. I'm so close. Tears blur my eyes. My pussy aches with the need to be filled with something other than his fingers.

"Not yet," Lyrick says, voice gravelly, sweat dripping down

a brow that's drawn in concentration. "You have to come first or I'll shred you."

A moment of icy clarity washes over me.

Is that what he's doing? Trying to make me orgasm so he can fit more easily?

Fuck that. Fuck him. I refuse to be complicit in my own rape.

"Is that what this is?" he asks. *"If you feel that way, why don't you take that blade and stab me with it? I know you have it."*

My eyes widen then narrow. Glaring at him, I squeeze the weapon impossibly tighter, but I don't move.

"That's what I thought." He lowers his head between my thighs, those thick eyelashes blinking up at me, covered in water droplets. The sight is so fucking profane—*so wrong*—but I can't stop staring at him, squirming with need.

Rain continues to patter against us, but I can't feel it's cold, just Lyrick's warm, damp breath against my skin. Lightning crackles overhead and his serrated teeth flash. He licks along their pointed tips, slimy venom dripping between my thighs, down my clit. I try to squeeze my legs together, but he easily pries them back apart.

"I think I know how to help you come. Hold still."

That fucker wraps his mouth around my clit, enveloping it in wet heat. Terror steals the breath from my lungs as I realize what he's about to do. *"Don't mark me there. Please."*

"I own you. I'll mark you wherever I want."

Spearing pain shoots through me as his teeth pierce my flesh, pumping hot venom deep beneath the skin. Sucking on me, Lyrick laps at my swollen clit in a way that sends tingles through every nerve ending in my body. I cry out. My muscles spasm as I come undone beneath him, hips grinding into his face. He sucks and licks me until every twitch, every moan has been wrenched from my body.

Boneless, I exhale deeply. My head falls back onto the

muddy ground and my eyes snap shut. I could sleep a thousand years and it still wouldn't be enough. But Lyrick has other plans.

Metal jingles, and my eyes snap open in time to see him unhooking his belt, shoving the leather from its buckle. Kneeling over me, he thumbs open his hide breeches and pulls himself out.

Absolutely not.

I shake my head at the sight of it. Most Hunters graft their genitalia to resemble ours; he hasn't. Lyrick's cock is just as monstrous as a Butcher's. Thick and wide. Grooved and bumpy from base to tip. It throbs a dark purple, its length nearly the size of my forearm.

"You're not putting that *thing* inside me," I hiss. My words sound firm and strong—much firmer and much stronger than I feel. The blade still lies in my outstretched palm, and I close my fist around its metal hilt. "Try it and I'll stab you."

He chuckles. "We've already established that you won't."

Is that so? I swing as hard and as fast as I can, angling for the bastard's neck. Sluggish and heavy, my arm misses the mark and pierces his bicep instead. Still, he recoils, his fingers wrapping around the braided hilt. Purple blood dribbles down Lyrick's armor when he pulls it free, but it's a shallow graze. Likely, it won't even scar.

Amused, he flicks his wrist and flings the dagger somewhere in the distance. Then, he unsheathes the blade at his hip and flings it, too. Booming thunder hides where they land.

I roll onto my stomach and try to crawl away from him. Fingers coil around my ankle and then—

Something thuds behind me.

Grasses squish as Lyrick crumples to the forest floor, his hand loosening its grip.

My brows furrow when strong arms coil around my stomach and throw me over their shoulder like a sack of rice. Through the downpour, it's hard to see their features, but I blink the blurriness away. Sheer harem pants plaster to their legs. Water slides off a poor excuse for a metal corset.

"Giara?" I ask.

She smiles up at me. "Later. We have to go."

In the distance, a dozen silhouettes dart through the blue-wood trees, searching for survivors. I cast a final glance at Lyrick, his skull bleeding—an enormous rock lying beside him. For the first time in five years, my palm doesn't burn.

XLI. Arden

"There's nothing we can do to protect our daughter from them, but that doesn't mean we won't try. Arden is resilient. She will survive."

—Clara of Ashwood, Former Starra'lee Priestess
Status: Deceased

Dawn crests the horizon and the rain clouds part, revealing a sky dusted in soft shades of pink and saffron yellow. Songbirds chirp overhead, and the sun's golden rays illuminate our walking path as Giara and I near the Aegis River. Neither of us speaks. It's never been our strong suit, and now years of time and circumstances have driven a wedge between us.

I asked her to save Fenris. It's my fault she got captured.

The truth of that weighs heavy on my shoulders.

Gravel crunches underfoot as we near our meeting spot, both of us dressed in clothing we stole off elgrew corpses along the way. The pants dig marks into my hip bones—a problem I've never had before—but they're functional enough. At least they're dry. Giara's leathers fit better, though.

"It's just around that bend," I tell her, pointing toward the wall of spine trees.

She holds her arm out to stop me. "Are you alright?"

The question shouldn't make tears well behind my eyes. So, I blink them away and pretend it didn't. "Are you?"

Our mutual silence is answer enough.

Giara wraps her arms around me and pulls me tight, squeezing me like she's trying to snap a rib. My eyebrows rise in surprise, but I hug her back, so fucking relieved to have her safe and home, away from Kariss. Almost no one goes there and returns, but we did. We made it. We're alive and mostly whole, despite everything.

"Thank you for saving me," I say, coughing to clear my scratchy throat.

"Just returning the favor." She lets go of me, taking the warm solidness of her body with her. "That was the most badass thing I've ever seen."

"I know. I'm pretty awesome." I shoot her a cheeky grin, though I doubt it reaches my eyes. Everywhere aches, and although we're leaving there victorious, we're not leaving without scars—both seen and invisible.

My palm no longer throbs, but I keep staring at it, this immense emptiness inside me.

I don't miss him—because missing him would be the actions of a psychopath—but he's been a constant presence in my life for five years. I know him almost as well as I know anyone in my squad, and now he's gone, and it's . . . odd.

"Lyrick?"

He doesn't answer.

I should be relieved, but bile rises to my throat when I think of that bloodied rock, his body lying prone on the forest floor. He deserved it. He drugged me. He tried to rape Giara. A moment earlier, I'd been willing to stab him myself, and yet . . .

"*Lyrick?*"

In my periphery, Giara watches me stare at those thirty-eight tooth marks. I shove my hand into my pockets so she won't ask about it.

The river burbles up ahead, and we squeeze past a row of spine trees to reach its gravel bank. Both of us move sluggishly, our injuries slowing us down. Giara doesn't ask about the blue blood that stains my crotch, and I don't ask about her broken nose or shattered front tooth. It's easier not to. Leading the way, I guide her over sharp rocks and shallow water to reach our campsite. There's no campfire or tent—nothing that could lure elgrew to us—but avra vines wind around trees to mark the route.

As we near the thinnest part of the Aegis River, my heart feels full for the first time in years.

It's not just Cheevy who's waiting for me, but Fenris too.

XLII. Lyrick

"This weekend, the cold-iron dam collapsed at our Grand Overseer's estate during the Ring Day celebration. Little is known about what caused the malfunction, but it is estimated that more than two thousand and three hundred elgrew lost their lives. May the rains bless them and the gods guide them on their next journey."

— *KARISS FORWARD*, CURRENT EVENTS COLUMN
AUTHOR UNKNOWN

Consciousness flits in and out.

Sabretooth fangs hook into my tunic, dragging me through leaves and grasses.

Darkness.

Underneath a green-and-white-striped tent, Stitchers roll me onto a cot. Hundreds of other cots lie beside mine, full of injured grays.

Darkness.

Needles poke and prod my squishy skull, and Yaklan's voice

cuts through a frazzled crowd of white-aproned apprentices. "I think he'll pull through."

Darkness.

Someone peels back my leathers. Cool water on a soft sponge dabs at my fevered forehead then my neck before it's wrung out, blood and dirt cascading into a wooden bucket below. It's so much blood, the water's purple with it.

Darkness.

I open my eyes to an unnaturally bright light and pain spears me. The light flashes over my face as someone rotates my head from side to side, pushing my cheeks together. "Hey, stop that." The command comes out slurry and cracked. My parched throat burns.

"You're awake." Yaklan releases my skull, and it sinks against a downy pillow, my neck not strong enough to hold it up. Groaning, I blink a half dozen times to try to get my bearings. In my delirium, it's hard to tell what's real and what isn't.

Up above, a blurry green-and-white-striped ceiling comes into focus. A bright kerosene lantern hangs from a pole beside my bamboo cot, swinging near my face under the supervision of some white-suited apprentice. She's still a child, but her clothing is covered in purple and silver blood.

"You've been asleep for a reaaaaallly long time," she says, crossing her ankles, poking the swinging light. "I've never seen someone sleep so long."

"Rashi, go fetch Lyrick a cup of water," Yaklan says. Grabbing her shoulders, he spins her in a direction and points her to where other Stitchers and their apprentices gather, ladling water out of an enormous metal bucket.

She pouts. "Yes, Dad."

"We're working." He groans.

Rolling her eyes, Rashi stomps off toward the others. "Yes, *Yaklan.*"

I smile at her, but then something sharp pierces my skull.

Wincing, I go to touch it and find wads of bandages and gauze wrapped around the entire left side of my head. Purple blood dots my fingertips, seeping through the cloth. Memories of Arden, Brawler, and that enormous fucking rock snap into place. "How bad is it?" I croak.

Yaklan grimaces. "The worst is over. It didn't reach your brain, but your skull was cracked in several places. It's been . . . challenging . . . to hold and piece it back together."

Hundreds of cots fill the tent, but most of them are empty now.

"How long have I. . . ?"

"Almost two weeks," he says, lips pursed in thought. "Rashi is right. I've never seen an elgrew sleep for so long. There were several days I wasn't sure . . ."

In my periphery, Yaklan reaches for something that I can't quite see. A moment later, a bamboo chair appears beside me, which he promptly sinks into. Dark circles line his eyes like he hasn't slept since the attack, and his sclerae are bloodshot. Sighing, Yaklan pushes the long silver hair from his face and twists it into a bun before grabbing a bucket of fresh gauze from underneath the cot. "I need to look you over and change your bandages."

Slowly, he peels the puffy cotton from my head and sucks in air.

Warm liquid dribbles down the sides of my temples, spattering the white silk sheets that cover my naked body. Yaklan snaps his fingers, and Rashi returns a moment later with the water cup. "Set that down somewhere and hold his head for me."

The child does as she's told, placing it onto the grassy floor. From the other side of the cot, she grips my cheeks in her palms the way Yaklan had been doing when I woke. Wordlessly, they work. Soaked bandages float to the floor. Yaklan rummages through his apron pocket and procures a set of tweezers. I feel a slight pinching, then hear crunching and grit my teeth.

"The trouble is getting all the pieces to stay in place so they can properly heal," Yaklan explains. He shoves the bloody tweezers between his teeth and reapplies the bandages, tightening and twisting them around my skull. It only takes a minute, and then my head's back against the plush pillow, my blurry eyes blinking at the green-and-white canvas above.

With Yaklan's help, Rashi scoots me into a sitting position, then retrieves the water cup and passes it to me. I guzzle the liquid down, hissing at the sharp but soothing burn of it. I'm about to ask for more when a Stitcher gasps and what sounds like a dozen metal objects clink to the ground. Near the entryway, orange fur and rippling muscle appear behind a fallen Stitcher, who crawls on hands and knees, gathering up a tray of fallen medical implements.

Prowler.

Gods, I missed that fucking asshole.

Yaklan rubs his forehead. "You don't know how many times I've had to kick him out. He keeps harassing my staff."

My verncat meows when he sees me, bounding past terrified Stitchers and their apprentices, who've more than likely never seen one up close, least of all for an extended period. I can't stop the smile from cracking my chapped and peeling lips when he roots between Yaklan and me and nuzzles into my elbow, soft fur brushing my skin.

"He's the one who found me, right?" I scratch the beast's chin and he purrs, closing his bright yellow eyes in gratification.

Yaklan nods. "You're lucky he found you when he did. He saved your life."

"Did they catch the elf who . . . ?" My stomach tightens into knots at the thought of anyone touching and imprisoning that which belongs to me. But my anxiety is short-lived.

Yaklan shakes his head, though his fingers coil into tight fists; it's the first time I've ever seen him show signs of anger.

"How many are dead?" I ask.

"You shouldn't worry about that yet," Yaklan says. "You still need to recover."

I stop petting Prowler long enough to glare at him. "How many are dead?"

"I don't know. Thousands."

And it's my fault.

I sink into the cot, letting the plush pillows and soft bedding consume me. The canvas tent blinks into and out of existence as I stare up at it. The scent of muddy water and mossy trees lets me know the makeshift surgery must be close to the wreckage of my family home. "Azerin must be furious."

Yaklan sets a hand on my forearm and squeezes. Voice low, he speaks to me like one speaks to a small child. "Lyrick, your father didn't make it back. He and Tyla—" The man swallows, soft gray eyes boring into mine. "He and Tyla sank with the estate."

My ears ring.

"No." I refuse to believe that. Yaklan is mistaken. He has to be.

"I'm so sorry, Lyrick." Glassy-eyed, he stares at me, willing me to see the truth. And I feel something crack inside my chest. My father—for all his faults, for all our disagreements—loved me. And now he's gone. And *she* killed him.

Tears well behind my eyes.

Yaklan pulls me to his chest as I sob into him.

"Azerin saved me from the tunnel and I . . . I should have stopped him . . . I should have. . ." My voice cracks.

"It's not your fault," Yaklan whispers.

But it is. Because I'm the one who let Blue go.

THE ESTATE IS LITTLE MORE than a wetland. The blue flowers, blue trees, and blue walkways of my youth are all gone. Still bandaged, I walk along the muddy edges, staring at the grim remains of my childhood home. In the estate's absence is a pool of muddy water covered in pond scum. Where the gazebo once stood are a handful of cracked tiles and glass from shattered kerosene lanterns. Everything I've ever known sits buried in millions of gallons of water that would take a lifetime to drain.

It seems surreal.

My father survived civil wars and incursions, hunting swamp dogs and slaughtering elven militias. More god than man, he outlived nearly every elgrew on Rayna, but in the end, a single elf brought him down. And Tyla . . . she never had the chance to prove me right and become just like my other siblings, but she never had the chance to prove me wrong either. Chalk died and lived for nothing, and that small child spent her last moments in pain.

They all did.

I should drown that creature like she drowned them. I should make her watch as I slaughter *her* friends, *her* family, *her* sister. But even that would be too kind for Blue. No, I think I'll finish what Azerin started.

Dressed in my father's armor, I turn on my heels and walk into the orangeleaf forest—my course set, my conscience clear for the first time in my life. I'm going to hunt Blue, breed her, and turn her into the myrie my father always wanted.

Epilogue

Julian

"I can see why Giara hid her. Arden is a gifted soldier—one of the best in my unit—and I'd be remiss to let her go. Furthermore, it is against Starra'lee policy to willingly place an undeveloped elf in Kariss, spy work or no. She will remain with me until she's reached her Age of Majority, and in the meantime, you can tell Elder Risha to kindly fuck off."

—Julian of the Drift, Starra'lee Squad Leader
Personal Correspondence to General Ustas.

Raucous laughter pours from the dining hall as we celebrate the return of Arden, Cheevy, and Giara, their new friend quiet beside them. I slip out the canvas flap covering the entryway before anyone in the gathered crowd can spot me. Tonight, they deserve to have their fun. Tomorrow, I'll find a way to punish them for defying orders. Right now, I have better things to do with my time.

Down and down, I descend, past the barracks and the armory, to the rickety metal ladder that leads to the Korring-Marr. It's been almost two years since I willingly stepped foot in the High Priestess Supreme's domain, but it's time. She fucked with my unit and a reckoning is at hand.

The ladder's metal rungs thrum beneath my thick leather boots. I jump off them and crawl into the hole that leads to our Great Tree. Like always, the Korring-Marr hums its soothing melody, but I can't be lured into a false sense of peace. Not tonight.

Priests, priestesses, and their apprentices gather around steaming water pools, dressed in their nondescript black cloaks, the hoods up to protect their identities. I elbow past them to one of the Korring-Marr's nine trunks, where Torvin, Elder Risha, and Nirissa sit at the edges of a murky green water pool, nutrients and muck burbling near the top.

Torvin's been hiding down here for weeks, ever since I found out about his little stunt and kicked him out of my squad. Dressed in black apprentice robes, he's clearly found a new home here. The snake stands when he sees me, dusting off his clothing.

"Julian—"

"It didn't work," I say, folding my arms over my chest.

Elder Risha clears her throat and inclines her head toward Nirissa, who hangs her feet into the water, kicking at the surface. Doll in hand, she ignores us, walking it across the glossy obsidian floor. "Not in front of the child," Risha says.

If Nirissa knew what her mentor tried to do, I have no doubt she'd never speak to her again. But my tongue is tied by orders from the higher-ups. I'm not to interfere in the High Priestess Supreme's affairs, and I'm not to punish Torvin for obeying her orders. I grit my teeth and take a deep breath, trying to cool my rising temper. Then, I beckon them away from the child and lower my voice. "It didn't work," I repeat.

Green glowflies blink around us, illuminating the cave as the apprentices carry out their daily chores—taking water samples, reading books, chanting. The Korring-Marr's opalescent glow reaches all the way to the cavern's borders, where canvas flaps hide study rooms that are off-limits to anyone not under Elder Risha's command.

The High Priestess Supreme takes me in, checking me from toe to head like we're preparing for combat. Narrowing her eyes, she tilts her long, birdlike nose up at me. "What didn't work?"

"Your plan. Arden destroyed the mine, and now she's home."

Beside her, the snake's eyes bug like saucers—as they should. I can barely control Arden on the best of days, and I have no interest in getting between her and her revenge—not when his petty scheme would have seen her raped and tortured at Azerin's command. I hope she rips the bastard apart, leadership and rank be damned.

"I spoke to General Ustas," I add. "He has agreed that she is not to be used for spy work now or in the future. After what she's done, sacrificing her would destroy soldier morale. Your plan backfired."

Elder Risha purses her lips in displeasure, but the expression is short-lived. "We'll see."

On tiptoes, she all but glides back to the glowing Tree and bends before Arden's sister. "Nirissa, could you please step into the pool? I need to see something."

Nirissa beams up at her, setting the doll aside. "Okay!"

She strips the black robes from her back and slides into the water, dressed in cotton fabrics Arden stole off a dead Hunter. As she reaches for the Korring-Marr's submerged roots, she closes her eyes and chants in a language that sounds just as snakelike as the priests and priestesses are. The roots glow brighter, and Nirissa shoves her head below the water's surface, past the mucky film that covers the top. The still water ripples and images flash across it—too fast for me to see, but not for Elder Risha, who's spent her life watching them.

I catch a bitten blue palm, a cave covered in red glowflies, cheering arena spectators, and eyes as opalescent as the Korring-Marr blinking up at us. A moment later, Nirissa bursts through the surface, hacking up water. As she scrabbles onto the obsidian, a feline grin creeps across Elder Risha's face. "Torvin, escort Nirissa to her quarters so she can dry off."

The snake nods, helping wrap Nirissa in her black robes. But they don't head upstairs to the room she used to share with Arden. They walk behind the forbidden canvas flaps. In her sister's absence, she stopped sleeping in the tunnels, and I suspect she never will again. Now that Risha has her hooks in her, it'll be all but impossible to rip them apart.

"Aren't you going to tell her Arden's home?" I ask, staring at the room they exited from.

"There's no need," Risha says, tucking a flyaway hair back into her bun. "She'll be gone soon enough. The Korring-Marr told me."

My nose crinkles in revulsion. "And what exactly did the Korring-Marr say?"

"Did leadership ever tell you why Clara left? They told Giara." My brows furrow. They did not, which she must surmise from my face because Elder Risha continues. "Two hundred years ago, the Korring-Marr gave Clara and me a vision. A blue elf would herald the creation of a new god. We didn't know how —the images were fuzzy back then—but we got started on manipulating it into place."

She leans against the Great Tree and places her palm atop it, shivering as she does so. Her black robes are more sheer than the others—layered and flowing—and in the light, it's almost ethereal. "Azerin had slaughtered all the blue elves, so we tracked down those with latent genes and convinced them to breed. Clara was so committed to the cause, she agreed to it as well. By the time she got pregnant, the visions became clearer. The blue elf would need to be in Kariss and they'd need to be given up as a pet." Her hand tightens into a ball. "When Clara realized that, she and her lover took off."

"It was never about spy work," I say.

She snorts. "No. It's more important than that."

"And you still don't know how this new god comes to be."

"I know enough." She presses her lips to the Tree and kisses it. "I've seen Arden's bite in the vision. I've seen her stuck in the mining tunnels as she reached her Age of Majority. I've seen her become that Hunter's pleasure slave. What's been set into motion cannot be taken back. Arden will be caught and returned to Kariss, no matter what steps you or her friends may take to protect her. My work here is done."

"You're a bunch of religious fanatics," I hiss. "The Korring-Marr speaks in riddles. This is all guesswork. Arden's *real*."

The High Priestess Supreme merely shrugs. "One girl isn't worth the fate of our people. I only wish leadership had allowed me to pursue it sooner, before she reached her Age of Majority. I could have trained her for the role."

For the role of spy? Or Lyrick's pet?

I don't want to know the answer. It makes me squeamish thinking about it.

"Arden's stronger than you give her credit for," I defend. "She won't let herself be taken."

"She won't have a choice. After what she's done to Lyrick, she'll never be free."

Afterward

ON HUMAN ETHICS AND ANIMAL RIGHTS . . .

I wrote this novel with an ecologist's lens in mind, incorporating what I hope to be realistic predator/prey dynamics between two intelligent species. It would be easy to read *They Call Me Blue* and paint the elgrew as the unequivocal villains, but I encourage everyone to dig a little deeper than that, and try to imagine what any person or creature is capable of when it necessitates survival.

From a human standpoint, evidence suggests that many of the animals we hunt and eat possess heightened intelligence. It's common knowledge that animals like dolphins, elephants, corvids, and great apes display human-like traits. It's less known, or at least less discussed, that our agricultural animals do too. For example, cows can problem solve, recognize faces, and learn from one another. They can even experience empathy, becoming distressed when another member of their herd is. Pigs can solve mazes, play video games, deceive others for personal gain, remember locations, and exhibit empathy as well. Turkeys form strong parental bonds, social hierarchies, and can use their voices to warn about danger or communicate their intent. I won't keep giving examples here ~ you get the point.

It is my belief that we humans often downplay animal intelligence to justify eating them. While I think it's great that we encourage free-range farming to improve their quality of life, and use humane dispatching/euthanization techniques to minimize their pain, we *are* still killing and eating them. I'm not a vegetarian either; I eat them too.

When writing *They Call Me Blue*, I wanted to take this concept to an extreme. What would happen if both predators and prey were intelligent species and acknowledged it? What if the predator species not only needed their prey to survive, but to procreate? What messy dynamics would come into play then, and how might both their cultures develop to accommodate this?

Like I said earlier, it would be easy to call the elgrew villains, but if I were a turkey, cow, or pig, I'd call us villains too.

ON THE CREATION OF ELGREW . . .

The elgrew are an amalgamation of several real-life species, alongside horror monsters like Mary Shelley's *Frankenstein*.

In nature, several plants and animals hybridize. Sometimes this hybridization results in a new species, as is the case with the prairie sunflower and the common sunflower. These two plants cross-pollinate to form the western sunflower, a reproductively viable species that can have offspring with other western sunflowers or with prairie sunflowers and common sunflowers. Their offspring maintain hybrid traits of both parents.

Similarly, animals may undergo hybridization, but with more limited degrees of success. For example, lions and tigers mate to form ligers, a hybrid group where the males are infertile, but the females can still reproduce with both male lions and tigers. Both ligers and their offspring often have several genetic disorders that reduce their quality of life, including: birth defects, neurological issues, obesity, and shortened lifespans.

To mirror these hybrid animal species with elgrew, their females are infertile, but their males can still mate with female elves (the inverse of ligers). Their offspring are always unhealthy and require several surgeries from an early age to improve their lifespans and quality of life. This is why the purples are portrayed so horrifically throughout the novel.

In addition to hybridization, I chose to mirror elgrew mating practices off of several real-life species too. For example, monarch butterflies only reproduce through violence, by grabbing a female mid-air and forcing her to the ground, then using their claspers to attach to her, which makes it impossible for the female to escape. Likewise, male bottlenose dolphins form gangs to isolate a female from her pod, and then force her to mate through body slamming, head butting, and biting. Dolphins will forcefully mount other males too in a show of dominance. Like humans, they don't have sex strictly for reproduction but for pleasure as well, mating even when they are not fertile. In this capacity, elgrew and dolphins are similar.

I mirrored elgrew social hierarchies and eating practices, as discussed in the *Human Ethics* section, on us: how we treat animals we view as inferior, how we create our civilizations and forms of government, how we use medical procedures for cosmetic purposes, and to increase our lifespans.

I think the cruelest thing about the elgrew, if one looks close enough, isn't how different they are to us, but how similar. They are the worst of "humanity," but they're still capable of empathy, friendship, familial love, and all our other human-like traits.

Elgrew aren't just predators; they're complex, intelligent creatures who will do whatever it takes to survive.

Acknowledgements

I'd like to thank my college advisors and graduate study professors for all the knowledge they've imparted to me over the years. They probably wish I'd used my coursework and research for something other than this, but I couldn't have written it without them.

I'd like to thank my graduate school colleagues and friends, Megan M. and Ashley G., who helped me develop the elgrew species and their societal structure, and who've served as valuable alpha readers and critique partners for both this novel and the *Seas of Paradise Series*. Their knowledge and time have been invaluable to me.

Lastly, I couldn't have done this without my critique partners Ali Breshears, Kaela Woodruff, P.C. Nottingham, Nic Scrim, Jenni Tayla, and Wes Ellis, or without my husband, who has supported me financially, enabling me to become a full-time author. He's my rock, and I'm truly blessed to have him in my life!

ABOUT THE AUTHOR

Before becoming a full-time author, Loren Huxley was a field biologist who specialized in stream ecology, environmental monitoring and sampling, animal physiology and reproduction, as well as toxicology. She has always been passionate about community outreach and education, especially when it comes to teaching the importance of other animal species and encouraging habitat restoration in sites that have been impacted by deforestation, pollution, and other human activities.

Loren completed her first novel in September 2023, and is now a full-time author, though she still volunteers with field work and research whenever possible. She lives in the Midwest with her husband and two dogs, and has a baby on the way.

When Loren isn't writing novels or working knee-deep in streams, she likes to play RPGs, read dark romances, horrors, and fantasy novels, as well as take her dogs on long walks. She is an avid swimmer and book collector, with display shelves that have gotten entirely out of hand.

Connect

If you liked this story, please consider reviewing it on Amazon or Goodreads.

For updates on new stories, you can sign up for Loren Huxley's newsletter at lorenhuxley.com, or you can follow her on her social media (links below).

Thank you so much for reading!

instagram.com/lorenhuxleybooks
goodreads.com/lorenhuxley
amazon.com/author/lorenhuxley